Being a P. I. --and, Again!

By

Alan Zacher

Dedication:

My mother and father, Lillian and Pat Zacher, have both passed. They always believed in my writing.

--In memory of them, I humbly dedicate this novel.

--Love always.

BEING A P.I.
ALAN ZACHER

Part 1

Chapter One

It was a dark, cold, rainy night, and I was sitting at my messy desk in my sleazy office above the long-shuttered Woolworth's store, gulping down shot after shot of bourbon from the half-empty bottle when, suddenly, there was a soft knock at the door. The next moment, in stepped the most beautiful blonde bombshell that these old gumshoe eyes had ever seen—oozing of raw sex appeal. She was wearing a red dress that was so tight it was making love to her hour-glass-shaped body. She leaned back hard against the door, as if to prevent herself from fainting, and then said, so softly, venerably: "Help me, Mr. Spade. I'm in trouble. I'll do anything you ask. It's murder."

Yeah, right.

Well, it is a dark, cold night. Hell, Monday is Christmas Eve, but it's not raining, and, no, I'm not at my office—hell, I don't even have an office. I'm sitting at my desk in my bedroom of my parents' two-story old house, which is in an old neighborhood of Lemay, which is in the county of South St. Louis, Missouri. My desk faces the street below, and I'm just staring mindlessly out of the window. It's almost midnight, and I'm bone-tired. And, no, I'm not drinking bourbon. I'm drinking warm beer from the cache of beer that I always keep hidden from my mother in my closet. And, no, I'm no P. I. Hell, I haven't had a job—of any kind— in years. If it wasn't for the kindness of my parents permitting me to live here, I'd be living on the streets. Damn, I'm fifty-five years old, and I got nothing . . . Well, I did solve two murders tonight—and I'm damn proud of having done that, too!

I can't believe I did that, solved those two murders. I mean, I don't have any experience or training at solving murders, but I did it. I solved them . . . Come to think of it, though, I am getting pretty familiar with being around where murders take place. A little over two years ago now, in 2005, a murder took place in this very house: My dad killed this crazed-guy, Fred—who was the manager of this grocery store where I worked part-time for a week—who had been terrorizing me by phone— threatening to kill me!—for two weeks, because I quit that job that Mom had gotten me without giving him notice: That's why I couldn't tell anyone that it was that Fred guy who was terrorizing me, because I told Mom and everyone else that he had fired me for working too slow. What? I should tell everyone my life and my lies because of that nut job? The guy was nuts. He told me that he had had it with life's shit. He had walked out of his job and was going on a killing spree. First, he was going to kill that bitch wife of his for running off again with his kids; then, he was going to kill me just for the hell of it—because I had pissed him off so much that day by quitting and leaving him short-handed; and then he was going to kill himself. He didn't give a fuck anymore. Well, at the end of those two weeks, he stealthily broke into our house at two a.m. and phoned our number. I came rushing downstairs still half asleep to answer the damn ringing phone in the kitchen—the phone sits on a wooden stand next to the entrance of the kitchen—and I heard him on the other end of the phone. He told me to turn around, and when I did, I found him standing there at the kitchen door with a cell phone in one hand and a gun in the other—pointing the gun at me! I knew in my heart that he was at the very point of pulling the trigger, when, all of a sudden, his whole body went stiff, and then he plummeted to the kitchen floor as stiff as a board.

"Damn burgermen," my father said, wiping the blood from the large blade of his old Army bayonet with the red handkerchief that he always kept in one of the pockets of his robe. "I killed a burgerman." About a year before this, at night, my dad began strapping on his old Army belt with its bayonet over his pajamas to check that the windows and doors to the house were shut and locked. He was afraid that the bogeyman—what he called "burgerman"—was going to get us.

Gosh, I miss my dad so much. This will be our first Christmas without Dad being here at home. You see, six years ago, Dad was diagnosed with being in the early stages of Alzheimer's. Four months ago, he caught a cold, which turned into pneumonia, and he had to be hospitalized. He was in the hospital for three weeks, and I guess because of the Alzheimer's, and because of having been bed-ridden for three weeks, he forgot how to walk. Well, that made up Mom's mind that we could no longer care for Dad at home. I mean, how would we have gotten him up the stairs of this big, old house? I had to admit to myself that even with my help, we could no longer care for him at home. Dad's a tall, heavy guy—he had worked at the gas company for years, digging ditches and such. So we had him transferred from the hospital to Living Care of South County, an assistant-living facility for the elderly, which is only two miles east of here.

Yeah, I miss him.

Now, I'm not saying that that nut-job, Fred, trying to kill me and Dad killing him "qualifies" me being a private investigator, but—well, no, it doesn't. So how did I get roped into becoming a P.I.? Because of whom and what I am—a pleaser. I'm always trying to please people. I get into one mess by lying and running away, and then I get into a bigger mess by telling more lies and running. In this case, it was Mom again, like when she had gotten me that part-time job at that grocery store.

It's just so stupid, too—how this all started. It was a joke. It was a harmless little joke that I was playing on Mom. Mom loves watching all of those old detective movies of the '40s. The Thin Man movies; Humphrey Bogart as Sam Spade; Alan Ladd, and on and on. She just loves watching them: I think it has something to do with the time period—you know, the '40s. Mom had once told me that Dad had taken her to see many of those movies when they were dating, after he had come back home from the war.

Anyway, I bought many of those movies for her, and she watches them endlessly. You should see that old, mahogany-wood, color TV set of ours in the living room. It sits between the north-corner wall and the fire place—the west wall, where our long, old, brown couch is, separates the living room from the kitchen. On the other side of the fireplace is Mom's old, also of mahogany wood, stereo console. It hasn't been played in years, and Mom now has all of the family pictures standing on its closed lids. Sitting on top of that old TV set, though, is a VCR, a DVD player, and three remotes: one to work the TV, one to work the VCR, and another to work the DVD player. I'll tell you, I didn't think Mom was ever going to figure out how to work all of that, but she finally did. She just kept at it until she mastered it.

I wish I had Mom's determination. When she sets her mind on doing something, she doesn't quit. She keeps at it until she achieves it. When I was—oh, twelve or thirteen—Mom decided that she wanted to go back to work, so she got a job as a checker at Kroger's. Well, those first couple of weeks, she came home every night crying about the mistakes she had made and how the manager had kept yelling at her and telling her she wasn't going to make it as a checker. Dad kept telling her to quit the damn job, but she wouldn't, and within four months, she was the best checker they had—the manager said so. Then, after she retired from there, at the age of sixty-five, she decided that she wanted to go back to school and get her GED. She enrolled in night school at my old high school, and it was tough. Night after night, Dad and I watched her as she struggled to study at the kitchen table. Dad thought she was nuts, and I did too. Having a fifth grade education was good enough for Dad, and Mom had graduated from the eighth grade, so he couldn't see why she wanted to go through all she was going through to get a GED—at her age! But she got it. She took the test a year later and passed.

She's something else.

After we had placed Dad in that assisted-living facility, and what with all of Mom and Dad's brothers and sisters and most of their friends being dead from old age—except for Aunt Rose—and what with Mary and Eve, my two older sisters, living in other states, I felt sorry for Mom. So, I began watching those detective movies with her in the evening. Well, for the past three weeks, Mom had been on this kick of watching those Thin Man movies that I had bought for her last year,—almost every night, and they had only made six of them!—and I've been watching them with her.

Now, Mom doesn't have Alzheimer's or anything like that, but it doesn't take all that much time to pass before she forgets the ending of the movie or who the killer is. I mean, c'mon, the poor, old, white-haired, pudgy, dear is eighty-four-years-old. So, out of sheer boredom, I began playing a joke on her. One night, as we were about to watch one of those movies, I told her that I had been thinking that I could be a P.I., that I thought I had what it takes to be a gumshoe. To prove this to her, I told her that before the movie was over, I would predict who the killer is and why and how he, or she, did it. This I did and she was very impressed.

I thought it was pretty funny. So, I did it again and again. Well, she finally says to me that maybe I should give some serious thought about becoming a P.I. "I had no idea, Tom," she said, continuing, "that you had such a gift. You're as good as Nick Charles himself." Then she added that I shouldn't give up on my obtaining my teaching certification— which she hasn't said to me in a year or so—and then asked me if I had recently called Dr. Burke, the Dean of the English Department at St. Louis University, or other colleges to enroll.

About five months after Dad had killed that Fred guy, his physical and mental health worsened. He now needed help getting dressed and undressed, with eating and going to the bathroom, and on and on. It began taking a lot of work taking care of him. I guess this was why she didn't seem to be so devastated when I told her—when I lied to her, again—that I wouldn't be returning to school in the fall, because Dr. Burke had told me that because of budget cuts there was now limited enrollment available and that I'd have to wait until an opening became available. I told her not to be depressed about it, that I'd keep in touch with the college and check out other colleges as well. She seemed to accept this, and I've been brushing her off about it ever since.

About two weeks ago, at around ten in the morning, I was lying on the couch in the living room still in my sleeping clothes—my gray sweatpants and T-shirt—watching TV. Watching TV lying down in there is the best way to watch TV. The couch is against the west wall, and what with the TV penned in between that north corner and the fireplace, if you watch TV sitting up, you have to keep your head turned at a ninety degree angle to the left—it's uncomfortable and looks goofy at best. Even though there are four tall, narrow windows that face the opposite wall, it makes more sense to me that that couch, and the coffee table, should be position there and the TV should be where the couch is. Well, there would be problems doing that—like right now, there's all of the Christmas stuff in front of the windows: the Christmas tree, all of Mom's miniature houses and buildings-- those houses and buildings all light up and they're supposed to be a representation of the town in that movie *It's a Wonderful Life*, with the train set and the white clothes underneath it all to give it a snowy Christmas feeling.

What with Dad not being here, I had thought about not putting up a damn Christmas thing, inside or outside. I mean, it's a lot of damn work putting up all of that Christmas crap. Christmas was always my parents' favorite time of the year, and it became something of a tradition with Dad and me that the day after Thanksgiving—and Thanksgiving this year was just horrible; it was so lonely without Dad here—we'd start putting up the Christmas stuff. It would take us three to four full days of working on it to get all of that stuff up, inside and out, but it was kind of fun. No matter what the weather was, good or bad, we'd get it up, and after it was all done, we'd feel so good. But now, with him not being here, I just didn't feel like doing it. I mean, it just doesn't feel like Christmas without him here. But I did it; I put it all up—shagging up and down the ladder outside, stringing the large-bulb, multi-colored Christmas lights across the gutters, ice-cycle lights inside of every front window, reindeers and sled in the front yard. It took me eight days to do it all, too. After Thanksgiving Day, Mom began hinting and hinting for me to do it, and when I kept putting her off, she began doing it herself—began putting up the Christmas tree. Well, I couldn't let her do that, so I started doing it, putting all of that damn Christmas junk up.

So, anyway, I was lying on the couch watching TV, and Mom came rushing in and said, all excited: "Tom, the Lord has answered your prayers again."

Mom's very religious. She belongs to several prayer groups, and we have pictures of Jesus all over the house, even in both bathrooms. Did you ever try to take a poop—or do something that a man who hasn't had a date in years sometime does—with Jesus staring down at you?

I once asked my sister Eve why Mom was so religious, and she said: "Because of James, you idiot." James was my older brother by four years. When he was ten, he was killed by a car while riding his bike in the street. At his interment, I kept pestering Mom to tell me how much longer James had to stay in that box. Finally, in tears, she bent over to me and said: "Until the end of time." I think that I am what I am because of James' death. Although I wasn't able to fully comprehend what my mother had said to me that day, I think a part of me vowed that day never to end up like James—never to be trapped in a box of any kind until the end of time.

Well, anyway, from past experience, I should have known right then and there that no good could come from Mom saying: Tom, the Lord has answered your prayers again!

Mom had been over at Mrs. Peterson's, who lived next door to us, to the right of our house. I've known Claire all of my life. She and her husband, Bud, were more than good neighbors to my parents; they were also good friends. Bud died suddenly from a massive heart attack about seven years ago—yeah, that's right, seven years. I remember that it was the millennium, 2000. He died at work. He was a clerk in an auto parts store.

Claire changed after Bud died. She became this nosy old busy-body, forever staring out of one of the windows of her two-storied, old house, always looking for any infraction committed by strangers or any of the neighbors of the neighborhood—like the ongoing battle she had had with Mr. and Mrs. McGuire, who lived directly across the street from her. Claire claimed that they kept leaving their front porch light on all night, and that it was keeping her up, shining directly into her bedroom. She kept calling the police on them; when the police would come and knock on Claire's front door, she would never open the door to them, what with it being night and she being an old lady and scared. Through the closed and locked door, she'd instruct the police to arrest her neighbors, or at least tell them to turn off the light so she could go to sleep. Leo McGuire vehemently denied leaving that porch light on at night, stating adamantly that that light was turned off every night at exactly nine p.m. "She's gone senile," Leo would shout, mad as hell that she had called the police again. "And even if I did forget to turn off the light, which I don't, there ain't no way in hell that it shines into her bedroom—the old goat." Again, this is an old neighborhood, and these people have known each other for years, and it was common knowledge that Claire's bedroom was on the west side of the house, so no, there's no way that that porch light could have shined into her bedroom. But in Claire's defense, from time to time, that porch light is left on all night. I've seen it. However, as I have said, these are old people, and old people forget.

Even we were not immune to Claire's busy-body eye. Whenever she'd see Dad standing on the sidewalk in front of our house, she'd call and want to know if we knew that Dad was outside all by himself. Mom would always reassure her that, yes, we did know that he was out there and that we were watching him, and on and on this went.

I got to tell you, though, that I always had the feeling that another reason Claire was always looking out of a window was that she was always watching, or waiting, or hoping—praying—for someone to come back home.

Well, on this day that I'm speaking of, Claire had called Mom over to her house to see if Mom could hear Mr. Fluffy barking with all of the windows and doors to the house shut. Mr. Fluffy is June

Neely's dog. Mrs. Neely lives to the right of Claire. I don't know what kind of a dog Mr. Fluffy is, but it's a cute little dog. It's snow white with curly fur. June's husband, Harold, died last year, and out of loneliness June bought Mr. Fluffy about four months ago. I'll tell you, everybody in this neighborhood is old, sick or dying. Claire's right, though. That damn dog barks incessantly, especially if someone passes by June's house; you can see it in the fenced-off backyard jumping up and down and barking like crazy—and that damn little dog has the most high-pitched, shrill yap that I have ever heard. June had apologized to Claire repeatedly for this, but what had really ticked off Claire was that she claimed that June was letting that dog out at six a.m. and that that damn barking kept waking her up. As with Mr. and Mrs. McGuire's front porch light, June vehemently denied this, stating that she didn't let Mr. Fluffy out of the house into the backyard to do his "duty" until well after eight a.m. Plus, she added equally as vehemently, that there was no way in the world that Claire could hear Mr. Fluffy barking with it being winter and with all of the windows and doors to her house being shut. Claire had told June that she didn't mind his barking so much at night when June let him out to do his "duty," but that if this barking at six a.m. didn't stop, she was going to call the police. Again.

Mom hadn't needed to go over there to Claire's house. I could have told her that, yes, you can hear that dog yapping. I hear the damn thing yapping from our house, with the doors and windows shut.

So after Mom had confirmed for Claire that one indeed can hear Mr. Fluffy barking with all of the doors and windows shut, she told Claire about me going into the detective business. She told her how good I was at solving crimes; she told her how I was having cards printed, how I was going to advertise in the newspaper, and how I had told her that with any business that the hardest part was getting your first customer, or in this case, your first client.

I couldn't believe my ears. I couldn't believe that Mom had told her about that—and I definitely couldn't believe when she said, after that business about how The Lord had answered my prayers again: "Claire wants to see you. She wants you to prove that John didn't murder Tyra."

The whole time Mom was saying all of this to me, I kept saying, screaming, to myself: Oh, shit! How do I get out of this one? Oh, shit!

After washing and dressing in my usual every day, old clothes—
my long-sleeved, plaid shirt, my jeans, and my black tennis shoes—
and after throwing on my old, green, puffy winter coat, I walked over
to see Claire. I walked slowly, racking my brain as to what I was
going to tell Claire to extricate myself from this mess.

At Claire's, I stood at the first step of the two-step cement porch
that led to the entrance of their house. I stood there staring at their
front door. It was a wooden door, painted white, with four small
windows towards the top half of the door. Their house was the same
as our house, only it was painted a light brown, with the trimming and
the shutters painted white. Actually, all of the houses on this block
look the same, only painted different. As I stood there, staring at their
front door, I was struck by two thoughts. The first one was how much
I love living here in this neighborhood. I thought of how much of my
adult life I had hated this neighborhood and wanted to run from it;
wanted to move to England, or Paris, and become a writer; or to New
York or Los Angeles and become an actor; or anywhere; just wanted
to get the hell out of this boring city, this boring neighborhood, and
become something—someone, anything.

I don't know when the change came in me. Maybe that Asian
psychiatrist that I had gone to for a while several years ago was right:
He had told me that the reason I don't try anymore—to get a job or a
girl—is that I'm retired, that I'm now too settled in my ways. Yes, he
said, you still want things, but you won't go after them now. I
countered this by telling him that I was thinking about returning to
college again—this time to obtain a teaching degree in English. "Jesus
H. Christ," he yelled. "Haven't you heard a single word I've said?!
You're retired. The boat has sailed. If you feel bad about quitting all
of those jobs—which you quit because your parents babied you all of
their lives—and telling your parents and everyone else that you got
fired, I can tell you right now that if you return to school, you're
really going to feel bad—because you will quit. You're retired. No,"
he continued. "The best you can hope for is that your parents live
until you can start collecting social security."

At the time I had thought that he had been a Chinese noodle off. I
mean, I think you have to have a job before you can retire. But now, I
think he had been right. Because now, I can't think of anywhere else
that I would rather live than here. I love the houses here; I love the tall

maple trees that line both sides of the street along the sidewalks; I love the people here—finally, at long last, the acceptance of age has replaced the chaos of youth's wants, and this place has become my home again, like when I had been a kid.

My second thought, as I stood there staring at Claire's front door, was that if the demeanor of a house is determined by those who live in it, then the demeanor of this house can be summed up in a single word: sad.

But it hasn't always been this way. There had been a time, as with our house, when this house had been young and full of livelihood and happiness. I thought of how Mom and Dad and Bud and Claire had been such good friends. I thought of how they had used to get together at each other's houses on the weekends and play cards; how they had used to have each other over to celebrate birthdays, wedding anniversaries, holidays, the births of their children, and of their children's children, and on and on. I thought of how Dad and Bud used to go fishing and hunting, and of how they, especially when they were drunk, used to swap war stories; although they didn't know each other then, and didn't serve together, they both had fought at The Battle of The Bulge. Bud had been shot in the right arm; gangrene had set in and the arm had to be amputated above the elbow. "Oh, you had it rougher than me," Dad would say, to which Bud would reply: "Oh, no, you had it rougher than I had it. And anyway," he would then always add with a smile and a wink, raising that stump of an arm towards Dad, "Uncle Sam takes care of me." I thought of how mad Dad used to get at Bud when they went out somewhere, because Bud, inevitably, would ask Dad if he could borrow a couple of bucks from him: The word "borrow" to Bud always meant "give." Dad would scream to Mom: "That guy is the cheapest, penny-pinching-est SOB that I have ever met. They got money, Lill. No one is goin' to tell me that they don't have money."

Dad was right on that one, about them being most frugal with a buck. Bud and Claire never went on vacations; almost everything they bought was second-hand—clothes, furniture, cars, and on and on. About twenty or thirty years ago, there was this ceiling fan that was all the rage at the time. It was a Casablanca fan. It was the Cadillac of ceiling fans—and expensive. Well, Mom wanted one for the dining room, wanted it to hang over the long, mahogany-stained dining room table in there. She bugged Dad and bugged him until he gave up and they finally bought one. She was as proud of it as she could be. Well, the next time that Bud and Claire came over, the first thing that Mom did was scoot them into the dining room to proudly show off their newest purchase. Both Bud and Claire were very impressed with it and both said how beautiful it was. Mom, as proud as a peacock, then added: "And, you know, it's a Casablanca." Well, for some reason, Bud took offence at this, and replied: "Well, we have a ceiling fan above our dining room table. It's not a 'Casablanca,' but it turns."

Good ole Bud.

As I stood there, still staring at their door, I thrust my hands in the pockets of my coat to ward off the coldness of the day. I tried to think of when it had all started to go so wrong for Bud and Claire. It certainly hadn't begun with Claire's illnesses—no, that's too recent, I had told myself. For the past five years, Claire had been battling colon cancer. Besides having had two mild heart attacks, Claire was having respiratory problems as well, having to almost use oxygen perpetually. No, that wasn't it, I had told myself. I guess it had to be the death of Bud. Then, it hit me. It had been none of that. God, I chided myself. I must be getting old. No, it had been none of that. The beginning of the end for this family had begun with the death of their only child, Karen.

Oh, Karen.

Karen was a year younger than me, and I guess if truth be told, she was the only girl I think that I truly ever loved. Barring Mom, Karen was the first girl I ever kissed. Out of the fear of me being hurt, Mom didn't want me playing with the other boys on the block, so that left me with little choice but to play with Karen, which Mom didn't mind at all. Mostly, we played Tea Party. Up in her bedroom, Karen had a miniature tea set, with cups, saucers, and a tea pot: they were white and made of plastic. Looking back upon it, I would say that they were cheap, but Karen took much pride in owning them. Karen was always the hostess of this tea party, and we would pretend that we were eating cookies and drinking tea. Sometimes we played husband and wife, and, yes, we kissed. As adulthood took root, we never mentioned the kissing to each other, but whenever we met, like any embarrassing moment of childhood, it was always remembered by both of us. You could see us remembering it on our faces. I wouldn't have mind talking about it, but out of respect to her, I never did.

Karen was always straight with me. She cared for me, but she just didn't care for me romantically. Once, when she was seventeen and had been dumped by Tim Logan—Mehlville High's star jock football player—she was feeling sad, and I took her to a movie. After the movie was over, we got back into my car and I tried to kiss her.

"Don't, Tom," she said, pushing me away. "You're my friend, my best friend. You're like the brother I never had. Don't spoil our friendship. It's so special to me."

Yeah, she was always straight with me, but it hurt. It always hurt. It hurt when she got back together with Tim Logan and went to the senior prom with him; it hurt when she went off to the same college that he did, in Springfield; it hurt when she married the prick; it hurt when she gave birth to Megan; it hurt that they had a great life together; it hurt when she and he were killed in an automobile accident one Saturday evening returning home from seeing a movie by a car of drunken teenagers— God, how long has she been dead now? Let's see, it was 1991; Bud and Claire had thrown Megan that Sweet Sixteen birthday party, and five months later, Karen and Tim were killed. My god, that was sixteen years ago! Yeah, it hurt. It all hurt. Because it was all supposed to be mine. I had fantasized that it was all mine for years. Karen married me; Megan was my child; life was good; I was the big-shot accountant for Anheuser- Bush; I was a man. Yeah, it all hurt. But do you know what hurt the most? I don't know when I started picking up on this, but sometime shortly after Karen gave birth to Megan, whenever I saw her, she always had this sound in her voice and a look upon her face and in her eyes of pity for me. She'd always give me this disgusting, patronizing kiss on the cheek and say: "Well, how's my old childhood buddy doing?" But I think if she would have said what was truly in her voice and on her face and in her eyes, she would have said: "My god, what the hell happened to you? How did you end up being this lonely, miserable, pitiful creature that you are?"

Yes, I think that that's what she would have said. Well, the only thing that I can say to you, Karen, is that I'm happy you got fat. I mean, after she had had Megan, she ballooned. I mean, she needed a "WIDE LOAD" sign on that two-seater ass of hers ... You should have seen her when she was younger, though. On her wedding day, in that long, flowing, white wedding dress, she was just vogue-model beautiful: that hour-glass figure, with those luscious, grapefruit-size breasts; her limpid, watery, blue eyes; her shoulder-length-long, thick, rich, golden blonde hair; her prominent forehead—Well, that forehead was never one of her best features. I mean, it wasn't a total turnoff, but it did protrude out. I guess she got that from Bud's side of the family, because his forehead was the same as Karen's and Megan's.

Anyway, I guess if truth be told, I still wish she would have been mine, even with that protruding forehead and getting fat and all.

I felt sorry for Bud and Claire. I think those three years after Karen's death were the most tumultuous years of their lives—because of Megan. Megan had been out partying with her high school girlfriends the night her mother and father were killed, and after their deaths, Megan came to live with Bud and Claire until she went away to college, and let the partying begin. Bud and Claire were too old to be taking care of a sixteen-year-old girl with raging hormones and dealing with the mental grief of her parents' deaths. She made their lives a living hell. Bud was constantly chasing drunken, or high on pot, boys and girls from their house in the middle of the night; he was constantly threatening her that he was going to call the police if she didn't stop not telling them where she was going and staying out until the wee hours of the morning, or not coming home at all. She wrecked three automobiles during the time that she lived with them, sports cars, they were—I think that Megan had gotten some type of financial settlement from the insurance company, or from the parents of the teenager who was driving the car that night that killed her parents. She got into fights at school and got poor grades. Megan was wild, fiercely independent, and rude, or troubled. In many ways, Megan reminded me of my sister Eve, who is also fiercely independent.

I'll give you an example. When Megan came to live with Bud and Claire, they gave her a-a-oh, let's say a house-warming party. Well, I was in their backyard drinking a beer, and I spotted her. I went over to her to speak to her. Now, I was feeling uncomfortable speaking to her for two reasons: One, her parents had just been killed, and, secondly, she looked so much like Karen—blonde hair, blue eyes, and that protruding forehead—that I was feeling very sexually attracted to her. Well, we were talking and, suddenly, she began fanning herself as if she were hotter than hell and said: "God, I'm PMS-ing like a racehorse." Then she started pulling at the crotch of the jeans she was wearing. I had just taken a sip from the beer I was drinking and, I guess, out of embarrassment, I started choking. I excused myself for chocking and spitting, and she said: "Why, did you fart?" Now that's just like something my sister Eve would have done and said.

Bud and Claire gave Megan several parties while she lived with them, but I bet the party that they were just beside themselves with joy to give her was her going-away party, her going off to college in Springfield, Missouri, the same college that her mom and dad had gone to. She wanted to be a dentist, and studied—well, dentistry, I guess. She only lasted two years in college before she quit, though. Much to the relief of Bud and Claire, she didn't come back home. She took a job as a barmaid in one of the local bars that she frequented and let it be known to Bud and Claire that she was living with one of the bartenders who worked there, John Jones. John—or "JJ" as he was known to friends— had also been a student at Springfield U., but had also quit in his second year of college—he had wanted to be an engineer. I always liked John. He was a very down-to-earth, easygoing kind of guy; always quick with a slap on the back, a joke; not my type of guy—loved fishing and hunting, hiking, all sports, anything that had to do with the outdoors or physical activity. They married and honeymooned in Durango, Colorado.

They loved it there. In fact, they loved it so much there that they stayed there after their scheduled two-week honeymoon was over.

They were both from St. Louis, but they didn't return here until Megan found out that she was pregnant. John accepted a position as a linesman for AT & T, and they purchased a real nice ranch-style house in a fairly new, middle-class, maze-of-a-subdivision in Kirkwood. By all accounts, though, their marriage was not a happy one. For one thing, Megan kept pestering John to take loans out on things that they really didn't need—like a big butt-ass boat; then a new car for her, a red mustang; she kept maxing out credit card after credit card; she hated being a stay-at-home mom; she still wanted to party, or at least go fishing, or hunting, or camping—she wanted friends—people that were alive, not like these "suburban drones." John came home from work one day, and she announced to him that she had taken a dental-assistant position for a high-class dentist in Clayton. John was certain that this was simply a prelude to her asking him for a divorce, again.

For about a year and a half, it was horrible. She loved the job with this "high-class dentist," but she and this dentist, a female, would work late; would go out for drinks after work; would take business trips. John was at his wits' end, as the saying goes, and was just about to ask for a divorce himself, when, suddenly, she seem to do a hundred-and-eighty- degree change. She didn't work late anymore; she didn't go out for drinks after work; she didn't go away on business trips; she wanted to stay home—and more than all of that, she was loving, again, to not only John, but to Tyra, their daughter, as well. John had felt that Megan had finally matured. John had felt, or believed, that Megan had finally matured into a wife, and, more importantly, into a mother. Life would now be good.

Claire always said that she was glad that Bud had died when he did, because his heart was broken enough with Karen's death, but the tragedies that followed Karen's death, she had always said, would have sucked out what little remaining life was left in him—would have made a living zombie out of him.

Five years ago, in the spring of 2002, Megan went missing. It was a Thursday evening. Megan had gotten off from work and had gone to West County Shopping Mall, and that was the last that anyone had ever seen her again. One of the clerks at the Famous-Barr there remembered her, because Megan had gotten angry and made a big scene about the store not carrying the type of stockings anymore that she was used to purchasing. "Are you not ordering them anymore because they are expensive?" Megan had demanded to know. "If that's the reason, start ordering them again, and I'll buy every goddamn one of them. I've got lots of money." Three days later, Megan's red mustang was found in a very seedy part of North St. Louis. Her purse and billfold were found on the passenger's seat, empty of all money and credit cards. The newspaper stated that a "substantial" amount of blood was on the driver's seat; DNA later confirmed that it was indeed Megan's blood. John and Claire were grief-stricken. Unlike that old platitude of "they never gave up hope," as the weeks turned into months, and the months turned into years, they did give up hope of Megan still being alive. Mom told me that

John had turned to the bottle for solace, and Claire, with Mom's help, found solace by acquiring a deeper meaning in God and religion. My heart felt for both John and Claire, but even more so for little Tyra. Mom told me that for months after Megan's disappearance, she cried herself to sleep while clinging to one of the many teddy bears that her mother had bought her, crying for her mommy to come home.

If all of those tragedies weren't enough for one family to endure, the next one that followed was the most horrific of them all, and I can honestly say that I don't know how poor Claire retained her sanity, let alone her very soul.

Two years ago, about a month after Dad had killed that Fred guy, John came home from work and found the house unusually quiet. Usually, he'd find Tyra, now nine years old, listening to that damn rap music on the radio while doing her homework at the kitchen table, or— and he had told her time and time again that he didn't want her doing it—cooking them dinner, usually soup or a pre-cooked pizza. This evening, though, she was nowhere to be found. He called out her name two or three times. No reply. He started walking down the hall towards her bedroom at the end of the hall, telling himself that she was probably lying on her bed doing her homework with those damn headphones on listening to that damn rap music. He got a little more than halfway down the hallway when his mind and body almost stopped thinking and breathing because of what he saw. There, upon the white-painted door of her bedroom, written in red spray paint and written vertically down the door, were the words: REVENGE IS MINE. With adrenaline of pure fear pumping through his body and mind, he raced to the door. He threw open the door, and what he saw inside, he said, made him pass out: Tyra was lying on her bed as if asleep. She was lying under the cover of her teddy-bear-printed quilt, with her arms and hands folded over the quilt. Her many teddy bears lined both sides of her body, as if keeping her company or watching over her. Yes, it was as if she were sleeping, as John had repeatedly told the police—except for the fact of the cord, cut from one of the lamps in the living room, wrapped around her young, thin neck. She had been strangled to death.

Two weeks after her death, John was arrested for her murder.

Because of knowing the family, I had followed John's trial in the newspaper and on TV with great interest. I even attended the trial one day: Claire desperately wanted to go and begged me to drive her, which I did.

The defense attorney for John stated that the State's evidence against John was "circumstantial" at best; the lead attorney for the prosecution stated that John was a cold-blooded murderer who murdered his own daughter because he no longer wanted to be saddled with a child; he, John, wanted to have a fresh start in life, wanted to move back to Durango, Colorado. They even produced a copy of an application to a telephone company in Durango that John had applied to recently.

To me, the most damaging evidence against John, besides him not taking a lie detector test—which he had wanted to do but didn't on the advice of his attorney—were four things: One, John had said that in a two-week period prior to Tyra being murdered, he had received three threatening phone calls. Although the calls were "muffled," he could tell that it was a woman's voice, and she always said the same thing and then hung up. She always said: "You know what you did. Revenge will be mine." The prosecuting attorney stated that they had those phone calls traced and that they all were made from a public pay phone at a Wal-Mart about five miles from John's home. It was their contention that John had made the calls himself.

Second, the unused can of red spray paint. Tyra was what in my day was called a "Latchkey Kid," meaning that until her father came home from work, she was left by herself at home. In the mornings, the school bus picked her up at the corner to the entrance to their subdivision and dropped her off in the same spot after school. John had given Tyra strict orders to go straight home, lock the door, and open it for no one. If she ever had any trouble or needed him, she should use their home phone or the cell phone that he had purchased for her. Well, two days prior to Tyra being murdered, she came home from school and found a package at their front door. It was wrapped in yellow wrapping paper with tiny brown teddy bears on it and had a large yellow bow on top. There wasn't any card to the package, but Tyra thought that it was a birthday present, or something, for her, but then she told herself that it couldn't be, that her birthday had been three months ago. Excitedly, she called her father and asked him about the present. John told her that he knew nothing about the package and told her not to open it until he got home. That evening, when he opened it, it contained a single item: that can of red spray paint. John had called the police and reported it, as he had after the third threatening phone call. The prosecuting attorney stated that that can of spray paint was another one of John's ruses in his attempt to deceive everyone that he was being framed for Tyra's murder. Although that had not been the actual can of red spray paint that was used to write those words on Tyra's bedroom door, the prosecuting attorney stated that John had purchased two cans.

Third, all of the doors and windows in the house were locked from the inside, and there wasn't any trace of a forced entry. The coroner's report stated that Tyra's time of death was between seven and eight a.m. On the day of Tyra's death, John arrived at work almost an hour late. John stated that the reason he had arrived at work late was that when he had gotten about a half a mile away from home he realized he had a flat tire from a nail.

Fourth, and probably the most damaging to John, was his girlfriend, Helen Dyer—and what John ever saw in her is beyond me. I mean, Megan was beautiful, but this gal was just plain butt-ass ugly: spare, stringy red hair, cut short; patches of freckles all over her face and neck; cheap-looking eyeglasses; yellow, rotting teeth from years of heavy smoking; a beer belly and flat ass; and a sarcastic personality of white trash. About the only thing this gal had going for her, to me, was her watermelon-sized breasts. I mean, they were huge.

The day that she had given testimony against John was the day that I had attended John's trial, had driven Claire there, and the moment I saw her, I thought: Boy, with breasts like that, I bet you have to stand at least three feet away from her to have a conversation.

Anyway, as I have said, after Megan went missing, John took solace in the bottle. I guess, he hit rock bottom about a year later. He kept missing work and coming into work drunk. His place of employment gave him an ultimatum: either get help or be fired. John began attending AA meetings, and it was there that he had met Helen Dyer. They began going out for coffee after the meetings, then they began dating, and finally, she moved in with John and Tyra. All was good for about six months, when they started drinking again. She was fired from her job as a housekeeper in a hospital for coming into work drunk, and one evening before John had come home from work, in a drunken stupor, she had had a fight with Tyra and beat her up. When

John got home and saw Tyra's black eye and swollen nose, he immediately called the police and had Helen arrested. Although Tyra was okay—she didn't have a concussion or anything serious—John would have nothing to do anymore with that Helen Dyer. He had all of the locks to the doors changed; packed all of her clothes into her two, tattered, old suitcase; set them on the front step of his home; and wouldn't permit her to return. She had vowed to get revenge.

It was John's belief that Helen had made those threatening phone calls, and that she had murdered Tyra.

I got to tell you, though, although you could tell that that Helen Dyer was terribly nervous that day that she testified—kept moving in the chair, and kept bringing her right hand up and then back down again, as if she desperately wanted, needed, a cigarette—to me, everything she said sounded pretty truthful.

She was wearing a nice, light blue dress. Her hair was nicely combed—parted on the right side and combed straight across. She wore just a touch of makeup to hide that freckled face. Except for those huge breasts of hers, she looked so small sitting in that witness chair next to the overwhelmingly large, raised, dark-wood bench of the judge, and lonely. I felt sorry for her.

She answered every question straight-forward. When John's defense attorney asked her if she made those threatening phone calls, she replied: "No, I didn't."

"But you did threaten Mr. Jones," he responded. "You told him that you'd get revenge. Isn't that right?"

"He threw me out of his house," she cried, shifting nervously in the chair. "I had nowhere to go. I was homeless. He—

"You fisted his little girl so badly that he had to rush her to the hospital. Isn't that right?"

"I was drunk," she cried, bringing her right hand up almost to her mouth and then bringing it quickly down. "I was sober for over a year before I met him, and he got me drinkin' again. That son-of—"

"But you wanted revenge, didn't you?" John's attorney interrupted her. "You wanted him to pay, and what better way to make someone pay than to murder a father's daughter. Isn't that—"

"I object, your honor," the prosecuting attorney stated, shooting up out of his chair. "He's leading the witness."

The judge agreed, and, then, it was the prosecuting attorney's turn to cross-examine Helen.

"Ms. Dyer," he began, "where were you on the morning that Tyra Jones was murdered?"

With much confidence, she stated: "I was in St. Andrew's Halfway House for re-reha-hab-bilitation for alcohol abuse. I was there, so there ain't no way that I could have killed her."

Yeah, like I said, I found her testimony to be pretty truthful, and most damaging to John. It's a good thing that John's attorney hadn't asked her if she could spell the word "revenge." Personally, I don't think an uneducated, low-life, like her could have. If he had asked her, and if she had misspelled it—well, I think that that would have damaged John's trial all the more.

In the end, the jury found John to be guilty of first-degree murder. He was sentenced to be executed by legal injection at the stroke of midnight on January 31st, 2007, which is next month.

Chapter Three

Anyway, as I stood there, still staring at Claire's front door, and beginning to freeze, I kept asking myself how I was going to get myself out of this mess. I'm no private eye, I kept telling myself. I can't solve who killed Tyra. Plus, I had my doubts as to John's innocence. This is all so silly, I told myself.

Finally, I told myself to just be truthful with Claire—and being truthful with people doesn't come easily to me, like when telling the police that that Fred guy was probably at our house that night to rob us because I had offhandedly told him that Mom and Dad always left lots of cash lying around the house; like with telling Mom and everyone else that that Fred guy had fired me; and like with telling Mom and everyone else that Dr. Burke from the college had told me that I had better withdraw from school and return in the fall because I was failing in three of my classes. No, I like telling lies to people because of whom and what I am: a fifty-five-year-old scared little boy. But I could be truthful to Claire. I mean, like I said, I've known Claire all of my life. She would understand. I'd tell her it was just a joke I was playing on Mom. I'd tell her how I conned Mom into believing that I could solve all of the murders in those Thin Man movies and that I was just teasing her about becoming a private eye. It was a joke. I was just having some fun. Yeah, that's what I'll tell her, I told myself. She'll understand. Hell, she might even get a laugh out of it, and Claire needs a good laugh.

After stepping up onto the porch, I rang the doorbell and then waited for Claire to answer the door. In an attempt to shut out the coldness of the day, I shifted my weight from one leg to the other. I brought my clenched hands up to my mouth and blew on them to warm them. Then, after what felt like a million years, Claire finally answered the door.

"Hi, Claire," I said.

"Hello, Tommy," she replied, tiredly. "Come in," she then said, waving me to come in with her right arm and hand, which seemed to take much effort.

Poor Claire, I said to myself as I passed her and stepped into the hallway. Claire's hair used to be thick and blonde, like Karen's and Megan's. Now, it was spare and white—not a pure white like Mom's, but a dingy white. I got to tell you, too. Her body used to sexually arouse me. Now, it was sickly pencil-thin—and this had bugged me for some time now: What happened to her breasts?! I mean, she never had BIG breasts, but she had them. Now, they were gone. She was as flat as the proverbial pancake.

She was wearing a light gray dress with large flowers printed on it— orchids, I would say—and the material of that dress was wafer-thin. It hugged that flat-breasted, thin, sickly body like a blanket. About the only things that gave any dimension to Claire now were the oxygen tube flowing from her nose to behind her small ears to the portable tank she held in her thin-fingered hands and the large rosary she wore around her neck. The rosary was made of translucent beads that looked like crystals, and the large cross itself was of a silver color, as was Jesus who hung upon it in agony.

Seeing her so ill and frail always saddened me. Claire had been like a second mother to me—well, she was always there for us if we needed her. My fondest memory of Claire was when I had been about thirteen or fourteen years old. I had a terrible flu, or cold—ran high fever, couldn't go to school, and felt like shit—and since Mom and Dad were both at work, Claire came over every day at noon and cooked me chicken noodle soup and toasted two slices of bread for me. What I found so touching about this was that she always cut the crust off of the toast. I mean, it was weird. I was thirteen, or fourteen, years old, and she always cut the crust off of the toast like I was a little boy. Why did she always do that?

I don't know why, but I have always felt that Bud and Claire's house always had a mustier smell to it than our house does.

"Why were you standing out there all that time?" she asked as I took off my coat.

Against the south wall, next to the hall closet, is a much-worn, old, mahogany-stained bench. Its back is about five or six feet high, and about a foot down from its top are five or six pegs to hang coats on.

"Oh, I was just thinking," I replied, hanging up my coat on the peg closest to the front door.

Suddenly, I felt more nervous than a husband being caught in bed with another woman by his wife. This had little to do with that detective business. Suddenly, a flood of old emotions came rushing back in my mind. All through my childhood, and my adulthood, too, I had always felt uncomfortable around Claire. Besides the sexual attraction that I had for her and Karen, Claire had this aura, or presence, about her of being better than everyone else. She never verbalized this, but I always felt it about her. Now, her mother, Madeline, did verbalize it. She took every opportunity to inform you that she was better than you. The house that Bud and Claire lived in had been Madeline's and her husband's. The husband had died before I was born, and Madeline ruled that house like a tyrant. She always wore dresses: "Only poor people and 'Ladies of the Evening' wear pants," she would say. Claire, too, wore only dresses until the day Madeline died in the early '60s; then she began wearing pants. The way Madeline wore her long blonde hair was about as straight-laced, and strict, as was her demeanor: it was always worn bundled tight and high upon the top of her head, like a beehive. Her husband had owned a bank, and she loved to say, or boast, how they had lost everything in the Great Depression and how he, her husband, from hard work and from sheer will, had rebuilt, and restored, their finances and social standing from nothing. "For years," she would say, "we lived on bean soup and homegrown vegetables from the garden. Isn't that correct, Claire?" She was also fond of saying, for my ears: "Little boys are such nasty creatures." There's a large painting of her that hangs at the end of the hall on the second floor of the house, and to this very day, when I see it, the thing gives me the heebie-jeebies. It was only after Claire became ill that I began to feel equal with her. It was as if, now, she had a flaw, like all the rest of us mere mortals. From the time when Claire became ill, she became more and more like her mother.

It was hotter than hell in there. I guess that's why my nose started running, coming from the coldness of outside into this hotter-than-hell house inside. My nose kept running the whole time I was there, too.

"Well, come on into the living room," Claire said, tiredly. "I can't stand for long periods now."

She turned around and went into the open living room. I followed her.

"Sit down," she said, tiredly, as she slumped down heavily into Bud's big old leather easy chair. It was positioned in the middle of the room, facing the street, and to the right of the chair was an oak-stained, wooden, nightstand. Upon the nightstand was a box of tissues, some medicine bottles, reading glasses, and a pair of old Army binoculars.

After stepping behind the old wooden coffee table, I sat down at the left end of the long, old, deep-upholstered, white sofa with a floral print to it. It was positioned against the four tall, narrow, windows that face the street, and, suddenly, I remembered something. Remember how I told you that all of the furniture, and such, in our living room is all wrong, and how it all should be positioned? Well, I hadn't organized that in my mind as I had always thought. I had unconsciously stolen that from Claire—the old sofa, her older-than-old TV set, the old coffee table, everything, was positioned as I had said everything in our living room should be positioned.

"Sssssh," Claire stated suddenly, bringing her right index finger to her thin, pale lips and tilting her head to one side to hear better. "Do you hear him? Do you?"

"Yes, I hear Mr. Fluffy, Claire," I replied, sniffing and wiping my nose with my hand.

"I called the police again and placed another complaint against June and that damn dog of hers."

"I know. Mom told me," I said, still wiping my nose and feeling terribly embarrassed.

Claire picked up that box of tissues from the nightstand, and after extending her right arm and hand out towards me, said: "Here, Tommy. Take some."

"Thanks," I replied. I leaned forward and ripped out five or six sheets from the box.

There was silence as I blew my nose.

After I had finished, Claire said: "Your mother tells me you're going into the detective business."

"Oh, about that, Claire," I said with a nervous laugh. "I think you're going to find this funn—"

"I'm dying, Tommy," Claire stated gravely, grasping the cross of that rosary in her right hand. "They're all gone—Bud, Karen, Tim, Megan, Tyra . . . Oh, my sweet, sweet, precious Tyra," she continued, and a single tear escaped from her left eye and did a rollercoaster ride down her aged face. "They're all gone," she repeated. "I should change my will and leave all of my money—what little money I have—and give it all to charity. I have nothing more to live for. When

Megan went missing," she said and extended that cross out towards me, "your mother gave me this cross. I never take it off. Never. Not even when I go to bed. I lie in bed holding it, and I pray and pray until I fall to sleep. I don't pray for my health to be restored or for salvation. I pray for death to come. I pray and pray to be reunited with my family. I have nothing more to live for, Tommy. But before I die, I want you to find who murdered Tyra. I owe John that much—I need to know the truth."

"Well, yes, about that, Claire," I started to say, sheepishly, moved back and forth nervously on that sofa and wiped my nose again— and it was so damn hot in that house. I could feel perspiration forming on my forehead.

"All of that monkey business about those phone calls, and that spray paint," she continued. "Why, John's not smart enough to think all of that up … Now, you could," she said, changing the subject. "I always told Bud that you are probably the smartest person I've ever known—lazy, but smart. Even when you were a boy, you were always reading. Yes, I always told Bud that you are probably the smartest person I've ever known. I want you to find Tyra's killer before I die. I'll pay you," she said, and then looked towards the nightstand. She then said: "I think my purse is on the kitchen table. Will you get it for me, Tommy?"

"Sure, Claire," I said, and then rose from the sofa.

As I walked to the kitchen upon the much-in-need-of-re-varnishing wooden floors, I silently screamed: How am I going to get out of this mess?! … And don't tell me that she's going to give me a damn dollar!

Over the years, whenever I had finished doing something for Claire, like driving her to the doctor, or to the store, or cutting her grass, she'd always hand me a dollar and say: "I wish it could be more, Tommy, but as you know, I'm on a fixed income, and money is tight."

Her purse was on the long, old, wooden, kitchen table.

After returning to the living room, I handed it to her and then sat back down on the sofa.

As I watched Claire retrieve a pen and her checkbook from her purse, I silently screamed: Are you for real?! Don't tell me you 're going to write me a check for a dollar?!

But that's just what she did.

"Here," she said, ripping the check from her checkbook, and then extended it out to me.

"Claire," I protected, holding my arms and hands out, holding those moistened tissues in my right hand with my thumb. "Claire, I can't take any money from you. Claire, I don't—"

"Please, Tommy," she said, pleadingly. "I have to know who killed Tyra before I die. Please, Tommy," she repeated, still holding that check out to me.

"All right," I said, surrendering. "I'll see what I can do."

I leaned forward and took the check from her.

I looked at it; folded it and was about to put it in my shirt pocket when, suddenly, something didn't seem right to me. I unfolded the check; looked at it again, and I was in shock. Shock! It wasn't for a dollar. It was for one thousand dollars—a thousand dollars! I was stunned.

"I wish I could give you more, Tommy," I heard Claire saying as if I were in a dream, "but as you know, I'm on a fixed income, and money is tight."

"No, no," I heard myself saying, "this is fine, Claire. I'll see what I can do."

"Can you see yourself out, Tommy," I heard her say. "I'm tired."

I folded the check again and then placed it in my shirt pocket.

"No, no," I said, rising. "That's fine, Claire. I can see myself out. I'll call you when I find something out."

Walking home, I was still in a daze. I mean, I haven't made a thousand dollars in years. Hell, what am I talking about—I haven't made a dime in years. I was stunned. I didn't even feel the coldness of the day—hadn't even zipped up my coat.

By the time I reached the first step of our porch, though, reality began to hit me. My God, I told myself, what's wrong with you? You can't keep this check. It's stealing. You 're no private eye. My God, why did you take it? You just stole a thousand dollars—and from Claire. You've known Claire all of your life, and you just stole a thousand dollars from her. She old and poor and you stole from her. You march yourself right back over there, mister, and give this check back to her and tell her the truth. "Okay," I then stated out loud. I turned around and started back towards Claire, but then stopped and thought: Well, wait a minute now. Let's think this out. I mean, it's not like Claire's going anywhere. I turned around again and started for our porch, but then stopped again and thought: No, this is wrong. You march yourself right back to Claire's and—Oh, just go inside and think this out!

Once inside of the house, I hung up my coat in the small closet that's just beyond the front door, on the inner south wall.

"Mom," I called out, looking in the living room, and then in the kitchen.

She must be upstairs, I told myself. I decided to go upstairs and lie down and think this thing out. I had about an hour before I had to drive Mom over to the facility Dad's in and spend some time with him and feed him lunch.

For the past month, I've been driving Mom everywhere she needs, or wants, to go. She mis-stepped and fell in the kitchen one morning while making breakfast. As she was falling to the black-and-white tiled floor, to break her fall, she thrust her arms and hands out in front of her and came down hard on her right arm and hand. I rushed her to St. Anthony's Hospital, and the doctor there told us that she had a hairline crack about three inches below the elbow. He said that it wasn't serious—no surgery, or pins, or anything. They simply placed a white plaster cast on her right arm that extends from her elbow to her wrist. She says, though, that that cast prevents her from having full control of moving the steering wheel of her car. So, she hasn't been driving.

As I passed the bathroom upstairs, the door to it opened and Mom stepped out wearing her full-length white robe and slippers. Her cut-short, snow-white, hair was damp, so I knew that she had just taken a bath.

"Oh, you're back," she said. "Well, so how did it go?"

"I told her that I would look into it—see what I could find out."

"Oh, Tommy," she stated joyously. "Your first case. I'm so happy for you."

"Yeah," I replied, somewhat flatly. "She even paid me."

"Claire gave you a dollar, huh?" Mom said, with a knowing wink, and then laughed.

"Actually, Mom, she wrote me a check for two hundred dollars."

"Oh, my Lord!" Mom replied, shocked. "Did you take it?"

"Well, yes, I took it."

"Well," she began, shaking her head and thinking deeply, "two hundred dollars isn't all that much money. But with Bud being gone, and her having little money, I—Well, you just do a great job . . . Isn't the Lord wonderful? Your first case and you got paid for it. The Lord is good."

As I have told you, throughout the house are large pictures of Jesus, the type with large, piercing, brown eyes that stare and follow you. There is one of those pictures of Jesus directly across from where we were standing that day. I glanced over at it and our eyes met. I looked deep into those large brown eyes to see if I could determine how He was feeling about me. I got nothing, though.

"He sure is," I replied, as my mind screamed: How in the hel-heck am I going to get out of this mess?!

I don't know why I lied to Mom about Claire giving me that money—giving me a thousand dollars and not two hundred dollars. Well, yes I do. If I had told Mom that Claire had given me a thousand dollars, she would have made me give it back to her, and I didn't want to do that. I wanted that thousand dollars … I sure began sweating bullets, though— that Mom would find out that I had lied to her.

Anyway, after we had gotten back home from seeing Dad and feeding him lunch, I went back upstairs and once again flopped down on my bed. I had decided to keep the money. I guess the reason for this was, actually, going down and seeing Dad—seeing him in that place always puts me in a real shitty mood. Seeing his body emaciating away in that damn wheelchair; him not knowing us anymore; placing a spoon filled with that pureed slop to his lower lip, and him automatically—by instinct, I guess—opening his mouth and accepting the food, and that blank stare of a dead fish in those once dancing, full of life, crystal-clear blue eyes of his. Seeing all of this, and more, always makes me feel mean and selfish. I told myself: Yeah, Claire's old and poor, but she has more money than I have— hell, who doesn't have more than what I got. I got nothing.

So, I would keep the money, and, yes, I would do some investigating. That doesn't mean that I have to solve the case, I told myself. What do the words "private investigator" mean? By the very definition of the words they mean to investigate privately, and that's exactly what I would do. I would do some investigating and then tell

Claire that, sadly, all the evidence pointed to John—because if truth be told, I, personally, as I have said, had a belief that John did, or may have, murdered Tyra.

The next morning, Wednesday the twelfth, I dashed to the bank and deposited that check into my checking account. Every month, Mom writes me a check for four hundred dollars to pay the household bills, and what money is left after I pay the bills, I secretively keep for myself, which is usually forty bucks. But that money—that check for one thousand dollars—was all mine.

I then went on one hell of a buying spree at Wal-Mart. I bought a cell phone. I have always wanted a cell phone. It's not an expensive or elaborate one, but I can take pictures with it and it has voicemail. I didn't get a contract or anything like that. I got the "pay-as-you-go" plan, in which one buys minutes as needed. Then, I bought a pair of miniature binoculars—well, I figured that if I'm going to be doing detective work, I might need them. Then, I thought that that cell phone might not take good enough pictures for detective work, so I bought a Canon 35mm camera. All in all, with taxes and everything, I spent three hundred-and-sixty-nine dollars and ninety-six cents. Wow!

That's the most money I have spent in years.

Driving back home, I suddenly felt damn angry at myself for buying all of that stuff. I mean, if I was only going to give a-lick-and-a-split to this investigation, why in the hell did I buy all of that stuff? But I, then, told myself that I can always use all of that stuff that I had bought. So, then, I felt better about having bought all of that stuff—especially that cell phone. Clipping that cell phone on to the belt of my pants makes me feel like a gunslinger out of the old West.

I got back home just in time to drive Mom down to visit Dad and feed him lunch again.

After we got back, I spent the rest of that day and evening playing with my new-bought "toys" and thinking about what I should do next— where do I begin with this investigation? The only thing that I could come up with was to begin at the source: John.

This displeased me for two reasons: One, I really didn't want to ever see John again. I mean, c'mon, the guy may have murdered his own daughter. Why would I want to see him again? Secondly, I didn't even know if I could see him. He's on Death Row at Potosi

Correctional Center. Can you even visit someone who's on Death Row?

The next morning, I called there—and for some reason I was very nervous doing that, too. My hand shook and my voice kept cracking. And after telling my name and that I was a friend of John's and asking if it would be possible to visit him, and after being transferred what seemed like a zillion times, I was finally told that if John agreed to see me, I could indeed visit him. I was then told that someone would get back with me later in the day.

Someone from there called back just as Mom and I were leaving to visit and feed Dad lunch. I was told that John had agreed to see me and that I could visit him today from three to six p. m.

After Mom and I got back from seeing and feeding Dad, I dashed up to my bedroom and Map-Quested the address of the prison on my computer. I have heard of Potosi, Missouri, but I had no idea of where it was or how long it would take me to dive there. It was seventy-two miles south of St. Louis and would take me an hour and a half to drive there.

I hated that, too. I hate driving long distances. I almost said to hell with it. I'll find some other way to convince Claire that I had done an investigation. But I couldn't think of what else I could do that would be as convincing as telling her that I had interviewed John.

So, after hastily dressing in my dark-blue suit—the only suit that fits me anymore … And how ironic is this: Mom had bought it for me to attend Tyra's funeral. I put on a white dress-shirt and a wide red tie, and after hastily throwing on my light-brown, full-length, topcoat—which I haven't worn in years, and which didn't fit me anymore. I couldn't button it, but for some reason I still wanted to wear it, to look the part of a private eye. And after hastily telling Mom goodbye and that I didn't know what time I would be home, I got into my car and headed for the entrance to the highway, Highway 55, south.

I had looked good in that suit and all. Mom had even said that I looked real dapper. Being all washed and shaved and in that suit and topcoat had put me in a good mood. I had this heightened sense of nervous anxiety, too—as if I were doing something that had meaning, purpose. I hadn't had that feeling in years. I used to get that same feeling of nervous anxiety whenever I'd first meet a girl and start dating her . . . Gosh, I kind of miss not dating—not that I dated all that much in my life. I was never all that good at "putting the make" on girls. Well, if truth be told, I was never even very good at making friends. I never wanted anyone ever getting all that close to me—for fear of them finding out how shallow of a person I am. I was always good, though, at making an initial great impression with girls—with snowing them is more like it—but then, as time went on, they would begin to catch me in my lies and too soon realize that I was a false person and dump me. It's sad. I never made it to the point with any girl in which it was a given that we were a couple, an item. I never made it to a point with any girl in which our relationship had reached that comfort level, or zone, that we could fart in front of each other and not be devastated about having done that. Oh, well.

Chapter Four

It was a butt-ass long drive. It was mostly rural after I had gotten past Arnold, Missouri—long stretches of rolling, hilly, landscapes of naked trees and naked woods on both sides of the highway as far as the eye can see, intermixed with stretches of open land. I saw farms along the way—some of them were quite impressive looking, while others were, well, what I would call "dirt farms." I didn't see a single cow or horse, though. I guess it was just too damn cold.

About after thirty or forty minutes of driving, I was getting damn bored to death. I don't like listening to the radio anymore. I've never been into listening to music. When I was young, I used to like listening to The Beatles, but that was about it. I turned on the radio anyway to a talk radio station just to hear a human voice and to drown out the continuous, monotonous hum of the heater. I remember thinking how I wished that I were into music, because the car has a CD player, and if I had some CDs, I could be listening to music that I liked. Then, that got me thinking of how much I hated that car.

An automobile should reflect a person's personality—-and that car is definitely not my personality. It's a snow-white 1997 Lincoln Continental. I hate the big old thing. Every time I get into it I think that I should have it painted pink and begin selling Mary Kay products. In my freshman year of college, in 1972, I had bought a 1971 Plymouth Barracuda—now that was my personality. It was green, but I had it painted black, and I loved that car. It had a stick on the floor and was made to move, fast. And I got the speeding tickets to prove it. Mom and Dad weren't too pleased with all of the speeding tickets I was gleaning, but it was my car—paid with the money I made working part-time as a checker at Kroger's, and I paid all of those tickets, too, and slowed down my driving, eventually.

But I sure had loved that car. Over the years, I had the engine replaced, and had a complete body overhaul done to it twice. I hated to sell it—and I sold it for next to nothing—but in 1999 it began using a lot of oil and I wasn't working and didn't have the money to have it fixed, so I sold it. It was about this time that Dad's eye sight began to fail to a point that he felt he shouldn't drive anymore. He gave me his car, a 1995 Mercury Village van. I hated that thing about as much as I hate that Lincoln Continental. I was almost happy when, about four months before Dad had killed that Fred guy, I was backing out of our driveway and, suddenly, the engine blew. I had the thing towed to a junkyard.

I didn't know what to do now. I mean, I didn't have a job or any money to buy a new—or used—car. I felt miserable, depressed. Mom said she didn't know why I was so depressed about it; she would just go to the bank and take a loan out for me to buy a car. This I adamantly refused. I didn't want her to go into more debt because of me. I told her that I just wouldn't have a car until I got a job.

My sister Mary called from California, and I heard Mom say to her: "Mary, Tom's not lazy, and that's not nice of you to say, 'Good. Maybe now he'll get off of his lazy ass and get a job.' Tom's in college, Mary, getting his teaching degree. That's rough."

A few days after that, my sister Eve from Chicago called, wanting to know how we all were, and such. Mom was at one of her many prayer meetings, and when I told Eve about the car and about what Mary had told Mom about me, she cried, "Where does that uppity bitch get off saying that about you! She has no—"

"She right, Eve," I said, interrupting her. "I should get a job. Mom and Dad pay for my car insurance. They let me stay here for free. I eat their food. They pay for my schooling. It's not right, and I keep stealing from them."

"What do you mean you keep 'stealing' from them?" Eve asked. "Do you mean money? Are you stealing money from them, Tommy?"

"Well, yes," I replied. "I'm constantly asking Dad, or Mom— sometimes from both of them in the same day—for a twenty here, and twenty there. It's not right, Eve."

"That's not stealing, Tommy," Eve stated, flatly. "Who's taking care of Dad, and Mom, around there? Who does all the household repairs around there? Who's always there to do whatever Mom or Dad need? You are," she continued. "I don't see Mary's uppity ass there helping out—or my fat ass there for that matter. So don't tell me you're 'stealing' from them, Tommy. You're not."

"Well, thanks for saying that, Eve. I appreciate it."

"If there's anybody that can get my dandruff up quicker than a fart out of your pants, it's Mary." After a few seconds of silence, she continued. "Okay, here's what we're going to do about the car situation. I got this coming weekend off. I'll drive down and give you my car. I'll bring the title—"

"Eve, Eve," I protested. "Don't do that. Don't make me feel even more depressed than I—"

"Tommy, listen to me," she insisted. "Listen to me. I only keep a car for about ten years anyway. This will be my way of thanking you for taking care of Mom and Dad. At least this way, I'll feel that I...."

I miss Eve . . . Well, I miss Mary, too. It's just that Eve and I have always been closer. I sure wish Eve hadn't felt the need to take that nursing job in that hospital in Chicago all those years ago. I guess she just got tired of it all, and decided to leave . . . Well, Mary was always the "pretty" one, the "intelligent" one, the "socially acceptable" one. Everything just always seemed to come so damn easily to Mary—school, friends, men, life. She married this great guy, Todd, straight out of college. She went to the University of Missouri at Columbia, and after they graduated, they moved to his home city of Santa Monica, California—and you should see the house that they live in. It's a beautiful, Spanish-style ranch, with palm trees and everything. He's some type of realtor developer, or something like that.

I don't know. I guess Eve was always the opposite of Mary. Eve was wild. She was always partying, always getting drunk, always with one guy after another, always in relationships that went nowhere. She drove Mom and Dad crazy. Then, when she was, oh, twenty-four or twenty- five, she laid two big bombshells on Mom and Dad. The first one was that she was pregnant and that the guy had told her that that was her problem and not his; being pregnant, that is. The second one was that he, the father, was black.

Now, my mom and dad are no more or less prejudiced than the next fellow is, but, well, yes; those two bombshells didn't sit well with them. The three of them were sitting at the kitchen table, and easy-going Dad just kept shaking his head, and looking despondent, while Mom kept shouting, "You just kept sinning, Eve. You sin, and you sin, and then you sin again."

Eve told them not to worry about it, that being a nurse had its "perks." She would have an abortion.

"You mean to tell me that on top of all your other sins, now you're going to add murder to them?!" Mom screamed at her. "Abortion is against the Lord's laws! It's murder in His eyes!"

"Well, what do you expect me to do, Mom?!" Eve shot back at her.

"I expect you to stop sinning, young lady," Mom stated. "I expect you to accept the Lord as you Savoir and stop sinning. I expect you to grow up! That's what I expect from you!"

In the end, Eve didn't have an abortion. Nine months later, she gave birth to a boy. She named him James, after my father's father. In time, Mom and Dad came to love Jim dearly. Life was good again.

But, then, Aunt Rose called.

Aunt Rose told Mom—and I bet it was Aunt Rose herself who had said it: the old busybody—that she had overheard one of the relatives say that Eve had better not ever bring that little black bastard around to their house; that Eve, and especially him, were not welcomed.

When Mom demanded to know who had said that, Aunt Rose told Mom that she didn't want to get involved in it, didn't want to be the bearer of rumors. But what with Mom being her baby sister, Aunt Rose felt it her duty to tell Mom what was being said behind her back.

Although this upset Mom greatly, when she told Dad about it, whatever despondency he had had left in him about it all quickly turned into a fireball of pure rage. Much out of character, Dad called the relatives on both sides of the family and gave it to all of them with both barrels: "I don't give a goddamn who said it, but if my daughter and my grandson aren't welcome in your home, then neither am I!"

It was a mess. It caused arguments and fights all around. I guess Eve just got sick of it all and took that job in Chicago to get away from it.

Yes, I sure miss Eve—and Jim too. He's a great guy. He's a surgeon in Chicago; has been one for about four years now. He has a wife and two children.

Anyway, that prison was about two miles south of the town of Potosi, and what was so overwhelming to me was the juxtaposition of it all. First, you're driving through rural land—woods, open land, woods again—then you pass through the little rural town of Potosi—modest, old, struggling to survive, looks like hundreds of other rural towns throughout the Mid-west: a water tower on the outskirts of town; a cemetery; a Baptist church; a VFW hall; Main Street lined on both sides with dying, narrow, brick, storefronts—then you're driving through rural land again—more woods, more open land, woods again—then the sight of that prison comes into view and splats you flat like from the pounding of a sledgehammer. It was huge.

It had to be three or four football stadiums long and wide. It's like aliens from another planet plopped this futuristic city, or fortress, down in the middle of nowhere. I don't know if it was because of it being a cold, gray, winter's day, or if it was because of now seeing it and coming ever closer to it, but the literal meaning of the word "prison" finally sunk into my insipid head. My heart began racing and my body began shaking. The whole place and the immediate area surrounding it—the plain, nondescript, white-cement, buildings; the ten-foot-tall chain-link fence with its top fanning out with razor wire, holding the perimeter at bay like a belt; the square, imposing, white-cement, guard-towers with its non-seeing-in, tinted-glass tops on both sides of the entrance and at all four comers of its existence—screamed two words: fear and suppression. If the damn thing could talk, I think it would say: "If you know what's good for you, stay away from here."

It was so quiet there, too. Not a serene quiet, but an eerie quiet. If it were music, it would be the type of music that plays in monster movies, just before someone gets eaten by the monster. For some reason, I felt that the silence demanded that I turn the radio off, so I did.

At the entrance at the gate, I stopped and through the now rolled-down window of my car gave the guard my name and then told him why I was there. After he had checked something off on the clipboard he was holding, he gave me directions to where I was required to park and the number of what building I was to enter: building 31.

After entering building 31, and after telling one of the two guards in there my name and why I was there, I had to pass through a metal detector.

The inside of this place was a cavernous--a long box with many corridors leading to-to, hell, I don't know; high ceilings, and walls made of cement, painted a bright white. The floor was a highly polished, black-and-white tile, which made me say to myself: Hey, we have the same tile in our kitchen at home. The ceilings were drop ceilings with continuous rows of fluorescent lights. The dull light emanating from them added to the coldness of the place, as did the pale light that oozed with forced indifference through the bare, wide-glass windows that banked the left wall about three-fourths of the way up. In all, the place was cold, in every sense of the word, with no smell or taste to speak of.

The only sign of humanity about the place was a small decorated Christmas tree to the right of the large wooden doors to the entrance of the building. There were a few wrapped Christmas presents lying under the tree, and I wondered if they were actual presents or simply empty boxes wrapped to give the illusion of presents. Seeing them also made me think of the Christmas present that I had purchased at Borders for Mom: about two months ago, that old movie "Friendly Persuasion," with Gary Cooper, had been on TV. Mom watched it, and it had made her laugh so much that I bought a DVD of it for her.

One of those two guards at the door told me to follow him. He, as did all of the guards that I saw there, wore a light-green uniform, with a wide, black leather belt that had a holster with a gun in it, a case with a walky-talky in it and a leather loop that had a long, slender, wooden club in it. That black leather case with the walky-talky reminded me of my newly-purchased cell phone with its black leather case clipped to my belt. I just love wearing that cell phone. It gives me a sense of status— like being a doctor or something. I know that it's a false sense of status, but so what?

That guard was a tall, lean fellow in his early twenties, I would say. He spoke with a rural accent, and his whole demeanor—in his speech, in his walk, in his thinking—seemed to be one of slowness, or one of the fact that nothing could disturb this guy, not even a fire lit under his ass. Now, I had never met a guard from a prison before, but this guy just didn't strike me as being tough enough to be a prison guard. I was glad he was with me, though, because as we walked across the floor, passing the large metallic doors of those corridors, I heard numerous voices emanating from behind them. Hearing those voices, for some reason, made me start fantasizing that at any moment some big, hairy, burly guy was going to jump out at me, grab me by the throat, and say: Hmmmm, fresh meat. You 're mine, bitch. Bend over and assume the position.

"This is sure a cavernous place," I said, wanting to make general conversation with him.

"C-cavernous, sir?" he replied languidly.

"Ahhhh, large," I stated.

"She's large, sir," he said. "That's for sure. Here we be, sir," he stated, stopping in front of a wooden door and then opening it. "Have a sit in here and I'll be bringin' Mr. Jones to you."

"Great," I said, passing him and stepping into the room, saying to myself, What a country hick.

He, then, shut the door, which I didn't like him doing at all. I mean, it was bad enough that the room was so small, and bare—just four walls and a ceiling, painted white, and a long, heavy, metallic table with four or five metal folding chairs surrounding it—and cold. Damn cold. And him shutting that door made that room feel even smaller, and barer, and colder. I felt claustrophobic and nervous, and cold chills ran up and down my spine.

I stepped to the back of the table and sat down in the first chair at the left end of the table, so that I could face the door.

As I sat there, I kept going over in my mind what that guard had said: Have a sit in here and I'll bring Mr. Jones to you. To me, that seemed impossible. I mean, John's a convicted murderer, in prison. I thought for sure that I'd be in a room with a glass partition and phones. You know, like you see in the movies. Am I really going to face him in this tiny room with no glass wall or phones? I had said to myself. Well, at least he'll have arm-and-leg shackles on.

To take my mind off of the smallness of that room, and the coldness of it, and all, I started going over again in my mind some of the questions that I was going to ask him. The first question I was going to ask him, the number one question—looking him straight in the eye, and being dead serious—well, being serious—was: "John, did you do it? Did you murder your daughter, Tyra?" Then, suddenly, I thought: Damn, why didn't you buy a recorder? One of those mini-recorders so that you could keep playing back everything that he says. Damn.

Time just seemed to drag in that damn, small, butt-ass cold room. I lifted back the sleeve of my topcoat and looked down at my wristwatch and I knew that at least ten, or fifteen, minutes had passed. I was getting damn fed up with sitting in that damn room, so I got up and started walking for the door. I was almost at the door when it opened. That same guard held the door open and John walked slowly, unsteadily, past him and entered the room. I was shocked—shocked!

John had always had a healthy, youthful look about him. But this guy's body was emaciated, and his unshaven face was gaunt. John's light brown hair had always been of a straight, fine quality, but this guy's long, dirty, uncombed hair was just plain thin—I could see skin on top of his head. But what shocked me the most about seeing him was his demeanor. There was no more care-free, happy-go-luckiness to him. Hell, it was like he wasn't even there at all. He just kept standing there—no arm-and-leg shackles, either: just an orange jumpsuit—staring at me with brown eyes that were-were lifeless. He looked like a broken old man—and I'm at least twenty-something years older than him. I felt like a kid looking at him.

"I'll be right outside the door if you need me, sir," the guard said to me, and then shut the door.

After a moment of silence, I said, hesitantly, nervously stumbling on my words: "Why-why don't we sit down, John."

I sat back down in the chair that I had been sitting in and John sat across from me in total silence with his head down. I thought: Is this guy crazy? Has he lost his mind? Have these guys in here beat him senseless?

"How have you b—" I began, but then stopped. "Do you know me, John?"

Staring intently at the top of the table and appearing as if he were struggling to find the answer to my question, he finally said: "Tom."

After a few moments had passed, he raised his head, and looking through me, not at me, he said: "What are you doing here, Tom?"

"Well—well, Claire has asked me—"

"Claire," he sighed, shaking his head from side to side, as if remembering. "Claire," he repeated. "She's been good to me . . . She's sick, too."

"Yes," I replied. "She's-she's sent me here to see if I can help you."

"Help me?" he said, flatly, and then laughed a hollow laugh. "No one can help me."

"Well, John, she still believes in you. Claire still believes in your innocence," I continued, and saying this seemed to bring a spark of life to John's lifeless eyes. "She-she wants me to find out who mur-killed Tyra."

"Tyra!" he wailed. "Tyra, my baby," he wailed again, grabbing the lip of the table in his hands and shaking it hard. "She's dead. She's dead," he repeated, tears now running down his tormented, haggard face.

"Who-who killed her, John?" I asked.

"That bitch killed her," he replied, straightening his arms and leaning back hard in the chair and throwing his head back and shaking it wildly from side to side. "That bitch Helen killed her. That goddamn bitch Helen killed her—murdered my baby!" he screamed, thrusting his whole body back at me. "She did it! She did it! Helen! Helen! She did it!" he continued and pounded his closed fists down hard upon the table.

Suddenly, the door flew open and that guard came rushing in.

"What be goin'on in here?!" he demanded, after coming to an abrupt halt at the edge of the table beside John, his hand gripping the handle of that slender, long club.

"It's all right," I said. "He's just upset."

"I'm goin' to have to ask that this be over, sir," he said, or stated, to me.

"All right," I replied, and then stood up.

I looked down at John. He had his arms and hands spread out on the table with his head slumped between them.

"John," I then said, "just remember that Claire still believes in you."

I then left, with my mind spinning and my whole body shaking—and my body wasn't shaking from just the coldness of that damn, small room, either.

Although I was overjoyed to be out of that room, and out of that prison, all the way home, I kept saying to myself: What a complete waste of time.

I hadn't learn a damn thing from the guy. He had given me nothing—and he certainly hadn't convinced me that he hadn't done it, hadn't murdered Tyra. The guy was nuts.

No, it was a complete waste of my time. The whole day had been wasted. Driving all the way out there and back, speaking with him—and on top of all of that it had cost me nearly fifty dollars in gas.

No, I told myself that I was done. I told myself that I know that Claire doesn't have much money and that she had given me a thousand bucks, but you know in today's world a thousand bucks isn't all that much money. Now, I had done some investigating—like I had said that I would do. I had done that, and I thought what investigating I had done was well worth a measly thousand dollars. So, no, I was done. Maybe tomorrow, or the next day, I would get on the internet, or maybe go down to the library, and see if I could look up some of the newspaper articles on John's trail and go over them, but other than doing that, I was done. I told myself that maybe I would wait until after Christmas, but then I would see Claire and inform her that my full investigation of the case had, sadly, brought me to the conclusion that John had murdered Tyra.

But did I do that? No. The whole thing was a mess. What a mess.

It was a little after six-thirty by the time I got back home. I had stopped off at Burger King and had a Double Whopper, a large fries, and a large coke … Well, I felt that I deserved all that because of all that I had been through that day.

I was dog-tired, miserable, and cold. All I wanted to do was go upstairs to my bedroom, take off that suit, get four or five beers from my cache of beers in the closet, crash on my bed, watch some TV on my small TV, get drunk, and fall drunkenly to sleep.

Mom was so excited to see me. She stopped me at the staircase just as I was going up. She wanted to know everything: What was it like being in a prison? What was John like? What did he look like? What did he say?

"Oh, Mom," I said. "I'm so tired. I just want to go to bed. Can I tell you all about John and everything tomorrow?"

"You poor dear," she said. "I bet you are tired . . . Say, you have got to be starving. I made a big pot of vegetable soup especially for you. Just the way you like it, with hamburger in it."

"Oh, I'm not hungry, Mom," I replied, feigning being more tired than I really was and thinking of those beers in the closet. "Thanks, but I just want to go to bed."

"Not hungry?!" she cried incredulously. "You haven't had anything to eat since breakfast." After giving me a curious look, as if she were trying to read my face, she said: "Oh, did you stop at a restaurant or something and have supper?"

"No, no," I replied. "I'm hungry, but I'm more tired than hungry."

"Oooooh," she then said, dismissively. "Then, you can have a little bowl of soup. It will only take me a minute to warm it up, and you can tell me as much as you can about John while I'm warming it and while you're eating. It will only be a few minutes. Come on into the kitchen."

"Well, okay," I replied, and then added: "How about buttering two slices of bread for me, too?"

"Sure," she replied, entering the kitchen. "This dang cast," she then said, inserting her left index-finger into the top of the cast. "I'll sure be glad when it comes off in two weeks. It's itching me like crazy."

So, I had a small bowl of vegetable soup, and then a refill, and four slices of buttered bread, washing it all down with a cup of hot tea. I told Mom all about my experiences of the day and all about John. By the time I was done, I felt like a stuffed pig—what with having eaten that hamburger and stuff—and I was now truly tired.

I rose heavily from the chair and was about to turned around and go upstairs when my whole body and mind froze solid from what Mom had then said to me. She told me that she had gone over to see how Claire was doing. She said that when she told Claire where I was and what I was doing, Claire was so happy. She said that she hadn't seen Claire that happy in years. Then, Mom looked me straight in the eyes and said: "I'm so proud of you, Tom."

My very soul silently screamed: Oh, shit! What a mess. What a complete mess! How in the hell did I get myself into this mess?! … And how in the hell do I get myself out of this mess?! What a mess!

I had to go through with it now. I had no other choice. I had to continue the investigation. God knows over the years I have given that woman precious little—nothing—for which to be proud of me. I had no other choice now. I had to continue. Damn!

What a mess.

Chapter Five

I was so stuffed that I wasn't able to drink my first beer until nine o'clock. After I left Mom, I want up to my bedroom, took off my cloths and flopped onto my bed on my back, wearing nothing but my underwear. I felt so uncomfortable. My stomach felt tighter than an overblown balloon.

As I lay there, wishing for death, or for at least a sheet-raising fart, I thought: Well, what do you do now? Where do you take the investigation from here?

After a few minutes of thinking about it, I told myself that John still believes that his old girlfriend, that gal with the gigantic breasts, that Helen Dyer, murdered Tyra. So, I told myself that that has to be the next step—to talk to her, to talk to that Helen Dyer.

From her testimony in court that day, I knew that she worked as a janitor at some assistant-living facility, but I couldn't remember which one she had stated that it was.

The next morning, Friday it was, I awoke at six forty—which shocked me; if I don't set the alarm clock, I usually don't get up until at least nine. I was thankful, though, because I wanted to get up early and get started. After washing my face and under my armpits in the sink in the bathroom, and after shaving, and after dressing in that suit again, I grabbed the binoculars and my cell phone off of my desk, and then I went downstairs and got the phonebook out of the kitchen pantry to see if there was a listing for a Helen Dyer. I put the coffee on and then sat down at the table and began flipping pages in the phonebook to the D's. Yes, there was a listing for a Helen Dyer. Her address was on Minnesota Street, which is in the city and not too far from the house. I thought that it must be an apartment, because following the address was written: apt. C.

Mom and I always keep a yellow notepad on the kitchen table to write each other notes. I wrote Helen Dyer's address onto the top sheet, ripped it off from the pad, folded it and shoved it into my right suit coat pocket. After that, I wrote Mom a short note telling her that I would be back by noon to drive her over to feed and visit Dad and that if she needed me to call me on my cell phone. Then, I filled my Starbucks thermos with steaming hot coffee and headed for the hall closet to get my topcoat, with those binoculars in my right hand.

The whole area around that apartment was pretty seedy—deteriorating, old, two-storied red brick flats, some lived in, some boarded up; a fallow lot here and there; a little wooden house that was burned down; cars on both sides of that narrow street that from the looks of them should have been sent, or hauled, to the junkyard years ago.

Minnesota Street was one block west of Broadway Boulevard, which is a major boulevard in St. Louis, connecting the older part of the City of St. Louis to the older part of the County of St. Louis.

The apartment building in which Helen Dyer lived was congruous to the neighborhood—it wasn't anything to write home about, if you know what I mean. An old, two-storied building constructed of what I believe is called cinderblocks, painted white long ago, with an iron-rod railing, also long ago painted white, on the second level of the building, and a wooden hand-railing, not painted and rotting, on both sides of the cement steps in the middle of the building and leading down to the sidewalk. All of the units of the building faced the street; all were narrow; each unit contained its own narrow white wooden door and a small window.

About the only redeeming thing to this whole deteriorating, decrepit area were the trees. They reminded me of the trees in our neighborhood—tall maple trees, or oak trees, lining both sides of the street with long branches that extended out above the street, and even though the trees were denuded of leaves, I told myself that I bet they provided plenty of welcome shade in the summer. But in a neighborhood such as this they might be used to hide secrets.

I got pretty lucky, too. I got a parking spot on the same side of the street of the building and just four or five cars away from it.

There were eight units in all to this building, four on top and four on the bottom. On each door was one of those reflective, metallic, black stick-isms of a letter of the alphabet, running from A to H.

With binoculars in hand, I could easily see the door to her apartment, which was the third door east of the building on the bottom level.

I felt pretty uncomfortable sitting there in my car with the engine running and watching her door with those binoculars, and I didn't need the binoculars at all. I kept thinking that any moment now someone is going to call the police on me, or that a Neanderthal-type of guy—with long, dirty hair and multiple tattoos; wearing a T-shirt and tattered jeans, and holding a beer-can in his hand—is going to come flying out of one of those doors and scream at me: "What are you doing in this neighborhood? I can tell you don't belong here. Are you a peeping Tom or something?"

After I had gotten her address and phone number out of the phone book back home, I had thought about just calling her. But then I thought: What if I call her and after telling her who I am and why I'm calling, she hangs up on me? So, I call her again and she hangs up on me again. I call her again and she hangs up on me again. I didn't want her to think that I was stalking her—like that Fred guy had done to me—and call the police on me. No, I didn't want that. And now, being at her apartment, I didn't want to go up and knock on her door, either. What if I did that and after telling her who I am and why I was there she got angry and got a bat—or a gun!—and tried to hurt me? Why, I'd be stuck there in her doorway. No, I didn't want any part of any of that. I mean, I saw and heard this person in court that day, and my opinion of her was that she was one tough broad—and uneducated. One of the things that I was definitely going to ask her was if she could spell the word "revenge."

So, my plan was this: I'd stay there, in my car, until she came out and I'd confront her on the sidewalk. This way, if she got angry and threw a punch or something at me I could block it or dodge it, and dash back to my car.

I told myself that if I didn't see her by eleven o'clock, I'd come back tomorrow, or Sunday, or Monday, or—well, until I saw her.

About an hour after being there—and suddenly I had to pee—I saw two little black girls come out of one of the upstairs apartments that had tiny Christmas lights on the inside of the small window of that apartment. These two little girls were all bundled up in winter attire— winter coats, gloves, earmuffs, and stocking caps. They both had backpacks strapped to their backs, and as they walked with playful stride west up the block, I thought: My god, that taller one can't be over ten years old. Where's the Mom? Where's the—and then, I saw the door to Helen Dyer's apartment open, and then she stepped out.

She was dressed for winter as well. She had on a dark-brown stocking cap that was pulled all the way down to her protruding ears and stopped at the upper rim of her clear-rimmed glasses. She had a black scarf that was wrapped tightly around her neck, and she covered her face with one of the ends of it like a shield to block the biting coldness of the day. Her coat was full-length down to her knees, light blue, made of cloth, and a bit tattered-looking. Underneath the coat, she wore worn jeans and white tennis shoes that had seen better days.

I wondered what size that coat was, because it looked too big for her in the shoulders. But with those watermelon-size breasts of hers, they threatened to pop the oversized blue button at the chest.

At the sidewalk, she turned and started coming my way, east.

I waited until she was almost abreast of my car before I got out. With my heart pounding away in my chest, and with sweaty palms on this butt-ass cold day, I said, "Well, here goes nothing" and got out of the car.

I went around the back of my car and stood on the cracking sidewalk, blocking her way.

"Helen Dyer?" I asked, giving an authoritative sound to my voice to hide my nervousness.

"Yes," she replied, hesitantly and cautiously, holding the end of that scarf to her face, and, suddenly, I felt sorry for her. She seemed so helpless, like a rabbit caught in the hypnotic freeze of headlights of a car at night.

"I'm Tom-Thomas Mayor. I'm conducting an investigation into the murder of Tyra Jones."

"Are you a cop?" she asked, questioningly. "You don't look like a cop—your hair's too long and messy, and you look too out of shape to be a cop."

"No, I'm not a cop," I replied. "I'm a—"

"A goddamn reporter," she stated, interrupting me. "A goddamn reporter," she repeated, shaking her head. "I don't have to talk to you. Get out of my way," she continued, shooing me away with her hand. "You're gonna make me miss my bus for work."

After saying that, she stepped around me and began walking away.

I spun around and said, "John still thinks that you murdered Tyra. Did you murder Tyra, Ms. Dyer?"

That stopped her dead in her tracks, and when she spun back around, her whole body and face was on fire with pure anger. If she had had ice icicles hanging on her, her anger would have evaporated them immediately like the hot summer sun.

She came at me like a damn steamroller, threatening to smash me as flat as an asphalt street. I didn't think she was going to stop,—I didn't know whether to run or to brace myself for impact—but, suddenly, she came to an abrupt halt a foot away from me—the tips of those mountainous breasts almost touching the chest area of my topcoat.

"Listen here, you motherfucker," she shouted angrily at me, pointing a jabbing index-finger at my face. "The person who killed that little brat is rottin' in jail and will be rottin' in hell next month … That's the thanks I got for takin' care of the little brat. He tossed me out of the house like a goddamn dog."

"You beat up his daughter," I replied, stepping back. "He had to take her to the hospital."

"Big fuckin' deal," she said. "So I slapped her around, some. So what? I was drunk—and he got me drinkin' again. I was sober for over a year before I met him ... I took care of him and the little brat; I fed them; I did the wash and cleaned the house; I fucked him. He said that I was the best fuck that he had ever had, had never been fucked like the fuck I gave him. And what thanks did I get? He tossed me out of the house like a goddamn dog . . . I'm only goin' to say this once to you: On the day that that little brat was killed, I was in St. Anthony's Halfway House. You can check with the police. So fuck off, you motherfucker."

With that, she turned and stormed off.

Well, that was a waste of time, I said to myself, watching her as she walked down the sidewalk. That was a complete waste of my time. I got nothing from her. Nothing. But I'm sure glad that it's over. That is one mean gal.

Then, I felt something cold and wet between my legs. When I lifted my topcoat up and looked down at my pants, I said: "Oh, shit." I had peed in my pants.

Driving back home, I kept chiding myself. I just couldn't believe that I had gotten nothing from her—and I definitely couldn't believe that I had let that bitch scare me so badly that I had peed in my pants.

Well, you're no P. I., I said to myself. No William Powell; no Nick Charles, the Thin Man. Do you think Nick Charles would have let an uneducated, low-life bitch like that get in his face and scare him so badly that he'd pee in his pants? No. He would have said something sharp and witty to her, like-like: "Listen freckle-face, unless you 're going to kiss me, take those 55-gallon jugs out of my chest. '' And he definitely would have gotten the information out of her that he wanted. No, you 're no Nick Charles.

Anyway, after I got back home, I told Mom all that had happened with Helen Dyer, how mean she was, and how I had gotten nothing from her. I also told her about peeing in my pants—how I had drank too much coffee and I hadn't realized how badly I had to go to the bathroom until just before I had pulled into the driveway and that was when I couldn't hold it any longer and peed in my pants.

Mom had wanted me to take the whole suit—pants and all—to the cleaners, because a label on the inside of the suit coat stated, "dry clean only." I told Mom that I couldn't do that, that I needed the pants and suit for the investigation. So, Mom told me to take the pants off and that she would "spot clean" the pants and lightly press them.

We had about three hours before we had to go feed and visit Dad, so after cleaning and drying myself and then putting on my plaid shirt and my jeans, I plopped down on my bed and thought about what my next move should be on the investigation, with half of my brain saying, shouting: You've done enough. No more. She 'II still be proud of you. What do you want to do, get beat up?--or pee in your pants again?

I was at a loss as to what to do next, really. I mean, John was so convinced that Dyer had murdered Tyra, but I was torn. As I have said, when she had given testimony against John at his trial that day, I felt that she was being truthful, and I felt the same way after confronting her on the sidewalk, that she was being truthful. I did keep going over in my mind, though, why she had gotten so angry with me when I had asked her if she had murdered Tyra. I mean, if she weren't guilty, or hiding something, why would she have gotten so angry with me?

Then, a thought struck me. What if she had fooled everyone? Her whole alibi was that she was at St. Anthony's Halfway House on the day Tyra was murdered. What if she had eluded everyone there that day, had snuck out, murdered Tyra, and then snuck back without anyone detecting her?

Suddenly, it all made sense to me. John was right. She had motive and means—and let me tell you, from what I saw of that gal that day, she could definitely murder someone. I'll admit it, the bitch scared me. Who the hell did she think she was anyway, getting in my face like that and screaming at me? I'm in my fifties, man. I don't have to take that crap— especially not from some sleazebag like that, that Helen Dyer.

What was that place like, that St. Anthony's Halfway House? I asked myself. Does it have bars on the windows? Does it have a guard? Do you have to sign in and sign out to come and go? Was it possible—could she have snuck out and back in without being detected? I had to know.

I changed back into my suit clothes, substituting my suit pants for a pair of black dress pants. With my topcoat on, I told myself that no one would know the difference.

My plan was this: After Mom and I had fed and visited Dad, I would drive Mom back home and then drive over to St. Anthony's Halfway House.

St. Anthony's Halfway House was about six miles north of Helen Dyer's apartment, on Broadway Boulevard. It was on a corner of the block. Big, it was: a tall, three-storied, red-brick, old building, with tall, narrow, windows and a flat roof. From the sidewalk, you had to look up to see it, because it sat upon a small hill. If you looked east, you could easily see The Gateway Arch in the not too far distance, and the Mississippi River just beyond that. I would say that the house had been the residence of rich people at one time—about a hundred years ago, that is.

The small front yard was in two tiers of un-groomed, now brown grass, with two tiers of cracking, concrete, steps. The steps were in the middle of the yard and came to an end at a short concrete sidewalk, which came to an end at a two-step concrete porch, which led to two tall, wooden, ornate, old, doors. There was a large wooden sign on the first tier on the left side of the yard which said in painted black letters: **Welcome to St. Anthony's Halfway House. Serving women's needs since 1972.**

After opening one of the doors and stepping inside—feeling the draftiness of a large, old place, and smelling the mustiness of an old place—I looked immediately to my left because of hearing the voices of girls. In a large room with a high-vaulted ceiling, four or five women, in their early twenties, I would say, were milling around each other, sitting on metal folding chairs that were positioned in a half-circle. Two of the women had babies in their arms. Upon seeing me, one of the women jumped up from her chair to greet me.

"Hi," she said, ever so coquettishly. She was wearing a white, pullover sweater that was way too big for her and jeans, and this girl was just bone-thin. "My name is Amanda. What's yours?" she continued, keeping up the coquettishness, and now taking a lump of her stringy, long, brown hair in a bony hand and twirling it at me while she moved her no-weight hips from side to side.

"Well, my name is—"

"Sir, sir," I heard a woman's voice say to the right of me, a tone of exasperated urgency in her voice. "May I help you?" I turned and saw a wide-faced, heavy-set woman, in her early twenties as well, I would say, sitting behind a large wooden desk that faced the door in another room with a high-vaulted ceiling. Directly behind the desk, against the south wall, was roll after roll of old, metal, filing-cabinets, painted white.

"Why, yes, you can," I said, and began walking towards her, hearing the planks of the highly-polished, old, wooden, floor making a cracking sound under the weight of my body.

"Go back into the room, Amanda," the woman behind the desk then ordered.

"Okay," I heard Amanda replied, disappointedly.

When I came abreast of her desk, she asked again, but this time more pleasantly, "How may I help you?"

"I'd like some information on one of your former patients, or former residents—a Helen Dyer."

"Oooooh," she replied as if in pain, "you will have to speak with our managing director, Mrs. Savage." She then turned her head to the right, to the front of the building, and pointed to a woman who was seated behind another large, wooden, desk that was facing this woman's desk and was behind one of the two tall, narrow, bare windows. She was on the phone.

As I walked over to her desk, I said to myself: This gal's name is 'Savage'? With a name like that, this can't be good—and it wasn't.

There were two green-padded chairs with wooden arms and legs in front of her desk, and after standing there for a few minutes and listening to her having a conversation with someone and her not acknowledging me and getting tired of just standing there like a dummy, I sat down in the chair nearest to me. After doing that, she then acknowledged me, giving me a very stern look of disapproval, looking at me over the top of her half-moon-shaped, black-rimmed, glasses, accompanied by a crystal-beaded chain, as if saying to me: How rude of you to sit down without first being given permission to do so. She was wearing a black pants suit and a white blouse, with a red-beaded necklace and matching earrings. Her hair was the color of that pants suit—a dye-job, I would say—and it was coiffed to her straight, narrow, shoulders like that little Dutch boy's haircut: a box with the middle-front cut out of it. She was in her late fifties—this I was certain of, what with all the make-up she had plastered on her skin to cover all of the age lines that mapped her narrow-shaped face. The scent of the perfume she was wearing was overwhelming. It smelled like pine, and I thought: You got to be wrong. Who would want to smell like a tree?

"Please don't feel that way," she said into the phone. She had a high-pitched voice, and if that wasn't bad enough to begin with, she made it worse by accenting the last few words of every sentence by raising that already shrilled voice about an octave higher. I found it to be very annoying. "You have been a devoted advocate for our cause here, and no donation is ever too large or too small . . . Have a good day, Mrs. Joyce, and I'll see you at the fundraiser next month. Goodbye."

"How may I help you," she said to me, flatly, or patronizingly, lacing her gloss-colored fingernails together and then placing her hands on the desk. "I'm Mrs. Savage."

"Yes, I'm doing an investigation into the murder of Tyra Jones, and I would like some information on one of your former patient, or resident, here—Helen Dyer."

"I heard you ask my secretary this," she said to me, equally as flatly, or patronizingly. "And you are?"

"I'm Thomas Mayor," I replied.

"In what capacity are you conducting this investigation?" she then asked.

"Capacity?" I asked.

"Are you with the police, or are you a reporter?"

"No," I replied, "this is a private investigation," as I thought: Why does everyone keep asking me if I'm a cop or a reporter?

"I see," she then stated. "Well, Mr. Mayor, all information concerning our residents here is confidential."

"But all I want to know is if Helen Dyer could have gotten out of here and back undetected on the day that Tyra Jones was murdered?" I asked. "Were you aware that she was a susp—"

"Again, Mr. Mayor," she stated, interrupting me, the irritation with me building in that high-pitched voice of hers, "all information concerning our—"

"Okay," I then stated, now interrupting her, "let's be hypothetical then. Could anyone get out of here and back without being—"

"Again, Mr. Mayor," she said, that voice of hers almost reaching crescendo-pitch, and making me wince, "all information con—"

"Do you have surveillance cameras here?" I interrupted hurriedly. "How about a guard—or a book to sign in and sign out?"

"Mr. Mayor!" she stated, shooting up from her chair, her voice shattering-glass-high now, and making me wince, again.

"Do you think she can spell the word 'revenge'?"

"Leave, Mr. Mayor," she demanded, pointing an outstretched arm and index-finger towards the door. "Or shall I phone the police?"

I was silent for a moment, and then said, flatly, "No, you don't have to do that. I'm leaving."

I rose from the chair, turned and started for the door. At the door, I turned back around and said to her: "By the way, thank you—for nothing," and then walked quickly out of the room and out of the building.

I couldn't believe it! I just couldn't believe that it had happened again to me! I got nothing from her—nothing! I didn't know any more about the case than when I had gone in there. It was frustrating. I mean, I kept asking myself how does a real private detectives do it: How do they get information out of people? Nobody wants to answer questions unless they're forced to—and when did women get so independent and aggressive? I don't like that. I like women who are vulnerable and helpless, and with a southern accent: Oh, Tom, help little ole me. I've broken a fingernail. . . Oh, Tom. Be gentle with me.

I love having you in little ole me, but you're so big, and I'm so tiny, and helpless, that little ole me is going to faint. Please, please, be gentle with little ole me … Now, that's the type of women I like.

It was a little after two-thirty by the time I got back home, and I was tired, frustrated, and fed up. It had been a butt-ass long day—no, it had been a butt-ass long week. I hadn't worked that hard in—in years. I decided to give myself a well-desired break and take the weekend off. Actually, where my thoughts were leaning was that Monday I was going to walk over to Claire's and tell her that my investigation had concluded that, sadly, John had murdered Tyra … I mean, yes, it's great to have your mother proud of you, but, damn, I had given that damn case almost an entire week of my time and life, and wasn't that enough for all that I had been through for a paltry thousand dollars?

Mom had cooked her homemade bean soup that night for supper. Although the Roman Catholic Church had repealed the rule, or law, forbidding the eating of meat on Fridays years ago, my parents—or at least Mom did—still adhered to Meatless Fridays.

I hate beans. Beans and beer and I don't like each other.

After eating two large bowls of bean soup, and several slices of bread, heavily buttered, I told Mom that I was going upstairs to lie down.

"Okay," she said, washing the supper dishes in the kitchen sink. "Oh," she then said, "remember you told me that *Home Alone* is on tonight at eight o' clock. You're coming back down to watch it, aren't you?"

Oh, crap, I said to myself. I had wanted to just go upstairs, unbutton my jeans and unzip the zipper, grab some beers from the closet, turn on my TV, crash on my bed, and get drunk. "Yeah, I'll come back down," I said to her.

Over the past three or four years, it has become somewhat of a tradition with Mom and me to watch all of the Christmas movies and Christmas TV shows together. I guess we started doing this when Dad's Alzheimer's really started to kick in and he stopped watching TV. I had enjoyed watching those movies and TV shows with Mom before. They never failed to make us laugh or to put us in the "Christmas Spirit," but for some reason, I just didn't want to do it this year.

I did do it, though. About fifteen minutes before eight, I got up from bed, zipped up my pants and buttoned them, and then went downstairs and watched the movie *Home Alone* with her. It did make us laugh, and it brought joy to my heart to see her laughing and enjoying herself.

I was glad when it was over, though—couldn't wait until it was over. More often than not, my laughter was hollow, and, no, it didn't ignite the "Spirit of Christmas" within me. How could it without Dad being here? Well, at least now I could go upstairs and get drunk.

Chapter Six

From time to time over the weekend, I did think about the case. I thought about getting in touch with the police detective who had arrested John upon Tyra's murder and talking with John's defense attorney—wanting to ask both of them what evidence did they have that Helen Dyer was telling the truth, that she had indeed been at St. Anthony's Halfway House on the day that Tyra was murdered. I told myself that if interviewing both of them brought nothing new to the case, then, it was over. I would, then, definitely, go over and tell Claire that John unequivocally had murdered Tyra.

Then, Sunday night, about a quarter-to-eleven, while I was lying on my bed, gulping down my second beer, a thought struck me … I was only on my second beer because of having watched the movie *White Christmas* with Mom. No, I hadn't wanted to watch it, but she loves that movie so much—with all of the singing and dancing, and with Bing Crosby and Danny Kaye—and I knew that she had wanted me to watch it with her. So, I had watched it. It was just simply easier to watch it with her than it was to make-up some lame excuse—and, no, it, too, failed to ignite the "Spirit of Christmas" within me. It didn't even make me laugh for that matter. I was in a bad mood. I kept thinking how stupid my life was, how here I am in my fifties, and I'm sitting here in the living room of my mother's house watching *White Christmas* with her when I should be in my own house with my own wife watching *White Christmas*. I just kept looking down at the wooden floor and shaking my head and feeling bad.

I was sitting at the far end of the couch, next to the entrance of the kitchen, and Mom was sitting at the other end of the couch, close to the TV. Well, I wasn't paying attention, and she looked over at me and catches me looking sad. She said, "What's the matter, Tom? Don't you like the movie?"

"No, no," I replied. "It's not that, Mom. I'm just thinking about the case, what steps I ought to take next."

"It's pretty rough, isn't it, Tom?" Mom said, and then set her cup of decaffeinated coffee down on the old, dark-stained, coffee table.

"Well, yeah, Mom," I replied. "It is. Nobody will talk with me— and none of the people I've interviewed has convinced me that John didn't do it. It's frustrating . . . Plus, I've done some investigating on the case that I haven't told you about," I continued, lying, "and none of it looks good for John. I'm afraid that my investigation is quickly coming to an end and—well, I think Claire may just have to accept the fact that John may have murdered Tyra."

"I pray not," Mom said. "Claire wants so much for him to be innocent ... I know this is rough on you, Tom, but in two weeks I'll have this dang cast taken off, and you won't have to drive me around anymore. It'll be easier on you then. You'll have more time to give to the investigation. I'm so proud of you, Tom—well, we all are; Claire and me."

I didn't need for her to say that to me again. Damnit. I didn't want two more weeks of this crap!

Anyway, like I said, a thought struck me. What if this whole thing wasn't about John or Tyra at all? What if it was about Megan? ... I mean, think about it. What if her kidnapping hadn't been a random act as we all had assumed? What if she had pissed someone off so much that kidnapping her and killing her wasn't enough? What if that "revenge is mine" spray painted in red on Tyra's bedroom door had nothing to do with John or Tyra but had everything to do with Megan?

Suddenly, I felt excited. I had to know.

I thought about interviewing John and Megan's neighbors. Then, I thought: No, when you work with someone, you really get to know that person ...What was the name of that dentist Megan worked for? What was her name? She was a pretty little gal. You saw her interviewed on TV a few days after Megan went missing. What is her—Williams. That's it. Williams. Dr. Teresa Williams.

I jumped up off of my bed and went over to my desk. After looking out of the tall, narrow window directly in front of the desk—looking beyond the set of Christmas lights in the window, which I had yet to turn on, ever; I just didn't want to—and seeing nothing on the street below, I Googled the local Yellow Pages on my computer and then typed the name: Dr. Teresa Williams. Bingo. Her name appeared with the address of her office and phone number. I, then, printed it.

After drinking two more beers, I set my alarm for eight-thirty a.m., and, then, fell into bed semi-drunk.

The next morning, I drank a cup of coffee first to wake me up, and, then, about ten-of-nine, I called her office. I got a recording, though, that stated the office didn't open until nine o' clock: the recording was of a woman's voice, in her forties, I would say, and who had the deepest, gravelly-sounding voice that I have ever heard of a woman's voice— sexy, it was. So, I had another cup of coffee and read some of the newspaper.

At precisely nine o' clock, I called her office again, and I got a hold of that woman with that sexy-sounding voice. I told her that I had a terrible toothache, but that I didn't have a dentist in St. Louis. I told her that although I had been born and raised in St. Louis, about ten years ago my place of employment transferred me to Los Angeles, California, but that I had gotten myself transferred back to St. Louis three weeks ago on a hardship case because of my elderly parent's failing health: I was going undercover on this one. I wasn't going to screw this one up by telling the doctor that I was conducting a private investigation into the murder of Tyra Jones.

That gal—the receptionist, Sarah, she said her name was—told me that I was in luck, that she had just had a cancellation for two o'clock this afternoon, and that if I could make it there at that time, I could see Dr. Williams today. I told her that I would take that appointment and thanked her for being so kind. After I hung up the receiver, I told myself: With a voice as deep as that voice is, I bet she's a smoker.

The address of Dr. Williams' office was 9100 Clayton Road—in the township of Clayton—so I knew that it would take me at least thirty minutes to get there. When I had passed by the bathroom to come downstairs, I had heard Mom taking a shower. Now, knowing that I would be under a time crunch to make it out to Clayton by two o'clock, what with having to drive Mom down to see and feed Dad lunch, I told myself that when she came downstairs I'd explain the situation to her and ask her if she would ride along with me to that doctor's office.

She said that she would—and she did, too.

St. Louis is a stupid place to live. We have two seats of local government in St. Louis. For the residents who live in the City of St. Louis, their local government is in downtown St. Louis, and for the residents who live in the County of St. Louis, their local government is in downtown Clayton. I like going to Clayton more than I do going to downtown St. Louis: Downtown St. Louis is old and dirty, whereas downtown Clayton is much newer and far cleaner.

Clayton Road is in the County, and it runs east and west. Dr. Williams' office was about seven or eight miles west of downtown Clayton, in a long section on Clayton Road that is a mixture of uppity businesses—lawyers, doctors, avant-garde shops and such—co-existing in total harmony with mansion after mansion. These mansions have to cost in the millions, easily.

The building that housed Dr. Williams' office stood alone on the north side of a pristine intersection. The building itself was modern-looking and expensive-looking—a one-story building of light-colored brick, with large, tinted-glass windows. Finely trimmed evergreen bushes stood sentinel at the lower-waist of the building and followed the graceful cure of the building around the block. Parking was to the back of the building.

You could tell that this place was expensive, because the driveway and the whole parking lot itself were paved with little rock that's glued to the pavement underneath. It's real shiny looking. I've seen it on the driveways of homes, and you just know that it has to be expensive to do that.

Directly across the street from Dr. Williams' office was a restaurant that had a circular drive that passed the entrance to the place. The entrance had a green canopy that led from the sidewalk to two, ornate, wooden-framed, stained-glass, doors. On the face of the green canopy was written the word, in white ink: Ferraro's.

"Okay," I said to Mom after pulling into the driveway and stopping to the side of a row of four-foot-high bushes that hid the sidewalk, "this is it. I'm glad that there's that restaurant back there. I'll drive you over there, and you can stay there while I'm in here."

"Why can't I go in with you?" Mom protested.

"Because you're my mother for one thing," I replied. "I'm undercover. I can't have you saying something that might blow my cover."

"All right," she then said, reluctantly. "What does that restaurant look like?" She turned half around in the seat and looked out of the rear window. "What's it say? Let me get my reading glasses," she said and began rummaging through her large, baggy, black, purse for her glasses.

"It says Ferraro's," I said, getting a bit angry with her.

"What kind of a name is that?" she then said, turning around again and looking at it.

"I think it's Italian," I replied, now getting damn angry with her.

"Oooooh, I don't like Italian food," she said. "And that place looks too expensive."

After pushing back the right sleeve of my topcoat and looking at my wristwatch, I said, "Mom, I only have ten minutes until my appointment. I have to go. Just go to the restaurant—just have a cup of coffee or something . . . Oh, I'm sick of this," I said, turning back around and throwing up my arms and hands in disgust. "I don't even want to do this. You're the one that got me into this. Why don't you go in there and interview her."

"Me?!" Mom cried and turned back around. "What would I say to her?"

"I don't know," I replied, feeling dejected. "You'd probably do better than I'm doing. Just secretively ask her questions about Megan … I don't know!"

"All right, Tom," Mom said, with an apologetic sigh. "Settle down. I'm sorry. Drive me over to the restaurant . . . She wouldn't have believed me anyway."

"Why wouldn't she have believed you?" I asked, looking at her.

"Because she's a dentist," Mom said.

"What?" I said, shaking my head, totally confused.

"Why would I be going to a dentist?" Mom said, looking at me as if I were the most stupid person on the planet. "I have false teeth."

After dropping Mom off at that restaurant, I parked in the parking lot behind the building.

Against the back of the building was a metal, white-painted, carport, of sorts. Under it were six or seven parking spaces that had "RESERVED" painted on the pavement in white block letters between the white lines. I assumed that these spaces were for the BIGSHOTS of the building. In one of these spaces was one of the hottest-looking cars that I have ever seen. It was a Porsche. The emblem on the side of the car read 911, Carrera. It was black and had a long front. It was sleek and elegant-looking, and you just knew that this baby had been built to run—fast.

After opening one of the two glass doors of the building and stepping inside, I checked the directory for Dr. Williams' office. Her office was the first office on the left side of the building, facing the street, and she shared this office building with a real estate agency and two different law firms.

I think the design of the door to her office is called Grecian—a heavy-looking, dark-colored, wooden door with embossed squares on it and flanked on both sides with trim that looked like pillars.

Opening the door and stepping inside, my ears were immediately met with the joyful sound of Christmas music being softly piped into the room from somewhere. The office was open and spacious. Directly opposite to the door was that row of those large, tinted-glass windows that curved with the shape of the building. The windows had retractable shades on them that looked like mini-bamboo, and there were large tropical plants in all the comers of the room in large terracotta pots.

The reception desk sat two or three feet away from the entrance to the office and was positioned two or three feet away from the south wall of the room—in front of four large metal cabinets—and what a weird-looking desk it was, too. It was in the shape of a tree stump. It had a hard, shiny surface to it, and the whole thing looked to be a petrified tree. The top of the desk was messy, with three stacks of manila folders, a multiplex office phone, a white ceramic cup in the shape of a dog that held many pens and pencils, and a small plastic Christmas tree that was festooned with paperclips.

"May 1 help you?" the receptionist said in a deep-sounding, gravel voice.

Ah, I thought. The voice has a face. Looking at the vertical lines running up and down her upper lip, I said to myself, She's definitely a smoker.

Don't get me wrong, though, she wasn't without allurement. Well, actually, it wasn't her face or body that I found attractive, but her snappy personality, which almost bordered upon being downright sarcastic. It was a personality that seemed to state: I do and say what I want, and if you don't like that, tough.

I was right when I had said that she sounded like she was in her mid-forties, because she did look to be in her mid-or late-forties. She had light chestnut-colored hair that hugged her roundish face and fell in frizzy, wild curls to her rounded shoulders. Her eyebrows were large and painted onto her face and were the same color as her hair. She painted her thin lips a bright red and she painted her face with much rouge. She had a stocky body and in a few years from now she will have what I call the "three-tire body": a body that looks like it's composed of a stack of tires three high.

This gal was definitely weird, too. She had on the largest pair of glasses that I had ever seen before, and the frames of them were a bright yellow. Plus, she was wearing a white, sleeveless dress of thin material.

I mean, it was a nice-looking dress, but it's winter. Shouldn't a dress such as that be worn in the spring? If she continued spreading, though, I don't think she would be able to fit into that dress come spring. It already looked a size too small for her.

"Yes, I'm here for my appointment," I said to her. "I'm Tom-Thomas Mayor."

"Here's some paperwork for you to fill out, Mr. Mayor," she said, handing me a clipboard with two forms attached to it and a pen.

"Thanks," I replied, and then said, "Say, with a desk like this, aren't you afraid of woodpeckers?"

After staring at me for a moment, as if she were trying to read me— her blue eyes magnified like a cartoon character's eyes popping out of their sockets by those silly-looking glasses—she placed her right arm and hand up and then with her index-finger motioned for me to come closer.

I did.

"I'm not afraid of any peckers," she stated with a wink, and then laughed.

"Great reply," I said, laughing.

As I walked upon the plush, light-beige carpet over to the northwest comer of the room, to the highly-polished, wooden coat rack that was standing next to one of those tropical plants, I said to myself: Was she flirting with me?

I set that clipboard down on the seat of the upholster armchair that was nearest to that coat rack. After removing my topcoat and hanging it on one of the pegs of the coat rack, I brushed off lent from my pants. Not wanting to look like a detective, I had decided not to wear my suit. But my equating the township of Clayton with being rich people, I didn't want to look like a slob either, so had I decided to wear those black dress pants that I had worn the other day while Mom was washing the pee out of my suit pants and the white shirt that I had been wearing and that red tie. I wore the topcoat, because the only other coat that I have is my old winter coat, and it looks far too shabby to wear to any place this hoity-toity.

Above the row of upholstered arm-chairs that flanked the west wall were prints—in metallic frames of gold color—of famous buildings— like the Eiffel Tower in Paris; Big Ben in London; Notre Dame Cathedral in Paris; the Leaning Tower of Pizza in Italy, and on and on. There were two long, glass-top coffee tables with wooden stands in front of the row of chairs, and both about four feet from each other. Lying upon them in no particular order were both ladies' magazines and travel magazines— but travel magazines mostly.

Besides me, there was only one other patron in the office, a business-type-looking woman in her mid-thirties, who was wearing a sharp-looking dark-brown suit coat and matching pants, and who was perfunctorily, as if bored out of her mind, flipping through one of those lady magazines.

I filled out those forms—and get this, where it asked for place of employment, I wrote: Johnson & Johnson—you know, the company that makes and sales bandages and baby powder. I don't know why I had listed that as my place of employment, or why I had listed my employment there as Sales. I just did. Plus, where it asked, "referred by", I wrote: *Mrs. Claire Peterson, grandmother of Megan Jones.*

I did that to get the ball rolling, you know. I figured that when Dr. Williams read that, she'd want to know how I knew Megan and then I could start asking her questions about Megan.

After I had completed those two forms, I happily returned them to the receptionist—I say "happily" because I was attracted to her and wanted to know if she had been flirting with me.

"If you will give me your insurance card, Mr. Mayor," she said after I had handed her the clipboard and forms, "I'll make a copy of it and give it back to you."

Just as I was about to answer her, a heavy-set woman, in her early twenties, and dressed in light-blue scrubs, suddenly appeared from the long, narrow, hallway to the right of the receptionist's desk, my right that is, close to the entrance, and said, "Hi, Mrs. Taylor. Nice seeing you again. Are you ready?"

"Well, I have health insurance," I then replied, lying, "but last year— and I'm still ticked off about it—the company discontinued dental insurance."

"Ouch," she said, crunching up her face as if in pain for me. "Sadly, Mr. Mayor, more and more companies are doing that."

"Oh, please," I said, "call me Tom. Any woman who isn't afraid of," I said, cupping my right hand over the right side of my mouth, "you- know-what needs to call me by my first name."

"All right," she replied, laughing. "Thank you, Tom. I'm Sarah. Sarah McClellan."

"Oh, you're Irish. Why isn't your hair red?"

Sarah looked at me through those oversized glasses with a deadpan stare, and then said, ever so coquettishly: "What makes you think that my hair isn't red—in some places?"

I was shocked—shocked! I was shocked by what she said, and I was shocked by the fact that this gal was, indeed, flirting with me. It's been so long since a woman has flirted with me that I can't tell you when the last time was.

I was getting sexually aroused. I told myself that I had to come back with a very witty reply, but I couldn't think of one goddamn witty thing to say. In fact, I couldn't think of anything to say. My mind was a blank.

Think, man, I chided myself. Think . . . Her dress. Yes, that's it! Tell her that that's such a pretty dress that you wished you had one like it. Yes.

"You know, Sarah," I began, being a bit coquettish myself, "that's such a pretty dress that I wish I—" and then that fatass broad in those light-blue scrubs suddenly appears back at the desk and interrupts me, saying, "Is this gentleman ready, Sarah?"

Can you believe it? Can you freakin' believe it?!

I angrily followed her down the long, narrow hallway, wanting to kick her in her fat ass.

The examination room that that gal sat me faced the street, but the examination chair faced the door—and was that room posh: everything looked new and expensive, but there were two things that impressed me most about the room. One, the large, flat-screen TV that was high-up on the wall above the entrance to the room, opposite to the long, well-padded, examination chair that I was comfortably sitting in—CNN was on—and, two, what I thought to be black sunglasses that were upon the silver-looking tray in front of me.

After Fat-ass handed me a page-sized, laminated, hard sheet of paper with writing on it, she says, real friendly, "This is a list of the movies we're featuring today. Would you like to choose one?"

"Wow, watch a movie?" I said, genuinely impressed, pointing to the TV.

"Oh, no, not there," she replied. "There," she said, and pointed to the sunglasses.

"You can watch a movie with these?" I asked, picking up the sunglasses and looking at the inside of them.

"Yes," she replied, and I said to myself: Now this is class. "Do you have any porn?" I asked, looking at that sheet again.

"What?" she replied, shocked. "You're joking, right?" she continued, hoping that I was indeed joking.

"Yes, I am," I replied, flatly, and handed her the sheet and the glasses.

"Is there anything I can get you that would make your time with us more enjoyable?" she continued.

"Well, since you don't have porn, I'll just watch TV," I replied and smiled at her.

"Dr. Williams will be with you shortly," she said, and after giving me a quick, patronizing smile, she walked quickly out of the room.

After she had left the room, I began thinking how this place was far different from the clinic where I go to have my teeth worked on. At the clinic, they even have an old ceramic white bowl right next to the chair that has a small metallic spigot that water continuously trickles out of, and the clinic smells like a dentist's office, smells of rubbing alcohol— but this place had no smell at all, other than clean, and new, and expensive.

"Shortly" turned into a good half hour before Dr. Williams finally stepped into the room, holding a manila yellow folder in one hand.

I was a bit shocked by her appearance. I mean, she was much shorter in person than she had looked at that time that I had seen her on TV. She couldn't have been much over five feet tall, and thin. I said to myself: How in the hell does a tiny thing like her pull a tooth? I could have sex with her by picking her up, pressing her against my body and moving my arms up and down.

She was wearing a white blouse, black dress slacks and black high-heeled shoes. It seemed to me that her total presence of authority came from the wearing of a full-length, white doctor's smock. I had a flash sexual fantasy about her. In it, that smock was buttoned, and when she stepped into the room, she ripped it open and revealed to me her perk, naked, body, and said, in a low, seductive voice: "Do what you will to me, big boy."

The biggest thing on her was her head. It was too big for that small body. Don't get me wrong now, she was a cute little thing: raven black hair, cut short, above her small ears—her hair was so black I would have said that it was a dye job, but its blackness matched the blackness of her eyebrows and the blackness of her pearl-black, watery raccoon eyes. I say "raccoon eyes" because they were so heavily lined with black mascara on an oval face with creamy white skin.

About the only thing about her looks that depressed me were her breasts—or the lack of them. Her breasts were really nothing more than two small protruding bumps. This depressed me because I was looking forward to having some breasts rubbing up against me while she worked on me. Well, at least it would be better than having old Doc Reese's cigar-breath, fat old body rubbing up against me as he works on my teeth at the clinic.

My first impression of her—besides being shocked that a dentist could be so small—was that there was a darkness to her—something not quite right about her, you know—that I just couldn't put my finger on. Then, as she moved closer to me and I saw the shrunken, closed holes of multiple piercings that ran vertically down her right ear, I said to myself: I bet when she was in college, she was into that gothic crap. That explains that darkness to her.

After exchanging that folder from her right hand to her left hand, she extended out her right arm and hand to me and said with a wide smile from those small, lipstick red lips: "Mr. Mayor, I'm Dr. Williams." And her voice was not low and seductive at all. It sounded small and mousey, helpless even, which I liked.

"Thank you for seeing me on such short notice, doctor," I said, having eye-to-eye contact with her. "As I told your receptionist," I continued, "I've recently returned home to St. Louis from living in Los Angeles for the past ten years and haven't had the time yet to choose a dentist. So, thank you."

"My pleasure," she replied, smiling. "I've been to Los Angeles a few times myself. It's lovely there."

"I was admiring the many pictures you have of Europe in your office," I then said. "I've never been to Europe, but I hope to go there someday."

"I've been to Europe so many times that I've lost count of how many times I've been there," she then said. "I love all of Europe, but Paris, France, is my favorite city of all of Europe. I always thought that when I retired I'd move to Paris, but I guess that's not going to happen. I guess it will be New Zealand." She then sighed longingly and said something in French, which, obviously, I didn't understand.

"Why New Zealand?" I asked.

"Oh," she said, somewhat flatly, "New Zealand has much pristine wilderness for hiking, camping and hunting—if you like such activities. I'm more into culture and social activities—which New Zealand has, especially in Wellington."

I couldn't believe this! I mean, I thought by now she would have said something to me about knowing Megan. I mean, that's why I had written Megan's name down on that form—so that she would start talking to me about Megan. It was as if she hadn't even read those damn forms. If you're not going to even read the damn forms, then why ask such questions as "Referred By."

"Well, maybe you'll get to Paris anyway," I said, dismissively. "I'm sure glad you're here now. You come highly recommended. You were recommended to me by my mother's neighbor, Mrs. Claire Peterson. Megan Jones was her granddaughter."

Well, this at least got a reaction out of her. It hit her like a hard, stunning punch right between those raccoon eyes of hers.

She was quiet for a moment, and then said, "How sad. It's all so sad."

"Yes," I replied. "Claire is devastated. She says that after John, Megan's husband, is executed, she'll have no one left of her family. She says she's going to change her will and leave what little money she has left to charity ... You know," I continued, " living in Los Angeles all of those years, I only met Megan once or twice. What was she like?"

"What?" she said, as if thinking of something else. "Oh, Megan. Why she was a dear person."

"Were you and she close?" I asked.

"Well, we had a good employer-employee relationship," she replied.

"Do you think Megan had any enemies?

"Enemies?!" she cried. "Why are you asking such questions?" she stated.

"Forgive me, doctor," I said. "Because of having known Mrs. Peterson all of my life, I've followed Megan's disappearance with special interest. You know, the police still seem to believe that Megan's disappearance was a random act—a robbery gone terribly wrong. I don't think that it was random, doctor. If it had been a random act, doctor, then why take the trouble of disposing of a body that hasn't been found for these five years now. No, I think that—"

"Please, Mr. Mayor," she said, interrupting me. Still holding that manila folder in her left hand, she waved her arms and hands at me to stop. "I'm sorry. This is upsetting me."

"Oh, I'm sorry, doctor," I replied.

She quickly opened that folder, and looking down into it, she said, "How long has it been since you have had x-rays taken of your . . ."

I walked out of that office furious—foaming at the mouth furious!— for three reasons: One, my lips and tongue were paralyzed from all the Novocain that she had shot me up with; besides taking x-rays of all of my teeth, and then cleaning them, she filled two cavities. Two, I had wanted to flirt some more with that receptionist, that Sarah gal, but when she asked me if Dr. Williams was painless, I opened my mouth and drooled on her desk. And, three, when she told me that "today's visit" was three hundred dollars—three hundred dollars!—I was so pissed that I just wanted to get the hell out of there.

If Mom had thought that the outside of that restaurant across the street looked expensive, the inside of it definitely was, or at least elegant- looking. Although the lighting of it was a bit too dark for my taste, the room was spacious, with chandelier after chandelier suspended from a vaulted ceiling with many dark wooden beams and flying buttresses to it. The main section of the room was a single-step-down sunken floor of some type of grayish-looking slat. This area was consumed with round tables covered with thick, white, table-clothes. Upon the tables were white-cloth napkins, with much highly-polished silverware upon them, and crystal glasses, and in the middle of each table was a lighted candle in an oval-shaped, tinted, glass container. The perimeter of the upper floor was consumed with booths made of dark wood, except for an area near the entrance, which was a large bar.

The smell of the place was of an overwhelming smell of pizza, or of bread baking—not a bad smell.

I found Mom sitting at one of the round tables towards the back of the room—looking very impatient. Beside her right elbow, on top of the table, were two plastic bags with a white foam plastic container in each bag.

When I approached the table, she said, "Good Lord, I didn't think you were ever coming. It's been almost two hours."

Through a closed mouth and closed teeth, I replied as best that I could: "I know. I'm sorry."

"Well, the food here," she said, tapping an index-finger of her casted right arm on one of the bags, "is delicious—simply delicious, expensive but delicious. I had a house salad, and something called linguine with creamy pesto. It was too much food for one person to eat, though. I had them to wrap it up for me so that I could take it home. You can have the rest of it for supper when we get home."

"I can't," I replied, again through a closed mouth and closed teeth.

"Why can't you?" she asked.

I opened my mouth to speak, but no words came out—all that came out was more drool, upon the white-clothed table.

Chapter Seven

After carefully having a can of chicken noodle soup for supper, and after watching two Christmas TV shows with Mom—"Rudolf the Red Nose Reindeer" and "Frosty the Snowman"—I went upstairs to my bedroom to crash. I turned on my TV, got a six-pack of beer from my cache of beers from the closet, and flopped on my bed. My gums and teeth were hurting, but I figured a few beers would take care of that.

Thinking back upon the day, I was pretty proud of myself. I mean, at least I had gotten something out of Dr. Williams—not like with John, or that Helen Dyer, or that Mrs. Savage. I got nothing from any of them.

No, I had definitely caught her telling a lie. When I had asked her if she and Megan were close, she had said something like they had a good "employer and employee" relationship. Well, that's not what I had heard. I had heard that John was always pissed about them going to nightclubs after work and going away on business conferences. So either John or she was lying, and why did she become so upset about talking about Megan's kidnapping and death? I mean, if they weren't close, why would that upset her then?

Then I told myself that maybe she wasn't lying, that maybe in her mind that was a good employer and employee relationship. I mean, I've never been in the "business" world. What do I know about what is or isn't a "good employer and employee relationship." As for her becoming upset about talking about Megan's kidnapping and death— well, she's a girl, with feelings, and what had happened to Megan was pretty horrific.

After turning it all over in my mind every conceivable way, and after polishing off my fourth beer, which was about at ten o'clock, I was fed up with it all.

I had wasted a whole week of my life with this crap, and I had gotten nothing. Next week would be Christmas, and instead of enjoying the Season, I was spending every waking moment of my time on this foolishness. No, I was done. I wanted my old life back. Yes, Claire had given me a thousand dollars; yes, it's nice to have your mother proud of you. But I was finished with it.

I told myself that out of respect for Claire and Mom, I would do one more thing—and one more thing only: Tomorrow, I would rise early and drive over to John and Megan's old neighborhood and talk to some of their former neighbors about John and Megan. But if that turned out to be a total wash, then I was done. Then, a few days later, I would walk over to Claire's and say, with heartfelt sincerity: "Claire, after a thorough investigation of this case—after interviewing all the people connected with this case; after reading all newspaper reports on this case; after reading and re-reading the transcripts of John's trail, and following up on all leads gleaned from that—all of the evidence confirmed, definitively, John's guilt. I'm so sorry, Claire. I, too, wanted very much for John to be innocent. I'm so sorry."

I'm not sure how many beers I downed. Nine? Ten? Did it matter?

The next morning, I woke up at ten-minutes-to-eight, but I had such a splitting headache from one of the worst hangovers that I have ever had that I turned back over, pulled the sheet and cover back over my head, and went back to sleep.

I was awakened by Mom's knocking on my door and then saying: "Are you all right in there, Tom? . . . Tom, are you still in bed? . . . It's nearly ten-thirty."

My mind felt like mush. My throat and mouth felt as dry as proverbial cotton balls.

Still hung over, and feeling cold, and like shit, I dragged my sleepy ass out of bed. I didn't even bathe or shave. I just lazily, feeling more dead than alive, by rote, threw on my old clothes—dressing in my jeans, my plaid shirt and my black tennis shoes—and dutifully went downstairs.

Since it was getting so late in the day, I decided to wait until after Mom and me had fed and visited with Dad before I'd drive over to John and Megan's old neighborhood and speak with some of their former neighbors. Hell, what with the way I felt, I told myself that I might not do it at all.

Dad was pretty good that day. He ate voraciously, and when I asked him if he knew my name, he said, heartily, child-like: "Tommy!" Hearing him say that put me in a good mood.

After pulling into our driveway and stopping the car parallel with the back porch of our house, I told Mom where I was going and what I was going to do. Seeing our small, wooden garage at the back-end of our small backyard, I made a mental note that if I decided to paint the house this coming summer, I would probably paint the garage as well. Dad had painted it white years ago and now it was blistering and peeling in spots. I don't know why he had painted it white, but I told myself that if I did paint it that I would paint it the same color as the house, a light blue.

The garage sits at the northeast end corner of the yard and has a three-foot-high chain-link fence that runs behind it to the two adjacent yards of our neighbors. There's an alley behind the garage, and over the years some of our neighbors have had garage doors installed at the back end of their garages so that they could use the alley to get in and out of their garages. I wish Dad had done that. It's stupid driving a car through your backyard to get to a garage. Mr. Neely had it done years ago before he died. I'd like to sneak over there one night while Mr. Fluffy's in the backyard and snatch him up and throw him into their garage and hope that he dies of carbon monoxide poisoning—the yapping little bastard.

Anyway, Mom wanted to know if I was going to be back home by four o'clock, reminding me that I had to drive her over to St. Paul's Church for one of her many prayer meetings. I told her that I was definitely going to be back home by four—not that I was excited about attending another one of Mom's many prayer meetings, but I wasn't about to waste the rest of my day talking with John and Megan's former neighbors. Ever since I've been driving Mom everywhere she has to go because of her broken arm, I've been attending her prayer meetings with her. Well, I don't want to waste gas leaving the engine running, and it's too damn cold to sit in the damn car. So, I've been attending them with her, praying and praising God while silently screaming: I hate this!

Frequently, while Mom rides in a car, she takes her little prayer book out of her large, baggy, black, leather purse and silently recites prayers.

She was doing this that day as I pulled into our driveway. After I had told her that I would definitely be back home by four o'clock, she started to replace the prayer book back into one of the compartments on the face of the purse where she keeps it, but she missed the opening and it fell to the seat beside the purse on my side. I leaned slightly to my right to retrieve it for her, and—POW!

It was like being in a goddamn movie, man! In an instant, the whole windshield exploded into a thousand pieces. Shards of sparkling glass came flying towards Mom and me, and this was immediately followed by an arctic blast of wind and coldness. All of this happened within seconds, but, I swear, it felt like it was all happening in slow motion.

I was so scared that I don't remember everything that happened. What I do remember is this: A second or two before the windshield exploded, I heard what sounded like a firecracker going off. Then, as I was raising my arms and hands to cover my face from the flying glass, I heard a car door in the alley being slammed. I heard an engine to a car being started—and if I live to be a hundred years old, I'll never forget the sound of that engine. It had such a distinct, singular sound to it. It had a high-pitched sound, like a high-performance engine, one that was made for moving fast, real fast. The last thing I heard was the sound of a car peeling rubber as it sped away.

I was thrown back into reality out of this surreal, slow-moving world by suddenly feeling this stinging pain on the left side of my head, about one or two inches above my ear. When I touched that area with my left hand, it hurt. I brought my left arm down and looked at my hand. It was covered in blood.

I felt light-headed and faint.

"Oh, Mom," I cried. "I'm bleeding! . . . Call an ambulance, Mom!"

Mom got out of the car and dashed around the back of the car to the driver's side as fast as her aging, pudgy, little, body would allow her.

After opening the door and leaning in to me, she said: "Here, Tom, let's get you inside."

"Oh, Mom," I cried, getting out of the car, "I'm dying. I don't want to die, Mom!"

"You're not dying, Tom," Mom replied. "I won't—Jesus won't let you . . ."

The police and paramedics were at the house within five minutes. The police didn't stay long at all. They left as soon as they realized that it wasn't a criminal matter, I guess.

Now I'm not gay—I'm not. I know that I'm not, but if I were ever to go gay, it would be for a guy like one of the two paramedics who came to the house that day. This guy was just butt-ass gorgeous—well, maybe I shouldn't say "butt-ass" when speaking of this. But he was damn good- looking. I had trouble taking my eyes off of him. I think he was Greek or Italian—raven black hair and black eyebrows that matched the color of his eyes. His skin was a warm olive complexion, with a lean-looking face and a straight, narrow nose. He was in his early twenties, I would say, and he wasn't all that tall of a guy, about five-seven or five-eight—but, boy, he sure filled out that immaculately clean and pressed, dark-blue uniform that he was wearing. He wasn't buffed-up like a muscle man is, but you could tell that he worked out a lot.

He didn't talk much, though. The other guy did that—the jerk. He was a short guy, about my age, with a protruding beer belly. He had salt-and-pepper hair with a matching full mustache, and although he was wearing the same type of uniform as the good-looking one had on, it was not clean or pressed and fit him like an overblown balloon ready to burst. He also had this annoying habit of prefixing many of his sentences with "Well, I don't know." But that's not what he meant when he said "Well, I don't know." What he meant was "Yes, I do know"—like when they had first came in and I had kept begging them to take me to the hospital, that I was dying. I'm sitting in the kitchen with a wet, blood-soaked, white dishtowel pressing against my wound.

He says: "Well, I don't know, sir. It's a larger wound than you and this woman have on your faces and hands, but it's still a superficial wound. It's not even bleeding anymore. Now, if you want us to transport you to the hospital, by law, we are required to do so. Well, I don't know, but if we transport you to the hospital, the doctors in the emergency room aren't going to do any more, or less, than what old Mike here is doing. They'll trim some of the hair away from the wound; they'll clean it and then they'll apply some antibiotic ointment to it. I don't know, sir, but do you really want to go through all of that there when we're doing all of the same things here?"

    See what I mean about that guy being an annoying piece of crap— and get this! After he had convinced me that I wasn't dying and that I didn't need to go to the hospital, and I'm feeling all embarrassed about being a baby about it all, and trying to save a shred of dignity, and say to Mike that that glass had really did a number to the side of my head, and give a nervous laugh, he jumps in and says: "Well, I don't know, sir. I've been a paramedic going on-oh, twenty-six years now, and I've seen a lot of wounds in my day. Well, I don't know, but that's too straight of a wound to have been done by glass. That's a bullet wound."

    "What?!" I cried.

    "Well, I could be wrong, sir," he replied, "but I don't think I am. That looks like a wound from a rifle to me."

    "Who would shoot at me?" I asked.

    "Well, that's a good question, sir," he said. "You got any enemies?"

    "No," I replied.

    "Well, I don't know," he said, "but there are a lot of crazies out there. Maybe it was just some kid getting his jollies off."

    After Mom escorted them out of the house, she came back into the kitchen with a very worried look upon her face and asked me if I thought that this had anything to do with the investigation. I told her that I was one-hundred percent certain that it had nothing to do with the investigation, which was a lie. When that asshole had said that that was a bullet wound, that was the first thing that popped into my mind—that it was someone from the investigation. But then, after thinking about it, I readily dismissed it. I mean, think about it. John's in prison, and the only other person who would have the balls to do something like that was that Helen Dyer gal, but she doesn't even have a car. She's too damn poor to own a car. She takes the bus, and where is she going to hide a rifle on a bus?

    Once Mom was assured that it had nothing to do with the investigation, she told me that all of the neighbors had been milling around the sidewalk outside of the house and that when she had stepped out onto the front porch with those two paramedics, Mr. and Mrs. Meyers, our next-door neighbors to the left of us, rushed up to her wanting to know what had happened. Mom said for some reason she didn't want to say anything about the possibility of a firearm being fired, so she simply told them that the windshield to my car had shattered and that I had gotten a pretty good size cut from the glass to the left side of my head.

I was glad that Claire wasn't home, because if she had been, she most assuredly would not only have been outside, she would have marched right in to find out what was going on. Claire had a doctor's appointment, and she had wanted me to drive her there, but her appointment was at one o'clock, and if I had agreed to drive her, Mom and me wouldn't have been able to visit and feed Dad. We could have gone down and visited and fed him at supper time, but I don't like being there in the evening. It's too depressing being there in the evening. To me, a person should be home at supper time, not in a "home."

So, Claire had no other choice but to take Call-A-Ride to drive her to and from the doctor: Not liking strangers, Claire always hated taking Call-A-Ride, but God forbid she should shell out good, hard-earned money on something as expensive, and frivolous, as taking a taxi.

I hadn't wanted to see Claire anyway, out of the fear that she would have asked me how the investigation was going, and because I had made up my mind. Now, it wasn't because I believed that someone was trying to kill me. No, that had nothing to do with it. I will admit, though, with that business of the windshield exploding, and with being shot at, maybe, had made up my mind for me. I had had it. I was fed up with it all. I wanted my old life back.

I had thought about waiting until after Christmas to tell Claire, but after thinking about it, I thought: No, I want my old life back and I want to enjoy Christmas. Tomorrow, if I feel okay, I'm going to walk over there and tell her. I'll tell her that the investigation is over. I'll tell her that after performing a comprehensive investigation—after interviewing everyone involved; after chasing down every lead; after going over and over all the transcripts of the trail, and after reading and re-reading all newspaper articles about the murder and the trail— all evidence confirmed John's guilt. "I'm very sorry, Claire. I'm very, very sorry."

Obviously, Mom missed her prayer meeting.

For supper, Mom opened up two cans of Campbell's vegetable soup and grilled some cheese sandwiches.

Right after supper, my head began to hurt more than what it had earlier, so while Mom was doing the dishes, I took two aspirins and lay down on the couch in the living room and began watching the evening news. Sometimes taking aspirins can really do a number on me, makes me real sleepy. I got up from the couch and told Mom that I was going upstairs to lie down and that I might come back down later on.

Sometimes I really hate this big-old-barn-of-a-house. It can be so cold and drafty, at times.

My room, to me, seemed to be freezing. I threw off my tennis shoes and got into bed, blood-stained clothes and all. I pulled the cover and the sheet up tight against my body and neck and prayed for warmth.

My head ached with a throbbing pain, especially on the left side of my head, and I had an echoing in my ears, which seemed to magnify my hearing. I could clearly hear the news still being broadcasted on the TV downstairs.

My body temperature started to warm the bed, and it started to feel oh-so pleasant under the cover and sheet. I started to drift off into a welcome, dreamy sleep state—and that's when it happened! Outside, from the street below, I heard that same engine that I had heard in the alley pass by our house. Terror gripped me. I thought: Oh, my God, is he—or are they—coming to get me again?

Then, it was gone. I didn't hear that engine anymore. My terror abated, some.

I told myself that I was being paranoid, that lots of people have cars with engines that sound like that one in the alley did.

I should have at least gotten up and gone to the window and looked out onto the street below, but I just hadn't felt like doing that. My head hurt, and I was tired and sleepy, and I didn't want to lose the warmth of my bed. I told myself that I should yell down to Mom to make sure that the doors are all locked. But if I had done that, it would have probably caused my head to hurt much more, what with my hearing being magnified: I was wishing Dad were here.

I started to drift off to sleep again. It felt so good—and wouldn't you know it: that damn dog, that Mr. Fluffy, became yapping its fool head off. It just kept barking and barking in that high-pitched yap. It was hurting my ears, and head. Shut up, Mr. Fluffy! I screamed,

silently. Shut up! ... C'mon, Claire, I said, call the police. I knew
Claire was home, because Mom had called her shortly before supper
to find out what the doctor had said and to tell her about what had
happened to my car and me. Mr. Fluffy kept barking. C'mon, I yelled,
someone shut that goddamn dog up!

Then, just when I had resolved to leave the warmth of my bed,
drag my tired, sleepy body, and hurting head, downstairs to call the
police myself, it stopped. Mr. Fluffy, finally, stopped yapping.

Except for the TV downstairs, silence returned. Moments later, I
began to drift off to sleep again, thinking: By tomorrow night, I'll
have my old life back.

I couldn't believe it! I woke up the next morning at six-forty—
six-forty! I woke up totally awake, and, well, I felt great. My head
didn't hurt much at all, and I didn't have the slightest trace of a hangover. Then, I remembered that I hadn't had a single beer the night
before—and I had slept throughout the entire night like the proverbial
log.

I tried to go back to sleep, but I just couldn't. I felt too awake and
felt too alive.

I got up out of bed, threw off my clothes, put on my robe and
went into the bathroom and washed and shaved at the sink: Before I
started washing and shaving, I inspected my face in the mirror. I
didn't like all of those marks on my face—they made me look like I
had the measles or a bad case of acne, but I did like that long, straight
wound on the left side of my head. It kind of made me look like a
tough guy. Then, I returned to my bedroom, put on another pair of old
jeans, a long-sleeved, blue shirt, my tennis shoes, and then went
downstairs.

I put the coffee on, retrieved the newspaper from the front porch,
and then I sat down at the kitchen table and began reading the paper
while I waited for the coffee to finish brewing. Two cups of coffee
later, and the newspaper half read, I fried myself two eggs and toasted
two slices of bread. After I finished my breakfast, I took the
newspaper into the living room, lay down on the couch and began
reading the rest of the paper.

Time really dragged. By seven-twenty, I had the newspaper all
read and didn't know what else to do with myself. I was bored out of
my mind. It's times like that that I wish I'd start writing the short

stories and the novels I want to write, but that I never do. I got some great ideas for stories and such, but I just can't stand the thought of facing that keyboard and a blank screen for some reason.

About eight-thirty, Mom comes downstairs, dragging herself into the kitchen for a much needed cup of coffee, dressed in her white flannel pajamas, full-length white robe and white slippers.

I was glad Mom was finally up. It was lonely in the house with nothing to do. I got up off of the couch and went into the kitchen to chat with Mom and to have another cup of coffee.

Standing by the coffee-maker at the counter, and after taking a couple of sips of coffee, Mom said to me: "How are you feeling this morning?" Mom's face didn't have as many marks to it as mine had, and I was glad of that.

"Actually, great," I replied, smiling. "I'm feeling pretty good. My head doesn't hurt all that much at all."

"Oh, praise the Lord," she said. "Do you remember what you said to me last night?"

"No," I replied, grabbing my coffee cup off the kitchen table and heading for the coffee-maker.

"You said that you might come back down last night, but you didn't. I got worried about you, so before I want to bed I knocked on your door. You didn't answer. I knocked and knocked and called out your name a couple of times, but you never answered. I got scared and opened your door. I saw you lying in bed with the cover on. I called out your name a few times, but you still didn't answer. So I walked over to you and started shaking you on the shoulder and kept saying: 'Tom, are you OK?' Well, you shot-up screaming: 'Listen here, Fred,' you said. 'If you're thinking about shooting me again, my dad will stab you to death again with his bayonet.' Do you remember that? And why did you have your clothes on?"

"No," I replied, grabbing the black handle of the glass coffee pot. "I don't remember saying that. I had my clothes on because I fell asleep with them on."

Mom placed her coffee cup down on the counter. Then, after pulling up the right sleeves of her robe and pajamas, she began scratching her arm below the elbow.

"This dang cast is itching me like crazy," she said, scratching away. "Well, what was that all about, Tom?" she continued, looking at me. "Are you still worried about that guy? You had some terrible nightmares after your father killed that guy," she said, shaking her head from side to side. "I used to hear you . . . Tom," she then stated emphatically, and with much resolve, "it's a fact—a dead guy can't hurt you. You know that, don't you?"

"Yes, I'm well aware of that, mother," I replied condescendingly, taking a sip of my coffee.

"Well, then, why did you say it?" she persisted. She stopped scratching her arm and lowered the sleeves of her robe and pajamas at the same time. Then, she picked up her coffee cup again. "Well, why?" she then repeated when I didn't answer her.

"I don't know," I said. "I guess it had—I don't know," I repeated. "It was a nightmare. Lots of people have nightmares."

"Thomas," she then stated firmly, looking at me straight in the eyes, "are you positive that what happened yesterday had nothing to do with the case? Tell me the truth. Because if this is dangerous, I want you to go straight over to Claire's, tell her it's too dangerous and give her back that two hundred dollars."

"Yes, mother," I replied, condescendingly again, "I'm positive that what happened yesterday had absolutely nothing to do with the case. It's like that guy said yesterday, it was probably kids."

"You're positive?" she said, a look of concern still mapping her aged, wrinkled, and now measles-like-marked round face.

"Yes," I replied. "I'm sure. I'm not a brave man. You know that."

"That's right," she cried, finding much joy and comfort in that.

"Well, thanks a lot for that," I replied flatly.

"I didn't mean anything by—"

"Listen," I then said, interrupting her, "I guess we're going to have to use your car to see Dad today, so I'm going to get my gloves and a rag and brush all of the glass off of my car seat so that I can move the car to the side and get your car out of the garage."

"OK," she replied, happily. "I'll get breakfast started."

I set my coffee cup down on the counter and then left.

Once outside, I was shocked to see that not only had my front windshield been blown to smithereens and gone, but the rear windshield was gone as well. I guess I had missed that yesterday because of me bleeding and my belief that I was dying.

It was a beautiful day. The sun was out, and it was much warmer and less windy than it had been in days. I was glad for this, because my coat wasn't now up to extreme bad weather, what with all of those small tears in it, especially in the sleeves, from all of that shattered glass. I kind of liked it, though. It added another element to my new tough-guy look. I felt really sorry for Mom, though. Her winter coat had about as many tears in it as mine had. She had really loved that coat. She had wanted that coat for some time, and Dad surprised her and bought it for her for Christmas seven years ago, a year before he was diagnosed with being in the early stages of Alzheimer's. He had paid a hundred-sixty-five dollars for it. It was a waist-long, shiny brown leather coat with a matching belt. I told her that we'd purchase new coats after Christmas when the prices would be reduced.

After brushing off most of the glass from the driver's side of the front seat—using what used to be a pair of my old underwear—I drove and then parked the car where I usually park it, pretty close to the garage, to the outer-left side of the two, narrow, worn cement tracks that service as the driveway of our house.

Boy, was I pissed after I spoke with the receptionist of the insurance agent with whom we have are cars insured. She told me, ever so professionally, and matter-of-factly, that all it would cost me to have the windshields replaced is for me to pay the deductible— two-hundred-and-fifty dollars. Two-hundred-and-fifty dollars! Can you believe it?! Boy, I was pissed. I sure didn't want to pay that much money on a car that I don't even like.

At noon, Mom and I drove down to feed and visit with Dad.

I don't know why, but I've always felt safe in Mom's car. Now, don't get me wrong, I can't say that I hate it as much as I hate that big, white, elephant of a car of Eve's, but it's not the car for me. I mean, it's a 1992, silver, Ford Taurus. It's a family car, and Mom has the two front-door pockets of the car filled with religious tapes from these TV evangelists and a miniature statue of Jesus right in the middle of the dashboard. So, no, I don't like it very much. I mean, it's not the black Jeep Wrangler that I have been fantasizing about owning for so many years now.

Anyway, after Mom and I got back home, Mom said that she had a basket overflowing with clothes to wash, adding that she would just throw away the clothes I was wearing the day before. Hers hadn't sustained as much damage, or blood, as mine had. I agreed with her about my clothes, and I told Mom that I was going over to Claire's to give her a progress report on the investigation.

"Oh, good," Mom replied. "She'll like that."

The reason that I didn't tell Mom that I was going over to Claire's to tell her that the investigation was over was that—well, I liked the feeling of Mom being so proud of me and I didn't want it to end. I told myself that I'd tell her later that night.

With much regret, and anxiety, I left the house and walked over to Claire's.

I had my speech all prepared. I had gone over it, acting it out in my mind how it would go, several times throughout the day. It was comprehensive, sincere, and contrite. Claire would be sad, but she would believe me.

At Claire's, I stopped at the bottom of her porch and stared at her front door, as I had done the day this whole thing had begun. It had only been the previous week, but it felt much longer than that, like months had passed.

"Well," I muttered under my breath, my heart racing, "let's get this over with."

I walked up to the door and pressed the small, white, vertical-line button of the doorbell with my index finger. I then heard the dull, metallic, ding-dong of the chimes echo inside for a few moments and then come to an abrupt stop. Silence.

Several minutes passed without Claire answering the door, so I pressed the doorbell again. Several more minutes passed and still Claire didn't answer the door. I didn't want to be rude, but I didn't want to just be standing there, either, so I knocked on the door and said: "Claire, are you home?" Silence. I pressed my fingertips against the door and stood on tippy-toes to see if I could see inside of the house through the four, small, square windows towards the top of the door, but I wasn't tall enough.

Now my anxiety and nerves were turning into frustration.

Well, where the hell is she? I stated to myself. She didn't tell Mom that she was going anywhere. She has to be home.

I rang the doorbell again.

Several more minutes passed and still no answer.

Well, this is just stupid, I said to myself. Damnit. I want this to be over—today. Angrily, I turned around and stormed home.

Not even taking off my coat, I went straight into the kitchen, picked up the receiver of the phone and dialed Claire's number. She never answered it—it just rang and rang and rang.

The door to the basement was open, and I could hear the sloshing sound of water in the washing machine moving back and forth.

I went over to the door and called down: "Hey, Mom, are you down there?"

"Yeah," she replied.

"Did Claire tell you she was going anywhere today when you spoke with her yesterday?"

"No, she didn't," Mom said. "Why?"

"Well," I replied, "she not answering the door, and I just phoned her and she's not answering that either."

"Do you think something's wrong?" she said, with a tone of concern in her voice. "Do you want me to come up?"

"No," I replied. "You know how Claire says that since she's had colon cancer she gets diarrhea and is sometimes on the toilet for hours. I'm thinking that it's something like that ... Do we still have that key to her front door?"

"Yes," Mom said. "It's in a small tin key-box in the utensils' drawer."

"Okay," I replied. "I'm going to use it. I just want to be sure that nothing is wrong."

"Well, let me know."

"I will," I replied.

After grabbing that key, I shot back out the door for Claire's.

The first thing that I did when I returned to Claire's was ring the doorbell again, but as with before, no reply. I then knocked on the door again, as I had done before, but this time, in a semi-loud voice, I said: "Claire, are you home?" Moments passed. Nothing. No Claire.

After taking a deep breath and then expelling it, I said: "Well, let's get this over."

My hand shook as I inserted that key into the lock of Claire's front door. I felt as if I were doing something wrong; like I was stepping across the boundaries of being a "good neighbor," as if I were committing a crime or something, like burglary. There was also something very sexual about inserting that key into the lock.

I opened the door and let it swing wide open. I then stepped inside and shut the door behind me. It was freezing in there, which was unusual for Claire. Claire and Bud were penny-pinchers, but after Claire became ill, heat was one thing that she didn't penny-pinch on: it was always as hot as a boiler room in Claire's house.

"Claire," I called out. "Are you here? . . . Claire."

Silence. The whole house was silent, and it had an eerie feeling to it.

I looked in the living room, in the kitchen, in the half-bathroom—the door to which was open—and in the dining room. No Claire.

At the bottom of the steps to the second floor, I paused and looked up. For some reason, the stairs and the distance to the top seemed mountainous to me. The dark-stained, worn, old, wooden, planks creaked at times under the weight of my body as I ascended the stairs.

Upon reaching the second floor, I stopped again. I gazed down the long hallway. The first thing that I saw was that large painting of Claire's mother, Madeline. It hung on the narrow wall at the end of the hallway about three feet above an old wooden stand that had a blue vase on top of it with plastic flowers in it. I didn't need to see her picture—I was spooked enough. Seeing that stern face of hers, and that penetrating stare of her eyes—-just like Jesus' eyes at our house—sent chills through me.

I could easily see the door to the bathroom, which was mid-way down the hallway and on the west side of the house, and the door to Bud and Claire's bedroom, which was at the end of the hallway and also on the west side of the house. Both of the doors were closed.

As I passed the first bedroom, which was on the east side of the house and faced the street, and which had been Karen's old bedroom— the door to it was opened, but I didn't look inside—my heart felt a sudden pang of regret and sorrow as memories of us as kids playing husband and wife in her bedroom, or drinking imaginary tea, swirled around in my mind's eye. I felt regret for opportunities not taken; regret because someone whom I had truly wanted, loved, hadn't wanted me, or loved me; sorrow because even if she had one day come to realize that I was her one true love, it was now too late. She was gone.

When I came to the closed door of the bathroom, I hesitated for a moment, and then knocked on the door and said: "Claire, are you in there?" Silence was my only reply.

Except for the front door of the house, all of the doorknobs to the house—which is the same at our house—look like sparkling diamonds with flat heads. I don't think that they are made from plastic, and I know that they aren't crystal, but when I was a boy, I used to daydream about taking one of them to the bank and the teller giving me a million dollars for it.

After expelling a heavy breath, I grabbed the doorknob, turned it and opened the door wide. Much to my relief, Claire was not in there. I mean, how embarrassing would that have been—to have caught Claire sitting on the toilet pooping and farting her old head off.

I started down the rest of the hallway to Bud and Claire's bedroom.

At the door to Bud and Claire's bedroom, I stopped again for a moment and just stood there, staring at the door. A closed door, especially the closed door of a bedroom, is an odd thing. It speaks of comings and goings; of beginnings and endings; of privacy; of things that you can say or do in there, but that you are not to say or do in public.

I knocked on the door and repeated: "Claire, are you in there?"

Again, nothing but silence was my reply.

With my heart racing and breathing heavily, I grabbed the doorknob with a shaking hand and turned it. I let the door fly wide open so that I could take in a full view of the room.

The first thing that caught my eye was the large, heavy, oak-stained, old dresser with its large, oval-shaped mirror against the west wall and between the two, narrow, tall windows. The windows were curtained with a heavy material of light brown color. Upon the dresser, underneath an ornate white doily, were framed photographs of the family—one of Bud and Claire together—they looked to be in their mid-sixties, happy, not a care in the world—one of Karen, her husband, Tim, and Megan together, and there was a much later picture of John and Megan, with Megan holding baby Tyra in her arms. Against the north wall was another dresser of similar design, minus the mirror. The large, heavy, oak-framed, four-post bed caught my view next. The head of the bed was against the south wall and there were two matching old, oak nightstands there, one on each side of the bed. The bed was covered with a heavy, patch-work quilt of multiple colors. I remembered how Claire had told Mom that she and her mother had made one for every bed in the house. And lying ever so peacefully in the bed, with the quilt pulled up to her thin, sagging, shoulders—her arms and hands above the quilt—lay Claire.

I think that I knew that Claire was dead even before I had knocked on her bedroom door. Actually, I think that I had known that she was dead even before I had inserted that key into the front door.

Slowly, quietly, I walked up to the east side of the bed, coming to a stop at the head of the bed, next to the nightstand that was on that side of the bed. What I saw next almost made me run mindlessly out of the room in horror. Claire's eyes and mouth were opened, and her face was contorted. It reminded me of a picture I once saw on the wall of a Psychology class I once took of a guy holding his hands to his face with a look of great horror on his face. I think the painting is called "The Screamer."

Her fish-dead, glazed-over, blue eyes stared up at the white-painted ceiling of the room, and I had the belief that she had died hard.

I told myself that I better check her pulse—just to confirm to myself that she was indeed dead. I extended my right arm and placed my index-finger and my middle finger on the sickly, ghostly-white skin of the side of her neck that was nearest to me, but I then removed them faster than as if I had just touched the burning flame of a kitchen stove: the touch of her skin was icy-cold—and stiff. I couldn't look at her anymore, and I turned my head to the left and looked down at the nightstand. Upon it was a small shaded lamp, a Bible, Claire's reading glasses, that rosary that Mom had given her, and a full glass of water. I then looked back at Claire.

I'm one mentally sick person, I'll admit it. While I was looking at Claire, a thought came to mind. I could see that Claire was wearing a white nightgown, and I thought about pulling back that quilt and lifting up the end of her nightgown and—well, looking at her. Now, in my defense, though, I mean, it has been years since I've seen a woman's naked body—and who would have known that I did that. I mean, it's not like I wanted to have sex with her. Now, that would have been sick. There's a name for people like that, who want to have sex with dead people. I can't think of what that name is right now, but that's just sick. All I wanted to do was just look at her—and in the end I didn't do it. I told myself that Claire had been like a mom to me, and the next mental picture I got after having said that to myself stopped me cold from now even wanting to look at her naked body. Yes, I'll admit it. When it comes to women, I've got the mind of a horny teenager. I'm a fifty-five-year-old man trapped with the mind of an adolescent when it comes to women.

"I'm sorry I took your money, Claire," I said to her, looking down at her. "I know how tight money was for you. I'm also sorry that I only gave a lick-and-a-split to the case. I know how much it had meant to you. I did put 'some' effort in to it, though, and all of the evidence does seem to point to John's guilt. If that's any consolation to you . . . Well, again, I'm sorry, Claire. I hope you can find it in your heart to forgive me."

I turned and started walking for the door, but when I came to the door, I halted suddenly. A thought popped into my mind—and it froze me solid with horror. I couldn't have been more frozen if someone had dropped me off naked at the Antarctic.

I turned slowly back around and looked at that nightstand—more specifically, at that rosary that Mom had given her on that nightstand. I thought back to the day when this had all begun, and in my mind I played back Claire telling me that she never removes that rosary, not even when going to sleep.

Could it be? I asked myself. No, that's crazy, I tried to convince myself . . . But she said that she never removes that rosary. Could someone have murdered Claire? I asked . . . That's insane. Who would murder Claire, and for what reason? ... I don't know, I reasoned. But she said that she never removes that rosary . . . Listen, stupid, she was an ill, dying, old woman. Old people get confused all the time. You know that . . . But she said that she— . . . Listen, you idiot, if she's been murdered, where's the blood? You don't see any gunshot wounds or stab wounds on her, do you? . . . No, I thought . . . Well, then, just forget it. It's over. You've been on pins and needles since this whole thing began that Claire would tell Mom about the thousand dollars that she gave you and you 'd get caught in that lie.

It's over. You've made a thousand dollars. You got your old life back. You're free again. Go home . . . But. . . No buts—go home. It's over.

Mom was upstairs in her bedroom. She was standing on the east side of their king-sized old bed, taking what clothes were hers from the wicker clothesbasket on the bed, folding them and then gently placing them on top of the thick material bedcovering of floral design.

"Mom," I said quietly after entering the room. She turned and faced me. I knew the moment our eyes met that she already knew what I was about to tell her. "Claire's passed away, Mom."

She was silent for a few moments. Then, as if in a hypnotic state, she turned around and sat down heavily on the edge of the bed. She began tearing up, and she quickly grabbed a large, white bath towel from the basket and buried her face in it before she burst into tears.

"Oh, Mom," I said, going to her. I placed my arms and hands around her at the shoulders and began hugging her, the left side of my chin touching the right side of the top of her head. "I'm so sorry, Mom. Claire was a good friend to you."

"Yes, she was," Mom stated, and then lowered the bath towel from her red, tearful face.

I released her and she said: "Well, at least she isn't suffering anymore. She's in heaven now with the Lord, and with her family. That's what she's been wanting."

"That's right," I said as cheerfully as I could. "She's in heaven."

"Oh," Mom said suddenly, as if remembering something, "Claire gave me her lawyer's card and asked me to call him when she-she returned home to heaven. He has all of the arrangements for her burial. I better call him."

"Do you want me to do it?" I said. "I don't mind."

"No, no," she replied. "I'll do it."

"I wonder if I should call 911?" I said. "You know, to inform the police of Claire's dea-passing."

"Let me see what the lawyer says," Mom replied.

The lawyer told Mom that he would handle everything. When Mom asked him where Claire would be laid out, he informed her that as per Claire's instructions there would be no wake. In a day or two, her body would be transported to St. Stephen's Cemetery, where she would be buried beside Bud's grave. Although Bud had been eligible to have been buried at Reavis Barracks National Cemetery because of having served in the Army, he had chosen to be buried at St. Stephen's in order to be beside the graves of Karen and her husband. Claire would be buried to the right of Bud's grave and to the left of little Tyra's grave. Before the lawyer hung up with Mom, he asked her if she would be kind enough to let the police and the paramedics into Claire's house when they came. Mom said that she would.

About an hour after Mom had called that lawyer, the police and the paramedics arrived at Claire's house.

Not that I'm gay—because I'm not!—I had hoped that the paramedics who showed up at Claire's would have been the same two paramedics who had come to our house the other day. They didn't, though. It was two different people, a heavy-set woman and a guy. That Mike guy had been so strikingly handsome that, well, I had just wanted to look at him again—that doesn't make you gay, you know.

Mom didn't want to see Claire's body in her bed, so I escorted the police and the paramedics into Claire's house.

All of the neighbors were there when those two paramedics carted Claire's body out of the house in a black plastic body bag.

Despite the tension, the hostility, and the sheer anger that Claire's busy-body ways had often caused throughout the neighborhood in the last several years, the heaviness of her passing was deeply felt by us all, like the oppressive, sweltering heat of a hot summer day. Upon the faces of us all, there was genuine sadness and sorrow at her passing—and silence. No one said a word. I don't know if it was out of respect for Claire's passing, or if it was because Mr. Fluffy was comfortably nestled in the arms and hands of Mrs. Neely, but it barked not a single yap.

Chapter Eight

About four o'clock that day, I suddenly thought of John—that he should be informed of Claire's passing. I called that prison that John's in, and after telling who I am and why I was calling and what I wanted, and after being transferred and repeating all of this a zillion times, again, I was finally connected with someone who told me that under the circumstances, and if John desired to speak with me, he would be permitted phone privileges and that I should expect a call from John between the hours of six and eight p.m.

At exactly six p.m., as Mom was washing and I was drying the pots, pans, plates, and such at the kitchen sink from supper, the phone rang.

It was John.

He asked me what I wanted, and I immediately asked him how he was doing.

"I'm better," he replied.

He sounded different, too. He sounded more sedate. For some reason, I even envisioned him bathed and shaved, with clean prison clothes on. I told him this, too, that he sounded better, and he replied that he was trying to make peace with himself.

My heart was racing, but I told him pointblank that there was no easy way of saying this, that Claire had died, probably during the early part of the last night, or that's what the paramedics had told me. There was silence on the other end of the phone, and then he said, "She was the only one who believed in my innocence. She was the only one."

"Yes, she did believe in you, John," I replied. "Claire was a good person."

"I sure hope I'm not in her will," he stated. Then, he added, "I don't want any of her millions."

"Excuse me?" I asked, believing that I hadn't heard him correctly. "What did you just say?"

"I said that I don't want any of her millions," he repeated.

"But Bud and Claire didn't have much money," I said.

What John told me next blew me away—simply blew me away!

It was a highly guarded family secret, but John told me that shortly after he and Megan were married, she had told him that her parents were wealthy. What income, or compensation, Bud received from the Army for having lost his arm and hand during the war went in to buying stocks and bonds. After bills were paid, what extra money they had left from his weekly income at that auto parts store went in to buying stocks and bonds. What money they saved by buying second-hand clothes, and such, and not taking vacations and always penny-pinching went in to buying stocks and bonds. John told me that when Megan had told him this, she had said that they were worth close to two million dollars, and he guessed that that had to be somewhere in the neighborhood of three million by now.

Mom had pulled out the stopper in the kitchen sink and was now drying her hands with a dish towel when I told her what John had just told me. She was stunned—stunned!

With the sound of dirty, soapy, water draining down the sink, Mom said, "Your father was a smart man!" She threw the dish towel down on the counter, and waving a fiery index-finger at me, she continued, "He always said that they had money, and he was right. When I think of the number of times when Claire and I would be shopping and she'd see something that she liked and I'd say, 'Oh, go on, Claire. Buy it.' And she'd say, 'Oh, no. We can't afford that.' And when I think of the number of times your father and I paid for their meals at restaurants because we felt sorry for them—why, I could just scream . . . Claire," Mom said, looking towards heaven, "if you was here right now, I'd slap you silly."

The movie *Home Alone 2* was playing that night on TV, and Mom and I watched it. It's not as good as the original movie, but Mom likes it a lot, especially when that kid tricks those two bumbling crooks with all of his traps and antics. Mom laughed a lot. It felt good hearing her laugh. I like the movie, too, and usually laugh, but I just couldn't get into it this time. Try as I did not to think about it, my mind kept drifting back to what John had told me about Bud and Claire being rich, and I kept wondering if that had anything to do with the case.

The movie ended at ten, and after it was over, I said goodnight to Mom and went upstairs to my bedroom.

After grabbing a six-pack from my cache of beers in the closet, I flopped onto my bed, ripped one of those beers from the pack, popped it open, and began drinking and thinking.

I told myself that since this whole thing began that I hadn't given motivation much of a thought. Claire being worth three million dollars is a lot of motivation, I told myself. Hell, for three million dollars I'd kill Mom. So who would be on that will? I asked myself. Well, Bud would be on it. But he's dead. Karen and her husband would be on it. But they 're both dead. Megan would be on it. But she's dead. John's probably on it—and Tyra would definitely be on it. But Tyra's dead. So that only leaves John . . . Holy cow! I said to myself, excitedly, realizing something. I think that you have just cracked this case wide open. You were right all along about John being guilty. I think you really are a private detective . . .

Wait a minute now, I said to myself, let's think this out. What if John and that Helen Dyer gal had planned this whole thing? What if he had met her some years before he said he had, in a bar or something, and he told her that his wife's parents were—Jesus! I shouted to myself, thinking of something else. He, or she, or both of them, murdered Megan. Her kidnapping and disappearance wasn 't a random act. He, or she, or both of them, murdered Megan. This whole thing was a diabolical plot to get Bud and Claire's money . . . But why didn't it work out? I asked myself. Well, somewhere along the way things went terribly wrong. Maybe that Helen Dyer got scared after he, or she, or both of them, murdered Tyra, and she wanted out. But it still makes perfect sense, right? ... Look, that's why John still claims that Dyer did it, and that's why she still claims that John murdered Tyra. They 're guilty— guilty of murdering Megan, guilty of murdering Tyra, guilty of doing all of this to get Bud and Claire's money . . .

If this is all true, I then asked myself, then why doesn't John confess his guilt? And why does he hope that his name isn't on that will? . . .

Well, maybe his brain is pickled from all of that alcohol abuse. Maybe he's deluded himself into believing that he truly didn't do it. It has to be John. There's no one left. They 're all dead. . . Shit! Shit, shit, shit.

I had polished off my second beer by now, and as I popped open my third one, I said to myself: Throughout this whole thing, there has been only one person that I got a bad feeling from, that I was being lied to, and that was that dentist—that Dr. Williams . . . Why did she become so upset when I started talking about—? Then, I remembered what Mom had said to me that morning. She said: "Tom, it's a fact—dead people can't hurt you." And then it hit me—it hit me right between the eyes like a clenched fist to the face! If I was right—it changed everything.

I had to know.

I knew exactly what I was going to do the next day.

I had polished off all six beers of that pack, and I woke up the next morning with one hell of a hangover. It didn't matter, though, because I wasn't going to do anything important until that evening.

I pretty much rested until it was time to go down and feed and visit with Dad. After we got back home, I took a nap until about two-thirty. Then, I got up and went downstairs.

Mom was in the living room, watching her favorite soap on TV, *The Bold and the Beautiful.*

I stepped into the living room and said: "Mom, don't make any supper for me tonight. I-I—Well, I have a date."

"With a girl?!" Mom cried, shocked. "Oh, praise the Lord!"

"Of course with a girl," I replied. "What do you mean by that?"

"No, no," she said. "I didn't mean anything . . . Well, who is she? Where did you meet her? What does she look—"

"Do you remember that dentist who I went to?" I said, interrupting her.

"You're going out with that dentist?!" she cried again.

"No," I replied. "I'm going out with her receptionist. We started talking that day, and I had the feeling that she liked me, and I asked her to have dinner with me tonight and she accepted."

"Oh, Tom," Mom sighed, joyously. "That's so wonderful . . . You know, Tom, I think you have finally found your calling in life. Becoming a detective has been good for you. You've made some money, you've got direction, and now you even have a date. It's all so wonderful. Thank the Lord."

"Yes," I replied. "It is all wonderful, isn't it?"

With my topcoat on, I headed out the door at three-thirty on the dot. I had showered, shaved, and changed into my suit clothes.

I hadn't lied to Mom all that much. I mean, no, I didn't have a date with that Sarah yet, but that was the plan. I felt it was best to ask her out on a date face-to-face. That way, she might be less inclined to say no.

I arrived at Dr. Williams' office a little after four o'clock. I parked to the back of the parking lot with the front end of Mom's car facing towards the building and that row of cars under that metal carport, directly opposite to that hot-looking, racy, black, Porsche 911 that I had seen the last time I was there. The front-end of it was facing me this time, and for some reason I couldn't take my eyes off of it.

I kept the engine running to keep warm and waited for Sarah to come out of the building.

At ten minutes after four-thirty, I spotted Sarah walking along the inner edge of the parking lot, close to the building. Night had fallen, but there was plenty of light from the streetlamps and from the overhead lamps in the parking lot.

She is definitely weird, I said to myself as I got out of the car.

She was wearing a full-length winter coat, but it was pink. Who wears a pink coat? It was unbuttoned, and I could see that she was wearing a velvet-blue dress. It was a nice-looking dress, but isn't that a bit fancy and inappropriate to wear to work? In her right hand, she had a cigarette, which she madly kept puffing on, and in her left hand, she held the handles of—well, I guess it was a purse. It was this basket-sized, floppy, purse made of weaved bamboo, with an embroidered picture on the outer face of it of a girl in a bathing suit on the beach.

I came abreast of her as she was passing by that Porsche.

"Hi, Sarah," I said, blocking her from moving any farther.

For a second, I saw fear in her, fear in the sudden tenseness of her body, fear on her face and in her eyes—those blue eyes of hers that were magnified by the thickness of the glass in those goofy-looking, over-sized, yellow-framed, glasses. The fear she felt was the fear that all women fear—the fear of being raped.

"It's me, Sarah," I said. "Tom Mayor. I had a toothache and you were kind enough—"

"Oh, yes," she stated, and gave a nervous laugh, her body relaxing a bit, "I remember you now. How are you? . . . Good Lord," she said suddenly, "what happened to your face and head?"

"It was bizarre," I replied. "My car,—my new, black Jeep Wrangler, the pride and joy of my life—the windshield exploded with me in the car. I had the heater going at full-blast, and I guess the coldness of the outside temperature and the extreme heat of the inside of the car made the windshield explode."

"Oh, you poor baby," she stated ever-so sensuously in that deep, gravelly, smoker's voice of hers.

"Yes," I said. "Listen, I know that this is short notice. But as I told you, I've recently returned to St. Louis because of my parents' declining health, and I don't know anyone in town anymore, and I was wondering if I could talk you into having dinner with me. I hear that that restaurant across the street has really good food. What do you say?"

"Well, I don't—"

"C'mon," I stated, coaxingly. "It will be nothing more than eating and talking. I promise."

"Well, where's the fun in only eating and talking," she said, and raised her painted-on brown eyebrows up and down coquettishly. "I'd love to have dinner with you."

"That's great, Sarah," I said. "Thank you."

For some reason, I looked over at that Porsche and said: "Boy, that's a hot-looking car, isn't it?"

After taking a long drag on that cigarette she was smoking and then letting it fall to the pavement of the driveway and extinguishing it by stepping on it with her right foot and giving a few sharp turns to her blue, pointed-toe, high-heeled shoe, she said: "That's Dr. Williams' car."

"That's Dr. Williams' car?!" I stated, incredulously, pointing to the car. "I wouldn't have pegged her for owning a car like this."

"She says she loves it," Sarah said, "but I don't believe her. I've been with her from the beginning, for twelve years now, and in that time she has owned two cars, both of them Volvos. She's a carefree person about some things, but driving isn't one of them. She bought it three years ago."

"I bet a motor like that has a very distinct sound—a very high-pitched whine."

"Yes, it does," she replied, seeming impressed with my guessing the sound of that engine.

"Well, shall we go? I'm getting cold, and hungry."

I didn't lie to Sarah. I told her that that car was my mother's car. I was going to tell her that it was a rental car, but I would have never gotten away with telling her that. I mean, what with all of those religious tapes and that miniature statue of Jesus on the dashboard, she would have never believed that it was a rental car.

The parking lot to that restaurant was behind the building. Because of this being a "date," and wanting to make a good impression, as we were driving over there, I told Sarah that I would drop her off at the entrance and then park the car. She declined my offer, though, stating: "No. Park the car. I'll walk with you. I can smoke while we walk. The restaurant has a goddamn no-smoking policy ... Do you smoke?"

"No," I replied. "But I don't mind it that you smoke. I hope you don't mind me saying this, but I think it makes your voice sound sexy."

"Awww, you're sweet," she said and reached over and moved her hand up and down my right arm, flirtatiously.

In the restaurant, we were seated at a table that was pretty close to the table that Mom had been seated the day that she ate there. The restaurant was crowded, noisy, and dark. We sat directly across from each other, with the lighted candle in the middle of the table. It casted shadows on our faces.

After our waitress, an overly enthusiastic college girl, in her early twenties, I would say, with light brown hair, gave us each a menu, she asked us what we would like to drink, and Sarah quickly asked me: "Do you like dry red wine?"

"Sure," I replied.

"Let's order a liter instead of two individual glasses," she said. "You get more for your money that way . . . Could you hurry up and bring the wine," she then said to the waitress. "It's been a long day for me. Thanks."

As Sarah looked-over the menu, she said, "They serve a steak here with a baked potato that's the best."

"Well, why don't we order that," I replied, congenially.

"My feet are killing me," Sarah said and then leaned down to one side and removed her shoes.

Our waitress returned, carrying a small, round, tray that had two wine glasses on it and a glass container that looked like a vase with a thin neck and was filled with red wine. She filled Sarah's glass first—holding and pouring that glass container by its thin neck—and before she had finished filling my glass, Sarah had gulped her glass empty. Our waitress, Debbie, I think she said her name was, refilled it and then left.

"I don't know what to do with my hands without being able to smoke," Sarah said and then took another long gulp of wine.

"Well, I know what you could do with your—-No, I'm sorry. Forget that I said—"

"You're terrible," Sarah replied with a smile and a wink at me. She then refilled her glass.

A male waiter passed by our table.

"So, Sarah, tell me something about yours—"

"Excuse me," Sarah said to the waiter. "I know you're not the person who waited on us, but could you find her and tell her that we need more wine . . . You don't mind, do you, Tom?" she said to me.

"No, no, not at all," I replied.

"Here, let me fill your glass, Tom," she said, filling my glass and emptying that vase.

"Thank you," I said. "So, tell me something about yourself, Sarah. I see rings on your fingers but none on your ring finger. I'm assuming you're not married—you're not, right?"

"No," she replied, with a disdainful chortle.

"Have you ever been married?" I asked.

Drinking, she answered me by holding up two fingers of her left hand.

"Twice," I said. "Wow."

Our waitress returned with another vase of red wine. We ordered the steak and baked potato, which came with a house salad and buns.

"Have you ever been married?" she asked me.

"No, I've never been married. I came close once. In Los Angeles, I lived with a girl for five years."

"What happened?" she said, refilling her glass.

"Well, I'm a salesperson for Johnson & Johnson, and I was on a two-week sales trip out of town. I finished my business sooner than I thought I would, and I came home unannounced and caught her in bed with my best friend."

"They were having sex?!" she cried, and then took a drink.

"Yes," I replied. "Now, you're a lady, and I don't want to be crass or inappropriate here, but they were doing it doggy-style, and she would never do it doggy-style with me."

"The whore!" Sarah stated angrily.

"Thank you for saying that, Sarah," I said. "Do you have any children, Sarah?"

"I have two children," she replied, her speech already a little slurred. "Would you like to see a picture of them?"

"I'd love to," I said, lying.

Sarah leaned over and slid her right arm and hand into that over-sized, floppy, bamboo purse and retrieved a large, sequin-covered billfold. After opening it up, she removed from one of the compartments a pocket-sized photograph and then handed it to me.

I looked at it for a moment and, confused, said: "I believe that you've given me the wrong picture, Sarah. This is a picture of you holding two small white poodles."

For some reason, Sarah found this hilarious. She laughed and said: "No, them are my babies, Snowball and Snowflake. Do you know why I named them Snowball and Snowflake?"

"Because they're white," I replied.

"Yes!" she cried excitedly, impressed with my mental prowess. "Fill your glass, Tom," she then said. "Don't make me drink alone ... I don't want any little goddamn brats. When I retire, I'm moving to Florida and buying a condo. I'll be one of those white-haired old broads you see playing shuffleboard."

"Oh, you're much too young to be talking about retiring, Sarah," I said.

"You're so sweet," she said and, suddenly, I felt a foot moving up and down my right leg below the knee.

Our food came and Sarah squealed excitedly: "I'm starved!"

We tore into it ravenously. I tore into it more out of the want of it soaking up some of that alcohol than out of hunger.

"I thought that I might be retiring last year, but it hasn't happened yet," Sarah stated between shoveling-in large bits of food.

"Why is that?" I asked.

"Well, last year Theresa, Dr. Williams, told me that she was thinking about selling the business and moving to New Zealand. She didn't want to lose me, but because of my years of faithful service, she felt she owed it to me to give me a heads-up. I told her that I was with her from the beginning and I'll be with her to the end. I'm not worried about it. I got plenty of connections in business."

This was the "in" that I was waiting for.

"What's Dr. Williams like?" I asked.

"She's a doll," Sarah replied with food in her mouth and then took a drink of wine.

"It's been my experience with doctors that they're dull people, all business and no personality."

"Theresa's like that now," Sarah said, "all business, but when she first opened the office, she was wild. She'd come in sometimes looking more dead than alive from nightclubbing all night. But she's changed. She's matured in the last four or five years."

"So-so, she's pretty easy to work for," I said, feeling a bit lightheaded.

"Oh, she's a doll," Sarah repeated. She leaned her glass a little too far to one side and spilled some of the red wine onto the white tablecloth: it looked like it was bleeding. "Oops," she said. "Oh, well, I'll refresh my drink." She refilled her glass, and as she did, she said: "Now seven or eight years ago was a different story. I almost walked out on her four or five times."

"Why was this?" I asked.

"Theresa hired this bitch who thought she was my boss. I told her, 'If Dr. Williams wants me to do something, she can tell me. I don't take orders from you.' I'd get mad and threaten to quit, and Theresa would talk to her and things would be fine for a while, but then she'd go back to ordering me around again. That bitch made my life a living hell ... I shouldn't call her a bitch. It's not polite to speak badly of the dead. She was kidnapped five years ago and hasn't been seen since."

"I think that I read something about that in—in the newspaper," I said. "What—what was her name?"

"Megan Jones," Sarah replied.

"It sounds—sounds to me like Dr. Williams and this—this Megan person were close," I said.

"Too close," Sarah replied with a disdainful, drunken, grunt, "like two peas in a—Hey, why all the questions about Dr. Williams? ... Are you interested in her?!"

Before I could reply, Sarah said, "Because if you are, you'd have to cut your dick off before she's go out with you!"

Bingo! That was exactly the type of thing that I wanted to know.

"Oh, my, God," she cried, in a panic, holding her hands to her chest. "What did I say? . . . I'm drunk. I drink too much . . . Please don't tell anyone what I said. Theresa is a good kid and I wouldn't harm her for the world. Please don't say any—"

"Sarah, Sarah, "I said, holding up my arms and hands dismissingly. "What someone's sex—sexu—What someone's sex orien-omiet—I won't say a word."

"Please don't," Sarah pleaded with me. "Please." She quickly scooted down in her seat, and then I felt a foot pressing hard against my groin and rubbing "it" with her toes. My body went tense, and I swear to you that my eyes bulged out of their sockets. And "it" rose fast, and hard.

There are times in one's life when you just know that something is going to happen—that it's a given certainty. I can't give you an example of this right now off the top of my head, but this was one of those times. In that moment, I knew that that night I was going to have sex with Sarah. It was a given.

I was so excited. For on this night, I wasn't having sex with downloaded porn; for on this night, I wasn't having sex with myself; for on this night, I was having sex with a warm, wet, living vagina: I was having sex—sex, sex, sex!—with a woman.

"That feels so good, Sarah," I cooed from across the table.

"Wolf," Sarah barked at me. "Wolf. I love doggy," she said ever so seductively in that deep, gravelly smoker's-voice of hers.

It was a damn good thing that I was having sex that night or I would have been pissed. That damn wine and dinner, plus tip, cost me one-hundred-and-twenty dollars. Can you believe it? One-hundred-and-twenty dollars!!!!

We stumbled drunkenly out of that restaurant, holding on to each other by the waist. She smoked a much needed cigarette while we walked back to Mom's car. My legs felt heavy, like 30-pound weights.

At the car, I unlocked the passenger's-side door and held it open for Sarah to get in. She passed by me, but instead of getting in, she turned around, suddenly. I knew she wanted to kiss. I leaned in and started to place my arms and hands around her solid hips, but she threw me to the side like a toy. I nearly fell. When I recovered my balance and looked at her, she was bent over at the waist, her left hand leaning on the open door of the car, holding that stupid purse in that hand, a hawser of vomit shooting out of her mouth like water streaming out of a fire hose. It was a disgusting sight. She kept puking and puking, and then she began farting, too. It was disgusting.

When she had finally emptied her stomach of sixty dollars of that wine and dinner—sixty dollars being half of a hundred and twenty—I gingerly helped her into the car.

"I need gum," she said after I had gotten into the car. She reached into that purse and got a package of gum. "That was un-lady-like of me, wasn't it," she said, stuffing two pieces of gum into her mouth.

"No, no," I said reassuringly, and lying. "You got—got sick from the food." I started the car and put it into drive.

The parking lot at Dr. Williams' office was empty except for one car. I don't know the make or model of the car, but it was yellow in color. I assumed that it was Sarah's. I pulled in front of it and came to a stop, without turning off the engine.

"You want to follow me to my place?" Sarah said.

"It's late and—and I have to get up early—early tomorrow," I replied. "Can I take a rain check?"

She looked at her flower-shaped, plastic wristwatch and cried: "It's not even seven! . . . This is because of me vomiting and farting, isn't it?"

"It has nothing to do with that," I replied. "I'm tired; I'm drunk; I have to get up early for work tomorrow."

"Men!" she stated angrily. "They're all shit. I should turn gay!" She, then, threw open the door and stormed out of the car. Slamming the door hard, she said: "Don't ever call. . ."

It seemed like it took me forever to get home. I haven't driven drunk in years, so I drove home slow and cautious.

I entered through the kitchen door. I had hoped—prayed!—that Mom had gone to bed early, but before I had entered, I looked between the two slits of the flower-printed curtains that cover the large glass window to the kitchen door and saw that the light in the hallway was on and that the lights in the living room were on, too. Plus, I could hear that the TV was on.

My only hope now was that she was upstairs in her bedroom, or in the bathroom, and I could sneak upstairs to my room.

Mom must have heard me opening the door, because by the time I passed through the kitchen and entered the hallway, she was standing in the hallway.

"You're back early," she said, the look of anticipated joy upon her face turning instantly to one of confusion and disappointment.

"Yes," I sighed, leaning on the bottom post of the staircase for support.

"What happened?" she asked. "Didn't she have a good time?"

"No, no," I replied. "It was nothing—nothing like that. It must have been the food. She got sick—puked and everything."

"Oh, the poor girl," Mom cried and brought her hands to her face in horror.

"I—I had to help her out of the—the car into her home," I said.

"That's terrible—what's wrong with you?" Mom, then, asked. "Why are your eyes so red? . . . Are you drunk?"

"No, no," I replied. "I did have a glass of wine, but I'm not drunk. I think I'm getting sick too," I said, wincing and rubbing my stomach between the sides of my unbuttoned topcoat.

Removing my topcoat, and handing it to her, I said, "Would you mind hanging up my coat for me? I'm going to bed."

I turned and started up the stairs, walking heavily and unsteadily.

"I'm sorry it didn't go well, Tom," Mom called out to me. "Are you two going out again?"

"Yes," I replied. "We decided to wait until after the holidays are over to go out again. Goodnight, Mom."

"Goodnight, Tom," she said, with a sound of deep sadness in her voice.

In my room, I removed my clothes mindlessly, by rote. After clumsily slipping into my sweatpants, I crawled into bed. I was never as thankful as I was that night to finally be in bed.

The sheets weren't all that cold, and it just felt so good to be in bed. Then, I thought of something.

"Shit," I cursed and ripped the sheet and cover off of me. I got up and went to my desk. I set the alarm to my clock for seven a.m.

I crawled back into bed, vowing that no matter how hung over I was, or how bad I felt, I was getting up at seven and leaving the house by eight.

I told myself that I now had all of the information that I wanted.

Now, let's see if I truly am a private detective!

Chapter Nine

To my joy, and surprise, I woke up feeling pretty damn good. I had just the mildest whisper of a hangover—my body felt relaxed and rested, and my mind felt sharp and clear. Thank you, Jesus!

I washed and shaved at the sink in the bathroom. Back in my room, I threw on the same clothes that I had worn yesterday—my old jeans, my old, long-sleeved, blue, shirt and my old, black, tennis shoes. I clipped my cell phone to my belt, grabbed my binoculars, and headed downstairs.

I put the coffee on and got the newspaper from the front porch. The weather had turned bitter cold again—well, it was colder than it had been the day before. The clouds were ink-black on a canvas of gray.

While I waited for the coffee to brew, I got the telephone book from the pantry to see if Dr. Williams' residence was listed. I should have Googled her name on my computer again, but I had forgotten to do that, and I didn't feel like going back upstairs. I thought that I might have to do that anyway, because even if her address was listed, I might not know the location of the address. But I lucked out on both accounts. Not only was her place of residence listed, but I knew exactly where it was. Her address was listed as being on Central Street, and by the zip code I knew that it was in the heart of downtown Clayton. She lived in suite 3031. I told myself that she must live in one of those fancy high-rises, apartment or condo, that's on that street.

The reason that I knew exactly where she lived was that the County Government building is on Central Street, in the middle of that long block on the west side. In order to get Dad on a Medicaid/Medicare bed in that facility he's in, Mom had to supply the state with a lot of personal documentation. One of the documents that the state required was a copy of their marriage license. Search and search for it as Mom did, she couldn't find their marriage license. So, I drove her to Clayton, to The Department of Deeds & Records, which is housed in the County Government building, and we got a copy of their marriage license.

I was hungry and wanted some eggs, but I didn't feel like making a mess or cleaning it up, so I just had two pieces of toast.

Sitting at the kitchen table, I wrote Mom a note, telling her that I had something that I wanted to investigate on the case, but that I'd definitely be back by eleven-thirty to drive her down to feed and visit with Dad.

I filled my thermos with coffee, grabbed my binoculars off of the table, and walked to the closet in the hallway.

My heart was racing. I was anxious, and nervous, to know if I was correct.

I threw on my old winter coat and headed out the door to face the day.

As I said before, I like downtown Clayton much more than I do downtown St. Louis—it's newer, clearer, and there's a feeling of energy and growth in the very air that has been lost to downtown St. Louis long ago.

Parking there is a bitch, though. There's next-to-no public parking, and it's very expensive parking there—like ten dollars a day—and the pristine, small-tree-lined, busy streets are lined with 2-hour parking meters.

Knowing this, before I arrived there, I stopped at a convenience store and bought a large bag of Lay's barbeque potato chips. Well, I was hungry. When I paid for it, I asked the clerk—a rough-looking teenager—to give me six dollars in quarters: I thought that that would be more than enough quarters to get me through the day. He didn't want to at first, telling me that he only had a limited amount of quarters. But when I told him that I had to go to Clayton to pay for a parking ticket, he said: "Say no more, dude" and gave me the quarters. Those quarters put a bulge in the right-side pocket of my front pants, and I thought of that line by May West: Is that a gun in your pocket, or are you just glad to see me?

I got to Clayton a little after eight-thirty.

The building that Dr. Williams lived in was on the corner of South Grand Avenue and Meramec. It was on the west side of the street with a bus stop in front of it at the curb. It was a neck-and-head-turning-up-tall building, about fifteen or twenty stories, I would say—very modern and sleek, made of glossy brown granite and tinted glass. In some respects, it reminded me of a pencil being held upside down, the pointed end reaching into the sky. I told myself that I bet if I stepped in there it would smell of success and money.

The entrance to the building was two, large, glass, doors. There was a doorman, dressed in a dark-blue uniform with matching hat. Because of the coldness of the day, he stayed inside, letting people in and out as they came and went.

I was having dam good luck that day. I got a premium parking spot, on the same side of the street of the building she lived in, on the opposite side of the corner. I had a straight sideways view of those two glass doors. I didn't even need the binoculars. It cost me two dollars in quarters, though, for two hours of parking—which pissed me off. Eight quarters! I poured myself a cup of coffee from my thermos, ripped open that bag of potato chips, sat back, and began watching those two doors.

The sidewalks weren't crowded with people like they are in the summer time, or in more hospitable weather.

At some point, as I sat there watching those doors, I began trying to think of a word that would describe downtown Clayton—all of the office buildings, the residential buildings, the Government building, the Court house, the County jail; all were ensconced so peacefully with and between fashionable restaurants—one that specialized in Indian food, another in Greek food, and another in food from Vietnam—and high-priced antique shops, and two art galleries.

The word that came to mind was "bohemian." Then I started a fight with myself.

But does "bohemian" have a connotation to it of being a "peasant"? I said. Yes, I answered myself ... At least, I think so. But it also has the connotation of—of being unusual, fashionable, which is what downtown Clayton is. But what about that peasant part of the word? I then said to myself. You can't have it both ways. There's nothing "peasant" about downtown Clayton. It's expensive here. I know, but. . .

At ten-thirty, I got out of the car to refill my parking meter with eight more quarters. I was just about to insert the first quarter when I heard a voice coming from my left side say: "Excuse me, sir. You can't do that."

I looked to my left and was immediately confronted by a meter-maid. She was a black woman in her mid-forties. She wasn't very tall at all, about five feet tall, I would say. She was wearing a black uniform and a fur cap with drooping ears, and a winter coat that matched the uniform with a fur collar. On her wide, black leather belt hung a black leather case with a walkie-talkie in it. In her right hand she held a long, narrow—but thick in volume—book. Something in me told me that that book was for writing parking tickets—and, boy, was she heavy. Her heaviness was threatening to split the seams of her pants and shirt.

"What do you mean 'I can't do that'," I said to her. "The parking meter is running out of time. I'm filling it with—"

"Sir," she said, interrupting me, "its two hours' parking only. You have been here two hours. You have to move your vehicle."

"Oh, c'mon," I replied. "I'm waiting for an elderly woman who lives in that building," I continued, raising my right arm and hand in the direction of the building I had been watching. "She very ill and I'm driving her to the doctor."

"I'm sorry to hear that, sir," she said. "But the law is the law."

"Well, where do I park?" I asked.

"Anywhere but here, sir," she replied, nodding her fat, round, face and head towards the direction of Mom's car.

"But there's no other place to park at in this—"

"Sir," she said, interrupting me again, "if you don't want me to issue you a parking violation, move the vehicle. Now."

"This is just stupid," I muttered out loud as I walked back to the car. When I got back to the car, I looked across the hood of it and said to her, "I'm going to call my congressman and tell him about this."

"Sir," she said, "that's your choice. I can't stop you from doing that."

I got back into Mom's car, slamming the door behind me.

I was pissed. As I drove away, I said to myself, I'm changing my mind. Downtown St. Louis is much better than downtown Clayton.

I had to circle the block three times before I found another parking spot, but guess what? My luck was still holding out. The parking spot I got was just two spots back from where I had parked before.

At eleven-fifteen, I told myself that I better get home and drive Mom down to feed and visit with Dad.

Feeling despondent, and unsuccessful—and not wanting to leave; I wanted to prove to myself that I was right!—I started the car and drove away, leaving my prime parking spot and the parking meter with an hour's worth of time still left.

At the facility that my dad's in, I was antsy. I wanted to get back to Clayton. I kept coaxing Mom to feed him faster.

"I can't do that, Tom," she kept replying. "Like I told you, I'm so proud that you're still investigating—Claire would be so proud of you, too, but I can't feed your father any faster. He'll start choking . . . Why won't you tell me what you're doing?"

"Because," I replied, "I just don't want to say anything until I'm certain."

After she had finished feeding Dad, I said, "Mom, do we have to stay as long as we usually do? Can't we leave earlier today? I want to get back to what I was doing."

"Praise the Lord, Tom," she said, shaking her head. "You've changed. You're so—so responsible now. I'm just so proud of—well, let's go."

It warmed my heart hearing her say that to me. I said, "Say, Mom, would you like to come with me? That way, I won't have to drive you back home, and I can get back to doing what I was doing all the faster."

"Sure, I'll come with you," she said, eagerly.

But did we leave earlier than we usually did? No. Dad was sitting in his wheelchair at the dining-room table, and for some reason he suddenly leaned forward and swept his right arm and hand across the table in front of him, tossing the tray and the remnants of his meal onto Mom's lap, soiling the black stretch pants she was wearing and the long-sleeved, pull-over, white blouse she had on. By the time Mom did a makeshift clean of her clothes in the bathroom, we left there at the same time we always do. I handed Mom her winter coat— her old, old, winter coat: A full-length, cloth, red coat—to put on and we left at exactly one-thirty.

I got to give Mom credit, though. I knew that she wanted to go home, what with her clothes being wet in places and it being winter and all. I told her that I'd drive her home, but she said she was fine. I turned the heater in the car on as high as it would go.

It was five-minutes-after-two when we got to downtown Clayton.

I think my luck was running out, too. The parking spot I found wasn't all that bad of a spot, but I wouldn't call it "premium." I had to keep my head turned perpetually west. I was parked right across the street from the doors to the entrance of the building that Dr. Williams lived in and in front of that Greek restaurant.

As we sat there, Mom listened to her religious tapes on the radio, sliding one tape after another into the cassette player.

Listening to all of that religious crap really began to piss me off. The one that pissed me off the most was this so-called "preacher" preaching on The Healing Powers of Jesus. He kept droning on and on about how sickness is the child of the devil, and if you're sick, all you have to do to be well again is to repent of your sins and ask Jesus to heal you, and you will be healed—not tomorrow, or yesterday, but now. By His stripes, you were healed. Notice the verb used here, 'were; ' it's past tense. You are already healed. Ask and you shall receive. The father of a child who wants bread wouldn't give the child a rock. Our Father in heaven shall do no less. Say but the Word and it shall be done ....

I thought of the day that Mom and I had placed Dad in that assisted-living facility. Driving back home that day, I was so sad and angry that I wanted to lash out at someone—anyone—and I took it out on Mom.

"All of your prayers and praying over Dad didn't work," I said. "If God loved us, He wouldn't have permitted Dad to have to go into that shithole of a place. I don't believe in God."

"Oh, Tom, don't say that," Mom stated, feeling sad and tired. Then, she gave me a standard, Baptist, Bible-thumping reply. "We can only ask God for the things we want in life, but in the end, the decision is always His."

"I'm getting hungry," Mom said, "and I have to go to the bathroom."

"Well, I don't know what to tell you, Mom," I began, somewhat irritated with her. "Why don't you go into that Greek restaurant and buy a sandwich," I then said, pointing to it, and then added, "and go to the bathroom."

"Oh, I don't know about that," she replied. "I never had Greek food," she continued. "I don't think that I'd like it."

"Well, you can at least go to the bathroom," I said.

"Well, all right," she said, and reluctantly started to get out of the car.

Before she got totally out of the car, I said: "Hey, would you buy me a cup of coffee?"

"Okay," she replied.

When she got out of the car, I immediately turned off the tape she was listening to. When she returned with two cups of coffee, she wanted to know why I had turned off the tape she was listening to. I told her that I must have done it without even thinking about it. She gave me a look of disapproval and disbelief and immediately turned it back on.

By four o'clock, I was fed up with listening to all of that religious crap and was about to angrily tell her to turn it off when I heard a tapping sound coming from the window on Mom's side of the car. I turned my head in that direction and saw "HER" standing there. I couldn't freakin' believe it! It was that damn meter-maid again!

I pressed the button on the side of the door to roll down the passenger's-side window. She bent down a bit and stuck her fat head a bit inside of the window.

"You again?" she said, real sarcastically. "Is this the woman you was waiting for? You got five minutes left on that—"

She suddenly stopped talking. Then, she turned her head and tilted it as if listening to something.

"Ma'am," she then said to Mom. "Are you a Christian?"

"I sure am," Mom replied, proudly.

"It does my heart good to hear that, ma'am," she said. "Five years ago, ma'am, I was in the claws of the devil. I was homeless, on welfare, my children gave me no respect, and I was on dope. It got so bad that I thought of killing myself. One night, all doped up, I saw him, ma'am—I saw the devil himself. I fell to my knees and shouted: 'Jesus, save me! Jesus, save me!' And He did, ma'am. He did. I got a home, a job, my children respect me, and I haven't touched dope in five years."

"Praise the Lord!" Mom rejoiced.

"Yes, ma'am," she said. "Praise Him . . . Sir," she then said to me, "I'm sorry. But the law is the law. Move this vehicle ... You have a good day, ma'am," she then said to Mom. "God bless you, ma'am."

"God bless you, too, dear," Mom replied.

She then waddled away, like an elephant.

As I pushed the button to roll up the window, Mom said, "Wasn't she the sweetest person, Tom?"

I shifted the car into drive and said flatly: "If you say so."

My luck started to change again. I made one pass around the block and got—get this!—my original parking spot on the same side of the street and just across the corner of the intersection. I could see those doors great. Plus, I didn't have any more quarters for the parking meter—which pissed me off greatly!—but Mom had exactly, and only, eight quarters in her coin purse.

Mom stopped listening to her tapes, but then turned on the radio.

"Do you have to keep playing around with everything in this car?" I said to Mom, snapping at her. "I'm trying to work here."

"Don't you use that tone of voice with me, young man," Mom snapped back at me. "I want to listen to my Christian radio station . . . Working? What 'work' are you doing? All I see you doing is watching the entrance to that building."

"This is what a detective does," I replied, defensively.

"How much longer are we going to be here, Tom?" she said, looking at me. "You told me that *It's a Wonderful Life* is on TV tonight. Am I going to miss that?"

"That's not on until eight o'clock," I replied. "You won't miss it."

"Well," she said, "it's getting dark—and I'm hungry."

"All right," I said, heavily and disgustedly, as a bus pulled in to the stop at the opposite corner. "I guess that's enough for today. I'll come back Monday. What a waste of a day."

I raised my right arm and hand to the arm of the gear shift and was about to grab it when I saw the doorman opening one of those doors for someone, and this woman comes sauntering out of it.

Even though it was getting dark, I could still see clearly. But I wasn't taking any chances. I wanted to see extra clearly. I grabbed my binoculars and brought them to my eyes.

What first struck me about this woman was that she was wearing this wide-brimmed, floppy, black hat that covered the sides of her face, somewhat. She was wearing a full-length, cloth, black, coat that matched the hat and had a belt that tied at the waist. She had on designer's jeans and a red blouse and black, flat-heeled shoes.

Although her shoulder-length hair was raven-black, as were her eyebrows, she looked like Karen, my Karen, and there was no hiding—even with hair dyed black and eyebrows dyed black—that protruding Peterson forehead.

"Bingo!" I cried, overwhelmed with joyous triumph. "I did it. I really did it!" I continued, still looking at her through the binoculars. "I'm a goddamn—gosh-dam detective, Mom. I've cracked this case wide open!"

"How, Tom?" Mom cried, happy excitement in her voice for me. "How did you crack it?"

"Do you see that woman getting on that bus?" I asked, looking at Mom.

"No, not really," Mom said, straining her eyes and looking in that direction. "I'd have to put on my glasses."

"Well, she did it, Mom," I said, looking in that direction again with the binoculars. "She murdered Tyra—and she murdered Claire, too."

"Claire was murdered?!" Mom cried, shocked. "Who is she?!" Mom demanded to know, her anger growing. She leaned angrily forward in the seat and repeated, "Who is she?! I want to know her name this instant!"

"Megan," I replied, looking at Mom again.

"Megan?" Mom said, incredulously. "Megan's dead, Tom."

"Oh, no she isn't," I stated. "That's just what she wanted everyone to believe."

"You have to be wrong, Tom," Mom said. "Why on earth would Megan kill her own daughter and Claire?"

"For the money," I replied—and then added: "And because she's gay."

"What does being happy have to do with anything?" Mom asked, very confused.

"No, no," I replied. "Look, in today's world being gay can also mean that you are a homosexual."

The bus pulled away from the curb.

"Megan is a homos—"

"Listen," I began, interrupting Mom and looking at her again. "I know you're hungry and tired, so am I, but I want to see where she's going. I think I know where she's going, but I want to check it out. It won't take long."

We followed the bus, keeping three or four cars between us and the bus. Once the bus left downtown Clayton, it turned west on Clayton Road. It was a short bus ride, seven to ten blocks tops. Megan got off the bus exactly where I thought she would—at the building of Dr. Williams' office.

I waited until she entered the building before I pulled into the driveway and parked in the parking lot behind the building. Except for that Porsche of Dr. Williams' and one other car, both of which were parked under that metal carport, the parking lot was empty.

Thank God, I said to myself, not seeing Sarah's yellow car. I didn't want to deal with her.

"You stay here," I said to Mom, and I reached for the handle of the door. "I'll be right back."

"What?!" Mom cried. "Wait a minute, Tom. Wait a minute," she repeated. "Where are you going?"

"In there," I replied, pointing to the building, "to confront them."

"Are you insane?!" she said. "You just got finishing saying that they murdered two people."

"They murdered a little girl and an ill, elderly woman," I replied. "I'm not afraid of them."

"Well, you sure picked a fine time to suddenly get brave, Tom," Mom said. "No, I don't want you doing this. Get on that toy phone of yours and call the police. Let them handle it."

"Mom," I began, "I've never finished one damn thing that I've ever started in my damn life, and it's about time that I started. I'm sick of it. I owe this to Claire, and to myself, to see it through to the end."

Mom was stunned, and so was I to tell you the truth. She said not a word.

"Look," I said, unclipping my cell phone from my belt and handing it to her, "if I'm not back in—in ten minutes, you call the police and tell them to come to the corner of Clayton and New Ballas Road, to Dr. Williams' office. Tell them it has to do with two murders."

"I don't know how to use this thing, Tom," she said.

"It's easy," I said, flipping on the dome light. "Put your glasses on."

She did.

"Now, here's the number nine, just press it with the tip of your index-finger. Here's the number one here. Press it twice with the tip of your index-finger. Now, you see this button here up in the left-side corner with the green check-like mark on it. Press that after you dial 9-1-1, then, bring the phone up to your ear and wait for the police to answer. It's that easy. Act like you're doing it. Go on, try."

"Okay," she replied, reluctantly. "I press the nine. Then, I press the one two times. Then, I press the button up here that has a green check-mark on it. Then, I bring the phone to my ear and wait for the police to answer."

"That's it exactly," I said.

"But where do I speak?" she then asked. "Where's the receiver?"

"It's built into the phone," I replied. "When you have it next to your ear, just speak. They'll hear you. I got to go."

I got out of the car, but before I shut the door, Mom said, "Thomas, wait."

I looked back at her, but she didn't say anything. She just kept staring at me.

"What, Mom?" I finally said, looking at her.

"Be careful, Tom," she said. "Just be careful."

"I will, Mom," I replied. I smiled at her and then shut the door.

My heart was pounding away in my chest like a jackhammer breaking up cement. I was nervous, but I wasn't scared. Darkness ruled the night; the air was cold and crisp and somewhere someone had lit their fireplace. I could smell the sweet embers of the dying logs, and as I headed quickly across the shiny pavement of the parking lot, I knew that I was about to face my most dreaded enemies—my own fears.

Chapter Ten

Once inside of the building and standing in front of the door to Dr. Williams' office, I stopped and turned my head and leaned in to see if I could hear voices inside. Nothing. All was silent.

Well, here goes nothing, I said to myself. I took a deep breath and after expelling it, I began pounding on the door.

"Dr. Williams!" I began shouting, moaning and groaning in pain. "Dr. Williams! It's me, Thomas Mayor. I know it's after office hours, but I chipped a tooth eating popcorn. I saw your car out there in the parking lot. I'm in terrible pain, Dr. Williams. Won't you help me? Please ... Dr. Williams. I know that I should have called first, but I—"

The door to her office swung open and she said hurriedly: "Come in, Mr. Mayor."

She was wearing a red dress and red high-heeled shoes, with a small pearl necklace and matching earrings. Even with that over-sized head of hers on the small, perk, body, she looked drop-dead gorgeous, and she smelt good, too.

"Sorry about this, Dr. Williams," I said after stepping into the office, my right hand on the right side of my face, feigning a look of being in pain.

Except for the overhead florescent lights in the hallway that led to the examination rooms, the office was dark and silent. That wooden, tree-stumped-shaped desk of Sarah's looked so empty and lonely without Sarah's effervescent, weird, presence sitting there. I don't know if it was because of what I was about to do, or if it was because of that office being dark, silent, and cold, but my body began to tremble. There was a haunting eeriness to the office that made my fingers tingle with fear. At any moment, I feared that a monster was going to jump out at me and devour me.

"Follow me, Mr. Mayor," she said, turned and started down the hallway. "What happened to your face, Mr. Mayor?"

"It was the strangest thing, doctor," I replied, following her. "My car, the joy of my life... my black...

Stopping at the doorway of the same examination room that I had been in when I had seen her the week before, she leaned in and flipped on the lights. She then stepped to the side of the doorway, indicating with her extended right arm and hand for me to pass her and enter the room.

I did.

"Why don't you take off your coat, Mr. Mayor, and set it on the chair," she said, pointing to a wooden-framed, upholstered chair in the southeast corner of the room, by the windows. "Then lie down on the examination chair and we'll get started."

She walked over to an ornate, white, wooden, cabinet with glass doors to it midway up. It was positioned against the southwest corner of the room. After opening one of the middle drawers on the lower section of that cabinet, she reached in and removed a box of latex gloves from it. She, then, ripped a pair of gloves from it and began putting them on.

As she did that, I walked behind the examination chair, turned around and stood there, with my back to the windows. I wasn't taking any chances. I wanted to be facing the entrance to that door.

Dr. Williams was to my left and her back was to me.

After taking another deep breath and expelling it, I placed my cold, sweating, shaking hands in my coat pockets and said, "Where's Megan at, doc?"

This hit her hard, like a fist to the face. Her whole small body went stiff.

"I don't know what you're talking about, Mr. Mayor," she replied, her back still to me.

"Oh, c'mon, doc," I said. "Never lie to a pathological liar. You'll always lose . . . Hey, Megan!" I shouted, looking towards the door. "Where are you, girl?!"

Dr. Williams spun around and said, "There's no one here but us, Mr. Mayor!"

"C'mon, Megan!" I continued. "I know you're here. I followed you . . . Don't you want to say hi to your ole neighbor?"

Like the phoenix rising out of its own ashes, Megan suddenly appeared at the door, minus that floppy hat and coat.

She was boiling mad. With her hands at her sides in tight, knotted fists, her whole body was tense, ready, and eager to do battle. Now, I was scared.

What scared me the most about her was the look of pure hate and steely resolve on that enraged face of hers. If she had been a cartoon character, steam would have been spewing from her nose and mouth, like a bull preparing to charge.

As much as I knew that I should revile and hate Megan, a part of me couldn't. She looked so much like Karen, except for the eyes. Oh, she had Karen's watery, blue eyes, but whereas Karen's eyes had always innately conveyed sincerity and compassion, Megan's were devoid of the slightest sincerity or compassion for mankind. Her cold, steely eyes stated: I take what I want, and no one stops me.

"There you are, girl," I said, desperately hoping that I was hiding my fear. "Long time no see."

"Please leave, Mr. Mayor," Dr. Williams said, a mixture of held-back threatening and pleading escaping from a slightly trembling voice.

"I'm leaving, doc," I said to her. Turning back to Megan, I said, "It must have been hard for someone like you to live in the shadows for five years . . . What was the plan, Megan? To suddenly reappear after Claire's death and claim that you have had amnesia for the past five years and suddenly you remembered who you are? Or that you had been kidnapped by some cult and were held against your will and was their sex object for these past five years and finally escaped? I got to tell you, Megan," I said, shaking my head, "I can't believe you've gotten away with it as far as you have. If someone like me figured it out, I can't believe that the police didn't figure it out.

"At best, it's all so sophomoric—the faking of your death, the framing of John, the threatening calls, the red spray-painting of the words 'revenge is mine' on the door of Tyra's bedroom. Those were all red herrings. This had nothing to do with Tyra or John, or even with that Helen Dyer. But it had everything to do with you … John had repeatedly warned Tyra never to answer the door when he wasn't there, never open the door to strangers, and she never did. So how did her murderer get inside of the house? How was she murdered when all of the doors and windows to the house were locked? It had to be an inside job. No, she would have never opened a door to a stranger, or even to that Helen Dyer gal. But she would have for you—she would have thrown that door wide open and ecstatically, joyously, shouted, 'Mommy's home!'"

Suddenly, as I was piecing this story together, my confidence returned. Suddenly, I wasn't scared anymore. Suddenly, I felt like a real detective. I felt like Nick Charles. Why, I even sounded like William Powell. Suddenly, I was—The Thin Man!

"It was the same with Claire," I said, stepping in front of that examination chair. "Claire was a dying, bitter, frightened, old, woman, who was especially frightened at night. Even when she called the police on a neighbor at night and the police came to her door, she never opened it. But like Tyra, at the sound of your voice, as ill as she was, she would have sprinted to open that door—the prodigal granddaughter has returned! She must have been so happy to see you again, even with Mr. Fluffy, the neighbor's dog, yapping its fool head off at the sight of you. And that's where you made a mistake, Megan—a big one. After you removed that rosary from around Claire's neck and dressed her in that nightgown and placed her body in her bed, you should have placed that rosary back around her neck instead of placing it on the nightstand: Claire never removed that rosary from around her neck, not even when going to bed.

"Now, I don't believe that your little girlfriend here," I said, nodding my head at Dr. Williams, "has the guts to murder an innocent little girl, but Claire was a dying, old woman. Either you, or she, injected Claire with something that killed her. I'd say that you were betting on the coroner performing a most summary examination of her body because of her being a dying old woman, which was probably the case. When I go to the police and tell them all of this, I'll be sure that a toxicology report is done on Claire's body, and I know that they're going to find a substance in her that shouldn't be there.

"I know that I should feel more remorse and sorrow about you murdering Tyra than I do about you murdering Claire, but I didn't really know Tyra. But Claire was like a second mom to me, and when I realized that I was responsible for you murdering Claire, because of that flippant remark I made to Dr. Williams about Claire being so despondent that she was thinking about changing her will and leaving what little money she had to charity—No, you couldn't have that. All of the planning; the hiding; the killing would have all been for nothing if she did that. No, you couldn't have that—and when I realized this, I got mad. I told myself that I was seeing it through to the end, even if that meant you shooting at me again like you did that day in my backyard.

"I don't get it, Megan. I really don't. All of the pain and suffering and death you've caused—for what? For something as paltry as money? Or so you could run off to New Zealand with Dr. Williams and live an openly gay lifestyle? ... Your mother has got to be shaking her head at you, Megan—in total shame."

I guess I crossed the line with that last remark. Megan exploded! The bull finally charged.

She sped across that carpeted floor at me with the speed and ferocity of a lion pouncing down on a gazelle for its lunch.

She got in my face. Her face and body was so close to mine that I could feel the nipples—which were rock-hard, too, probably because of the coldness of the room—of her grapefruit-sized, supple breasts pleasurably pressing up against my chest. She forced me to bend the upper half of my body so far back that I had to reach behind me and place my left hand on that examination chair to prevent myself from falling backwards.

"What does a loser like you know about my life?" she stated, screaming in my face. "What does a loser like you know anything about shame or love, true love? All you ever wanted out of life is a free ride— free room-and-board; not to work."

"Now, let's calm down here," I said to Megan, my mind racing and my body visibly shaking. Then, I felt this sharp, stabbing pain on the side of my left leg, about a foot up from the knee.

"Ouch!" I cried and looked down to my left. I saw Dr. Williams rising. In her right hand, she held a syringe with a hypodermic needle. The syringe was empty. "What did you do?" I said to her, panicking. "Did you poison me?! ... I was joking," I said to Megan. "I won't tell anyone." I started to feel lightheaded. "Am I going to die?" I said to Dr. Williams. My whole body, suddenly, felt heavy. I couldn't breathe. I turned my head to heaven, for comfort. Then, I said it. I'm so embarrassed to tell you this. In my defense, though, maybe I said what I did—No, I know that was why I said what I did!—because of what Dr. Williams had injected with. I was speaking out of my head. I cried: "Mommy!" and then I passed out.

I was unconscious, but I could hear everything that was said. I heard Megan say: "Help me get him into the chair."

Actually, I don't think that I was unconscious. To me, I say that my body was paralyzed. Other than that, though, I felt fine. Then, things started to get weird. First, I saw these huge colored disks in front of me—red, green, blue, orange, and so forth. Then, suddenly, I was in this tunnel. It was pliable and felt like skin. It was almost like being squeezed inside my mother's womb, attached to an umbilical cord,, and when I looked up, I saw a light at the end of the tunnel. Well, I have read or heard enough about that to know not to go into the light. Because if you do, you cross over, and that's all she wrote. You're dead. I told myself that there was no way in the world that I was going into that light. Then, I felt wind. It felt good at first, refreshing. Then, it started to blow harder and harder. Then, it reversed itself. Instead of blowing, it began sucking, harder and harder. I felt my presence, my essence, my very soul, being sucked upwards against my will. I wanted to fight back, but how could I? I was sucked higher and higher towards the light, and then, like a person opening a bottle of wine, and giving one final heave to that corkscrew and popping that cork out of that bottle, I popped out of that tunnel and was thrown against the ceiling and splattered onto it.

I said to myself that it was over, that it couldn't get any more bizarre than what it is. But I was wrong. I couldn't see them, but Megan and Dr. Williams turned into animals. They were wearing the same clothes that they had on, but they were animals. Megan was this furry, brownish-red fox, with a tail coming right out of the butt of those designer jeans, and Dr. Williams was a mouse—a teeny-tiny gray mouse, with this huge, over-sized mouse's head.

"Let's run, Megan," I heard Dr. Williams say from directly below me. "He'll only be out for an hour—two at the most."

"I'm not running!" Megan barked at Dr. Williams. "You go get the car and bring it to—"

"No, Megan!" Dr. Williams cried. "You're not thinking about killing him, are you? No more killing, Megan. When does it stop?!"

"It stops when this piece of shit is dead, and after I got my money," Megan replied. "That's when it stops! Now do what I said, Theresa, and get the—"

"Megan! Look out!" Dr. Williams screamed.

Then, I heard this loud, dull, cracking sound, and I got the feeling that someone fell to the floor.

"Ooooooh, my arm!" I heard Mom cry. "I broke my cast!"

Gee, it was great hearing Mom's voice. Mom was a black bear—a big, furry, loveable, black bear.

"Little girl," I then heard Mom say, panting and out of breath, "I'm a God-fearing woman, but you better tell me the God's truth, or I'll do to you what I did to her. Were you telling the truth when you said that my son was okay?"

"Yes," Dr. Williams replied, nervously. "He's fine. He's unconscious, but he's fine."

"Here," Mom then said to Dr. Williams. "You take this phone, dial 911, put that phone to your ear, wait for the police to answer and then give them this address—you better tell them to send an ambulance, too. Tell them that it's murder. I'd do it myself but my arm hurts."

Within less than ten minutes, that room was buzzing with police and paramedics.

I don't know how many police and paramedics were actually there, but I counted three different voices that I knew were policemen and two that were paramedics. The police were gorillas, dressed in police uniforms, and the paramedics were—I'm not gay; I'm not!—well, both of them were that good-looking Mike guy that had treated me back at the house the other day, and both of them were naked except for the wearing of a sparkling, dark-blue G-string and a stethoscope hanging from both of their necks like neckties.

Because of all the talking going on in the room, I didn't catch all of it, but I heard Dr. Williams tell one of those paramedics that she had injected me with Keta-something.

I heard Megan talking again. I heard the other paramedic telling her that the contusion to the back of her head wasn't all that large, and that he didn't believe she had a concussion. He would transport her to the hospital if she chose to go, though. She declined to go.

"What about my son?" I heard Mom say, and then I heard that paramedic who had spoken to Dr. Williams about me say, "I'm monitoring his vital signs, ma'am. I want to see if he wakes up on his own. If he doesn't, I'll wake him, ma'am."

"Let me see if I got this straight," Sergeant Robert Seaton said. "You two were going to have dinner together when this man, Mr. Mayor, faked having chipped a tooth and begged for you, Dr. Williams, to fix it. You stayed in the waiting room while you and Mr.

Mayor came into this room. You heard screaming coming from this room and you rushed in here and found Mr. Mayor on top of Dr. Williams in this chair, ripping at her clothes and attempting to rape her. You wrestled him off of her and Dr. Williams subdued Mr. Mayor by injected him with a sedative. Mrs. Mayor here took offence at you doing this to her son and snuck up behind you and knocked you out with the cast on her arm.”

“That’s right,” Megan said.

“I never heard such lying in all my life,” Mom said. “Your nose should be as long as Pinocchio’s when he lies with all of the whoppers you’re telling. You liar.”

“You’re the liar,” Megan snapped at Mom.

“Ma’am,” Sergeant Seaton said, “what’s your name and address? You didn’t tell me the last time I asked you.”

“Why should I have to give you my name and address?” Megan said. “We’re not the criminals here. They are.”

“I’ll tell you her name, officer,” Mom said. “It’s Megan Peterson, and she lives with her.”

“That’s not my name, you senile old woman,” Megan snapped again at Mom.

“Don’t you call me senile, you Jezebel,” Mom snapped back at Megan. “Officer,” Mom continued, “I’ll tell you the same that I told that officer there. My son is a private investigator. He solved two murders tonight. She murdered her own daughter and her own grandmother, Claire Peterson.”

“Yes, he informed me that you stated that, Mrs. Mayor,” Sergeant Seaton replied. “But why did she murder her daughter and grandmother?”

“Because she’s happy,” Mom replied. “No, that’s not right,” Mom then said. “She’s—she’s joyous . . . No, that’s not right, either . . . She’s—she’s—oh, she’s living in sin. She’s living in homosexuality.”

“Ma’am,” Sergeant Seaton said, “homosexuality isn’t against the law.”

“Oh, I beg to differ, young man,” Mom said. “It’s against God’s laws.”

"Bob, come here," I then heard a man's authoritative, rough-sounding, no-nonsense voice say, coming from the door of the room. I hadn't heard his voice before.

After a few minutes had passed, I then heard that man speaking from directly below me.

"I'm Detective Frank Romper," he said. He was an orangutan, dressed in a three-piece suit. "Here's the deal. A lot of people in this room could be arrested tonight and go to jail. You could be arrested for trespassing, for assault, for attempted rape, for injecting a person with a substance against his will, and for obstructing a police investigation. But I don't think anyone should be charged tonight with anything and go to jail. There's something damn fishy about all of your stories. So, listen carefully to me: I'm going to investigate—real hard—all of your stories ... So, what do you want to do, people—get arrested or go home?"

Everyone chose to go home.

Suddenly, that sucking wind was back. It grew stronger and stronger, and sucked me off of that ceiling like a vacuum cleaner. Suddenly, I was back in that tunnel. Then, I was thrown back into my body.

I awoke coughing and choking, with that paramedic that had spoken to Mom about me waving something under my nose. It smelt horrible, like rotten eggs. It left a foul taste in my mouth for the rest of the evening—and that paramedic was no Mike. He was big, husky and hairy. He looked more like an ape than I had envisioned any of those cops looking like apes. And I had one of the worst headaches that I have ever had in my entire life. It was so bad that it made the worst hangover I've ever had seem like a picnic in the park.

That paramedic had previously examined Mom's arm and had told her that it was completely healed.

It felt good being outside. The night air was cold and crisp. I drank it in thirstily.

There wasn't a star in the sky, which disappointed me. For some reason, I wanted to see stars.

As Mom and I walked back to her car, I thought of how Mom had saved the day and my butt. I was so proud of her. I looked over at her with much affection for her in my heart. Then, she morphed back into that black bear—I'm not lying. I saw it with my own eyes. She was that black bear again!

I stopped, stunned, too dumbfounded to move or think, and I just stared down at her.

It stopped, turned, faced me and began staring back up at me.

"Tom," it said in Mom's voice, "what's wrong with you? Are you sick?"

It reached out and touched me on the shoulder with one of its paws and said, "Why are you looking at me like that, Tom?" Then, as instantly as she had changed into that black bear, she suddenly changed back to her old self.

"Oh!" I shouted, stunned again.

"What's wrong with you, Tom?" she said.

"I—I nothing. Nothing," I said. "I'm just so happy to see you."

We passed under a streetlamp, and feeling good, in my best Humphrey Bogart voice, I said: "Louie, this looks like the beginning of a beautiful friendship."

Imitating Bogie, too, Mom says: "Play it …"

Chapter Eleven

Well, that's my story. It's a little after twelve o'clock now. As I said at the beginning, I'm sitting at my desk in my bedroom, staring out the window at the night sky and going over it all again in my mind. I'm on my fourth beer and feeling only mellow-drunk. I'm still feeling super hyper about what all I have done. All through supper, and all through watching that movie with Mom, that *It's a Wonderful Life*, it all felt so surreal, like being in a dream. I had to keep telling myself that it wasn't a dream, that I had really done it—that I had actually solved two murders. I, me, Thomas Mayor—I did that.

All the way home, Mom kept saying how proud she was of me—how I had solved two murders and saved an innocent man from being executed. I sure hope that that detective does what he said he was going to do and investigate the case. If I don't hear from him in a week or two, I'll go to the Post-Dispatch Newspaper and see if I can get a reporter interested in my story.

I, too, am feeling pretty proud of myself. I have finally accomplished something in my life—something meaningful. I kept my word to Claire and solved the case. Funny thing, though. How do real private detectives make any money being detectives? I've done a quick calculation in my head of all that I spent of that thousand dollars that Claire gave me— including what I'll have to spend to have both windshields in my car replaced—and I'm pretty sure that I spent all of that thousand dollars that she gave me. I don't think that I made a dime being a P. I.

Oh, well. At least Mom's p—Oh, my God! . . . It's snowing. It's coming down hard. It's turning everything white—the street below, the sidewalks, the cars on the street, the trees and the rooftops— everything is covered in snow, white snow . . . It's so beautiful.

I don't know if it's the beer talking, or if it's because of what I have accomplished today and feeling so proud of myself, but seeing this snow, it finally feels like Christmas. I'm going to turn on the icicle lights in my window . . . Oh, it looks so beautiful. It's giving off a warm, inviting white glow to the inside and outside of the window. It's the only Christmas lights on in the house now, being so late. I wonder if it's serving as a beacon to others who are passing by—a beacon of hope to those who are lost and are desperately seeking answers to life or self. I hope so.

I guess because of having to place Dad in that facility and him not being here, I just haven't been able to get into the "Christmas Spirit." Putting up the tree and the decorations, and putting up the lights outside, and watching all of those Christmas movies and Christmas TV shows with Mom and buying her a Christmas present—none of it put me in the "Christmas Spirit." When anyone said Merry Christmas to me, I just replied, flatly, "Yeah, right back at you."

But now, being mellow-drunk, and feeling so proud of myself, and seeing this snow and the lights in my window, the Christmas Spirit is alive and in me.

Goodnight, Dad. I'll see you tomorrow.

Merry Christmas.

Being a P.I.--Again
ALAN ZACHER

Dedication

To all who suffer--from diseases, poverty, homelessness, hunger, despair.
Don't give up! For all of you, I humbly dedicate this novel, with my love and
prayers.

Chapter One

"Oh, Mom," I cried. "I don't want to die!" I, like Mom, was bound with gray duct-tape to an old wooden chair. We were about three feet apart and facing each other. We were in a dusty room on the third floor of a long-ago abandoned factory on Wharf Street, near downtown St. Louis. Against the north wall of the room was an old metal table. On top of the much dust-covered table was an old alarm clock, with large, black numbers on its face. I could see that the alarm was set for 8:00 PM, which was in seven minutes. Attached to the clock, by duct-tape, were three sticks of dynamite.

I should never have involved Mom in any of this. I mean, the poor, pudgy, white-haired, old dear. She's eighty-six years old.

"After all of those years of wasting my life," I cried, "I finally have reasons to live—I got money; I'm finally healthy and in shape; I'm dating—and now I'm going to die!"

"Stop your crying, Tom, and get us out of this!" Mom shouted at me angrily. "You're a detective—a famous detective; so, think! Think! Be a man! Get us out of this!"

Well, let's back up a minute here. This happened a few nights ago, so, obviously, we didn't die.

It's twenty minutes after midnight, Saturday, Halloween, and I'm sitting at my desk, which is butt-up against the wall under the window, and faces the street below, in my bedroom of my parents' old two-story house in Lemay, South County of St. Louis, Missouri. I have lived here all my life. I'm fifty-seven years old, and up until two years ago, in 2007, I was a real loser—a bum who never worked, secretively got drunk in my room night after night, told lie after lie, never dated or left the house unless I had to, and had no future at all. Then, two years ago, that all changed; I solved two murders.

Now, I'm no P. I., gumshoe. No. It was a joke. A joke that I was playing on Mom. See, two years ago, my dad's Alzheimer's got to a point in which Mom and I couldn't take care of him any longer. We hated it, but Mom placed him in a nursing home: Living Care of South County, which is only two miles east of here. Mom placed him in there at the end of summer, and, boy, was that first Thanksgiving and Christmas without Dad here awful. Just awful. It was so lonely. Mom and I drove there every day to be with Dad and feed him lunch.

Mom still does that, but I don't anymore. About a year ago now, I just couldn't look at him anymore, being like he is—a vegetable; a body with no mind; a zombie. Anyway, like I said, those two holidays were rough on us—well, especially rough on Mom. What with all of Mom and Dad's brothers and sisters being dead from disease and old age, and what with my two older sisters, Mary and Eve, living in different states—Mary living in Santa Monica, California, and Eve lives in Chicago, Illinois. So, yeah, it was rough on Mom. Two weeks before Christmas, I was really feeling lonely and sad, really missing Dad, and I knew Mom was feeling the same—sad and lonely. So, instead of going directly up to my bedroom after supper and getting drunk, I began staying downstairs and keeping Mom company, watching TV with her. And, boy, was that boring.

We'd sit on the old, long, brown-cloth sofa and watch old movies. And this is what got me into that mess. Mom loves watching old detective movies from the '40's—like Humphrey Bogart as Sam Spade or Basil Rathbone as Sherlock Holmes, and on and on. But the ones she likes watching the most are "The Thin Man" movies, with Myrna Loy and William Powell. They made six of them, and two Christmases from the time we are speaking of, I bought Mom the entire DVD collection of them for her—and I bet that she has watched them a million times.

Now, Mom doesn't have Alzheimer's—well, for the past six months now, Mom has had an all-consuming fear that she now does have Alzheimer's, and we're going to deal with that. But two years ago, no, she didn't have Alzheimer's; no, she just forgot things. I mean, come on, she was eighty-four years old! People that old forget things. Well, I started watching those Thin Man movies with her, and by the third night of doing this, I got bored out of my mind. So, I played a little joke on her. Knowing that she always forgets the ending of them, I told her that I was fed-up with my life and wanted to finally do something with it. I told her that I thought I had what it takes to be a private eye, and to prove this to her, by the time this movie was over, I'd name the killer and why he, or she, did it. This I did. Mom was quite impressed. I thought it was funny. So, I did it again the next evening, and again the night after that night. Mom says to me, "Why, Tom. You're as good as Nick Charles. Maybe you should go into the detective business."

Still keeping the joke going, I replied, "Yes, I want to, Mom. If I could just get that all-important first customer. The word-of-mouth would get out about me, and I'd be set."

And the next morning, the 'word-of-mouth' did get out, and I regretted having played that joke on Mom. I regretted ever having even heard of "The Thin Man" movies and, most of all, I regretted ever having been born. What a mess!

Like I said, the next morning, about ten o'clock, I was lying on the sofa, still in my pajamas—which is a white T-shirt and my gray sweat-pants—reading the newspaper, and harboring my usual morning hangover, when, suddenly, Mom comes flying into the house, all out of breath and excited, and shouts, "Tom, the Lord has answered your prayers. Claire wants to hire you. She wants you to find out who really murdered Tyra. Isn't that great?!"

"Yeah," I replied, feigning joy, but silently screaming: *Oh, shit! What do I do now?!*

Chapter Two

Claire—Claire Peterson—was our neighbor, and I had known her all my life. She was like a second mother to me. She and her husband, Bud, who died of a heart attack in 2000, had been good friends with my parents ever since Mom and Dad had moved into the neighborhood shortly after Dad came back from the Army after World War II and bought our home.

Claire was a few years older than Mom, and she was dying from colon cancer. It was sad. She was as thin as a pencil, frail, sickly pale, had to be on oxygen, and I guess because of sickness and old age, she didn't have breasts anymore. I mean, she was as flat as the proverbial pancake.

After Bud died, Claire changed. She became this nagging, demanding, old busybody—always sticking her nose into others' business. She had binoculars, and she would sit in her living room and spy on the neighbors through the window. And make no bones about it, she was quick to complain about any wrongs done by neighbors— to them directly and to the police. She had an ongoing feud with Mr. and Mrs. McGuire who had lived directly across the street from Claire. Claire claimed that they were intentionally leaving their front porch light on at night just to keep Claire up all night; Claire's bedroom was on the second-floor on the west side of the house, so, no, there wasn't any way that the porch light was keeping her up at night. And then, there had been her ongoing feud with Mrs. Neely. Claire lived to the left, or south, of us, and Mrs. Neely had lived to the left of Claire. Mrs. Neely had this little white dog, Mr. Fluffy, that yapped incessantly, and Claire was forever complaining about this to Mrs. Neely, June, and to the police. Mr. Fluffy's yapping was the reason Mom wasn't there that morning when I was lying on the sofa reading the newspaper. Claire had called Mom and wanted Mom to come over to confirm that the dog's yapping in the backyard could be heard before she called the police, again. Mom didn't really need to go over there to confirm that, because, yes, whenever that dog was in June's backyard, even we could hear its yapping. But Mom went over there just to please Claire.

I tried my best to get myself out of this stupid mess. I went over to Claire's and spoke to her. I was going to be honest with her—and being 'honest' with people didn't come easily to me: I had lived in telling lies so long—and tell her that I was just playing a joke on Mom; that I'm no P. I. But that didn't happen. As she held onto the cross of the rosary that Mom had given her—which she told me she never removed; not at night when sleeping or even when bathing—she started crying; telling me that she was dying; telling me that she had nothing more to live for; telling me that all the people that she had loved were dead; telling me that she was going to give all the money she had—what little money she did have—to charity, but before she died she wanted me to find out who really murdered Tyra. She had never believed that John had murdered her, saying that he wasn't smart enough to think up all that monkey-business with the threatening phone calls, and that red spray paint on her bedroom door of "REVENGE IS MINE." No, she said. He just wasn't smart enough for that. Now, me; yes, I was smart enough to think up all of that, she said. She always told Bud that I was one of the smartest people that she had ever met—lazy, but smart. I took the case.

I took the case because after she had said all of that to me, she wrote me a check. I was furious. I couldn't believe it! See, usually whenever I would do something for Claire—like drive her to the doctor, or cut her grass—she would always hand me a dollar, saying, "I wish it could be more, Tommy, but money is tight." So, I couldn't believe it. I couldn't believe that she had written me a check for a dollar, but when I had looked at the check—I was shocked! It wasn't a dollar, but a THOUSAND dollars. In a complete daze, I folded the check, placed it in the pocket of my shirt, and heard myself telling her that I would see what I could find out about Tyra's murder.

Chapter Three

Tyra was Claire's great-granddaughter; she had been only nine-years-old in 2005 when she was horrifically murdered—strangled with the cut-off cord of a lamp from the living room, and placed in the bed of her bedroom, covered by a blanket, and surrounded lovingly by her many stuffed teddy bears. Tyra had been what in those days was called a "Latchkey Kid," meaning that she stayed at home by herself until the parents got home, which in this case was her father, John Jones, or "JJ" as he was known to friends. He had come home from work that evening and found these words spray-painted in red across the face of her bedroom door: "REVENGE IS MINE." Two weeks later, John was arrested for her murder, and then, he was found guilty of her murder and sentenced to be executed.

But they had it all wrong, and I finally figured it out. See, John's wife had been Megan—and Megan had been wild; even as a kid she had been wild. Her mom and dad, Karen and Tim Logan—and if truth must be told, I think Karen had been the only girl that I had truly ever loved—had been killed in an automobile accident when Megan had turned sixteen years old. She then lived with Bud and Claire until she left for college—and she had made poor Bud and Claire's lives a living hell. Megan had looked just like Karen—beautiful: a slender body, shoulder-length blonde hair, grapefruit-size breasts, and a protruding forehead that—well, that protruding forehead wasn't so great looking. It was a Peterson's trademark that they all had inherited from Bud; Karen and Megan had both had it.

Megan went missing in 2002. It had not been a good marriage. John had been a linesman for AT&T, and they had had a real nice house in Kirkwood. But Megan hated staying at home all day, doing nothing. She hated being a wife and mother. She wanted to enjoy life—party; spend money; go places; do things; live, live and live. In college, she had studied to become a dentist; she and John had both quit, but she'd had enough training in the field that she took a dental assistant's position with a high-class, female dentist who had an office in Clayton. She worked there for about a year-and-a-half, and then suddenly went missing. Three days later, the red Mustang convertible that she had purchased some months before was found way up in North St. Louis. Her purse and wallet were on the front seat of the car, with all her money and credit cards gone. The police believed it had been a carjacking and robbery that had gone tragically wrong.

At the time of Megan's disappearance, Claire had said that she was glad that Bud was dead—all of this would have been just too much for him.

Poor Bud. Dad had sure loved him. He was like the brother Dad had never had, Dad coming from a family of four sisters. They had gone fishing and hunting together and had enjoyed each other's company. They hadn't known each other at the time, but they had both fought in the Battle of the Bulge during World War II. Bud got shot in his left arm; the wound became gangrenous, and the arm had to be amputated above the elbow. But Bud had made a good living. He was a salesclerk for a family-owned auto parts store in the city, and he received money from the government because of having been injured while serving his county and because of his disability, his amputated arm.

About the only thing that Dad hadn't liked about Bud was his frugality with money—and he WAS a penny-pincher. They never went on vacations, bought everything second-hand—cars, clothes, furniture, and on and on—the house that they lived in they had inherited it from Claire's parents, and whenever Mom and Dad would invite them to go to a restaurant or a movie with them, it was usually Bud's convention to say to Dad: "Hey, Pat. Do you have a few bucks you can lend me? I'm kind of short of money." The word "lend" actually always meant "give, and not be given back." Dad would scream to Mom, "Lill, they have money! I know that they do. Bud is just a cheap SOB."

Good ole Bud. I miss him, and Claire too.

Anyway, I took the case. I mean, how could I not take the case? I hadn't made a thousand dollars in years—well, I hadn't made a dime in years. If it hadn't been for the kindness, or stupidity, of my parents, I would have been living on the street years ago. I can't begin to tell you the number of times Mom screamed at me for quitting jobs and college. I was just always scared—scared of people, scared of life.

So, anyway, I took the case. My plan was this: I would just make a few inquiries, and after about a week, I would tell Claire that I was sorry, but everything that I checked out confirmed to me that John was guilty; that he had, in fact, murdered Tyra, which, at that time, I had thought to be true. Now, don't get me wrong. I had thought John to be a good guy—kind, easy-going and such—but I, like the prosecution, had thought he was guilty. There had been just too much evidence against him to think otherwise: no break-in; the doors and windows all being locked; the police finding in the basement, hidden, that empty can of red spray paint that was used to write those words: "REVENGE IS MINE"; John having been two hours late for work on the morning of Tyra's murder, saying that he got halfway to work when a tire on his car went flat from a nail; and his ex-girlfriend testifying that he was always saying how he didn't want to be a father anymore, that he wanted to be free. John kept saying, sobbing, that he was innocent, but I remember how the judge called him a "cold-blooded killer."

The day after Claire had given me that check for a thousand dollars, I had gone on a shopping-spree at Wal-Mart's. I purchased a cheap flip-cell phone, a pair of binoculars and a .35mm camera. Although I was only going to give this investigation a lick-and-a-spilt, I wanted Mom to think that I was serious about it, and I had for some time wanted a cell phone: everybody was getting them. So, armed with all of that, I began the investigation.

It was awful. Just awful. I got nowhere. I visited John in prison, and I got next to nothing from him. He was like a zombie, more dead than alive—a man who had given up on life and wanted to die. He kept crying, wailing, that his precious baby was dead, and that that bitch, his ex-girlfriend, Helen Dyer, had killed her. No, I got nothing from him. I interviewed Helen Dyer, and I got nothing out of her— and, boy, was she a low-life. I don't know what John had ever seen in her. She was ugly, with thick glasses and thinning brown hair, a stocky body to the point of being fat, and she cussed like a drunken sailor. About the only thing that she had going for her were her breasts: Boy, they were the size of watermelons. I'm not kidding. Those things made Dolly Parton look flat-chested. When she found out from me that I wasn't with the police or a reporter, she angrily told me that if I ever bothered her again, she'd beat the "F" out of me.

The reason John had believed that she had killed Tyra was that John had beaten her up and had thrown her out of his house. See, after Megan had gone missing, John took to drinking heavily, so-much-so that he almost lost his job. He began going to AA meetings. It was there that he met Helen Dyer. They began dating, and then she moved in with John and Tyra. Well, one evening, John came home from work, and Tyra came running up to him crying. She and Helen had had an argument and Helen, drunk, had slapped her, giving her a black eye. In a rage, John beat Helen up and threw her out of his house. She went to a halfway house for homeless and battered women.

It was awful. Just awful. I got nowhere. Like I have said, I interviewed John, and that Helen Dyer, and I even went to that halfway house where she had been—and, man, I got nothing from any of it. I was done. I figured that I had given enough time and energy to it. I had decided, the next morning I would go over to Claire's and tell her that after my intensive investigation—which was of seven days—it was my conclusion that John had in fact murdered Tyra. Sorry.

But did that happen? No!

That evening, after supper, Mom said how proud she was of me—that I was finally doing something that was important with my life. I could have killed her. I mean, how could I stop now, after she had said that to me? Goodness knows, I had given that poor woman next to nothing to ever be proud of me for. So, I didn't stop. But, truly, I didn't know what to do next. Then, a thought came to me.

A few days after Megan had gone missing, a local TV reporter had interviewed that dentist that Megan had worked for—a Dr. Teresa Williams. I decided to interview her, but this time I would go undercover—act like a patient who had a toothache, and who just happened to have been a friend of Megan's.

The next day, I called and made an appointment with her. Her office was several blocks away from downtown Clayton, which is several miles northeast from where I live and is a high-class section of St. Louis County—and, boy, was her office fancy with modern décor. I had always gone to a clinic for my teeth, so I felt nervous about being in such a fancy place, and nervous about what I was doing. But the receptionist made me feel comfortable. In fact, she began flirting with me, and no girl had flirted with me in years. So, I flirted back with her. It was fun. She wasn't good-looking at all: shoulder-length red hair that was just too red, a stocky body that would be fat by the time she was in her late fifties, and her round face was a map of freckles. But I found her to be most sexy. She was a chain-smoker, and her voice had this deep, gravel-sounding quality to it that I found to be appealing, and she had a 'brassy' personality. Her desk was made of wood—I mean of REAL wood; it was some type of a petrified tree stump, with a sheet of glass on top of it. After I handed back the forms that she had given me to fill out, I pointed to the desk and said, "Aren't you afraid of woodpeckers?" She replied, in that deep, smoker's voice of hers, "I'm not afraid of any *peckers*."

Now, as to that dentist, that Dr. Williams, I had forgotten what a tiny person she was. She couldn't have been much over five-feet tall, and tiny. When she came into the examining room that I was in, wearing a white doctor's coat over a white blouse and black dress pants, I remember thinking: *How in the hell does this mouse pull a tooth?* And she was no help at all.

When she had first come in, she was friendly enough, but after I told her that Claire Peterson, Megan's grandmother, was my next-door neighbor, and that I had known Megan for years, she got real nervous and quiet. She didn't want to answer any of my questions about Megan, like: What type of an employee was Megan? She just kept shaking her head and saying, "It's sad. It's too sad to even talk about it." And you should have seen the look on her face when I said, "Yes, it is sad. Claire is dying from colon cancer, and she says that she's going to give all of her money to charity." The look on her face was of-of—well, of total panic.

I left there feeling extremely pissed, in pain, and miserable. It had been a total waste of time. I got nothing from her, and because of not having any insurance, with x-rays taken and the filling of two cavities, it cost me three-hundred and sixty-two dollars.

Things really stared to move fast from this point on.

A few days after I had seen that doctor, I got shot at. See, six weeks prior to that time, Mom had fallen on her right arm. I rushed her to the hospital. She was fine. She had a hair-line crack in her arm just above the wrist. She didn't need surgery or pins—just a white plaster cast on the arm. But she said that she couldn't drive her car with that cast on. It interfered with her ability to control the steering-wheel. So, I drove her—everywhere: to the store, to her many prayer groups, and every day at noon to visit Dad and feed him lunch. Now, we don't have a garage that's attached to the house. Our one-car, wooden garage sets to the end of our backyard, just before the alley.

Even now, I usually park my car on the street in front of the house, but for some reason, I just began parking it in the driveway, right in front of the two wooden doors of the garage.

Well, like I said, Mom and I had gotten into my car, and I'm backing out of the driveway, and POW! The windshield of my car suddenly exploded. Glass went flying everywhere. Amidst the chaos of what was happening, I felt a burning sting on the left side of my head, and when I touched that side of my head, and then looked at my hand—blood. My hand was covered in blood, my blood. I cried, "Oh, Mom! I'm dying!" She helped me into the house and called 9-1-1.

An ambulance came, but I didn't go to the hospital. It had been only a slight wound—but get this! When I had said to the paramedic who was treating the wound, "Boy, all of that glass really did a number to my head." He replied, "This wound wasn't caused by broken glass. The wound's too straight to have been done by that. No, it's a gunshot wound."

I was shocked and scared. I mean, who would want to shoot at me?!

After the two paramedics had left, Mom said, "Tom, do you think that this has anything to do with the case? Because if it does, I want you to stop right now."

I told her no, that it probably was like that paramedic had said; it had probably had just been teenagers in the alley who had a gun. I think Mom accepted that, but I didn't. I didn't want to admit it, but I DID think that it had something to do with the case. I just didn't know why or who. But Mom was right. I had had it with that case. I had decided the next morning, I was going over to Claire's and tell her that I was done.

But did that happen? No.

The next morning, I went over to Claire's, and I knocked and knocked on her front door, but she never answered. I couldn't believe it. Claire never went anywhere. I went back home and got the spare key to Claire's house that she and Bud had given us years ago—and guess what? She was dead. I found her in her upstairs bedroom, in her bed, dressed in a white nightgown. It was awful. Her eyes were open, and she had a tortured look upon her face of having suffered. Seeing it upset me—well, like I had said: Claire had been like a second mother to me. But at least I had kept my word to her. I had done some investigating on the case, and I had seen it though. Now, it was over. So, I turned and began to walk out of the bedroom. But I didn't make it out of the bedroom. At the door of the bedroom, I stopped suddenly. A thought had occurred to me. I turned back around and looked at her again. Then, I looked on top of the wooden nightstand next to her bed. The large, crystal-looking beads of the rosary that Mom had given her was there—on top of the nightstand. I thought of the day that this had all began. She had been so adamant. Holding the cross in her right hand so tightly, she had told me that she never removed that rosary from around her neck, never. But there it was, on the nightstand. Why?!

Throughout the rest of that day, I kept thinking about that rosary not being around her neck.

Mom burst into tears when I told her that Claire was dead. Some years before that time, Claire had given Mom the name and phone number of her lawyer. She had told Mom that upon her death to call him and he would carry out all the arrangements for her death. Mom called him. Mom and I were both sad, quiet, and shocked by her death, and Mom went about her usual tasks of cleaning, washing, and cooking by rote.

About 3:00 PM, a thought occurred to me. I thought that John should be informed of Claire's death. I called the prison that he was in—which was in the township of Potosi, Missouri—and after telling a representative there why I was calling, I was told that if my request to speak with John was granted that he would be permitted to call me at 6:00 PM. At exactly six o'clock, the phone rang: our phone is an old black phone that sits on the top of an old wooden stand by the entrance to the kitchen. Mom was at the kitchen sink, finishing up doing the supper plates and such. It was John, returning my call.

He sounded a lot better—more alive and calmer—than he had when I had visited him at the prison. After I told him of Claire's death, I heard him sobbing. Through his tears, he said, "Claire was the only one who believed that I didn't kill my baby. The only one … I hope my name isn't on that damn will of hers. I don't want any of their millions." I thought that I hadn't heard John correctly. So, I asked him to repeat what he had just said. He did. I was shocked. Shocked! John then told me that it was a much-guarded family secret. For years, what money Bud got from the government for having been injured during World War II, Bud had invested it—and any extra money there was from living so cheaply—in the buying of stocks, bonds and annuities. John told me that Megan had told him that Bud and Claire were probably worth about three million dollars. Again, I was shocked.

After I had gotten off the phone, I told Mom what John had told me.

"Your father was a smart man," she said, drying her hands with a dishtowel. "Pat always said that they had money." She then looked up at the ceiling and stated, "Claire, if you were here, I'd slap you silly."

I went up to my bedroom, popped open a beer from my stash of beers hidden in my closet, and flopped down on my bed and started thinking about all of this. Again, I kept thinking about that rosary not being around Claire's neck, and I kept thinking about what John had said about hoping that his name wasn't on their will. I just kept going over all this again and again. It didn't make any sense, though. All the people whose names would be on their will were dead—Tyra was dead; Megan was dead; Bud was dead; and John was going to be executed next month. So, nobody would get Bud and Claire's money. It probably would indeed go to charity. Then, I thought of how I had said that to the dentist, that Dr. Williams, and I remembered the look upon her tiny face of sheer panic when I had said that. Thinking about that, a thought occurred to me. It had been just a thought, but it changed everything. I decided to act upon it.

The next day, about 3:00 PM, I washed, shaved and dressed in a suit and tie. Mom was in the living room, watching TV, and asked her if I could use her car, that I had a date.

"With a girl?!" she cried, shocked and overjoyed.

"Of course, with a girl!" I countered.

She wanted to know all about her—her name, where I had met her, and on and on. I told her that the girl's name was Sarah, and that she was the receptionist of that dentist, that Dr. Teresa Williams, and that I had called her and had asked her for a date. Mom was so happy for me. She told me to have a great time, and I left.

This had all been a lie.

I didn't have a date with that gal, but that was the general idea. There was a real fancy-looking Italian restaurant directly across the street from that dentist's office, and I was going to wait around in the parking lot of the dentist's office until Sarah came out, and then ask her if she wanted to have dinner with me at that restaurant across the street, which was exactly what I did.

Man, that gal was weird—and could she drink. We had liter after liter of red wine.

When I asked her if she had ever been married, she, gulping down that wine, raised up two fingers of her left hand, and then when I asked her if she had children, she showed me a wallet-size picture of them. But the photo was of her with three white poodles.

"I don't want any damn brats," she said, between taking drinks of that wine. Then I told her that I had known Megan, and I began asking her questions about Megan. Anger mixed with sarcasm, and by this time mixed with drunkenness, she told me that Megan was a smart-ass bitch who thought she owned the place because of how close she and Teresa had been. Then, when I started asking her questions about Dr. Williams—boy, did she get pissed. She said, "Hey, what's with all the questions about Teresa?! … Do you like her?! … Do you want to date her?!—Because if you do, you're going to have to cut your dick off!"

Bingo! That was just what I had wanted to know.

I got back home a little before 9:00 PM, and I was as drunk as a skunk. I set my alarm clock for 6:30 AM. I was determined to rise at that time, and I did. I was terribly hung-over, but I dragged myself out of bed; washed; got dressed; Googled Dr. Williams' home address on my computer on my desk; grabbed those binoculars I had bought; went downstairs; gulped down two quick cups of coffee; wrote Mom a note that I would be back by noon to drive her down to feed and to visit Dad; grabbed my winter coat out of the hall closet; and then headed out the back door to the car.

Dr. Williams lived in a high-rise apartment in downtown Clayton—and, boy, was it fancy. It had uniformed doormen who stood there at the glass double-door entrance to the place, opening the doors for people as they came and went. I got a real good spot to watch those doors too. I was parked directly across the street from the building. I didn't even need those binoculars. I could see those doors fine.

Time dragged on and on, though. Nothing. No luck. Knowing that it would take about twenty minutes to drive back home, I left there at 11:30 to drive Mom down to see Dad. I hated to leave—I really wanted to know if I was correct—but I had no other choice.

Mom and I visited and fed Dad. I was antsy the whole time. I wanted to get back to Dr. Williams' apartment. Mom could tell that something was bothering me, and as we were leaving the nursing home at 1:00 PM, she asked me what was wrong. I told her that there was a "loose-end" to Claire's case that I had wanted to "tie-up." She asked me what that "loose-end" was, but I told her that I didn't want to say until I knew more. Mom said that she was so proud of me. She said that I had changed, had become so "responsible."

Hearing Mom say that about me brought tears to my eyes. I was so pleased, that I asked Mom if she wanted to go with me, back to Clayton and be with me to check out that "loose-end." She readily agreed to this.

A big mistake. In less than two hours back at that apartment building—and I had lost my really good parking spot and had to park on the same side of the street that the building was on, and an intersection away—Mom started whining about being tired, hungry, cold and bored. She wanted to go home. It was awful. I couldn't concentrate on why I was there—and she kept playing with the radio, trying to get her Christian radio station. I got angry and told her to stop, that I was working.

Mom and her damn being religious. When I had been sixteen years old, I had asked my sister Eve, "Why is Mom so religious?" She replied, "Because of James, you idiot."

James was my older brother by four years. When he was ten, he was riding his bike and was struck and killed by a car. At his burial, I had kept pestering Mom, wanting to know when James was going to get out of that box. With tears streaming down her grief-stricken face, she finally said to me, "Not until the end of time."

I had been too young to rationalize the meaning of what she had said, but it had scared the shit out of me. I think that his death and the thought of "being in a box until the end of time" made me who and what I was to become in life—a coward. I guess I had vowed never to be trapped in a "box" until the end of time.

"What working?!" she cried. "All I see you doing is looking at the entrance to that place through those binoculars. That's working?"

"Yes," I replied. "This is what a detective does."

"Well, it's dumb—and I'm not going to miss that movie, am I? You told me that *It's a Wonderful Life* is on TV tonight."

"No, you won't miss it," I stated, flatly.

Another hour passed, and I had just had it with her nagging and whining. Now, the cast on her arm was itching like crazy and she wanted to get home and spray some anti-itching ointment into the cast and onto her arm.

I gave up. I was disgusted.

"Okay," I said. "It's getting dark. I'll come back tomorrow." A bus pulled up to the curb in front of the building. I started the car, saying, "What a waste of a day."

Just then, suddenly, I saw that doorman open one of the doors and a woman came sauntering out. I grabbed my binoculars again and brought them to my eyes.

She was wearing this wide-brimmed, floppy, black hat that covered the sides of her face somewhat. She was dressed in a full-length, cloth, black coat that matched the hat. She had on designer jeans, a red blouse, and black, flat-heeled shoes. Although her shoulder-length hair was raven-black, as were her eyebrows, she looked like Karen, Claire's daughter, and there was no hiding that protruding Peterson forehead.

"Bingo!" I cried with joy. "I did it! I really am a freakin' detective. I've cracked this case wide open!"

"How, Tom?" Mom cried, happy for me. "How did you crack it?"

"Do you see that woman getting on that bus?" I asked, now looking at Mom.

"No, not really, Tom," she replied, squinting her eyes and looking in that direction. "I'd have to put my reading glasses on."

"Well, she did, Mom," I said, looking in that direction again through the binoculars. "She murdered Tyra—and she murdered Claire too."

"What?!" Mom cried, shocked and angry. "Claire was murdered?! … Who is she?! I want her name right now!"

Looking at Mom again, I replied, "Megan."

"Megan?" Mom stated, incredulously. "Tom, Megan's dead."

"Oh, no she's not," I said. "That's just what she wanted everyone to believe."

"You have to be wrong, Tom," Mom said. "Why on earth would Megan kill her own daughter and Claire?"

"For the money," I replied—and then added, "And because she's gay."

"What does being happy have to do with anything?" Mom asked, confused.

"No, no," I replied. "Look, in today's world being gay also means being a homosexual."

The bus pulled away from the curb, heading south.

"Megan is a homo—"

"Listen," I said, interrupting Mom, "I know that you're tired and hungry, but I want to see where she's going. It won't take long."

She went straight to where I was sure that she was going—to Dr. Williams Office.

Chapter Five

The parking lot to Dr. Williams' Office was around the back of the building. After I was certain that Megan had entered the building, I then pulled into the parking lot.

"You stay here," I said to Mom and started to reach for the handle of the door of the car.

"Where are you going?!" Mom cried.

"In there," I replied, pointing to the building. "I'm going to confront them."

"Are you insane?!" she said. "You just told me that they murdered two people."

"They murdered a little girl and an ill, elderly woman," I stated. "I'm not afraid of them."

"Well, you sure picked a fine time to suddenly get brave, Tom," Mom said. "No, Tom. I don't want you doing this. It's too dangerous. Get on that toy phone of yours and call the police. Let them handle this."

"Mom," I said, closing my eyes and shaking my head, "I have to do this."

"But why, Tom?"

"I just have to, Mom," I replied.

"But why?"

"Oh, Mom," I said, feeling sad. "I-I—Mom, all my life I've-I've ran from life. I'm sick of it. I can't run anymore. I must see this through to the end. I got to."

She was silent for a moment, and then said, "Be careful, Tom. Be careful."

After I reached into the pocket of my coat and removed my cell phone, I handed it to Mom, saying, "Here, take this, and if I'm not back in, say, ten minutes, call 9-1-1."

"But I don't know how to work this thing," she stated.

"It's easy," I said. "Here, I'll show you. Put your reading glasses on."

After showing her how to use it, I got out of the car and headed for Dr. Williams' Office.

At the wooden door to her office, with my heart pounding in my chest, I began pounding on that door, saying, "Dr. Williams! Dr.

Williams! ... It's me, Tom Mayor. I know that you're in there. I must see you. I cracked a tooth, and I'm in terrible pain. Please, open the door. Dr. Williams, I must see ..."

The door to her office swung open and she said hurriedly, and flatly, in that tiny, mouse-like voice of hers, "Come in, Mr. Mayor."

She was wearing a red dress and red high-heeled shoes, with a small pearl necklace and matching earrings—and for being so tiny and as flat-chested as a pancake, she looked good.

"Sorry about this," I said to her after I had stepped inside.

It was dark in there and silent.

"Follow me, Mr. Mayor," she said. She turned and started down the hallway. She led me to the same examination room that I had been in the first time that I had seen her. She flipped on the lights and motioned for me to enter the room. I did.

"Take off your coat, Mr. Mayor, and set it on the chair," she said, pointing to a wooden chair that was in the corner of the room, next to the windows. "Then lie down on the examination chair and we'll get started."

She walked over to an ornate, white, wooden cabinet that was in the opposite corner of the room. A box of latex gloves lay on top of it, and she ripped a pair of gloves from the box and began putting them on.

As she was doing this, I walked behind the examination chair, turned around and stood there, with my back to the windows. I wasn't taking any chances. I wanted to be facing the door.

Dr. Williams was to my left and her back was to me.

After taking a deep breath and expelling it, I placed my cold, sweating hands in the pockets of my coat and said, "Where's Megan, Doc?"

This hit her hard, like a fist to the face. Her whole tiny body went stiff.

"I don't know what you're talking about, Mr. Mayor," she replied, her back still to me.

"Oh, come on, Doc," I said. "Don't ever lie to a pathological liar; you'll always lose ... Hey, Megan!" I shouted. "Where are you, girl?!"

Dr. Williams spun around and said, "Please, Mr. Mayor! There is no one here but us."

"Come on, Megan!" I continued. "I know you're here ... I followed you ... Don't you want to say hi to your ole neighbor?"

Suddenly, like the phoenix rising from its ashes, Megan appeared at the door, minus that floppy hat and coat.

She was boiling mad. With her hands on her hips in a tight fist, she stood there, tense, her whole body ready, prepared, and wanting to do battle. Now, I was scared.

"There you are, girl," I said, desperately hoping that I was hiding my shaking-body fear. "Long time, no see, Megan. How have you been?"

Silence. She just stood there, staring angrily at me as if she was going to eat me alive.

"It must have been hard for you living in the shadows for as long as you have," I began. "What was the plan, Megan? To-to suddenly reappear after Claire's death and say that you had amnesia, but suddenly remembered who you are? I got to tell you, Megan, I can't believe that you have gotten this far without someone figuring this all out."

"At best, it's all silly—the faking your death, the framing of John, the red spray-painting of the words "REVENGE IS MINE" on the door of Tyra's bedroom. Those were all red herrings. This had nothing to do with John or Tyra. But it had everything to do with you. John had repeatedly told Tyra never to open the door to strangers—but she would have joyously thrown that door open for you and would have shouted, Mommy! Mommy!"

Suddenly, as I stood there, piecing the story together, I wasn't scared anymore. Suddenly, I did feel like a private detective—Why, suddenly, I was Nick Charles, *The Thin Man!*

"It was the same with Claire," I said, now stepping in front of that examination chair. "Claire was a dying, bitter, frightened old woman, who was especially afraid at night. She never opened her door at night. But, like Tyra, she would have for you. And that's where you made a mistake, Megan—a big one. After you removed that rosary from around Claire's neck and dressed her in that nightgown and placed her body in her bed, you should have placed that rosary back around her neck: Because she never took it off. You should have never killed Claire, Megan. Claire was like a second mother to me. I don't even mind that you shot at me and tried to kill me—but not Claire. When I realized that my flippant remark to your 'lover' here," I said, pointing to Dr. Williams— "about Claire giving all her money to charity—well, you just couldn't have that. So, you killed her."

"I swear, Megan," I said, shaking my head, "your mother would be so ashamed of you."

I guess that I must have crossed the line with that last remark, because Megan came charging after me like there was no tomorrow.

She got in my face and screamed, "What does a loser like you know about my life?!"

"Now, let's calm down here," I said, my mind racing and my body shaking. Then, I felt this sharp, stabbing pain in my left leg, right above the knee.

"Ouch!" I yelled. I looked down, and I saw Dr. Williams rising from her knees. She was holding a syringe with a hypodermic needle; the syringe was empty. "What did you do?!" I said, in a panic. "Did you poison me?! … Am I going to die?! … I was joking," I said to Megan. "I won't tell anyone. Honest!" My whole body started to shake. My heart began racing wildly. I couldn't breathe. Then, I felt light-headed.

I'm embarrassed to tell you this—but I guess I will. I-I, well, let's get one thing straight. I thought that I was dying. I cried, "Mommy!" and then I passed out.

Actually, I was paralyzed but conscious—because I could hear everything. I just couldn't move.

"Let's run, Megan," I heard Dr. Williams say. "He'll only be out for an hour or two."

"I'm not running," Megan replied, angrily. "Help get him into the chair, and then you go get the car, bring it to the front, and then help me carry him to it."

"You're not thinking about killing him, are you?" she asked, with fear and desperation in her voice. "No more killing, Megan. When does it stop?"

"It stops when I get my money!" she barked. "Now, go get the—"

Then, I heard this loud cracking sound, and I got the feeling that someone just fell to the floor.

"Oooooh, my arm!" I heard Mom cry. "I broke my cast!"

It was Mom! It was so great to hear her voice—it was like hearing an angel's voice from heaven. She later told me that she just couldn't get my cell phone to work. So, when I didn't return, she got so worried about me, that she decided to find out for herself what was happening. She had heard much of what was said. She then crept up behind Megan and knocked her in the back of the head with her cast.

"Here," I heard Mom say. "Take this cell phone and dial 9-1-1—and listen to me good, little girl," Mom warned. "I'm a God-fearing woman, but if you give me any trouble, I'll slap you silly. Now, dial 9-1-1!"

Mom saved my life.

Chapter Six

Yeah, good ole Mom had sure saved my "bacon" that night—and, boy, did life change after that. It got wild. Megan and Dr. Williams were arrested, trialed, sentenced to life-in-prison. Megan got killed in prison: She got into a fight with another female inmate, and the gal stabbed her to death with a spoon that she had beat into a homemade knife. John was granted a pardon, and I became famous.

Yeah, I became famous. Boy, you should have seen all the reporters—newspaper and TV reporters, both local and national—that kept pounding on our front door wanting to interview me. Why, I was even featured on an episode of that TV show "48 Hours," and everybody was so proud of me. Mom was proud of me; the people in the neighborhood were all proud of me—why, even my sister Mary, who always called me a lazy bum, was even proud of me. And, man, did that old black phone of ours keep ringing off the hook. People kept calling and wanting me to do investigating for them. Much to the slight anger of Mom, I kept refusing. Well, I didn't want to be a P. I. again: I kept telling Mom that I was just holding out for the right case to come along.

It was crazy for about two months. Then, things began to slow down and get back to "normal" life again: The knocks on the front door became less and less; people didn't say that they were so proud of me anymore; the phone calls of people wanting me to investigate for them turned from a gushing hose to a trickle. It got bad. Mom began nagging me more and more to do things to get my detective business up and running. Then, when all looked hopeless, something great happened—something unbelievable! If I had thought that solving those two murders had changed my life, well, this truly did.

Last year, a week before Christmas, just as Mom and I were finishing supper, the phone rang. It was John. He wanted to know if he could come by and see us. I told him that we'd love to see him.

About an hour later, he came. He looked good, too. He was bathed, clean-shaven, smelled good, and he was dressed in real snappy clothes: he had on a black leather coat that looked to be at least three hundred dollars—and I guess if you're worth close to four million dollars, as John is, well, yeah, you can afford to be a snappy dresser. Besides the clothes, John was much different than when I had visited him in prison. He was calmer, more animated, his happy-go-lucky, easy-going demeanor had seemed to return, and he generally seemed to be at peace with himself.

Mom had made a chocolate cake earlier in the day and we all sat at the old wooden table in the kitchen, eating cake and drinking coffee.

After we had all had our fill of eating and drinking, John told us that in two days he was moving to Durango, Colorado. After he and Megan had quit college and married, they had honeymooned there. They had liked it so much—camping, hiking, fishing and hunting—that he had decided to return there. He just wanted to be at a place in which he and Megan had been happy. He made no excuses for Megan. She was, simply, "evil." But before he left, he wanted to repay me for all that I had done for him. From the pocket of his dress-shirt, he removed a folded check and handed it to me. I took it, unfolded it and read it. I was stunned! I-I felt like I was going to faint! Are you ready for this?! The check was for one million dollars! That's right. One million dollars.

In a daze, I heard my mouth telling him that I couldn't accept this, and I saw that my hand kept trying to hand him back the check, but my mind kept screaming: *Oh, please. Let me keep this check!*

John wouldn't hear of it. I had saved his life—and the money was mine.

I was a millionaire.

Chapter Seven

Yes, I was now a millionaire. I was no longer a worthless bum. I was whole, complete; my life was set—or so I had thought at the time, and I went on one hell of a shopping spree. I bought clothes, a new computer, a laptop, an AT&T Blackberry cell phone, and a car.

Buying a different car was a big deal for me; I hated the car that I had been driving: a long, snow-white Lincoln Continental. It had been my sister Eve's car, and she had given it to me. I hated that big old thing. Every time that I had gotten into it, I always thought that I should have had it painted pink and started selling Mary Kay Cosmetic products.

See, about six years ago, I had been driving my Dad's car. Well, one morning, I had gotten into it to go somewhere, and the engine had caught on fire. It was toast. I had it towed away to a junkyard. Now, I didn't know what to do. I didn't have a job or any money. I just didn't know what to do. Dad and Mom had said that they would give me the money to buy a new, used car, but I didn't want to do that. They had already done too much for me.

I had overheard Mom talking to my sister Mary about "my car" situation. I had overheard Mom saying, "Oh, Mary, don't say that. Tom isn't a lazy ass. He wants to return to college and become a teacher."

I had always hated it whenever Mary would say such things about me—but she was right. So, I didn't know what to do, and, as always, it was my sister Eve to the rescue. Good-natured Eve; the mother to all. Even as a kid, Eve was always bringing home stray dogs or cats. When Eve had called, and I told her about not having a car and about what Mary had said about me, she angrily stated, "That uppity bitch. I don't see her there, helping Mom and Dad! Boy, she steams me … Okay, here's what we'll do. I'm ready to buy a new car anyway. I'm off from work next weekend. I'll drive the car down and give it to you."

And she did.

Gosh, I miss Eve. I sure wish that she hadn't felt the need to take that nursing job in that hospital in Chicago. I guess that she had gotten fed-up with all the arguing and trouble that she had caused within the family and amongst Mom and Dad's brothers and sisters. When Eve had been twenty-four, she had laid three BIG bombshells on Mom and Dad. One, she was pregnant; two, the guy wouldn't marry her; and, three, he was black. Now, my mom and dad are no more prejudice than the next fellow is, but, yeah, it had caused arguments. It had gotten back to Mom and Dad that Eve and that "little black bastard" were not welcome in some of my mom and dad's sisters' and brothers' houses. Dad had told them all off good. So, I guess that Eve had just gotten sick of it all and moved with James, her son—and he's a great guy, too—to Chicago.

Anyway, I bought a new car. For the past several years now, I have dreamed of owning a black convertible Mustang. That's the car I wanted. I could just see myself in it, driving down the street with the wind in my hair; but I didn't get it. Isn't that just like life—something that you always thought that you'd love to have, and when you finally can have it, you find out that you don't want it. That's just what happened.

After John had given me that check, and spring came, I took a drive up to Lindbergh Boulevard, by South County Mall, which is only a few miles south of here, and which has multiple car dealerships on it. I had stopped in at Steve Smith's Ford Dealership, and he had the very car that I wanted: a black convertible Mustang. I took it for a test drive—and I hated it. I just didn't like it. I got back in my car and started driving further down Lindbergh. A few blocks down, I spotted a car that caught my interest: a black 1999 Jeep Grand Cherokee with thick, mean-looking tires on it. I pulled into the lot to give it a second look.

It was on the lot of Cowboy Jim's Auto Dealership. Cowboy Jim was something of a local TV celebrity in St. Louis—known for his "colorful" personality and for his outrageous TV commercials. He once sat on top of a live bull, saying, "Come on down and see Cowboy Jim for the best deals in St. Louis—and that's no bull." He always wore a white Stetson hat, cowboy clothes, and white cowboy boots, and he favored using the words "powerful" and "partner."

He was sitting on a rocking-chair on the small wooden porch, with a picket fence, all painted white, in front of the trailer that served as his office. When I got out of my car, he came trotting down the three wooden steps to greet me.

"Well, how are you, young man, on this most beautiful day?" he said, offering me his right hand. "Now remember," he then went on to say, holding up the index-finger of his right hand, "Cowboy Jim is in a powerful giving mood this morning. What's your pleasure?"

Turning around, I said, "I'm interested in that car there." I then pointed to the black Jeep Cherokee.

"That's a powerful car, partner. A powerful car," he said. "Let me get the keys, and you take it for a ride—but remember," he continued, holding up the index-finger of his right hand again, "Cowboy Jim is in a most powerful giving mood this morning."

From the moment that I stepped into that car, I loved it. I loved the smell of the inside of it; I loved the feel of the seat; I loved the feel of the steering wheel. About the only thing that gave me some concern was that when I pulled out of the lot, I had barely tapped the accelerator and shot out of the parking lot like a bat out of hell. I told Cowboy Jim about that when I had gotten back.

"Well, partner," he said with a laugh, "that's a most powerful funny story. This car was previously owned by a family who had a son who was a student at the University of Rolla, studying Engineering. Well, partner, the parents give him the car, and he started getting so many traffic tickets for speeding that he lost his license. The parents come to find out that he and his buddies tweaked the engine. They placed a hemi in it … Now, listen to Cowboy Jim," he said. "Cowboy Jim prides himself on knowing what people want in a car, and I'm telling you what you want is control and power. Am I right?"

I nodded that he was indeed correct.

"Well, partner," he continued, "then, there she is. That's the car for you … Come on, let's go inside and get the paperwork done—but remember," he said, holding up the index-finger of his right hand again, "Cowboy Jim is in a most powerful giving…"

Chapter Eight

It was about two months after I had bought my car that my troubles first started for me. It was weird. I now had more money than I had ever had in my life. I had new clothes; a new computer; a new cell phone; health insurance; respect and fame; a new car; and on and on. Yet, suddenly, I was miserable. I kept being plagued with depression—sometimes to the point in which I start crying for no reason. It was awful.

I thought that it might have something to do with my years of excessive drinking. So, I stopped drinking—and let me tell you that that was hell. But, I did it. I stopped and, boy, did I get fat. I turned to food and soda for comfort. I just ate and ate and ate and drank soda too. Then, I was depressed about becoming so fat, and if all of this wasn't bad enough, it was about this time that I had refused to go down and see Dad anymore. I just couldn't do it anymore. I just couldn't stand to see him like a zombie—alive on the outside, but dead on the inside. There was nothing to him anymore. He was just an empty shell; a nothing. It was too hard to see.

Anyway, I bought some jogging clothes and a pair of tennis shoes, and in the mornings, I began walking around the neighborhood in the hope of losing weight. It worked, too.

Soon, my walking turned into a trot, and then the trot turned into walking real fast, and then the walking real fast turned into light running. It was great. I began losing weight, getting some muscle definition, and I began feeling better mentally.

I love being on the street of our neighborhood in the early morning too. I love these two-story old houses, and the tall maple trees with long branches that stretch out into the curbed street. The feeling of familiarity, of belonging, of home.

There had been a time, long, long ago, when I had wanted so much to run away from here—to New York or England or Paris. Now, I couldn't think of anywhere else I'd rather live but here. And the neighborhood is really changing too. Claire is gone; Mr. and Mrs. McGuire are gone; all dead; Mrs. Neely and her little white dog, Fluffy, are gone; Mrs. Neely moved to Arizona to live with her eldest daughter. Yes, the neighborhood is changing. Why, there are even little children living here now. It's all bittersweet: Sweet to see and to hear children at play; bitter to know that it's 'out with the old and in with the new.'

Yes, the neighborhood is changing, and I knew that my time in this neighborhood, and in this house, was changing as well. What with Dad's illness—being gone, and never returning—and now with Mom's all-consuming, overwhelming fear of having Alzheimer's as well. We never openly speak of it, but it's always there between us. Well, except for one morning about three months ago. I came downstairs that morning to find the kitchen flooded in about an inch of water. Apparently, before Mom had gone to bed, she had turned the faucet on for some reason and had forgotten to turn it off. I had tried desperately to wipe it up before she came downstairs, but that didn't happen.

I was almost done when she entered the kitchen and cried, "Oh, my Lord! Did I do this?!"

"It's okay, Mom," I replied. "It's no big deal."

"Yes, it IS a big deal," she sobbed, angrily, "if I'm becoming Dad!"

"You're not Dad, Mom," I countered. "Look, why don't you get tested? Then, you'll know."

"Never!" she screamed, and then ran out of the kitchen. "Never!"

So, anyway, I was feeling good mentally. Like I said, the running in the morning really helped. Then, about three weeks after that incident with Mom in the kitchen, I crashed big time.

One day, I had decided to give myself a treat. I have always loved Burger King's Whoppers. With being on a "health kick," I hadn't had one in several months. So, I stopped in at Burger King and got one. While I was sitting at one of the tables there—and just ENJOYING my Whopper, I happened to look to my left and saw a teenage boy and a teenage girl kissing. I-I couldn't take my eyes off them, and the more that I sat there, watching them, the angrier I got. I became so jealous of that boy that I saw myself beating the hell out of him. I left—having only eaten less than half of my much-wanted Whopper.

My raging anger turned to depression—deep, deep depression.

Chapter Nine

This happened in the first week of May and, boy, was I ever in the throes of a deep depression. I just kept seeing and thinking about that boy and girl kissing—and I wanted it! I wanted a girl. I didn't want to look at porn on my computer anymore; I didn't want to daydream about having a girl anymore—I wanted, and needed, a real, live woman. I wanted sex. I wanted hot, sweaty, dirty, animal sex.

When Mom asked me what was bothering me, this time, I told her that I wanted to start dating. She had wanted me to date some of the women from some of the many prayer groups that she belonged to, but I didn't want that. I had met many of those women and they just didn't appeal to me. Too mild, dull. I wanted someone with flare, a passion for life, zest, and GOOD in the bed.

I thought about hiring high-class prostitutes, but, no, I wanted more than just that. I know, I know, I'm not making sense, but it's complicated.

I got on my computer and began looking up dating services and such. I narrowed my search down to three or four singles/divorce clubs for people in their 40's or above. I began attending the meetings and going to all the activities that each sponsored—such as going to the St. Louis Zoo, or to Forest Park, and on and on—and I found all of it, and the women, to be just dull and boring.

By the end of the month, I had had it. I didn't want anything more to do with singles/divorce groups.

Then, one night, just by chance, I happened to watch on TV a re-run of that Bruce Lee movie "Enter the Dragon." As I was watching it, I thought: *Yeah, that might by fun.*

I have always shied away from fights. Well, if truth be told, when it comes to any type of fight, I've always been a coward. So, I thought—yeah, I'd like to learn how to defend myself.

I got on my computer and looked up local places that taught karate. I narrowed my search to three places. Over the following two weeks, I visited all three. The first two that I visited, I didn't liked that much—there was a lot of exercise to them, such as doing push-ups and such. But the third place that I visited—well, by the end of the class, just watching it and listening to the instructor speak, I was hooked. I mean, the guy who owned and ran the place was just so awesome; he knew so much about martial arts and life.

His name was Master Hu, or, at least, that's what I and everyone else knew him by. He was Asian, from a rural village in northern China. He was in his late fifties, I would say, with thinning, black hair; a moon-shaped, flat face; slender body, but well-defined muscles, and not tall at all; and couldn't have been much over five feet tall. He spoke with a broken accent, but the man seemed so wise that I could listen to him speak all night.

His school—Master Hu's Tai Chi Jung Kung-Fu—was in a small corner, brick building, with a glass edifice, in a connecting three-business strip-mall—a smoke shop and an agent's office of Farmers Insurance—on Hampton Boulevard, almost in what, in the city of St. Louis, is commonly referred to as "Little Italy" because of all of the Italians who had migrated to this state in the late 1800's and settled in that section of St. Louis.

His style of Tai Chi Jung Kung-Fu was based upon Tai Chi itself and in the philosophy of Buddhism. Therefore, he stressed the taking of both Tai Chi and Jung Kung-Fu. He taught Tai Chi on Tuesday evenings—for the "spiritual" aspect of Tai Chi Jung Kung-Fu—and on Thursday evenings, he taught Kung-Fu; how every Tai Chi movement had a "fighting application" to it. He would spend hours of class time talking about how Tai Chi and Buddhism are applicable to everyday life.

On more than one occasion, he had told us students how Tai Chi and Buddhism had saved, and changed, his life.

As I have said, he had been born and raised in a poor, rural village in northern China. His mother had died giving birth to him. He was raised by his father and older brother. His father eked out a paltry living as a country doctor in that poor, rural village, and from an early age, Master Hu believed that his father hated him for his wife having died giving him life. Consequently, he grew up feeling unwanted and alone. He got into trouble repeatedly. His father and brother—who also became a doctor there—were both Tai Chi masters and followers of Buddhism. They both believed in living the "simple life" of Buddhism in the hope of one day achieving nirvana—a higher consciousness of life, heaven, if you will. Master Hu wanted no part of any of it. When he was seventeen, he ran away and joined the army. He was intelligent and ambitious. He rose through the ranks quickly. He began working for the government of China as a high-ranking agent. He stated that in that capacity he did many "unspeakable" things. The position made him drunk with power—power over men, women and life. Then, during a most "secretive and most dangerous" assignment, he was injured. His injuries, in the beginning, were life-threatening, and he was hospitalized for almost a year.

It was winter when he had been injured. Just beyond the window of the hospital bed in which he lay was a dwarf cherry tree. The tree was bare and seemingly lifeless. Master Hu became obsessed with staring at that tree. It seemed to him to reflect his life—barren, empty and fruitless; self-serving; producing nothing but pain, suffering and death; no growth; no change; just torpid existence; day after day, year after year. Then, spring came. Life returned to the tree—first green; then blossomed; then produced fruit; produced fruit in all of its life-giving, natural glory. Master Hu had an epiphany. His father and brother had chosen the correct paths in life—the only true path in life: The path of simplicity; the path of Buddhism; the path of peace and change; of moving from one plane of existence, or consciousness, to a higher plane of existence—until nirvana. He vowed to adopt this life, and he did.

He went back home for a short time, but then moved to begin his new life.

His brother had taken some graduate courses in medicine at St. Louis University, and he had told Master Hu how much he had liked St. Louis and its people. So, he moved here and began his new life. He loved it. His only regret was that his father's life-long dream had been to someday build a hospital in their village. Sadly, with Master Hu's life of simplicity now, he didn't have extra money to send his father to make his dream a reality, and, even sadder, his father had been recently diagnosed with having cancer.

Yes, by the time I finished watching that first class of Master Hu's, I was hooked. I was more than eager to sign a year's contract and begin taking classes.

Master Hu seemed just as eager to have me join as I was eager to join. From the moment that I walked through the glass front door of his studio, he was overly respectful and kind to me. He knew me, from having read about me in the newspapers and from having seen me being interviewed on TV. He kept bowing and calling me "Mr. Mayor." He seemed most interested in wanting to know if I were working on a case. I replied that, for the moment, I wasn't.

As he graciously ushered me into his closet-size office, which was at the front of the building, I kept hearing the smacking sound that the flip-flops he wore kept making. The wearing of those flip-flops was as usual to him as was the wearing of the slick-material, black Tai Chi Jung Gi.

His office was "spare," to say the least. The long, metallic desk consumed most of the room. Behind the desk was a wooden chair. In front of the desk were two metal folding chairs. In the northeast corner of the room was a waist-high, white-painted, metal filing-cabinet. On top of the desk was a small flag of China, a small statue of Buddha, a phone, and a pair of odd-looking shoes—soft, wafer-thin, leather, black, no soles; almost like ballet shoes: he later told me that he only wore those shoes in the winter, mostly.

His office was part of the glass, front edifice of the building, with a black-and-white image of two males sparring etched upon the glass. Looking through the black-and-white sketching on the glass, I could see that the summer sun had fallen.

From the file-cabinet, Master Hu took a stack of forms. He graciously but enthusiastically urged me to take the "premium" plan. This plan included not only the teachings on Tuesday and Thursday evenings, but private lessons with Master Hu—just sign your name and time on the sheet of paper on the clipboard hanging on the nail at the door to the office. Plus, for the "premium" plan, one got a key to the front door: Whenever there wasn't a class being taught, or whenever Master Hu wasn't teaching a private lesson, one was free to come at any time to work-out.

I took the "premium" plan. Master Hu was extremely pleased that I did, saying, "Good plan. Good plan—and someone as rich as you can afford two-hundred a month. Yes."

"What makes you think that I have money?" I asked. He told me. I had forgotten that in one of the last interviews I had given, I had mentioned John giving me that check for a million dollars.

Boy, I never signed my name to so many forms before. By the time I was done, I had muscle cramps in my right hand.

Yes, I enjoyed the classes and listening to Master Hu speak of life. It helped much with my struggles of bouts of depression. About the only thing that I didn't like about the classes was a guy in them—a Micky Cane. A real jerk. A twenty-two-year-old punk who thought that he was the center of the universe. He worked as a clerk in a grocery store, but he wanted to be a cop—and he had the demeanor of a cop, too: narrow-minded; saw the world and everything in it, and everyone, as black-and-white; no shades of grey.

He didn't like me at all. Probably for two reasons: One, because of Master Hu's liking and respecting me so much, and, two, I didn't take much of his shit. Like, this extremely shy, plain girl who came to about four classes and then didn't come anymore. Well, he was forever whispering things in her ear and following her out to her car after class. I can only image what "things" he was whispering in her ear. About two weeks after she had stopped coming to class, he says, "I wonder what happened to Brenda?"

I replied, "I guess she got fed up with you bothering her."

"Nobody's talking to you, Mayor," he stated sarcastically. "Mind your own business—or let's take it outside."

"Anytime you want to do that is fine with me," I said, and I was shocked that I had said that, I had meant it, too. But nothing came of it.

In class, I had sparred with him three or four times, and he had beat me on points every time. I just couldn't beat the guy. It was frustrating. I hated the guy and wanted to kick his ass.

One time after I had sparred with him—and, yeah, he had beat me good—Master Hu took me to the side and said, "You lose because you fight. No fight. Your heart, your chi, although troubled, is of intelligence and peace. No fight."

"But how can I defend myself if I don't fight?" I asked.

"Be water," he stated simply. "Water is soft; no fight. But water can destroy whole cities, populations. When water of a stream on its journey comes to a big boulder in its path, it no fight boulder; it splits and passes around boulder and continues its journey. Bringing peace to all."

"But how do I split?" I said, confused.

"Soon, Mr. Mayor," he began, "you must adopt the style of animal—tiger, mantis, monkey, crane. Choose crane. Crane with its graceful movements. It does not oppose or attack. Stretch out your arm and fist, Mr. Mayor," he commanded.

I stretched out my right arm. With his left arm and hand, as if they were the wing of a bird, he lightly followed the length of my arm down to the wrist, and then, he spun around behind me and touched my lower back at the left kidney with his opened left hand. From behind me, he said, "Be water; be crane, Mr. Mayor. No fight. The way of Tai-Chi-Jung is of peace. Accept the other person's energy and, ultimately, defeat himself."

The guy was good, I'll say that much.

Chapter Eleven

At the end of the month, June, my life changed again. I was feeling okay about myself; hardly any depression, but I wanted to do more: go places, date girls—have a life. Then, in the mail, I received a flyer from one of the divorce/singles groups I had joined of a dance being held that coming Saturday evening at the Concord House, which is about ten miles west of our house.

I had received that flyer that Wednesday morning, and for the rest of that week, I kept toying with the idea of going to that dance. I had told Mom about it, and she kept saying, "Oh, go, Tom. It will do you good to go. Go."

So, having mixed feelings—I just thought that it might be boring, and I'm not much of a dancer—I washed, put on a suit and tie, and went to the dance.

It was a hot, humid evening, typical of St. Louis summers. I arrived there at six-twenty, because the flyer had stated that the dance would begin at seven, after the half-hour of dance lessons. Since I'm not very adept at dancing, I thought that I had better take the lesson.

The Concord House was off Lindbergh Boulevard, and just behind Spring Middle School. It stood alone on a parking-lot made of small rock—a big, two-story, wooden, old house. The first floor of it had been gutted and converted into a HUGE dance floor, made of dark wood, with tables and chairs lining three walls of the place. At the far-end of the west wall, was a raised platform on which a DJ played recordings of revised, or updated, 40's-style music, and in the southwest corner was a bar.

The dance lesson was something called "The Imperial Swing." I didn't much care for it, and after I had returned home and had shown Mom what I had been taught from having taken that lesson, she said, "Why, Tom. That's almost like the jitterbugging that your father and I used to do at Casa Loma's Nightclub on Cherokee Street after the war ended."

After the lesson had ended, I hung out at the bar, having a Coke, and having to speak to that damn Melvin, the pest!

Don't get me wrong, Melvin is a nice enough guy, he's just an odd duck, who had latched on to me from the very first meeting that I had attended. He knew who I was, and he was most impressed and interested in me. He considered himself an "amateur sleuth aficionado." His passion in life, besides "bird watching," was solving murders. He had read all the detective classics by Author Doyle, Agatha Christie, Chandler, and on and on—and he was excessively BORING about it all. I always tried to get away from him, but that always proved to be as impossible as trying not to think about the pain you are experiencing from a boil on your ass.

He was in his late forties—short, pencil-thin, balding and always wore the same clothes: A Seersucker's suit and red bowtie; it was his "trademark." Besides him being a pest, the guy was so crossed-eyed, even when he was looking straight at me, I could never tell if he was looking at me. He had been divorced for two years. He had told me that his ex-wife got tired of their BORING life of twenty-some years together and asked him to leave. They were both teachers at Forest Park Community College in the city—he taught Chemistry and she taught Math.

Yes, he was odd—but, boy, could he dance! He danced to every song that was played, with a different girl each time, too. I just stood there at the bar, feeling too inadequate to dance—well, one lesson of that "Imperial Swing" wasn't enough to ask someone to dance.

Then, about an hour into the dance, she came in: a breath of fresh air, and as hot, or as "hot-looking," as a pistol.

Her name was Cindy Farmer, and from the moment I saw her, I wanted her. She was in her late thirties, about five feet, six inches tall, with short, white hair (she later told me that her hair was light-brown, but she had seen a female Country singer with white hair and liked it), an angular-shaped face with large, piercing blue eyes, a full body, and full-size breasts to match. She was wearing a light-yellow, summer dress, with matching high-heel shoes, and, boy, could she dance. She really shook that body of hers and that yellow dress. All the guys there were staring at her, and even many of the women there were staring at her, jealously, I would say.

There was one other thing about her that I just found to be captivating. She was a free spirit. She was her own boss. She had an aura, and a demeanor, that shouted to the world: *I do what I like, and if you don't like that—screw you!*

Yeah, I wanted her.

When she came in and was immediately bombarded by guys to dance, Melvin returned to the bar and me. As I, and almost everyone else, watched her as she danced, I said to Melvin, "Who's she?"

"That's Cindy," he replied with some regret, and with his damn cross-eyes, I couldn't tell if he was looking at me or at her.

"She's H-O-T, hot," I stated.

"Yeah, she is," Melvin replied sarcastically, "and she knows it. She only goes out with the 'top' men here. I'm still trying to get a date with her, but nothing yet. I'll keep trying—I'm told that if you get a date with her, she'll give you a blowjob that will blow your mind."

"Introduce me to her," I said.

"Okay," he said. "I don't mind having seconds or thirds or—"

"Just introduce me to her," I repeated, more forcefully this time.

As that song that she was dancing to with another guy was ending, Melvin and I pushed our way through the crowded dance floor to where Cindy and the guy whom she had been dancing with were standing. Melvin gave me a big introduction to her, telling her, and that guy, that I was a famous private eye—had solved two murders—and was rich. Sadly, for me, she didn't seem to be the least bit impressed by this.

I asked her if she wanted to dance, and after shrugging her well-shaped shoulder, she said non-enthusiastically, "Sure. Why not?"

Then the music began playing, and it was a fast song. Knowing that I couldn't dance to it, I told her that I would catch her on the next slow dance, and that damn Melvin moved in and began dancing with her. Damn him!

Well, I'll tell you, when the next slow dance was played, I was right there beside her. I grabbed her quickly in my arms and began dancing with her. It was great, having her in my arms and pressing her vivacious, sexy body against mine—and she smelt divine, too. Even her breath smelt good: she was a heavy smoker and almost always had a stick of gum in her mouth. I was in heaven, but nothing came of it. Well, it was too noisy in there to talk with the music playing and with the den of dancers dancing and talking.

I didn't stay much longer after having danced with her. It angered and depressed me to see her having so much fun dancing with others. So, I left. I had found out through Melvin that that place had dancing every Saturday evening, and as I walked out the door of that place, I vowed to return, knowing how to dance, and make Cindy mine.

The next day, I went to a music store at South County Mall and happily, and eagerly, purchased the two DVDs that the store had on Swing dancing. Then, I spent most of the rest of that day in my bedroom, repeatedly playing those two DVDs on my laptop. By supper time, I was tired of watching, listening and practicing to them: I needed a dance partner. So, after supper was over, I told Mom what I was doing and asked her if she would mind helping me learn Swing dancing. Her old eyes got as big as quarters at this, and her face lit up and was even youthful-looking again for a moment, and she said joyously, "Sure, Tom. I love dancing."

We have a long, mahogany-stained, wooden stereo that is positioned against the northeast wall in the living-room, on the east side of the fireplace. It's decades old and hasn't worked in years. For many years, Mom had kept saying that someday she was going to have it repaired, but she never did. Now, its closed-top serves as some type of odd cabinet for all the framed photos of the family.

I got my laptop from the desk in my room, and after repositioning a few of the pictures from the top of the stereo and placing my laptop there, Mom and I started dancing. She was great! At first, I tried to explain to her the basic steps of Swing dancing and some of the moves—like the Lindy, Balboa, and such—but she said that she knew all of that, saying, "I told you before, Tom. This is the same as jitterbug." And, boy, was Mom good!

We danced and danced. We danced until we both were exhausted. We plopped down on the couch, totally spent. This really helped with my learning of Swing dancing, and Mom had so much fun that we did it again the next evening, and the evening after that, and—why, we did it every evening, and by Friday night, I was ready to dance with Cindy.

The only thing, though, is that she didn't show up at The Concord House that Saturday evening. I was devastated. I stayed for a while. I talked with Melvin some, and I even danced a few dances with a few women, just to see how I did—and I was damn good! But I didn't stay long: I wanted Cindy!

Chapter Twelve

But she came the next Saturday evening, and I was in heaven seeing her, and, as usual, the moment that she entered, the guys swarmed around her like she was honey and they were working bees.

I didn't let that stop me, though. I worked my way through them, took her in my arms, and began dancing with her, saying to the guys, "That's right. I got the first dance with her." It was great. That practicing dancing with Mom had really paid off. I twirled her and spun her and everything.

Throughout the evening, I danced with her three times. The last time that I danced with her, which was towards the end of the evening—almost eleven o'clock—she said that she was hot and needed another beer. I escorted her to the bar and ordered two beers: they came in bottles. She took a long, much wanted gulp from the bottle. With no waiting, fear or trepidation—which shocked and surprised the hell out of me—I said, "How about a date?"

After wiping her mouth with the back of her right wrist, she shrugged her shoulders and said, as if she didn't care one way or the other, "Okay. Sure."

Hearing her saying that she would go out with me sent me to heaven. I was euphoric! And I came prepared. From the right pocket of the dark-gray suit coat that I was wearing, I withdrew a pen and two small blank pieces of paper.

"Here," I said, handing her the pen and one of the pieces of paper. Using the top of the bar, she wrote her name and number on the paper, and then handed the pen and the paper back to me. I quickly did the same with the other piece of paper. I hardly had enough time giving it to her when that damn Melvin came up to her and said, "Come on, Cindy. Dance with me." And away she went.

I left after that, waving goodbye to her as I left.

Mom usually goes to bed about nine or ten o'clock, but each time that I had come back from dancing, I had found her sitting on the couch in the living-room, watching TV, and each time she had anxiously asked me how the dancing went and had I met any nice girls. That night was no different. I finally told her about Cindy. Mom wanted to know all about her.

"Actually," I said, "that's all I know about her—other than she's hot-looking. She was wearing a sleeveless, green dress tonight, and she looked good in it. I have her phone number, and I'm going to call her Monday or Tuesday evening."

"Well, I hope it all goes well, Tom," Mom said. "She sounds nice … I'm so proud of you, Tom. You're really changing."

Wednesday evening, sitting at my desk in my bedroom, I phoned Cindy. Holding my cell phone to my ear, I could feel my hand shaking from fear as I listened to her number ring.

"Hello?" a young girl's voice said.

"Is Cindy there?" I asked.

"MOM?!" I heard her shout. "It's for you!"

A few seconds later, Cindy answered the phone.

"Hello?" she said, matter-of-factly.

"Hi, Cindy," I said, trying not to sound nervous. "It's me. Tom."

"Oh, hi, Tom," she replied, sounding a bit more enthusiastic. "How are you?"

"Just great," I replied. "Except I didn't run this morning. It was just too damn hot."

"Yes," she replied. "I sweated buckets of sweat at work."

"What kind of work do you do, Cindy?"

"I own my own landscaping and lawn service."

"Wow, I'm impressed," I said, and I meant it too. "How did you get into doing that?"

"Oh, about ten years ago, I got sick and tired of working in factories and taking orders from shit, dumbass bosses, and I just started cutting lawns."

"That's just great, Cindy," I said. I told myself: Enough of the small talk. "Say," I then began, "would you like to go out Friday?"

"I have plans Friday," she said, and the way she had emphasized the word "plans" I took to mean that she had a date.

"Well," I countered, "are you going to Concord's, dancing, Saturday?"

"Yeah," she said. "I'll be there."

"Well," I persisted, "how about a Sunday afternoon lunch—maybe even take in a movie?"

"I have three daughters," she said, "and I like to keep Sundays open for them. Sorry, Tom."

"Okay, then," I said, feeling depressed and rejected. "I guess that I'll see you at Concord—Now, you don't mind, do you, if I ask you out again?"

"No; not at all, Tom," she stated, flatly, I thought.

"Okay, I'll see you Saturday," I said and hung up.

And that's the way our relationship went—me seeing and dancing with her at Concord, and me calling her and her having "plans"—until the first Saturday in August. Then everything changed.

I was at Concord's, and it was about 8:30. I had already danced once with Cindy, and she was hot-looking. She was wearing a red dress that hugged and accented her full, shapely body, but she didn't seem to be her feisty, self-assured self. She seemed troubled and sad. Then, when I was dancing with her for the second time, she suddenly burst out crying. I asked her what was wrong, but through her tears she said nothing was wrong. I then said, "Come on, let's get out of here and go somewhere where we can talk." She agreed to this, and we left.

There was a Denny's restaurant a few blocks away from Concord's, on Lindbergh, so we went there. We drove there in separate cars: She owns a long, butt-ass big, white, several years old Ram truck with a trailer-hitch on the back bumper.

At Denny's, over having coffee, she told me why she had been crying.

She has three daughters: Faith, Hope and Charity. I had once asked her how her children had gotten their names, and she told me that that was one of her ex-husband's older brother's favorite sayings—that everyone should always have Faith, Hope and Charity. Anyway, for the past year, her oldest daughter, Faith, fourteen-years-old, has been struggling with the eating disorder anorexia nervosa. She was getting worse—not eating; losing weight; depressed; separating herself from life; not wanting to go to school or anything. Cindy was at a loss as to what to do. When I asked her if Faith was seeing a doctor for this condition, she replied that she was seeing only their family physician, who had prescribed for Faith the taking of antidepressants, which was only making her sleepy and zombie-like. I told Cindy that that was wrong—that Faith needed a physician who specializes in treating eating disorders. I told her that I would investigate it and see what I could do to help. Cindy was most grateful for this and asked me if I wanted to sit in her truck for a while and listen to music. Well, hell yes! I readily agreed to this.

After we had gotten into the cab of her truck, Cindy drove it and parked it at the far end of Denny's parking lot.

Cindy loved Country music—and she also loved the smoking of coke; the drug coke. From the glove compartment, she removed a small, glass vial, which was filled with a white powder. She licked the filter-tip of a cigarette and then, after dipping it into the vial, would begin smoking. While we were together in her truck, she did this repeatedly—it made her quite mellow, talkative, and horny.

Cindy was thirty-six-years-old. She had been born and raised on a small farm in the rural township of St. James, Missouri, which is about a hundred-and-ten miles south of St. Louis. Her mother had died of cancer when Cindy turned ten. She said her father was nothing more than an uneducated, dull dirt-farmer. When she turned seventeen, she left, hitching a ride by thumb from total strangers to downtown St. Louis. She stayed at a homeless shelter until she got a job in a factory and was able to save enough money to rent a dive-of-an-apartment in the worst, and in the poorest, section near downtown. "It was just full of crackheads, low-lives, roaches and niggers."

Cindy had been married three times. The first marriage to a man she worked with in that factory, who was two years older than she. He was a drunk, abusive to her, and was killed in a barroom brawl a year after they had married. Her second marriage was to a man who was the foreman of the factory in which she had worked. He was much older than she and did nothing more than work by day and get stinking drunk every night. Why, he got so drunk at night that he could rarely "get-it-up." She divorced him within the year of the marriage. With the money she got from the divorce, she got an apartment in a much better neighborhood than before—near Bates and Grand Street, in the city—and began working at a different factory. She began hanging out at nights in one of the neighborhood bars near her apartment. It was there that she had met her third husband, Jeff Farmer.

At first, she had dated Jeff's older brother by three years, Jerry, but Jerry kept dumping her for other women. He didn't like being "saddled" to one gal. It was all for the best, because Jeff was better looking than Jerry was. Jerry was bigger, stockier, hairier and more "ape-ish-looking" than Jerry was. Both brothers were wild. Both had barely graduated from Roosevelt High School, which is in the city. Both had been in and out of prison for street-fighting, taking and selling drugs, and public disturbances. Besides selling drugs, they had made their living by being auto repairmen of a dingy little auto repair shop that they had inherited from their father. Jerry no longer took or sold drugs or anything. Four years ago, during his last time in prison, he nearly died from a heart attack, and he became a "Jesus freak."

Jeff, at first, had not wanted to get married, but Cindy got pregnant, and Jeff thought that he should do the right thing. So, they got married, bought a nice house in Kirkwood, and fought like cats and dogs most of the time. The marriage had produced their three children: Faith, Hope and Charity. This was something that their marriage had none of—no faith, hope nor charity. It had been violent and abusive. Five years ago, Cindy had had enough. She divorced him. He wanted her back, but she wanted nothing to do with him—or to be "chained" again to any other man.

After Cindy had smoked four cigarettes—all prepared as the first one had been, with coke—she got as horny as hell. And, boy, did we DO it. I satisfied her with my hand, and she satisfied me—Well, let's just say that Melvin had been right about Cindy: she had blown my mind away.

I can't even remember having driven back home. It was all a blur. I was in love. Before we parted, I reminded her that I would see what I could find out about the treatment of eating disorders. She was most appreciative. She gave me the number of her cell phone, and told me that I could call her anytime, except on Thursday evenings: She was beginning taking an accounting course at Meramec Community College.

Yes, I was in love. Well, maybe not in LOVE. I mean, okay, I didn't like it that she took drugs, and I didn't like it that she was prejudiced. But what the hell, lots of people take drugs—and lots of people don't like black people. That doesn't make them monsters. Right? And-and look how concerned she was about her kid. Why, she even cried. So, no, when you add it all up, she was just what I wanted—a hot, sexy gal who made love—sex—like a starving wolf.

As usual, when I got back home, Mom was waiting up for me. I told her all about what had happened—all about Cindy and all about her kid having an eating disorder. Obviously, I didn't say anything about her taking drugs, or about her not liking black people, or about her having been married three times—and, obviously, I didn't tell her about us having sex.

"The poor dear," Mom said after I told her about it all. "I'll pray for her and for that child."

As we started upstairs for bed, Mom began sniffing the air. "What's that smell?" Mom asked, still sniffing the air. "Tom, have you been smoking?"

"No, Mom," I replied. "Cindy smokes. I think she needs to because of all that she's going through. I think it helps her to relax."

"Oh, yes," Mom said. "I can understand that. The poor woman."

Chapter Thirteen

The next day, I got on my computer and began searching sites about the treatment of eating disorders, and for doctors and places, both locally and nationwide, that treat such disorders. I spent about two hours doing this. Here in St. Louis, I found a few doctors who treat such disorders, and Barnes-Jewish Hospital, which is in the city on Kingshighway Boulevard, even had a treatment clinic for young adults who were suffering from such disorders. The best one I found, though, seemed to be the one at the Mayo Clinic in Minnesota. It had a four-to-six month program for young adults who suffer from eating disorders.

I wrote most of what I had found out down on a tablet of white paper, and I planned to give her the tablet the next time I saw her. I called her the next day, Monday evening, and I told her much of what I had found out. She was grateful and thanked me. I then asked her if she'd like to go out Friday—and I'll be damned, she told me that she had "plans" for Friday. I got to tell you; I was a bit pissed at that. I mean, come on, give me a break.

"Sorry, Tom," she said. I didn't reply, and I think that she could sense my disappointment and slight anger. After a few seconds had passed, she said, "Listen, I don't feel like going to Concord's this Saturday. Do you like Line Dancing?"

"I've heard of that," I said. "Isn't that Country dancing?"

"Yes, it is," she said. "Well, there a Country nightclub, 'The OK Corral', that I love going to. It's in Earth City. Do you want to go Saturday?"

"Sure," I said enthusiastically, thinking of the sex that we had had, and of the sex that we might have. "That sounds great, Cindy."

"Okay, then," she said. "It's a date. Pick me up at about six."

Before I hung up, I got the address of her home in Kirkwood—and then it all started again. The next morning, I went back to that music store at South County Mall and purchased the three DVDs that the store had of Line Dancing and on Country dancing. Then, I drove into the city, on Gravois, to Bob's Country Store, which has been around longer than I can remember (How could anybody made a living by having a business that sells Country clothes in St. Louis?!)

and purchased a white Country shirt, a pair of blue-jeans, a pair of brown leather cowboy boots, and a black cowboy hat.

When I got back home, I dressed in all the clothes that I had purchased—and, boy, did I look and feel silly, and I kept falling in those damn cowboy boots too!

During supper that evening, I told Mom all about my upcoming date with Cindy, and I asked her if, like before, she'd help me learn Country dancing. She readily agreed to this; so, wearing those cowboy boots, Mom and I practiced dancing in the living-room again to those DVDs I had bought. Mom was a real trooper about it all. Although she didn't like dancing Country as much as she liked dancing Swing, she gave it her all, and by Friday night, I was as ready for my date with Cindy as I would ever be.

Chapter Fourteen

Saturday, at 5:00 PM, dressed in my Country attire, and looking and feeling stupid at how I was dressed, and with butterflies of nerves having a fight in my stomach, I headed to Cindy's home in Kirkwood.

Kirkwood is an old township in the County of St. Louis. It's about fifteen miles west from our house. As with most townships anywhere, Kirkwood is no exception. It has a poor section, a rich section, a middle-class section, an old section, and a new section. The old section has houses in it that are like the houses in our neighborhood: old, two-story, well-kept homes. The newer section of Kirkwood is a maze of subdivisions with homes in them that are about forty, fifty or sixty years old. Cindy's home was in one of the newer subdivisions.

Even though it was the second weekend in August, the hot, humid, stale air of St. Louis' summers was still holding us in its summer misery as I pulled my car behind Cindy's pickup truck, which was parked in the curb-less street in front of her house.

Her home, which was towards the far-end of the block, on the west side of the street and faced east, was typical of all of the other houses in the subdivision: a small, ranch-style, light-red brick house with a cement driveway and a one-car garage. The driveway and the garage were to the north end of the house. On the driveway was parked a long trailer. In it was a walk-behind lawnmower, a regular lawnmower, three weed-wackers and a large, plastic gas container.

I really liked her front yard. It was beautiful, with all types of flowers. On both sides of the covered porch of the entrance to the house, a two-foot-high garden bed had been constructed made of large, flat, white rock. Both extended from both ends of the porch to both ends of the house. They were both about six feet wide and contained red and white rose bushes. Halfway up the driveway, on the south side of the house, was a sidewalk made of large, white boulders that were positioned deep in the ground and led to the cement step of the porch. Flanking both sides of the sidewalk were multi-colored irises—reds, yellows, purples and orange. There were also three small trees in the front yard. Cindy later told me that they were dwarf dogwood trees, and in the spring produced tiny, white blossoms. Also, to the north end of the house was another cement sidewalk that led to the back yard.

My hand was shaking as I stood upon the front porch, staring mindlessly at the red-painted, wooden front door, and rang the doorbell.

A few seconds after hearing the chiming of the doorbell from within, I heard the voices of young girls. Then, suddenly, the front door swung open wide. A dwarf of a girl wearing black-framed glasses stood before me.

"Hi," she said. "You must be Tom?"

"Yes, I am," I replied.

"Come in. Mom told us you were coming," she continued. I stepped into the living-room, onto the light beige carpet. Then she yelled behind her toward the back of the house, "Hey Mom! That Tom guy's here."

About six feet straight in front from where I was standing, to my left, was a hallway that led to the bathroom and three bedrooms. From somewhere down that hallway, I heard Cindy's voice say, "Hi, Tom. I'll be with you in a moment. Say hello to the kids … Get a beer from the fridge in the kitchen if you want one." The kitchen lay straight in front of me. Looking toward it, I saw two glass patio-doors at the opposite wall of the kitchen. Beyond the two glass doors, was a huge raised wooden deck, painted a dark brown. The chain-link, fenced-in back yard was about a half-acre long and wide.

To the immediate right of me was a wooden-framed chair with white upholstery and a floral design to it. Feeling terribly uncomfortable, I sat down in it. Directly opposite to me, against the brightly painted white wall of the living-room, was a long sofa that matched the chair in which I was seated. Seated at the end of the sofa, next to a wooden end table with a shaded lamp upon it, and closest to me, was Faith—Cindy's daughter who had the eating disorder. She was fourteen years old and was a freshman at Kirkwood High School. Dressed in blue-jeans and a red blouse, she sat there in silence, reading a paperback book of *Anne of Green Gables*. She was about five feet, four inches tall, sickly thin, and pale-looking. She looked much different than her two younger sisters. Hope, who had answered the door, was twelve and very animated and talkative. Charity, who was ten, was a bit pudgy and took pride in her ability to belch and fart at will. Both Hope and Charity looked like Cindy, except that their shoulder-length hair was light brown. Faith's hair was dark brown and the structure of her face was different than her two sisters—it was rounder, and her eyes and eyebrows were so dark compared to Hope's and to Charity's.

The almost floor-to-ceiling TV, which was wedged in the corner of the room, between the fireplace and the white-curtained bay window that faced the front yard, was playing loudly. Both Hope and Charity were wearing shorts and colored T-shirts. There was a dark-stained, wooden coffee-table in front of the sofa. Charity was kneeing between the sofa and the coffee-table; Hope was kneeling on the other side of it. They were playing a board game. A large plastic bowl sat on top of the coffee-table to the side of them. It was filled with buttered popcorn. There were also two glasses filled with soft drinks.

I don't know why, but I suddenly felt the need to speak with Faith. I said, "Anne of Green Gables. That's a good book."

"Have you read it?" she replied flatly, without even looking up at me.

"Well, no," I replied. "But I know that it's a classic."

"Come on, Charity," Hope said. "It's your move."

Faith finally lowered the book a bit and, looking at me, said, "Yes, it is. My girlfriend and I are taking a break from reading R. L. Stine. We're in a contest. She has read fifty-one of Stine's novels, and I have read—"

At that moment, Cindy appeared, wearing a white cowboy blouse with tiny brown tassels hanging from it at the chest area, a pair of white denim-jeans, brown leather cowboy boots, and small gold-colored earrings—and she looked HOT! Slung over her right shoulder was a waist-long, thin, gold-colored chain attached to a white purse.

As she entered, I stood up. She took one look at me and burst out laughing. "Oh, Tom," she said, laughing uncontrollably.

"What?!" I said in protest. "What?! … Do I look that bad?!"

"No, no," she said. "It's just that I've only seen you wearing suits, and this," she continued, waving her right arm and hand at me, "is SO different."

"Wait for it," I heard Charity say. "Wait for it … Wait for—"

"Charity!" Cindy warned, looking sternly at her. It was too late, though. Charity ripped a loud one. Then both Hope and Charity began laughing uncontrollably.

"Not funny at all, young lady," Cindy admonished Charity. "We're leaving now, and I want you two girls to listen and do all that Faith tells you to do … Faith?" she then said, "I'll be back a little after eleven. If you need me, just call. Okay?"

Faith just nodded okay, without even looking up at Cindy.

"Okay, then," she said to them all, and she then took another look at Faith. "We're leaving."

We left—and I was grateful to get out of there. It was too uncomfortable. It had been too long since I had been around kids.

Chapter Fifteen

When we had gotten into my car, I immediately gave Cindy that tablet with all the information on it that I had found out about eating disorders and doctors and places that treat such disorders. Cindy was most grateful that I had done this. As I drove, she viewed all of it intensely. When I told her that I thought that the best of them was the Mayo Clinic in Minnesota, she said that I was probably right, but that it was just too far away. She said that she was going to check out the doctors here at Barnes-Jewish Hospital.

The Ok Corral Nightclub was about thirty minutes away from Cindy's house—driving west on Highway 270, then farther west on Highway 70 to Earth City, which is mostly an industrial area, filled with modern-looking factories and office complexes. The OK Corral Nightclub was in one of the industrial parks on the southwest side of the Missouri River, which if one crossed over the bridge, you would be in St. Charles County. By the time that it had taken us to arrive there, Cindy had smoked two cigarettes; both had been prepared with coke as she had prepared them the last time we had been together— licking the filter-end of the cigarette and then dipping it into the small vial of coke.

The OK Corral Nightclub had been a factory that was converted into a Country nightclub. The place was HUGE! It was mostly a dance floor, with table and chairs surrounding the outer perimeter of the dance floor, with Western paraphernalia everywhere. The place was packed with people, too.

As with Concord, from the moment we had entered, Cindy was bombarded by men wanting to dance with her. She was in heaven— and I was in hell.

Needless to say, I hated it. I hated all those guys constantly asking her to dance; I hated being in those damn uncomfortable cowboy boots, and I hated Country music and Country dancing. Oh, I did dance, some. I line-danced to that song *Boot Scooting Boogie*.

So, I had a bad time. But Cindy made up for it after we had left that place, in my car, on the back parking lot of that place. Boy, did she make up for it!

I can't decide if my relationship with Cindy deepened the last weekend in August, or if it was on the first weekend in September.

A week before the last weekend in August, I had seen on TV that the Country singer, Martina McBride, was appearing at the outdoor Amphitheatre at Silver Dollar City in Branson, Missouri. I had heard Cindy say how much she liked her, so I asked Cindy if she wanted to go. She readily agreed to this. There was only one problem. Branson is about a hundred-and-thirty miles south of St. Louis. We would have to stay the night there—Saturday night and return home Sunday. Cindy wouldn't leave her kids alone all night, and she wouldn't permit her ex-husband to stay with them: We needed a babysitter. I resolved this by turning to the only person whom I knew could help me: Mom. Mom was super. She was more than happy to help, and she said that it would be great to have children in the house again—a BIG mistake!

Cindy and I had a great time. We stayed in a log cabin, had a great time at the concert—and the sex was wild, and often. Boy, though, I sure got an earful from Mom after we had returned; after I had returned home after picking up Cindy's kids and dropping them all off at Cindy's. Mom was furious.

When I stepped into the house though the front door, Mom rose from the couch and began giving it to me with both barrels.

"Those kids are the unruliest, most unchristian brats that I have ever met!" Mom cried angrily. "And that middle one—that Hope," Mom continued, getting even more steamed, "she went over to the stereo, looked at the pictures, and turns back to me and said, 'Who's the little nigger-boy?' She said that about James—and they didn't want to go to church this morning. They said that their mother didn't believe in going to church! ... I'm getting a bad feeling about that woman, Tom."

"They're only kids, Mom," I said, trying to make peace here. "How was Faith? Did she eat?"

"Well," Mom began, "she's the only one of the three of them who has got brains and some manners. She kept her nose in a book, mostly. Yes, I got some food in her. I had cooked a roast, made a salad, green beans. She just poked at it. So, I said to her, 'How would you like a banana split?' She said that she'd very much like to have one. I told her, 'Alright, then, you take just three bites of the food on your plate—and I'll go into the kitchen and make you a banana split with three scoops of ice-cream, nuts, whipped-cream and cherries on it.' She did what I said, and when I got up and started to leave the dining room, that Hope says 'Hey, what about us? We want banana splits, too.' I said, 'Well, if you can start behaving yourself, you and Ms. Farty-pants there may have one as well.'"

Mom told me that she would never babysit them again, and I assured her that I would never ask her to ever babysit them again.

Now to the other event.

For some reason, I wanted Cindy to begin thinking of me as a-a "rugged" man, an outdoors man. Cindy had told me that she liked fishing, camping, hiking and such. So, one evening when speaking with her on my phone, I told her that I had this deep urge to go fishing—that I hadn't gone fishing in years, and that I really wanted to go again. She replied that she and her kids had been thinking about going fishing—that they love going to Meramec State Park, in Cindy's old hometown of St. James, Missouri, which, according to Cindy, is only about eighty miles south of St. Louis. I told Cindy that I knew that she liked to keep her Sundays open for her kids, so why didn't all of us go fishing the next Sunday at that state park? She agreed to this.

On the first Sunday in September, at 7:00 AM, we, all in my car—Cindy in front with me, and Faith, who was reading the paperback edition of the novel *Little Women,* was in the rear seat with Hope and Charity, both of whom had fallen back to sleep—headed down Highway 44 for St. James, Missouri.

I got to tell you; I don't know if going there "deepened" my relationship with Cindy, but it sure did with her kids. We had a great time. We fished, played softball, ate fried chicken that Cindy had cooked, saw deer, swung on swings, and on and on. Yeah, I had a great, great time—and no sex neither.

About the only thing that happened that I didn't like was what happened when we all had first started fishing. I guess that I was trying too hard to impress Cindy with my fishing skills—which are none!—and I kept casting my line out to get it farther out and I got too close to Cindy's line and got them all tangled up. After trying unsuccessfully for some time to untangle them, Cindy finally said, "Let's just cut the lines. Give me your pocketknife."

"I don't have a pocketknife," I replied.

Mocking me, she said to the others, "Do you hear that, kids? Tom doesn't have a pocketknife."

Leave it to Hope to say something rude about that. She said, "Dad says you're not a man unless you carry a pocketknife."

"Well, EXCUSE ME for not having one," I replied flatly.

Yeah, except for that, I think we all had a great time. As I said, I know that I sure had, and I felt especially good about becoming friends with Faith. She had been sitting at one of the park benches, reading, and I just came up and sat next to her and we began talking— about books; about life; about what she wanted to do when she grew up (which was become a writer); about what she was going through with not wanting to eat (she had told me that she doesn't eat because when she doesn't eat she doesn't feel as nervous and depressed); about going to college; and on and on. We even exchanged cell phone numbers, and from time to time, she began calling me.

The following Saturday evening, Cindy and I went dancing again at that OK Corral Nightclub, and when I stepped into the living room of Cindy's house, I got a surprise. Cindy and all three of the girls were all standing in a line waiting for me, with ear-to-ear grins on their faces.

"Give me your car keys," she said.

I reached into the front pocket of the blue-jeans that I was wearing, and handed her my key ring that has the key to my car on it and the key to the front door of our home; it's all attached to a small, black, leather clip.

"Now," she said, "close your eyes and hold out your hand."

I did, closing my eyes and holding out my right hand. A few seconds later, I felt something being placed in my hand.

"Open your eyes," Cindy then stated, to the sound of the girls giggling.

There in my hand, on my key ring, was a tiny red pocketknife. The blade of it couldn't have been over a half-an-inch long.

"Now you're a 'man,'" Hope said.

"Gee," I replied, "I'm SOOO thankful."

Now, we've come to almost the core of my story. I have one more thing to tell you—before the killings started.

Chapter Sixteen

Yes, one more thing to tell you—before the killings started.

It was the third Sunday in October, October eighteenth, at 7:00 AM. My cell phone, which was on my desk in my bedroom, woke me up. It was Faith. She was all excited. It was her birthday. She was fifteen. Cindy was throwing her a birthday party in the back yard of their home at one o'clock, and Faith wanted to make sure that I was coming. I quickly reassured her that I was coming and hung up real fast: I had to pee—now!

With my cell phone still in my hand, my AT&T Blackberry, I dashed into the bathroom across the hallway from my room. I pulled down the sweatpants that I sleep in and my underwear, and joyously relieved myself with the first pee of the day. After pulling up my underwear and my sweatpants, I flushed the toilet. That's when it happened: I dropped my cell phone into the toilet! I was furious. I retrieved it from the toilet—with my hand!—and dried it out with a towel the best that I could, but it was toast. It didn't work at all. I hated that because it had all of my favorite numbers in it, and I had given that number out to all of my important contacts—like to Cindy and Faith; doctors and my lawyer, who is also my financial adviser; Master Hu, and on and on. Well, for over the past year, I hadn't been giving out the number to the phone in our home here. That damn old, black thing in the kitchen is so old that it doesn't even have an answering machine. When John had first given me that check for a million dollars, I was going to get everything new for the house—new furniture; new TV; new phone: everything new; but Mom had become so upset with me wanting to do that—it was like I was taking her life away from her—that I just didn't do any of it.

From the middle drawer of my desk, I got out my old flip cell phone that I had purchased at Wal-Mart when Claire had given me that check for a thousand dollars. Surprisingly, it still worked. I charged it and got some minutes on it.

At twelve o'clock, I left the house to attend Faith's birthday party.

It was a beautiful day. The sun was out, a cool, refreshing breeze was in the air, and the leaves of the trees were all in their autumnal glory.

As I drove to Cindy's, I thought about how I had wanted to talk with Cindy about Faith. I had told Faith about me taking Tai-Chi classes on Tuesday and Thursday evenings, so not to call me then. She had called me that Wednesday evening, and I was upset and worried about what she had said. Although I was glad that Cindy was taking Faith to a physician at Barnes-Jewish Hospital who treated young people suffering from eating disorders, I felt that that doctor wasn't giving her the treatment that Faith truly needed. According to Faith, she, this doctor, had only changed, and increased, her anti-depression medication. From what I had read, and now getting to know Faith, I felt that Faith was suffering from having a chemical imbalance, and that she should be getting treatment for that. Plus, and I had promised Faith that I wouldn't tell her mom about this as long as she called me first, but Faith had told me that she was thinking about cutting herself to stop her nervousness and depression.

I parked my car in front of the neighbor's house to the north side of Cindy's house. Directly behind Cindy's truck was a rusted-out, banged-up, black, old pick-up truck. From the moment that I had first seen that pick-up truck, I had a bad feeling about it—and I had been right. It belonged to Cindy's ex-brother-in-law, Jerry Farmer.

The birthday party was being held in the back yard, on the raised, wooden, dark brown patio that was attached to the back of the house.

Faith had expressed the want of a wristwatch, so I had bought her a thin, gold-colored Citizen wristwatch. Mom had wrapped it for me, with a red bow on top of it.

I walked up the driveway to the garage, and then I followed the cement sidewalk on the north side of the house that led to the back yard. As I approached the back yard, I heard many voices talking. For some reason, as I crossed into the back yard, my heart began to race from nerves.

On the north end of the raised patio, butted-up against the waist-high, wooden ledge of the front end of the patio, was a long, metal barbeque pit, which was smoking like crazy: Faith was standing in front of it with a long spatula, busy barbequing hamburgers and hotdogs. Directly behind her, against the house, was a long, wooden picnic table with two benches attached to it. The four wooden steps to the top of the patio were at the south end of the patio. Two large blue coolers were at the top of the steps. They were filled with ice for the soda, beer and wine which was within them. Behind them were two green lawn chairs. The lawn chairs were facing towards the barbeque pit and the bench. In the one nearest to the coolers sat Jeff Farmer, Cindy's ex-husband. In the other one sat Jerry Farmer, Jeff's older brother.

With Faith's present in hand, and with my heart pounding away in my chest, and with all eyes upon me (Well, at least Jeff's and Jerry's eyes were on me, staring at me hard, as if saying, "Who is this guy crashing our family party?!") I began climbing the stairs. When I had reached the top step, Faith shouted with joy, "Tom, thanks for coming!"

As I stood upon the patio, both Jeff and Jerry rose lazily from their chairs. Jeff had a bottle of beer in his hand. Cindy had been right: He was much better-looking than Jerry was. He stood about a foot shorter than Jerry; about five feet, seven inches tall; slender, lean build; an angular-shaped face, with light-brown hair and matching eyebrows and eyes. He was clean-shaven and his hair was cut short and nicely combed. He was dressed in blue-jeans and a denim shirt. It was his demeanor which I had found to be so disturbing: an uneducated, arrogant low-life who thought of nobody else but himself and what he wanted; you didn't matter; only he mattered, and if you didn't toe the line with him, he'd beat the shit out of you, or worse. Oh, he was street-tough, for sure.

Now, his brother, Jerry, was a different duck altogether. Oh, he had been like Jeff, but having almost died from that heart attack in prison had changed him. He had found religion and was now a Jesus Freak. Everything was about and for Jesus. He was nicely dressed, wearing a nice pair of blue-jeans and a bright, white, clean shirt. He was a big guy, though—heavy, stocky, with a hard, round body and round face to match. His hair was dark brown, curly, unruly, shoulder-length and matched his beard. Around his thick neck, hung a large, beaded rosary, with a large wooden cross with Jesus upon it in agony.

I gave an indifferent hi and nod to them. Both shook my hand, but in Jeff's grease-and-oil-stained hand, and in his eyes, was sheer hate—for me.

I walked over to the picnic table and placed Faith's present with the other presents that were upon the cloth-covered table for her.

Hope and Charity were seated at the picnic table, opposite to each other, engaged in arm-wrestling. Except for Hope, who was wearing brown shorts and a white T-shirt with the emblem on it of: KIRKWOOD ELEMENTARY—both Charity and Faith were wearing beautiful, flowing, white dresses.

I, then, walked up to Faith, hugged her and said, "Happy Birthday. How does it feel to be fifteen?"

"Oh, okay," she replied.

"Where's your mom?" I asked

"Inside, making the potato salad and coleslaw … Should I get her?"

"No, no," I replied. "She's busy. I'll see—"

"Faith!" Jeff yelled sternly. "Pay attention to what you're doin'. The hamburgers are burnin'."

Faith turned back to the barbeque pit.

There was another lawn chair by the two sliding glass doors of the back entrance to the kitchen. I sat down in it—feeling very uncomfortable.

"Do you want a beer?" Jeff said to me flatly.

"No, no," I replied. "Thank you."

"Perhaps you would like some wine," Jerry interjected. "The libation of Jesus."

"No, no," I repeated. "I'm fine. Thank you."

After taking a long gulp from the bottle of beer that he was drinking, Jeff said arrogantly and sardonically, "What's the matter? Are you too good to drink with us?"

Looking at him, I said, "No, I just—I'm fine."

Leave it to Hope to say something DUMB! She said, "Dad, Tom knows karate and is rich and famous."

Not taking his eyes off me, he said, "Well, baby girl, a bullet between the eyes can stop anyone—even the RICH AND FAMOUS."

"Dad," Faith chided him, with a pleading tone in her voice to *please-be-kind*.

This was followed by a few moments of silence—which I much welcomed! Then, he said, "So, how do you like screwin' my wife?"

I was beginning to have my fill of this guy. I said, "Look, man. This is not the time or the place to discuss this."

"Well, then," he replied, flipping his right hand towards the yard. "Are you 'man' enough to take it out there?"

"Dad, stop it!" Faith yelled. "Please!"

Rising quickly from the chair, I said to Faith, "Happy birthday, Faith. I'm leaving."

I left to the sounds of Faith begging me to stay and screaming angrily at her father—and to the sounds of him cackling like a chicken, mocking me.

I was pissed. Pissed! I couldn't believe that asshole had said those things to me—and in front of his kids. Cindy wasn't his "wife"; she was his "ex-wife" … And I wasn't afraid to fight him either. Now, the "old Tom" would have been afraid to have fought him; would have found a way to have talked himself out of it or would have ran—but not the "new" me. Hell no! No, I wasn't afraid to fight him, but I wasn't going to fight him in front of Cindy's kids. Kids shouldn't see adults acting like-like idiots.

I was so angry that I didn't go directly back home. I drove around for a while to calm down. Before I did go back home, though, I first stopped at a gas station and bought a six-pack of beer. I felt like getting drunk.

I returned home about 3:30. When I stepped through the front door, I saw that Mom was standing at the door-less, arched entrance of the kitchen, speaking on the telephone. She looked up at me. Placing her left, liver-spotted hand over the microphone part of the phone, she said, "It's for you. It's Cindy."

I took the receiver of the phone from her.

The first thing that Cindy said to me was that she wanted to know why wasn't I answering my cell phone—was I avoiding her? She had called me several times now. She finally got the number of our home phone from Information. I apologized to her and told her all about dropping my cell phone into the toilet and it being toast. She then apologized copiously for Jeff's behavior, saying that the no-good SOB ruined the whole birthday party—and Faith had been feeling so good, too. She went on to say that as soon as she had found out what he had done, she had cussed him out and then told the fucker to get his no-good ass out of her house. She also said that I should have knocked the shit out of him.

I explained to her my reasons for not fighting him: One, it was Faith's birthday party, and I didn't want to start trouble. Two, I wasn't about to fight him in front of her kids. She thanked me for this, but stated that I still should have knocked the shit out of him. She would have LOVED to have seen me do that. I then asked her how was Faith taking all this that had happened? She replied that Faith had taken to her bedroom and wasn't speaking; she was depressed and sad. I gave Cindy my old cell phone number and told her to give it to Faith—and that she could call me if she wanted to talk.

This is what I had wanted to tell you—now let the killings start.

Chapter Seventeen

I woke up the next morning feeling like crap. I was hungover, and I slept until 8:30—I didn't get up to run or anything. As soon as Mom had gone to sleep, I crept downstairs and out of the house. I got that six-pack of beer out of my car that I had purchased and brought it up to my bedroom and drank all six of the beers. Boy, I hadn't drunk that much, or snuck alcohol up to my room, in over a year. Don't get me wrong, I always had a beer or two at Concord's, or whenever Cindy and I went out, but not that much anymore at one time.

I just stayed at home all day, lying on the couch watching TV, or going up to my room and taking a nap.

After Mom and I had supper, though, I began to feel better. I decided to drive to the AT&T store where I had bought my Blackberry and buy a new one—or, at least, see if they would replace my old one.

The AT&T store where I had purchased my phone was only several blocks south from where we lived, in a strip-mall on Lemay Ferry Road, called Dierberg's South County Shopping Center—Dierberg's is a local grocery store chain.

It was a little after 6:30 when I had pulled into Dierberg's parking lot. Besides Dierberg's and that AT&T store, there are about ten to fifteen other stores there, such as a fingernail shop, a beauty salon, a family-owned restaurant, a pet store, and on and on.

The AT&T store was three stores to the north of the Dierberg's store, and, boy, was that parking lot crowded for a Monday evening. I had to park three or four lines of parking lanes away from the store. It began raining lightly when I had gotten out of my car with my toasted Blackberry in my right hand.

I was wedged in between my car and a car to my left, and I was about to lock my car when, suddenly, I saw a sleeveless arm come up from behind me and wrap around my neck. I was spun around and thrown up against that car that was to my left. Then, I saw another arm and hand come up to my throat—but this hand was holding an opened pocketknife. I grabbed the arm that was holding the knife at the wrist with my left hand. Dropping my cell phone that I had in my right hand—so that I could make a fist—I swept my arm backwards, hard, hitting whoever it was behind me in the chest with my elbow. I felt the upper section of the person's body concave away from me. I was about to spin around and push the person away from me and face him, when I heard a snapping sound; then a moan of pain; then, with the person still holding on to me, I was thrown to the ground, or to the cement of the parking lot.

I had gone down hard, hitting my forehead on that car to my left as I fell. Something, though, had broken my fall when I had reached the cement. I was lying on my back. I flipped over and saw what had broken my fall—it had been the body of a man. He was unconscious. His legs were lying underneath that car to my left. I was facing the rear of my car. I looked up. Something was dripping into my left eye, blocking my view. It was blood. Apparently, when I bumped my forehead up against the side of that car to my left, I had cut my head just above my left eyebrow. With blood dripping down my left eye, blinding my vision somewhat, what I had seen when I had looked up was the left leg of someone disappearing behind the bumper of my car. Whoever it had been was wearing black pants and black shoes— and the shoes (and, granted, I had only seen one shoe) were odd. The leather of the shoe looked to be of very soft leather, and the shoe didn't seem to have a sole.

Then, from behind me, a woman began screaming, "Murder!" She screamed, "Murder! Someone call the police!"

For the first time, I looked at the face of the person whom I was lying on top of. It was a man. It was Jeff Farmer, Cindy's ex-husband.

Chapter Eighteen

Yeah, it was Jeff Farmer, Cindy's ex-husband.

He was wearing a grimy white T-shirt and old jeans. The clothes were wet from the sudden burst of light rain that had suddenly started and had stopped just as suddenly. He smelt of nicotine, body odor and whiskey. I called his name a few times, telling him to wake up. I even slapped him on the face, trying to get him to get up. When this all failed, I took his pulse at the wrist of his right arm. He didn't have a pulse. That's when I knew that woman had been correct. He was dead.

I rose to my feet—wondering what the hell had just happened here?!

I didn't have all that much time to think about it, though. Within seconds after I had risen to my feet, five police cars came to a screeching halt in front and to the rear of my car. Quickly exiting the cars, with side-arm weapons drawn and pointed at me, they, in union, ordered me to lie back on the ground and place my hands behind my head. This I did, quickly.

I was then handcuffed, and after that, two of the officers helped me to my feet and began questioning me.

An ambulance came and the two paramedics knelt beside Jeff and began examining him.

I told the three officers who were surrounding me everything— that I had come here because my cell phone wasn't working; that I was going to the AT&T store, and when I had gotten out of my car, Jeff jumped me from behind and then somebody must have jumped him.

Just as I was finishing telling my story, one paramedic told the officers that Jeff was dead; that it looked like his neck had been broken. Then, a new-looking Ford Impala, black in color, pulled up to the rear of my car and stopped. Two men, one white and the other black, exited from the car. Both were wearing suits and ties.

The white guy stayed behind the black guy, as if the black guy out-ranked him, which he did. As the black guy came abreast of Jeff's body, one of the paramedics stood and the two men began speaking. Then, that black man motioned with his right hand for one of the three officers who were all standing by me to come to him. The officer did and they began talking. After this was done, the black man stepped to me and stated, with authority in his toneless, no-nonsense-sounding voice, "Mr. Mayor? I'm Homicide Detective Anthony Carpenter. What happened here?"

So, I tell this guy the whole story—again!

Homicide Detective Anthony Carpenter was in his late thirties, I would say. He was about two or three inches taller than me; maybe five feet, seven inches or so; a sender, muscular built; chiseled-shaped face, which was always clean-shaven. His clothes were "snappy"—as if he had them dry-cleaned every day before he would even consider wearing them. His head was shaven. I think that he did that for two reasons: One, to give himself an even more clean-look, and, two, he was balding.

From the first moment that I had seen the guy, something about him told me that I was going to have trouble with him—and I had been right.

No, from the get-go, I hadn't liked the guy. He was too arrogant for my blood; too into himself; too straight-forward; too much "by-the-book"; too black-or-white—you were either good or bad, innocent or guilty, my friend or my enemy; no shades of gray. Later, he let it quickly be known to me that he had been a Marine. He kept coating his sentences—like spreading icing on a cake—that he could tell that I had never been in the military; no "respect" for authority.

No, I didn't like the guy, and he didn't like me.

"I need for you to accompany me back to the police station, Mr. Mayor," he stated after I had finished telling him what had happened.

"Am I under arrest?" I said to him flatly.

"At this point, no, Mr. Mayor," he replied. "But I do need for you to answer more questions."

"Fine," I said firmly, getting angry. "Then take these handcuffs off of me."

He motioned again to one of those three officers, and the officer turned me around and removed the handcuffs.

"Follow me, Mr. Mayor," he then said, and I followed him and that white man that he had gotten out of that car with, to the back of that Ford Impala. He opened the back passenger door, and I got into the back seat. The white guy drove, and we left Dierberg's parking lot. Just before we left the lot, I spotted a rusted-out, banged-up, black, old pick-up truck. It had been the same truck that I had seen parked behind Cindy's truck. I knew that truck belonged to Jeff Farmer.

Chapter Nineteen

St. Louis is an odd place to live. We have two seats of local government here. One for residents who live in the city of St. Louis, and one for the residents who live in the county. Both have their own mayor, their own police department, their own fire department, and on and on. For those who live in the city, the seat of government is in the heart of downtown St. Louis; for those who live in the county, it's in the heart of downtown Clayton. This was where Homicide Detective Anthony Carpenter took me—to the headquarters of the police station on the first floor of the Court Building in downtown Clayton.

It was dark outside by the time that we had reached there. The inside of the first floor of the Court Building was huge—cubicles and desks were everywhere; people in plain clothes and police officers, both male and female, were constantly on the go, moving from here to there; the place was in constant flux. For some reason, I found the fluorescent lights from the white, drop ceiling to be blinding.

Homicide Detective Anthony Carpenter's desk was towards the back northeast corner of the enormous but crowed room. I sat in a very uncomfortable metal folding chair that was positioned at the left side of the desk as he filled out a report of me on the computer that was on the top of the desk. After he had finished the report, he escorted me down a long, narrow hallway to an Interrogation Room— and that's where the "fun" truly began. The room was closet-sized and bare. It had nothing in it but a wooden table and three or four metal folding chairs. I sat behind the table, facing the narrow, wooden door. Detective Carpenter sat, when he wasn't standing, towering over me, directly opposite of me.

He wanted me to tell him what had happened—again, from the top. I did. Then, he asked me what I did for a living. I told him that I didn't do anything—that I didn't have to do anything. That I was rich. I told him all about how I had played that joke on Mom of me telling her of how I thought that I had what it takes to be a private detective, and how I had gotten roped in to investigating Tyra's murder, and how I had solved the case, and how John had given me that check for a million dollars. Detective Carpenter was not impressed. He then wanted to know how I had met Cindy and how long have we been seeing each other. I told him. Then, he just got mean and nasty. He wanted to know how "good" Cindy was in bed—and I told him that was none of his damn business. Then, frustrated, exasperated, angry, and seemingly fed-up with me, he said, "Come on, Mayor. Why don't you just come clean? Admit it. You killed the guy. Just admit it."

"How many times do I have to tell you that I never touched Jeff? It was the other guy. The one who had come up behind Jeff and—"

"Oh, come on, Mayor!" he screamed at me angrily. "There wasn't any other guy. It was you. You did it. You killed him. You, you, you—you!"

I had had it. I looked at my wristwatch. It was ten minutes to eleven o'clock. I had been there for approximately four hours. No, I was through with this.

"That's it!" I shouted angrily. "I'm not talking anymore ... Aren't I entitled to one phone call? I want to call my lawyer."

"In a moment, Mayor," he said, "but first, I want—"

"No!" I shouted at him again. "I've been asking for a lousy cup of coffee for the past two hours, and you have just kept saying: 'In a minute'—No, I want my phone call. Now! This minute, Detective!"

I had my old flip cell phone in the front pocket of the jeans that I was wearing, but Detective Carpenter wouldn't permit me to use it. I had to make the call on the phone that was on top of his desk. I did.

I called my lawyer—Mr. Douglas Green. Mr. Green is a kind, gentle, little man, with one of the most soft-spoken voices that I have ever heard. He's in his early sixties, I would say, and is always nicely dressed in a suit and tie. He's a lawyer and CPA. He had been Claire's lawyer, and after John had given me that check for a million, and not knowing where I could go for advice on how to invest it and such, I went to him, and he's been my lawyer ever since.

I guess that the poor little guy had been in bed, asleep. The phone on the other end kept ringing. I bet that it had rang ten times—and my nerves were shot! —before I heard the sleepy, groggy whisper of "Hello?"

I told him who I was and immediately apologized for calling him so late. He said that it was "okay" and I then told him of my situation. He informed me that he wasn't that type of lawyer, that I needed a criminal lawyer. Luckily, though, one of his closest friends, a Mr. Raymond Goldstein, was one of the most skilled criminal lawyers in

St. Louis. He would call him. He told me to "be strong" and he would take care of everything.

The entire time that I had spoken to Mr. Green, Detective Carpenter had sat there, at his desk, listening to every word that I said—which had REALLY ticked me-off! I told him what Mr. Green had said, and he then escorted me back into that same interrogation room and then left the room.

For the next forty minutes, I sat there in that bare, tiny room, all alone. It was terrible. I kept thinking: *Did they all forget about me?! How much longer do I have to stay here?!*

Then, finally, the door opened, and in walked Detective Carpenter—and he was smiling, and in his right hand was a white, styrofoam, steaming cup of coffee.

"Here you go, Mr. Mayor," he said, placing the cup of coffee down on the table in front of me. "Not knowing if you took cream and sugar in your coffee, I brought you some packets of powdered cream and sugar." He then produced these from the left pocket of the dark-blue suit coat that he was wearing.

Usually, I do drink my coffee with cream and sugar, but I just didn't feel like fooling with that. I just wanted to drink that coffee. It was strong—boy, was it strong! It tasted like it had been re-brewed a thousand times.

Detective Carpenter sat down in one of the three metal folding chairs that were on the opposite side of the table from me. He stared at me for a few moments, smiled again, interlaced his fingers together, placed them down on top of the table and said, ever-so politely, "Things got a little heated before, Mr. Mayor. Let's start over ... This is a tough job, Mr. Mayor. One meets all types of people in this line of work—mostly low-lives. Now, I can tell that you're not that type. You seem to me to be a decent fellow, and I'm here to help you: I can help you. I can speak with the prosecuting attorney and see what type of a deal I can get you—maybe it would come down to being nothing more than justifiable homicide: self-defense. But you must work with me on this, Mr. Mayor. You must work with me before lawyers, forensics, and others get involved in this and really complicate this. You must come clean about it, Mr. Mayor. You did it. You killed him. Just admit it."

Either I had been just that tired, or worn-out or slap-happy or whatever, but I found him to be funny—hysterical. I burst out laughing uncontrollably. Through my tears of laughter, I said, "What-what are you trying-trying to do here, Carpenter? Play 'good cop/bad cop'?"

"Stop laughing, Mayor!" he demanded, returning to his mean, old self. He shot-up from the chair, pounded the clenched fist of his right hand down hard on the top of the table and said, "I said stop laughing! … Confess, Mayor! Confess! You did it! You killed him! Confess!"

Still laughing, I replied, "Why? What are you going to do? Beat me with a rubber hose?"

He looked me straight in the eye, and shaking that right fist at me, stated, "How about I knock some of your teeth—"

At that moment, the narrow door to that room swung open and that white guy, Carpenter's partner, I guess, stuck his head in the room and said, "Goldstein is here."

"Shit!" Carpenter cussed. "Shit!"

Next, standing at the open door, was the widest man that I had ever seen before. I mean, he was big—wide! He was so wide that he had to turn sideways to pass through the door. This was Mr. Raymond Goldstein, criminal lawyer.

The guy had to be at least three-hundred-pounds. He was in his late thirties or early forties, and although, I would say, that he bought the largest clothes for himself that he could find, they were still too tight for him. Not only was the light-blue suit that he was wearing too tight on him, it was wrinkled, and the white shirt that he had on was soiled with food stains—and the guy was red. His hair was red--which was curly and combed straight back—his, large, round face was red; his big-lobed ears were red, and his neck was red: He later told me that he was Irish on his mother's side of the family. He was a sight to behold.

In the sausage-like fingers of his right hand, he held a white handkerchief—he sweated like a leaky hose—and the handle of a leather, black briefcase.

His demeanor was of NO NONSENSE.

Breathing heavily, he lumbered in like an oversized steamroller, bypassed Carpenter without even acknowledging him, grabbed one of the folding chairs and tossed it next to mine, and then slapped his briefcase and handkerchief down on top of the table. I started to rise to greet him, but he stopped me by placing his left hand on my right shoulder.

Extending his right hand out to me, he said, "I'm Mr. Goldstein, Mr. Mayor."

After we shook hands, he plopped down, heavily, into the chair. If that chair could speak, I bet it would have screamed: "Get this guy off of me!"

Now, looking straight into the face of Carpenter, and with a total demeanor of authority, dead-pan-face seriousness, and of DON'T MESS WITH ME, he said, "I've read the report. You don't have anything, Detective. Mr. Mayor has been here now for approximately six hours. Either charge him or we're done here. We're leaving."

Carpenter stood there, shaking his head—and fuming. Boy, he was pissed.

Leaning on the table directly in front of me, cowering or towering over me, he said, "Fine. Leave … But hear me, Mayor: This isn't over—far from it! Bye."

He turned around and stormed out of the room, slamming the door shut as he left.

Mr. Goldstein looked at me and said, "Let's get out of here, Mr. Mayor. I do need to speak with you for a few moments … Do you like donuts, Mr. Mayor?"

Chapter Twenty

There was an all-night donut shop, or café, that was just two blocks east of the Court Building. We went there. Mr. Goldstein drove. I told him that my car was still at that Dierberg's parking lot, where all of this had happened.

That donut shop, or café, was nice—there were a lot of college-age kids there.

Mr. Goldstein just wanted to get my side of the story. I told it to him. We were only there a short time, no more than twenty or thirty minutes. But within the short time that we were there—boy, that guy sure put it away! He had bought for us a dozen donuts, each one different, and within that short amount of time, he not only wolfed down eight of those donuts, but four small cartons of milk and two cups of coffee. I had only one donut and one cup of coffee.

Before he left, he had asked me if I wanted a ride to my car. I thanked him, but declined his generous offer, telling him that he had done enough for me. I told him that I would call a taxi to take me back to my car. He told me that if I needed him, not to hesitate to call him, day or night. As he left, he popped another donut in his mouth, saying, "One for the road."

By the time that I had gotten a taxi, had gotten my car, and had returned home, it was almost 2:00 AM. When I entered by way of the front door, I was shocked: Mom was still up, lying on the couch in the living-room in her nightgown, bathrobe and slippers. As soon as I entered, she shot-up from the couch and said, greatly concerned, "Tom, where have you been?! I was so worried."

Although I was exhausted, frustrated, confused, angry, and wanted nothing more than sleep, I took Mom by the arm, led her back to the couch and said, "Sit down, Mom. Something happened tonight that I need to tell you."

I told her everything that had happened, and when I was done speaking, she said, boiling angry, "I knew it! I just knew it! I just knew that that-that Jezebel, that-that Cindy wasn't any good. I knew that she would be trouble! And here we are—in trouble."

"This isn't her fault, Mom," I replied.

"Well, then, I don't know who else's fault it is," she stated, still angry. "No, Tom. This is her fault." She was silent for a moment, and then said, "Tom, you know how proud I am of the changes that you have made in your life—but I'm not at all happy with you going out with somebody like that Cindy … I don't think that you even like her, Tom. I see how depressed you get when she refuses to go out with you—and don't think that I'm too old and feeble that I don't know why you're going out with her. You're going out with her for one reason and only one reason: sex. And look what it's got you."

For some reason, what she said ticked me off. I snapped at her.

"Well, what in the hell would you have me do?!"

"'Do'?!" she cried. "What would I have you do? I think it's about time that you DO what you do best. Put on your detective hat and find out who killed that guy before the police arrest you for his murder—and stop seeing that Cindy. Start seeing someone who has the same likes and dislikes as you; you need companionship. Right?"

Wanting to end this and just go to bed, I said, "Okay, Mom. I'll do all of that."

Chapter Twenty-One

The next morning, I didn't rise from bed until ten o'clock. I felt tired, but okay. I went downstairs and into the kitchen and turned the coffeepot on for some much-needed coffee. While the coffee was brewing, I stepped out onto the front porch and got the morning newspaper—Well, in St. Louis, we only have one newspaper, The Post-Dispatch, and it only delivers once a day. Anyway, back in the kitchen, while drinking my first cup of coffee of the day, sitting at the kitchen table in my pajamas, my T-shirt and sweatpants, reading the paper—and bang! Right there on the damn front page: me!

No picture of me, but it told all about Jeff being killed and how I was a "person-of-interest."

Just as I finished reading that article of Jeff's murder, Mom came dragging herself into the kitchen, wearing the same clothes that she had had on when I had entered the house—her nightgown, bathrobe and slippers; she looked more dead than alive. Mom was a die-hard, avid reader of the newspaper: read it every morning. If there had been any way of preventing her from reading that article about Jeff's murder, and my being mentioned, I would have prevented it. So, she read it, and she was good about it. All she said was, "I hope that you're going to keep your promise and start investigating this?"

I assured her that I was, and after we both had another cup of coffee, Mom got up from the table and made us some oatmeal and toast.

After we had eaten, I went back upstairs to my bedroom. I sat at my desk, thinking about what I should do first to begin investigating this case. I hadn't wanted to, but I felt it necessary to call Cindy. Man, I hated the thought of doing that. I mean, I didn't even know whether she even knew about Jeff's murder, and if she did indeed know, how was she reacting to it? Was she angry or depressed or—Well, what? No, I didn't want to call her, but I did.

Not knowing if she was at home or if she was working—it was a little after 10:00 AM—I called her on her cell phone.

As I listened to her cell phone ringing, I was nervous and my heart was pounding away in my chest.

"Hello?" she said flatly.

"Hi, Cindy," I replied, trying to sound cheerful. "It's me. Tom."

"Oh, hi, Tom," she stated flatly again, or so it had sounded flat to me.

"Can you talk, Cindy, or are you busy?" I asked.

"I can talk for a few minutes," she replied. "I'm just getting ready to cut another lawn. I'll probably be working until dark. Jerry and me are having a one-day funeral for Jeff. He'll be laid-out tomorrow and buried Thursday."

"So, you know all about his death?" I asked, softly.

"Yes," she replied, bluntly. "That damn nigger—that Detective Carpenter—was knocking on my door at seven o'clock this morning. He told me what had happened. I'm sorry, Tom."

"No, no," I replied, quickly. "It's not your fault. Was Carpenter hard on you?"

"No, he just asked me a ton of questions—like where I was last night, and I told him that I was home, with my kids. He asked, besides you, who would want to kill Jeff?"

"Well, Cindy," I interjected, "I want you to know that I did not kill Jeff." This was followed by silence. I took a few seconds of it, and then said, "You believe me, don't you, Cindy?"

After another few seconds of silence, she finally said, with me hearing doubt in her voice, "Yeah, I believe you."

"Who do you think did this, Cindy?" I asked.

"Well, I don't know," she replied. "He was a no-good SOB. He sold drugs, and I know that he was sleeping around a lot. Jerry always told me of that. He was even sleeping with married gals."

"Who were these women?" I asked, thinking it could be a good lead. "Where would he meet them?"

"Oh, they are all bar-flies that hangout at this neighborhood bar called the 'Water Hole' on Spring Street in the city; it's near Grand Street, just a few blocks from where Jeff and Jerry have apartments— or Jeff had an apartment."

"Well," I continued, "how are you holding-up?"

"Well, I-I-I'm shocked!" she said. "I don't know how I feel. I'm numb … I'm upset. For one thing, the lawn-cutting season is done. I should be wrapping it up by the end of next week. I was hoping that from what money I have made this season, and from Jeff's child support money—when the asshole paid it!—that I wouldn't have to do temp work this winter. But, I guess I'll have to."

"I'm sorry to hear that, Cindy," I said. "Say," I then said, "how's Faith taking all of this? Is she okay?"

"Well, no she's 'not' okay," Cindy stated bluntly and a bit sardonically. "I mean, yes, her father was a no-good son-of-a-bitch, but he WAS her father. She loved him."

"Yes, I understand," I said. "If she would like to talk, tell her that I'm always here for her."

This was followed by more silence.

After a few seconds had passed, I said, "Okay, Cindy? Will you tell her that?"

"Tom," she, then, stated, bluntly and sardonically again, with sprinkling of anger, "Faith doesn't want to talk with you. Okay?!"

"Oh," I said, feeling hurt. "I understand."

"Listen, Tom," she then said hurriedly. "I have to go."

"Okay," I replied. "I guess I'll see you at Concord's Saturday?"

"No," she stated firmly and quickly. "I'm not going anywhere for a while. My kids need me."

Before I could even say goodbye to her, she hung up. Boy, that ticked me off! She could have at least said goodbye to me. The bitch!

Chapter Twenty-Two

So, for the next two days, I did next to nothing. Cindy, I told myself, had been not much help to me in wanting to do some investigating. So, here was the plan: By Friday, Jerry, Jeff's brother, should be back to work at the auto repair shop that he and his brother co-owned. Friday, I would pay him a visit there and see what I could find out. I just couldn't think of anything else to begin this investigation. I keep drawing a blank.

I had skipped going to Master Hu's Tai Chi class Tuesday evening. I just hadn't felt like going, but I did go the Kung-Fu class on Thursday evening.

It had not been all that good of a class either. Master Hu was just not his usual self.

The raised wooden floor of the school ran from Master Hu's small office at the front of the building to the back wall. The north side of the building was a wall of floor-to-ceiling mirrors. On the south side was a three-foot-wide floor of tile that led from the entrance of the building to the back of the building, to a wooden door, painted white. There were three small rooms back there: a bathroom with a toilet and shower, a room for changing from our street clothes into our Martial Arts uniforms, and Master Hu's sanctuary. He loved that room and had decorated it with much thought and care. It faced south, and against the north wall, about midway up, hung two long, thin swords. The swords were crossed and, to me, looked to be Japanese. Directly in front of the swords was a three-foot-high and three-foot-wide statue of Buddha, sitting in the lotus position. The statue looked to be made of ivory, but this had to be some type of imitation ivory: ivory is just too expensive for that to have been real ivory. A furry brown rug lay at Buddha's feet, for one to sit and meditate. The room was always dark, lit by many candles, and always smelt of the sweet, heady scent of incense burning. The doorway to this room was covered by multiple strands of large, black, stringed beads.

It was not uncommon to find Master Hu sitting on that rug in the lotus position in front of that Buddha, deep in meditation. That Thursday evening had been no different. Except on this Thursday evening, he didn't want to leave the room or stop his meditation. It had taken some gentle coaxing from us to get him to leave the room and teach the class.

As I have said, it hadn't been all that good of a class. Except for time-to-time showing each of us moves of our individual animal styles—like I had chosen Crane style and Micky had chosen Tiger style—and commenting on each student's execution of the move, he said or did little else—no philosophizing about life or Buddhism.

Towards the end of the class, he apologized to us for his sadness and lack of teaching. He told us that a few days ago his brother had phoned him and had told him that his father's cancer was getting worse.

Well, then, his sadness was most understandable—and yet, I don't know, to me, it had just seemed that something else was weighing heavily on his mind. He had just seemed so preoccupied and troubled—and a dying father just didn't seem to be the reason to me.

Anyway, I was glad when Friday morning came. I was anxious to interview Jerry. To be honest with you, if it hadn't been for Faith, I don't think that I would have done any investigating at all. I mean, let the police do it—that's why we pay them! But I had to prove to Faith that I hadn't killed her father. I just had to!

Chapter Twenty-Three

It was a beautiful day—bright sun, cool breeze, and the trees in such glorious autumnal glory.

The auto repair shop that Jerry owned was just several blocks north of the Des Peres River. The Des Peres River, which runs east and west (well, flows east into the Mississippi River), is the line of demarcation that separates the County of St. Louis from the City of St. Louis. Jerry's shop was at the corner of Loughborough and Morganford. I drove down Morganford until I reached Loughborough. Then I turned right and parked my car on the right-hand side of the curbed street a few feet east of Jerry's shop. The damn place was so small that it didn't have a parking lot, really.

It wasn't a "bad" neighborhood; old, but with nicely kept, small, red brick homes with hardly any front yards.

Directly across the street from Jerry's shop was a beauty salon, and next to it was a shop that sold and repaired violins, which I thought to be very odd. I mean, how did the person who owned that place make a living at doing that? I don't know of anyone who owns, or who even plays a violin. Strange.

Jerry's shop was nothing to write home about. It was a small building made of brick, painted white, with two large garage doors with small-paned glass windows, and a tiny office to the west side of the building. Above the garage doors hung, precariously, an old, wooden sign. The sign was very sun-bleached and worn. It had black-painted letters on it, but the passage of time and neglect had destroyed some of the letters. I think the sign had read: FARMER'S AUTO REPAIR.

The two garage doors were open. Beyond each door was a lift and a well, a pit, for working beneath a car. Both lifts were raised high off the dirty cement floor. Both had a car on them, and a man was under both lifts, working on a car. Both men were dressed in dark-blue work jumpsuits.

As I entered through the open garage door that was nearest to the office, my nose was immediately assaulted by the overwhelming smell of gasoline and oil. I gazed to my right, and through a side door to the office, I saw Jerry sitting in a padded rocking chair in front of a much-cluttered wooden desk. The desk was butted-up against the south wall.

"Can I help you, Bud?" the guy in the pit closest to the office asked me. He looked to be in his late fifties, with salt-and-pepper hair and full beard.

"No," I replied. Flipping the thumb of my right hand in the direction of the office, I said, "I just want to talk to Jerry."

Jerry had heard me speak—well, the office was only about five feet from where I was standing—and when I looked back towards the office, I now saw that Jerry was staring at me. He was wearing the same type of work jumpsuit as the other two men were wearing. Plus, he also had that large-beaded, black rosary around his neck, the same one that he had had on at Faith's birthday party. His wearing that made me think of Claire. I wondered if, like Claire, he, too, never removed it from around his neck.

"Okay, Bud," that guy said.

I turned and took a few steps toward Jerry's office, stating silently: *The name's not 'Bud', asshole.*

As I stepped into Jerry's office, he said, his tone neither friendly nor unfriendly, "What are you doin' here?"

I stepped to the left side of the door and said, "First, let me say that I'm sorry for your loss. Second, let me say that I didn't kill your brother."

"No?" he stated. "Well, the police seem to think that you did."

"They're wrong," I replied.

Pointing the index-finger of his right hand at the large headshot of Jesus hanging on the wall above the desk, in a gold-colored frame, he stated, "Well, God knows the truth."

"Yes, I would say that He does," I stated. This was followed by silence. After a few moments had passed, I then said, "So, who do you believe killed Jeff?"

He shook his head from side to side, as if saying that he didn't know, then said, "I have prayed so long and so hard for Jeff's soul. I told him and told him to give up the selling of drugs; the gambling; the womanizing." For some reason, he had emphasized the word "womanizing." "But he wouldn't … I can only think of one person who would have killed Jeff—'Cause he had already threatened to kill him. Jeff owed him eight thousand dollars. His drug dealer. A young, dangerous, Vietnamese hoodlum, Ty Nguyen."

"Do you have his address?" I asked.

"Yes. It's 54333 Nebraska Avenue, off Cherokee Street." He paused for a moment, and then said, "Why? You're not thinkin' of—"

Just at that moment, that guy who had called me "Bud" came charging into the room. In his right hand he was holding a clipboard that had several sheets of pages clipped to it. He slapped the clipboard down on top of the desk in front of Jerry and stated angrily, "What the hell does that work order say about the Och's car? Does it say to replace the brakes?"

Jerry flipped a couple of pages with his right hand, read what was written on that page, looked back up at that guy and said, "Yes. Replace the brakes."

"I swear, Jerry," he said, shaking his head exasperatedly. "You got to go back to writing with your left hand again or get a secretary in here—a blonde with big tits. Your writing is chicken scratch. Just chicken scratch."

Holding up his right hand to that guy, dismissively, Jerry said, "My writing is getting better. It's getting better."

"It ain't either," that guy countered. "It's chicken scratch. Go back to writing with your left hand—the hand that you were born to write with."

"The left hand is the work of the devil. No. Never."

Grabbing the clipboard off the desk, that guy said, "Well, then let the damn devil do all the fuckin' work around here." He turned around and stormed out of the room.

Wanting to leave, I said, "I see you're busy, so I better go. Again, I'm sorry for your loss." I then left.

The next morning, Saturday, I had risen from bed about 7:00 AM. I donned my jogging clothes and went for a nice, slow run around the neighborhood. When I had gotten back home, Mom was seated at the kitchen table, drinking a cup of coffee. Knowing that after a run I like to drink some orange juice, Mom had a tall glass of orange juice waiting for me on the table. As I thirstily gulped down the orange juice, Mom asked me if I was hungry. I told her that I was, and she made us some oatmeal and toast.

My plan for the day had been this: I wasn't looking forward to meeting Jeff's former drug dealer, but I knew I had to meet him and question him. So, after Mom and I had finished having breakfast, I was going to shower, dress and then leave to drive over to that Ty Nguyen's apartment. But Mom had other plans for me.

Mom wanted me to go to Wal-Mart's with her.

Because of next Saturday being Halloween, and because of there now being children in the neighborhood again, Mom wanted to buy candy, pumpkins and Halloween decorations. She also wanted me to get Charlie from the basement. I don't remember how Charlie got its name. Years ago, Dad had gotten a male mannequin from somewhere, dressed it in old clothes and a straw hat, and sat Charlie on a bale of hay on the front porch. He was our scarecrow.

I had really wanted to get over and meet with that Nguyen guy, but I couldn't disappoint Mom. So, I drove her to Wal-Mart.

We didn't get back home until about noon. At Wal-Mart, we had bought a large, orange-colored plastic pumpkin and five large bags of assorted candy bars: the candy bars would be placed in the plastic pumpkin for Mom to reach into it and to give candy to the little trick-or-treaters. We also bought three pumpkins, a bale of hay for Charlie and a string of small, orange-colored pumpkins for the living-room window.

By the time that we had carved the three pumpkins, got Charlie all cleaned-up and sitting on that bale of hay on the front porch, and strung the lights in the living-room window, it was ten minutes to 3:00. I was hungry, and so was Mom. She opened two cans of tomato soup and grilled a couple of grilled cheese sandwiches.

It was a little after four o'clock when I had finally left the house to drive to Ty Nguyen's apartment.

Right before I had left, Mom had asked me if I was going dancing later at Concord's. I told her that I wasn't, that I had a few leads on the case, and I wanted to check them out. Nothing dangerous, I had told her—Boy, had I been wrong about that!

Chapter Twenty-Four

Cherokee Street is an historic street in the city of St. Louis. Running east and west, it is only a few miles south of Anheuser-Busch Brewery and of downtown St. Louis. In the forties and fifties, it was a block-long district of thriving, family-owned businesses of all types—clothing shops, shoe stores, meat shops, grocery stores, pharmacies, and on and on. Husbands and wives who worked long hours in their store, or shop, by day, and at night, lived and raised their family upstairs above the business. Proud people—proud of their neighborhood; proud of their heritage; proud of their business, and proud to be an American!

Casa Loma's Nightclub is there, too, on Cherokee Street. In the forties and fifties, it was THE place to go dancing on a Saturday night; big band music, Glenn Miller, Tommy Dorsey, and such. After Dad had come back home from the war, World War II, and had met Mom and they had started dating, why, they went there almost every Saturday night.

I had read that when he was young, the playwright Tennessee Williams lived in an apartment on Cherokee Street with his mother and sister. It has been said that his living there inspired him to write the play *The Glass Menagerie.*

In the sixties, Cherokee Street and the neighborhoods surrounding Cherokee Street began to decline and to deteriorate. For a moment, the "Hippy Movement" moved in and gave some renewed life; a much different type of life than before, but, yes, it was short-lived. The seventies brought more decline and deterioration to this section of St. Louis. In the early eighties, though, there was renewed hope for Cherokee Street and for the surrounding neighborhoods. A large population of Asians, who our government had helped come to this country—fleeing the failed war of Vietnam—settled and began living in the neighborhoods of Cherokee Street. For a time, that area even got the nickname "Little Saigon." This, too, was short-lived. By the nineties, most of the Asians who had settled there moved on to live elsewhere.

Today, Cherokee Street and the neighborhoods surrounding it—although no one has given up on it, totally—is a seedy place at best. Abandoned, boarded-up, long-closed and forgotten shops and stores;

high crime rate; a street filled with the poor, the uneducated, the disenfranchised, the lost, the scavengers, running-out-of-hope people of society. Sad. Just sad!

All the buildings in that area on Nebraska Street are the same: two-story, red brick, old buildings that are separated from each other by only a three or four foot space. Some of the residents on the block own and live in the whole building, some of the buildings are two-family flats, and some of the buildings are separated into four apartments per building.

I had got lucky. The narrow, curbed street of Nebraska was packed with parked cars on both sides of the street when I reached the address that Jerry had told me. I made two passes around the block, and on the third pass around, I got a parking spot on the same side of the street of the building where Ty Nguyen lived and just a few feet north of the wooden, old front-door entrance to the building. I had parked behind a banged-up, old yellow Chevy Camaro. How ugly! A yellow car?!

It was almost 4:30 when I stepped into the building. The weather outside was getting cloudy. It looked like rain.

One of the eight metal mail slots that were midway up the south wall near the entrance had Ty Nguyen's apartment listed as B-4. As I walked up the creaking wooden old steps to the second floor, I said to myself: *Gee, someone is cooking cabbage for supper.* The smell of it was overwhelming.

The apartment B-4 was at the end of the hallway on the south side of the building.

Standing in front of the wooden door, painted a dingy beige color, with the metallic indicators on it, B-4, I was breathing heavily and as nervous as a cat being thrown from a roof. I kept thinking how Jerry had said that this Ty Nguyen was "a dangerous hoodlum." I took a deep breath, expelled it, and then knocked on the door. From within the apartment, I heard a TV playing loudly and the voices of guys talking loudly.

No answer, so I knocked again.

The door was quickly thrown halfway open and a tall, thin, young black man, probably in his mid-twenties, stood before me. He was wildly dressed, wearing an orange-colored suit, a white dress shirt—which was mostly unbuttoned, and he had some type of gold chain and a medallion hanging from his neck—and a white Fedora; he was also sporting an afro under the hat. Plus, he was wearing white leather shoes. He was a sight. I immediately, silently, called him "Superfly."

"What you want, man?" he said in a low, deep, rough-sounding voice, eyeing me suspiciously.

Jerry had said that Ty was Asian, Vietnamese, so I knew that Superfly here couldn't be Ty.

"Is Ty here?" I asked.

"Who's askin' for me, Tyrone?!" I heard someone yell from within the room. "Open that fuckin' door wider and let me see who wants Ty."

Tyrone did and I stepped inside the apartment. Tyrone shoved me a bit to my left, so that he could close the door. I was standing in front of a 24-inch, flat TV that was attached to the east wall, midway up. The movie "Iron Man" was playing.

Across from me, sitting arrogantly on an old, tattered, cherry-colored, leather couch, with his legs and feet upon a dark-stained coffee table that was cluttered with empty beer bottles, empty pizza boxes and two ashtrays filled with ashes and smoked cigarette butts, was Ty Nguyen. He was wearing a cotton, sleeveless, white T-shirt, jeans and new-looking, white, Nike tennis shoes. His shoulders were broad and his body lean. His hair was shoulder-length and raven black. His face was round and flat, and his demeanor was of an arrogant punk. Behind him was a window that had a white bed sheet covering it—a makeshift curtain.

The place was small. To my left was a tiny kitchen, and just beyond that was a bathroom, and directly opposite that was a bedroom.

To the immediate left of the couch was a winged, old armchair with blue upholstery. Sitting slumped in it was an average-height, pencil-thin, white guy of about twenty years of age. His withdrawn-from-the-world face was covered with sores. He seemed high on drugs—meth or PCP. The dude was "out-of-it."

It was sad. I mean, these guys were just kids, really. Mean, violent, street-tough kids who had never been given the time, care, love or help to mature into law-abiding, good citizens. Sad.

"Who are you, man, and what you want of me?" Ty said, puffing on a cigarette.

"I'd like to buy some coke," I replied.

"Man, I don't know you. Are you a cop?"

"No, man," I replied. "I'm not a cop. I just want to buy some dope."

"So, why you comin' to me, man?" he barked. "I ain't no goddamn common pusher on the street. I'm a businessman. How did you find me? Who's your street dealer?"

"Well," I began, trying to think of what to say, "I usually buy my coke from Jeff Farmer, but he got killed last week. He told me about you … Some people are saying you killed him."

"That's bullshit, man," he cursed, and then he reached around behind himself and withdrew a large pistol from his pants. "When I kill a rat—EVERYBODY knows that I did it—I want everybody to know it. It breeds fear … There's somethin' not right about you, man … Tyrone," he then stated, "search him."

Tyrone moved in front of me. Suddenly, I didn't want these guys to know a thing about me—I didn't want them having my name and driver license. Tyrone started patting me down. When his long arms and hands came to my waist, with the open palm of my right hand, I brought it up hard against his wide, flat nose. His head snapped backwards. Using a Crane movement, I brought my arms and hands up above my head, then, stepping back and then quickly forward, throwing my whole body into it, I brought my arms and hands down in a sweeping motion. When the palms of my open hands made contact with his chest, I thrust my arms and hands forward. Superfly sailed backwards. He flew across the room, over the top of the coffee table and landed on top of Ty.

Amid the confusion of the moment, and amid the yelling and the cussing "to get me', I spun around, grabbed the handle of the door, threw it open and got the hell out of there.

It was dark outside—not dark from the lateness of the day. It was storming. Raining hard. Torrentially. Just from dashing from the front door of that building to my car, I got soaked.

My mind was racing, and my hands were shaking. Quickly, I started the car. I turned the wipers and the headlights on, and then pulled away from the curb.

I drove to the end of the block and then glanced in my rearview mirror. "Shit!" I cursed. In the rearview mirror, I saw all three of them piling into that yellow Camaro.

At the end of the block, I turned right, heading east on Cherokee Street. On Broadway Boulevard, I turned south. That old Camaro wasn't any match in speed to my car—not with the super-charged engine that was in mine, but with it raining so hard, I didn't want to drive all that fast.

I got on Highway 55, heading south. Checking the rearview mirror again—"Shit!" They were still chasing me. They were some distance away from me, but, yeah, they were still after me.

All I could think about was getting back home and being safe. Then, I thought: *Are you crazy! You want them to follow you home?!* Then, I thought of that police station at the next exit of the highway, on Loughborough. If I could just make it to there, I would be okay. Then, I thought: *Are you insane? Do you want to get involved with the police again?!—and have those guys know your name and address?!*

Now, I didn't know what to do. Then, another thought came to me.

I slowed down. I wanted them to catch up with me. Pulling up behind me fast, Ty stuck his body out of the passenger's side window, flashing that gun at me as he had back at his apartment. I sped forward. When I placed a distance of about fifteen feet between us, I slowed down again and sharply yanked the steering wheel to the left. The rain caused the car to slip a bit, but the car turned around, 180-degrees! I started driving north on a south-bound highway. The Camaro was coming at me head-on and at full speed. I swerved to the right and missed it.

The idiots! It had worked like a charm.

With it raining so hard, and with the pavement being wet and slippery, and what with them driving at top speed, when they had tried to turn the car around—it flipped! It became airborne and landed on its top, upside down.

Slowing to a crawl, I turned my car back around and began driving south again.

As I came abreast of their car, I saw that they were trapped inside of it. Then, suddenly, it burst into flames right before my eyes. It had happened so fast and furious that all I actually viewed was a fireball of fames.

Mom had been right when she said that I had changed.

Had the "old Tom" seen that, he would have become physically sick, would have pulled the car over and would have gotten out to help them, to save them—but not the "new Tom." No, the "new Tom" was glad that they were dead.

Yeah, Mom had been right about me having changed—and not for the better.

Chapter Twenty-Five

The next day, Sunday, I stayed at home all day—I never even left the house. It hadn't been so much that I was scared about what had happened the day before as it was-was—Well, alright, I was scared! I mean, come on, I had been responsible, technically, for three people being killed.

I'll admit it. I hadn't gotten much sleep that night. Had just kept tossing and turning, thinking about what had happened over and over.

So, by the next morning, I was sleepy all day and nervous. Besides not being able to get that picture out of my head of those three guys being trapped in that car, I kept fearing a knock at the front door. I kept thinking that any minute now Carpenter would be at the front door, saying, "Well, now you did it, Mayor. You finally did it. You murdered three people—and we caught you red handed. You're under arrest."

No, I just wanted to stay home where it was safe. I didn't listen to the news or think about the case or anything. I just wanted to feel safe.

I had stayed in my bedroom most of the day. From time to time, Mom would knock on the closed door and, without opening it, ask me if I was alright. I always told her that I was just tired and wanted to rest—which hadn't been a lie, really.

For supper, Mom had fried chicken, corn-on-the-cob, mashed potatoes, and apple pie—and nobody can fry chicken like Mom. It was delicious.

By six o'clock, I began feeling better—wasn't all that tired anymore, and I was mostly over my fear that Carpenter was going to arrest me. I had felt so bad about avoiding Mom all day that I said to her, "Say, I know that it's a bit early for Christmas, but I feel like having some Christmas joy. Let's watch 'White Christmas'?"

Mom eagerly agreed to this. "White Christmas" with Bing Crosby and Danny Kaye is one of her favorite movies. A few years ago, I had bought a DVD of it for her for Christmas.

So, we watched "White Christmas." She enjoyed watching it again, greatly. I was glad of this. For what was to happen to us in the next few days—she, we, needed the welcomed relief.

Chapter Twenty-Six

The next morning, I awakened at 7:00 AM. It was the beginning of a new week, and I felt good. I felt like having a run. I donned my jogging clothes and left the house. It was a beautiful fall morning, and I had a great run—nice and slow. I ran around the block at least twenty times.

Breathing a bit heavily, and not too sweaty, I returned home, feeling even better than before I had run. Before I entered our house, I even had a chat with Mr. Trim. Mr. Trim was our neighbor who had bought Claire's house. He was leaving for work. He and his wife, Emily, are both teachers at Washington University. They're good people, young, with two children, both of whom are girls.

It was almost 8:30 by the time that I stepped back into the house, with the newspaper in my hand.

I found Mom sitting on the couch in the living-room, nervously waiting for me. Still dressed in her night clothes—her bathrobe, nightgown and slippers—the moment I entered, she rose hurriedly from the couch to greet me, saying, "Thank God you're back, Tom. I did something awful."

Still feeling good, I replied heartily, "Well, now, what could my lovely mother have possibly done that is awful?"

"Sit down on the couch with me, and I'll tell you."

We did, and she told me.

As Mom had passed by my bedroom this morning, the door to it was open. She had looked in, and not seeing me, she had figured that I had probably gone jogging. She came downstairs and into the kitchen and put the coffee on. After it had finished brewing, she poured herself a cup and then sat at the kitchen table. When she had finished drinking her first cup of coffee for the day, she had decided to get the newspaper and then have another cup of coffee while she read the paper. Just as she was about to rise from her chair, the phone began ringing. She walked over to it—that old black-colored phone on that wooden stand by the entrance to the kitchen—and answered it.

It was weird, she said. The voice didn't sound human. She said that she couldn't tell if the voice was male or female: It, the voice, sounded like a robot's voice. It said if I wanted to know who killed Jeff Farmer, to come to this address tonight at 7:00 PM. Mom didn't have a pencil or a piece of paper to write the address down. She had asked the voice to wait a minute while she got a pen and paper, but the voice had hung up.

Mom said that she had quickly gotten a pen and a piece of paper and had written the address down. The piece of paper with that address on it was on top of the kitchen table.

"Oh, Tom," Mom sighed. "I was so nervous. I don't even know if I got the address right. What if I messed this up for you?"

"Stop worrying about it, Mom," I said, trying to comfort her. "Come on, let's go into the kitchen and look at that address."

We did.

The address was 655 Wharf Street.

"655 Wharf Street," I stated after reading the address. "This must be near downtown … Well, I'll look it up on the computer and go there tonight."

"And I'm going with you!" Mom interjected most emphatically. "If I messed this up for you, I want to at least be there for you—and don't argue with me about this, Tom. I'm going!"

And she did.

Chapter Twenty-Seven

At 6:00 PM, Mom and I got in my car and headed north on Highway 55 for downtown. I had looked up Wharf Street on my computer and it was several blocks past the Gateway Arch and Laclede's Landing. Laclede's Landing—named after one of the Founding Fathers of St. Louis, P. Laclede—is an entertainment spot along the Mississippi River, filled with restaurants and nightclubs. The buildings are all old, from the 1800s when that section of downtown St. Louis had been a major player in the fur business: red brick buildings with tall, narrow, wooden-framed windows, and with cobblestone streets and retro-looking streetlamps.

Before Mom and I had left the house, I had been sitting on the couch in the living-room, anxiously and angrily waiting for Mom to come downstairs. I had kept looking at my wristwatch and yelling, "Come on, Mom! We're going to be late!"

When she came downstairs, finally, I was shocked. She was dressed to kill. She was wearing one of her favorite dresses—a dress of floral design. In her right hand, was the white handle of her white leather purse. She had white leather flat shoes on that matched the purse, as did the white dot clip-on earrings.

I looked like a bum compared to how fancy she was dressed. I was only wearing my jeans, a plaid shirt and my tennis shoes.

Rising from the couch, and meeting her as she reached the bottom step of the stairs, I said, "Why are you so dressed up?"

"Well," she sighed exasperatedly, "what does one wear to meet a killer?"

"I haven't a clue," I replied. I looked at my wristwatch again and said, "Come on. We have to leave."

I got off the highway at the Market Street exit. Market Street is one of the busiest main streets in downtown St. Louis. I didn't get on Market Street. I took a service road that took us past the Arch and then past Laclede's Landing. Laclede's Landing is four blocks long and four blocks wide. Knowing that Wharf Street ran parallel to those four streets of Laclede's Landing, and knowing that I would have to drive past all those four streets to get to Wharf Street, and knowing that 655 Wharf was farther north than Laclede's Landing, I stayed on the service road that I was on until I came to the end of it. Then I turned right, drove past the ends of the four blocks of Laclede's Landing, and then made a left turn onto Wharf Street.

After I had driven a few blocks on Wharf Street, I began looking for the address 655. I'll tell you, though, we had driven no more than a block up Wharf Street when it began to get seedy and dark. The buildings were all abandoned and boarded up with sheets of plywood over the windows and doors. I began to get nervous. Then, about five blocks from having been on Wharf Street, in the near distance, about a half a block away, emanating from a building on the corner of an intersection, was a beacon of bright lights and people milling around the front of the building and some standing in a line on the sidewalk.

There were many cars parked on both sides of the street near that place. I got a parking spot across the street from it, about thirty feet north from it.

The place was like all the rest of the buildings were around there: four or five stories tall, old, red brick buildings. Except that the corner building had been given new life and had been refurbished. Above the ornate-looking, dark-stained wooden entrance to the place was a neon light that kept flashing in red, white and blue lights: **"COMIN' OUT!"**

Sitting in the car with Mom, and staring at that place, I finally said: "Something is very, very wrong here."

"Well," Mom began, "that has to be the place, Tom. There's nothing else around here." She looked through the window of the passenger side and said, "It's too dark. I can't see an address."

"The last address I saw was 649," I said. "Yeah, I think you're right. That must be the place. But it doesn't make sense to me. Why on earth would that person want me to meet him here? This is a restaurant or a bar—and it looks crowded."

"Well," Mom began again, "maybe it's like that old saying, 'In numbers there's safety.' Maybe that person thinks that you won't start any trouble with so many people around."

"Yeah, you could be right … Alright," I then stated, "let's get this over with. Let's go."

We exited the car, crossed the street, and headed for the entrance to that place.

We had gotten in the short line with the others who were also in line to get into the place.

When Mom and I had reached the door of the place, a very well-built, beefy guy with a shaved head and wearing a blue bandana tied around his forehead said, with a lisp in his high-pitched voice, "If she's with you, Sweetie, that will be twenty dollars, ten dollars apiece."

I couldn't BELIEVE that! Ten dollars apiece just to get in there! I paid it, though.

The guy was wearing jeans and a blue T-shirt that had the same writing on it as was on the neon lights: **COMIN' OUT!**

"Say," I said to that guy as I had handed him a twenty. "Does this place serve food?"

"No, we don't, Sweetie," he replied. "Just music, dance and alcohol."

As Mom and I stepped out of the darkness of the outside and into the darkness that was in there, I turned to Mom and said, "Did you hear that jerk keep calling me 'Sweetie'?"

My first impression of the inside of that place was that it wasn't any different than Concord's or that Okay Corral Nightclub—but, boy, was I wrong. I mean, it was like Concord's and that Okay Corral because it had a raised, wooden dance floor in the middle of the room that consumed most of the space. Tables and chairs consumed the outer perimeter of the dance floor against three walls of the room: the fourth wall, the west wall, was a full-length bar, and nestled into the northwest corner of that wall was a DJ's booth. But that is where the comparison, for the most part, ends. It was wild.

The ceiling of the place was of bare rafters of wooden beams and cement beams, with the belly of the wooden floor of the second level of the place showing. Throughout the room, large domes hung from the ceiling on a single strand of wire. These domes were made of tiny squares of mirrors, and from somewhere the multi-colored beams of light would strike the domes and a burst of rainbow colors would shower all.

From the moment that Mom and I stepped inside of there, my ears were immediately deafened by the loudness of the crowd of people—and by the loudness of the music playing. I recognized the first song that I heard. It was that song by Prince: "Let's go Crazy."

As soon as that song by Prince stopped playing, the DJ started speaking over the speaker, saying, "All-righty, girls. Make sure to tip our gorgeous waitresses. They're working so hard to please you. Be generous." Then, he stopped speaking, and that song by Cindy Lauper, "Girls Just Want to Have Fun," began blasting over the speakers.

I didn't know what that DJ had been talking about. The only "waitresses" that I had seen in there, so far, had all been men. They were all carrying round serving trays, and they were all dressed the same: leather, black, dress-shoes; short-short, black shorts; no shirt, just cuffs at the wrists, and a black bowtie held to the neck by an elastic, black strap. And that's when it hit me! That's when I knew. Mom and I were at a gay nightclub.

Not that there was anything wrong with us being there—because there wasn't. If you're gay, you're gay. That's fine. But I was just so confused! I mean, at first, I couldn't understand why that guy had selected such a crowded place to tell me of Jeff's death—but now it was also at a gay nightclub?! And not that there's anything wrong with that! I had just found it all to be so confusing.

The place was so packed with people that Mom and I had to keep moving, and we kept getting shoved, too. We were to the front of the place, between the east wall, which was red brick like all of the walls were, and the dance floor. The many tables and chairs there made it impossible to maneuver with any freedom. Mom was right behind me—and she was so close to me that I could feel her body pressing up against mine. When we had reached about halfway inside the room, I heard Mom shout, "I'm falling!" I spun around just in time to witness the top half of her body smack on top of the table to her right, which was a table by the east wall.

Fortunately, that part of the table on which Mom fell on was absent of people, and there were two empty chairs there. The four or five people who were sitting there stood up, and the man who was nearest to Mom came to her aid.

Placing his slender hands on Mom's shoulders, he helped her straighten up.

"Are you alright, ma'am?" he said to Mom, caringly. He was a good-looking man, with light-brown hair, which was cut short. He was about as tall as me, but he was of a slender build and had soft features, what some people might call a "baby face"; very pleasing to the eye. He was wearing a white, long-sleeved, puffy shirt and yellow dress pants. "Here," he continued to say to Mom, "you sit down for a moment."

He scooted one of the two empty chairs back and helped Mom be seated.

"Thank you, young man," Mom said.

Pointing to the empty chair, which was to the right of Mom, he said to me, most politely, "Please. You sit down too."

I did and let me tell you: I thought that I had sat down at a Village People concert. One guy at the table was dressed like a cop; another guy at the table was dressed as a hard-hat-wearing street worker; another guy was dressed as if he were in the Navy; and then there was Priscilla.

Priscilla sat in the chair to my right. She was short and stocky—almost to the point of being fat, especially around her rotund belly. I couldn't make up my mind about what she was wearing. Either she was trying to be Dorothy from the "Wizard of Oz" or a human-size Raggedy Ann doll, shoulder-length red-colored wig and all. And she was no "lady." Yes, when I had first sat down and had looked at her, I did a double-take, but you can apply all the make-up, red-colored lipstick, fake eyelashes, and rouge that you want, but if you're a man, it will show. And it did. When we all had exchanged introductions with each other, and when she had told me that her name was Priscilla and gave me the back of her right hand to shake, I said to myself: *Lady, if you're trying to be a girl, you should really shave the black hairs from your hands.*

"I just love all of your costumes," Mom said.

The one dressed like a cop said, and I think he had said that his name was Dave, "Who's wearing a costume?"

This got a big laugh from everyone—except me. I was in a bad mood and didn't find anything to be funny.

The guy who had helped Mom, Fredrick, said, "Well, it is Halloween, Lill. But here," he continued, raising up his arms and hands, "we have the freedom to be who we truly are."

They were all drinking red wine. Fredrick had jokingly told Mom that the wine was "sweeter" than anyone at the table. There were three empty glass liters on the table. Fredrick told Mom that he was going to order three more liters of wine and that he would ask the waitress to bring two empty glasses so that Mom and I could have some wine too. But that didn't happen. After Fredrick said that, the song "Boogie Woogie Bugle Boy" by the Andrew Sisters began playing.

"OH!" Mom cried joyously. "That's my song!" She began moving to the beat of that song in her chair.

"Well, Lill," Fredrick said, placing his right hand on top of Mom's left hand. "Should we go 'cut-a-rug'?"

"You bet, Daddio," Mom replied eagerly. "Let's go."

Rising from their chairs, Fredrick said, "Let's all dance. Come on."

Mom gave me a look and I raised my hands dismissively. I was in no mood for dancing.

Sitting now alone at the empty table, I looked around to see if anyone was watching me. No one was. After a few moments had passed, I began to get bored and got up, turned around and walked to the round, waist-high, brass rail that separated the dance floor from the rest of the room. I leaned on the rail and watched as Mom, Fredrick and the rest of them and everybody else danced. Mom was having a great time.

When that song had stopped playing, it was immediately followed by the song "In the Mood" by Glenn Miller. That song was another one of Mom's favorite songs. They all kept dancing.

Suddenly, I felt a presence by my right side. I looked that way and saw a man standing so close to me that our arms were touching. He looked at me looking at him, and nodded hello with a shake of his head. He was about the same weight and height as me, and I would say that he was about the same age as me. His hair was cut short and combed straight back; it was salt-and-pepper in color and matched the small mustache under his thin nose. He was wearing what I would call a Hawaiian shirt; very colorful, and black dress pants, and black slip-on loafers.

To be honest with you, I had no idea if this guy was "the guy" or not. I had never seen that guy before in my life, and he didn't seem like a guy who could kill someone, but you never know. So, I leaned into him and said above the noise of the crowd and above the loudness of the music, "Are you the person who I'm to meet?"

Getting close to my ear, he said, "Yeah, I could be your man. Let's dance."

I had no idea what that meant, but I followed him onto the dance floor. We began dancing in place, very close to each other. After a few moments had passed, I thought: *This is just stupid! I don't even know if this is the guy who I was supposed to meet!* So, I leaned in close to him again and said bluntly, "So, who killed Jeff?"

"What?" he replied, not really able to hear me above the din of voices and above the music. Then, he said, "Oh Jeff. Okay. I'm Richard."

Oh, shit! I cursed. *This is just butt-ass stupid!*

I leaned back into him again, and in his left ear I yelled, "Can't we go somewhere where it's private and we can be alone?!"

"Sure," he replied, more than friendly enough. "Follow me."

I did, thinking: *Well, at least now I'll get some action!*

He led the way to the back of the place, passing beyond the south end of the bar, in which there was a short hallway that led to a heavy-looking, metal exit door at the end of the hallway. On the left side of the hallway, midway down the hallway, on the south wall, were the bathrooms, both for MEN and WOMEN, which surprised me that they would have bathrooms for both men and women, what with it being a gay nightclub and all, but it was probably required, because of it being a public place.

That exit door had a long, horizontal handle to it, and when that Richard guy had reached it, he had to put all of his top weight into it to get it to open. After he did, he held the door open for me and I passed through.

I was outside once again, staring up at the night sky. This must have been an area for deliveries to the place. There were two cracked, unlevel, old strips of concrete that led to an alley. To the north side, the building extended out to that alley, as did a six-foot high red brick retaining wall. There was about a four-foot space in width between the building and that retaining wall.

As soon as Richard had passed through the door, and let it slam shut with a bang, he stepped in front of me and immediately shoved me up against that exit door. Then—then!—he started kissing me and running his roaming hands up and down my butt. Well, needless-to-say, I was shocked and uncomfortable, but I wanted to find out what this guy knew about Jeff's death.

I turned my face away from his lips and said, "Alright, now, who killed Jeff?"

Silence. He just kept trying to kiss me, and then he began licking me on the neck with his tongue.

"Come on, pal," I stated flatly, getting upset and angry. "Answer me. Who killed Jeff?"

More silence. Then—then!—I felt one of his hands TOUCHING me—and you know where!

"Did you call my house this morning?" I asked, getting more upset and damn angry. More silence. "Hey, Pal!" I yelled, pushing him away. "Talk!"

"What's your problem, man?!" he replied, angrily. "You're the one who asked me to come out here. Now, get with it!" He returned to licking my neck—and "touching" me.

This was when I knew that this guy didn't know a damn thing about Jeff's murder. I felt so stupid and violated.

"There's been a terrible mistake here," I said. "Sorry, Pal."

I started to turn around, to leave, but before I could, he grabbed me by the shirt with his left hand and said angrily, "Man, have you been teasing me?! Are you a teaser?! I came out here to get pleased and satisfied." He then brought up his right fist to my face. "Now, do I have to hurt you, or am I going to get pleased and satisfied?"

I reached out and placed my arms around his neck lovingly. Smiling, I slowly and coquettishly began moving my arms and hands down along his chest. When I had reached the middle of his chest, his solar plexus, I placed the palm of my right hand over it. Then, I placed the palm of my left hand on top of my right hand. I shifted my weight to the right, and then shifted back and then suddenly forward, throwing my entire body into it as I thrust the palms of my hands in a hard downward motion. This is called a Tai Chi one-inch punch. As with that guy Tyrone, Richard went flying backwards. He hit the back of his head on that retaining wall and slid down it like the proverbial sack of potatoes. He lay there unconscious.

"There!" I said. "You have been 'touched' and I hope you're 'satisfied.'"

I had then tried to get back into that place by that back door. It was locked, though. I pounded on the door several times, but no luck.

I walked down to the alley and then back around to the front of the building.

There was a different guy standing there at the door, and he wouldn't let me back into the place unless I gave him the ten dollars admission. I told him that I had already paid, that I had just stepped out of the back door to smoke a cigarette. But no deal. If I wanted in, I had to pay ten dollars. I did.

Boy, I was pissed! It had been a complete waste of time; I had been groped—by a man, and on top of everything else, I had to pay another ten dollars to get back into the place. That's thirty dollars I had paid!

And this was so appropriate. The song "Y. M. C. A." by the Village People was blasting away, and on the dance floor, everyone was dancing in a line together. They were all holding on to each other by the shoulder or with their hands around the waist of the person in front of them—and Mom was not only in the parade, she was leading it.

When she saw me, she gave me a big smile and a hearty wave. Being in the shit-mood that I was in, I gave her an angry wave of my right index-finger to COME HERE!

She did.

I stated, angrily and flatly, "Let's go!"

She grabbed her purse off the table, and we left.

Driving back home, I was silent—and still fuming about what had happened and about what hadn't happened. Mom, sensing my anger, remained silent too. But then she finally said, "Well, did you find out anything about the case? I saw you leave with that guy."

"You saw that, did you?" I stated sarcastically.

"Yeah," she said. When I didn't reply, she said, "Well, what did he say?"

"Nothing," I replied. "He didn't know a damn thing. Not a damn thing. It was a complete waste of time."

"I'm sorry, Tom," Mom said. She was silent for another moment and then said, "Was he—aaaah, you know, that word 'funny?'"

"You mean gay?"

"Yes," she replied. "Gay."

"Yes, he was."

"They were all gay back there, weren't they, Tom?"

"You figured that out, did you?" I replied, again flatly.

"Now, don't be mean, Tom," she said, getting a bit angry with me. "I said I was sorry. This is all my fault … But you have to admit that Fredrick and the rest of them were nice—and I had, get this, a 'gay ole time'!"

"Now that I can believe!"

Chapter Twenty-Eight

I awoke the next morning, Tuesday, a little after 7:00 AM, and I felt rested. Boy, had I slept soundly. I have no idea why, but having gone to that gay nightclub, and all that had happened there, and all that had not happened, had really exhausted me. So, when my head hit my pillow, man, I slept.

I didn't do a damn thing Tuesday. I didn't go running or do any investigating on the case or even go that evening to Tai Chi class. I kept thinking—even hoping—that the person would call back: the one who had called the day before and who was going to give me information about who had killed Jeff. I really needed for that person to call back—because I had nothing. I couldn't think of anything else to do that would put me closer to solving who had murdered Jeff. So, I never left the house all day. I just kept waiting for that person to call again.

The person never did—and that day was spent in anxious hope, anxious anxiety, and boredom. It had been one of those days in which the phone had not rang once. Damn it!

The next day, though, Wednesday, at exactly 8:30 AM, the phone began ringing.

Mom and I had been sitting at the kitchen table, eating our breakfast of oatmeal and toast, when the phone started ringing. We exchanged glances of both joy and fear: joy because it might be that person calling back, and fear because, yeah, it might be that person calling back.

Mom had felt so bad about possibly having messed-up that call the other day that she had stated that she wasn't answering the phone again until all of this was resolved.

Feeling very nervous and steeling myself for what I was about to do, I walked over and answered the phone.

Yes, it was that person calling back—and Mom had been correct: The voice on the other end didn't sound human. It was an electronic-produced voice, which had really confused me. I mean, it would have taken someone who had much intelligence and had knowledge of electronics to produce something as high-tech as that, and I couldn't think of anyone that I knew who had that intelligence or skill. For a second, I thought of Master Hu, but quickly dismissed it: That was just crazy!

The voice stated that I was being given one more chance to find out who had killed Jeff. Come to this address tonight at 7:00 PM. And, yes, Mom had gotten the address wrong. It hadn't been 655 Wharf Street, but 955 Wharf Street.

After I had hung up the phone and told Mom what had been said, she threw her arms and hands up in the air, praising Jesus and rejoicing. "Thank you, Lord! You alone are holy! Thank you! ... Are we leaving at six to meet that person?"

Trust me when I say this: I had tried hard to stop Mom from going with me. I just didn't want her going with me—it might turn out to be too dangerous. But she was ADAMANT! She WAS going!

And she did.

Dressed in the same clothes that she had worn the night before: that floral-print dress, white shoes and matching purse—I wore the same jeans and tennis shoes, but a light-blue dress shirt—at exactly 6:00 PM, Mom and I left the house. I took the same route that I had the night before.

There wasn't any difference in the drive there than there had been the other night, until we had passed that gay nightclub. As we passed by it, I thought: *Damn, I wish we were going back in there now.* When we did pass it, I started getting scared—for me, but especially for Mom.

Those three blocks on Wharf Street from that gay nightclub to the place in which we were going sure made a difference. It was a most appropriate place for Halloween. Besides night taking over, it was beginning to rain lightly; the wind was kicking up and howling; the moon was almost full; the buildings—two-centuries old, four-to-six stories tall, red brick buildings with tall, narrow, small-paned windows—were all deteriorating, decaying, dead; doors and windows all boarded up with a sheet of plywood, and not a living thing in sight—not even a stray dog or black cat. It was, in a word, spooky.

Except for the eerie light emanating from the almost full moon, which kept being hidden by slow-moving, dark clouds, the only other light came from the more-often-than-not busted-out, retro-looking (but not "retro"; they were just that old) standing streetlamps that lined both sides of the cracked, uneven, concrete sidewalks.

As I have stated before, in its heyday, all of this section of downtown had been a thriving and prosperous business district; again, back then, mostly in the fur and clothing business. Now, many of those long-forgotten, abandoned buildings had eight-foot-tall chain-link fences and gates surrounding the perimeter to keep out the vandals, the hoodlums, the drug addicts, the drunks, the poor and the homeless.

Our destination, 955, was no different: It was a five-or-six story, old, red brick building, with its front door and most of its windows boarded up with a sheet of plywood, and it had a tall chain-link gate and fence surrounding it.

The building was on the west side of the street. It faced east, facing the abandoned buildings across the street from it and the Mississippi River behind them. The two swinging gates to the place were wide open, as if giving me and Mom an official invitation to enter.

I was uncomfortable about it all. I didn't like it.

There was a parking area in front of the building, upon the once finely-paved cement lot, but I wasn't about to pull my car behind those gates and fence and be trapped inside of there. No way!

So, I drove a bit past the place, turned around in the middle of the street, drove back, and parked on the street in front of the place, just a few feet from the north side of the gate.

For the longest time, Mom and I just sat there in the car, silently, just staring at the place. Finally, Mom broke the silence and said, "Well, I guess that we better get in there, Tom. It has to be getting close to seven o'clock."

After looking at my wristwatch, I said, "Yeah, I guess we better. It's fifteen until seven."

For some reason, Mom decided to leave her purse in the car. We got out of the car and started walking toward the gates.

Above the entrance to the place was a wooden sign. It was much like the sign at Jeff's and Jerry's business—about three feet long and three feet wide; white, with black-painted letters stating: Barlow's Grease Company. I got the feeling that this had been the last business here. By the condition of the sign—now much sun-bleached, worn and grimy—I'd say that it had probably been in business in the fifties.

A sheet of plywood covered the door to the place. It looked as though there had been a padlock attached to the door and to the wooden door-frame, but it had been recently broken off. Taped to the door by two short pieces of scotch tape—in the middle of the door, midway up—was a sheet of white paper. Written on it in block letters from a black marker was: **COME IN. FOLLOW CANDLES!**

For some reason, I ripped that piece of paper from the door, crumpled it up in my hands, and tossed it over my right shoulder.

In that moment, I wished for one thing—and I have never wanted this one thing before as much as I wanted it now—a gun.

Mom was standing beside me to my left. I looked at her. She looked concerned, but not scared.

"Why don't you go back to the car, Mom," I said. "This is too dangerous."

She whispered angrily, "Absolutely not! I'm not afraid of this jerk!" To prove this to me, she reached for the round, rusting, brass handle of the door, turned it and opened the door wide. The door creaked as she opened it. She stepped to the side, and with a sweeping gesture of her right arm and hand, whispered, "After you."

As I passed by her, I said, "Why are you whispering?"

Once inside, Mom let the door shut with a bang. We were suddenly in almost total darkness, and in that moment, I suddenly wished for another thing besides a gun; I wished that I had a flashlight.

I found it cold in there. I had goosebumps, and I can't honestly tell you if the goosebumps were caused from the coldness of the place or from fear.

It had taken several minutes before my eyes adjusted enough to the darkness before I could finally see a bit better.

We were standing in an enormous room that was much cluttered with old furniture; tables and chairs; both wooden and metal desks; machines of some sort—and everything was covered in dust and cobwebs. On the cement floor of the room, there had to be at least an inch of dust covering it. I sneezed three or four times.

About fifteen or twenty feet from where Mom and I were standing, midway, and against the south red brick wall of the room were wide, dark-stained, wooden, old steps. They, too, were heavily covered with dust, and they led to the floors above. Beside the wall of almost every step, sitting on the face of the step, was a lit candle in a glass container—guiding the way, inviting us upstairs.

With it being so dark in there, and not knowing if Mom was having any trouble seeing, I took her right hand in mine, and we then headed for the stairs.

We ascended the first two floors of the building, and on the third floor, the lit candles turned to the left, south, down a narrow hallway. We followed the line of candles. As we walked, passing closed, wooden doors on both sides, our footfalls made squeaking sounds upon the dust-laden, wooden floor.

The candles ended at the last door on the west side of the building.

For a moment, I just stood there, still holding Mom's hand, and just stared at that door. Then, after taking a deep breath and expelling it, I released Mom's hand, grabbed the round doorknob, turned it, and opened the door.

The room was far better lit than the rest of the building had been. There were lit candles everywhere—on the black-and-white tiled, dust-covered floor; on the three or four wooden chairs with arms; on the five-or-six foot tall metal filing cabinet that was shoved up against the northeast corner of the room, and on top of a metallic desk that was to the right of us. It was not a large room at all.

After Mom and I had walked to the middle of the room, I turned around and faced Mom and said, "Well, where is this guy—"

Before I could finish the sentence, though, the door to the room quickly shot open. I caught a brief glimpse of an arm as it threw a white-looking ball into the room, and just as quickly, the door slammed shut.

That ball exploded and the room was quickly filled with white smoke.

I sidestepped Mom and ran to the door. But I didn't make it to the door. Suddenly, I felt weak and light-headed. I heard Mom cry: "Oooooh!" I spun back around and saw Mom fall to the dust-filled floor. I took one step towards her, and then all went black for me. I was gone; unconscious—in Never-Never Land.

Chapter Twenty-Nine

I had awakened hard. I felt like I was in a fog. My mind felt confused, and I had a sharp pain in my head. It took me a few seconds before I remembered where I was and what had happened. Then I saw Mom. She was about three feet from me, facing me. She was still unconscious. Her head was thrown back and her mouth was open—and, like me, she was bound to one of the wooden chairs with duct-tape. The gray duct-tape held both of her arms and hands to the arms of the chair at her wrists, and her legs were bound as well; more duct-tape around her ankles—just like me.

I looked around the room—and that's when I saw it. Sheer panic rose up within me. I was frozen stiff with fear.

On top of the metal desk was a plain-looking alarm clock with large, black numbers on its face. I could see that the alarm was set to ring at eight o'clock, which was in eight minutes. Attached to the clock with more duct-tape were three sticks of dynamite.

"Mom," I called to her. "Mom! Wake up, Mom! ... Mom! Mom, you have to wake up! ... Mom! Mom! Come on, Mom! Wake up! Mom!"

Slowly, she finally began to awaken. She closed her mouth and brought her head up. Then, she opened her eyes.

She shook her head from side to side a few times, as if trying to get cobwebs out of her mind, and said, "Where am I?" She looked down and saw that she was bound to the chair by duct-tape. "What in the hell is this?!" she cried, fuming mad.

"Listen to me, Mom," I said, interrupting her, a sense of urgency and downright fear escaping from my voice. "We have to get out of here—now!" I looked over at the makeshift bomb on top of the desk. "That's a bomb, and it's going to explode in eight—now, seven minutes!"

"Well, get us out of here!" she stated.

"How?" I replied. "We're tied to these chairs! How can we get out?! ... I was hoping that you could think of a way out of this."

"Me?!" she bellowed. "I can't think of anything. You're the brains here—so, think!"

"Think of what?!" I replied.

"Well, think of something, Tom!" Mom cried again, demandingly. "Think of anything. Just get us out of here!"

"I'm so sorry for getting you into this, Mom," I said, giving up. "It's useless. We're going to die …"

"After all of those years of wasting my life," I cried, "I finally have reasons to live—I got money; I'm finally healthy and in shape; I'm dating, and now I'm going to die!"

"Stop your crying, Tom, and get us out of this!" Mom shouted at me angrily. "You're a detective—a famous detective; so, think! Think! Be a man! Get us out of this!"

"Oh, it's hopeless, Mom," I cried again. "I've tried so-so—" I stopped speaking. I thought of something—something Hope, Cindy's kid, had once said to me, about being a man.

Like I have said, Mom was about three feet in front of me, facing me. Hopping and scooting in the chair that I was in, I got it up against the chair that Mom was sitting in. I tried to stand up in the chair and leaned forward. It worked! I fell forward on top of Mom.

"Tom!" Mom screamed. "Have you gone crazy?! What are you doing?!"

With my face buried between Mom's large, sagging breasts, I said, "Now, listen to me very carefully. In the right, front pocket of my pants is my keychain. I'm going to position my body so that you will be able to reach into my pocket with your left hand and remove the keychain."

I shifted the right side of my body until the pocket of my pants was touching Mom's left hand.

"Tom," Mom sighed. "I'm not at all comfortable with this."

"Just do it!" I shouted.

I felt her hand moving in my pocket. Then, I felt that she had the keychain in her hand and was pulling it out.

I turned my face to the right so that I could see and speak more clearly.

"Now, Mom," I said. "Hold that small pocketknife in your hand with the blade-part of it facing up—and whatever you do, don't drop that keychain."

She did as I asked.

I scooted my body down. It was rough doing it, but I managed to do it. I got my mouth right at the blade of that pocketknife. With my teeth, I opened the blade. Mom made another fuss about me moving back up again against her body, but it had to be done.

When I got my right wrist next to Mom's left hand, I said, quickly and emphatically, "Start cutting, Mom, fast!"

She did.

When she had cut halfway through the duct-tape that was holding the right wrist of my arm and hand to the arm of that chair, I yanked my arm hard. It worked! My hand was free. Quickly, I took the pocketknife from Mom and plopped back down in the chair. I freed my left wrist and then freed my ankles. I stood up and glanced over at the alarm clock with the three sticks of dynamite attached to it. Three minutes! Three minutes until it exploded.

I immediately started working on freeing Mom.

Sensing my panic, Mom looked at me and said, "Save yourself, Tom. Go!"

Not even answering her, I worked faster at freeing her. When I had gotten her free, she tried to shoot up out of the chair, but she couldn't do it. She plopped back down heavily into the chair.

"I can't do it, Tom!" she cried. "I can't! GO!"

I moved to her left side. Bending down a bit, I lifted up her left arm and hand. Throwing my right shoulder under her left shoulder, I yanked her up and out of that chair. Dragging her more than helping her to walk—we got the hell out of there!

Being outside of that building was HEAVEN. The cool night air felt so great.

We didn't stop for a moment. I kept dragging Mom. When we made it back to the car, I felt Mom begin to move away from me, probably to get into the passenger's seat of the car.

"No!" I shouted, and I kept dragging her. We passed in front of my car, and by the door on the driver's side, I shoved Mom down and then I squatted down.

"Why are we doing this, Tom?" Mom asked.

And then—BOOM!

Those three sticks of dynamite exploded.

"That's why," I replied. Standing, I said, "Come on. Let's get out of here before the cops and fire department get here."

Driving back home, Mom said, "Well, I'll say this much for you, Tom. When you take a girl out, it's never 'dull.'"

"That's for sure, Mom," I replied. "That's for sure."

Chapter Thirty

I awoke the next morning, Thursday, at a little after 8:30 AM. I had slept hard. By the time Mom and I had got back home and had calmed down our jangled nerves, we were both exhausted. We had both turned in for bed about 9:00 PM.

It was a horrible morning, weather-wise—dark, cloudy and raining hard. Every few moments, it seemed like claps of thunder rocked the house with their heavenly sonic booms.

I was sleepy and still DAMN angry. I had had a tough time, at first, falling to sleep. I had just kept going over and over again in my mind what had happened the night before—now that was a REAL game-changer for me. I had started investigating Jeff's death, was just going to give it a most cursory look into, really just to get Mom off my back about Cindy. Then, when Cindy had told me that Faith believed that I had murdered her father—Well, I had wanted to prove to Faith that I hadn't done it. But, now, NOW, with what had happened the night before: That made this a real game-changer. Yes, Sir! It was bad enough this asshole was trying to kill me—but don't you dare even think about messing with my mother! I wanted justice; I wanted revenge; I wanted to keep pounding and pounding my fist into this person's face. I wanted blood.

After drinking my second cup of coffee at the table in the kitchen, I walked to the front door and got the morning newspaper. It had stopped raining, but the newspaper was toast, soaking wet and beyond being readable—which angered me. I had wanted to see if there had been anything in the paper about that bomb having exploded in that building. I had thought about turning the TV on, but I just didn't feel like doing that. I went back into the kitchen and had another cup of coffee.

Close to 10:00 AM, Mom comes dragging herself into the kitchen, in much need and want of coffee. About ten minutes later, and two cups of coffee later, she asked me if I was hungry. Wanting to be healthy, Mom and I usually have hot oatmeal and toast for breakfast, but because of what had taken place the night before, Mom wanted something a bit heartier than just oatmeal. We had scrambled eggs, bacon and toast—and it was good, too.

I did the clean-up of the plates, pans and such after we had finished eating. Mom went upstairs to get washed and dressed. She was going down to the nursing home that Dad's in and feed him lunch and visit with him awhile. Then, at 1:30, she had a prayer meeting at the church. I told her that I wasn't going anywhere, so I didn't mind cleaning up.

After Mom had left, I got damn bored. I didn't know what to do—about the case or anything! I just couldn't think of anything. Most of me kept hoping that the person would call back and give me another chance to meet up with him, or her, again. And this time it would be different. This time—no Mom; this time, I'd have a gun or a knife or something; this time would be the end: we would fight to the death.

But that never happened. The morning simply dragged on, in BOREDOM, into the late afternoon. I even went for a run. It helped. The sun was out, but because of raining in the morning, it was cool. Many of the autumn-colored leaves of the tall maple trees that line both sides of the streets in our old neighborhood had been ripped from the trees by the heavy rain, and the trees now looked empty and embarrassed by their sudden nakedness.

Mom got back home about three o'clock. I was glad that she was back. I was just so damn bored—and getting damn antsy, nervous, depressed and angry. Well, I wanted all of this to be over; I wanted to get to the bottom of all of this; I wanted to know who this person was; I wanted answers and I wanted them right NOW! That was it! I was fed up with it all! ... Mom made meatloaf for supper. ... But do you know what I suddenly wanted most of all?! Sex. Yeah, I was suddenly going crazy for the want of it. I ached; I burned; I needed it and wanted it—and I knew (or at least, I had hoped so) where I could get it. Cindy!

Chapter-Thirty-One

Now, come on. Don't judge me. I'm a man like any other man: I have needs—and wanting sex is one of them. So, don't judge.

By the time Mom and I had supper and I had bathed, shaven, and had changed clothes—wearing my jeans and a plaid dress shirt—and had said goodbye to Mom, it was almost 6:20 PM.

I told Mom that I was going to the library to do some investigating of Jeff Farmer's financial and property records, hoping that in doing that I might get a new angle on the case. Of course, that was all bullshit. I don't even know if libraries carry such things as personal financial and property records. It had sounded good saying it, though, and Mom seemed to have bought it. With a look of doubt on her face, she had told me to be careful and I had told her that I'd be back home about ten.

I had always told myself that I would never bother Cindy during the week—what with her being busy with work, her kids, and going to school one evening a week, but I didn't care. I needed a much-needed diversion from all that I had gone through—I needed Cindy's hot body and animalistic passion for sex. That's what I needed, and that's what I was going to try and get.

Cindy had told me that the accounting class that she took at Meramec Community College on Thursday evenings was from 6:00 to 9:00 PM. Not knowing if she had not gone because of Jeff's death, and because of being concerned about Faith and her other kids and all, I had first swung by her home to see if she had gone or not. She had. Her white Ram pickup truck wasn't there, not in front of her house or parked in her driveway. Not stopping in front of her house, I proceeded to drive to Meramec Community College.

Getting back on Lindbergh Boulevard, I drove west on it until I had come to Big Bend Boulevard. Once there, I turned left and drove a block down to Geyer Street.

Meramec Community College is a fairly large community college. I would say that it's a block long and a block wide, with four or five parking lots—at each end, east, west, south and north. Not knowing in which building her accounting class was located, I slowly drove through each parking lot, looking for her pickup truck. My goal had been to park my car as close as I could to her vehicle and just wait for her, and then plead with her to be with me for a short time—that I was so worried about her and that I cared so much for her—while secretively hoping, praying, that she would invite me to sit in the cab of her truck; that she would begin smoking coke; that she would get as horny as hell, and that we'd have some hot, nasty, animal, dirty, filthy sex. Oh, yeah.

But that didn't happen. No.

When I had got fed up with looking for her pickup truck—and never finding it!—I decided to park in the Visitors' Parking and go to the Registrar's Office and find out the building and the room of that accounting class that Cindy was taking.

At the Registrar's Office, I stepped through the open glass door of it into a large, long, brightly-lit office—brightly lit from the multiple florescent lights from the drop ceiling. The room was packed with desks from the front to the back wall. Directly in front of me was a waist-high barrier that separated students and visitors from the workers on the other side. I leaned over and placed my arms and hands on top of the Formica-top of the barrier or counter. There were three or four young people there—probably students working part-time for extra money.

"Can I help you?" said the young lady who was seated at a desk nearest to me. She had been staring into the screen of a computer that was on top of the desk.

As she rose to meet me, I said, "Yes. My girlfriend, Cindy Farmer, is here taking an accounting class. She called me. One of her tires seems flat, but I can't remember the building or the room in which she had told me to meet her."

The girl had shoulder-length blonde hair and the most beautiful blue eyes that I had ever seen before—she was just strikingly gorgeous. She stepped three or four feet to my left, to a computer there on top of the counter. After a few seconds of typing, and then viewing the screen, she said, "No, there isn't any accounting class tonight … What did you say her name is again?"

"Cindy," I replied. "Cindy Farmer."

She began typing on the keyboard again. Then, she viewed the screen again. "No," she then stated. "There's nobody even registered as a student here by that name."

My mind began racing. After a moment, I said, faking it, "Boy, I'm getting stupid; just plain stupid. This is Meramec College, isn't it? She said Jefferson Community. I'm sorry. I'm just getting stupid."

"No problem," she replied.

I turned around and left—fuming angry! … Well, I sure had no desire for sex anymore.

She had lied to me—and if she had lied about taking that class, what else had she lied about?!

Tomorrow, I vowed. Tomorrow I would find out! Tomorrow would be D-Day. Tomorrow the truth would be told. Tomorrow that low-life bitch would tell me the truth, or I'd beat it out of her. Tomorrow!

Chapter Thirty-Two

Yesterday, Friday, October 30th, I had awakened feeling good. The morning sun had come shining brightly through my bedroom window, beckoning me to rise and meet the day—and I was determined to do just that. Oh, don't get me wrong. I was still fuming angry about the night before; about finding out that Cindy had lied to me; had all that time been lying to me, but I was resolved, determined, and just plain damn angry enough to face her and find out everything.

I had got back home about 9:20. I had driven around for a while, thinking and trying to cool down. When I had entered the front door, I found Mom on the couch in the living-room, watching TV and waiting up for me. She had immediately asked me what I had found out at the library about Jeff. I lied to her and told her that it had been a complete waste of time; that I had found out nothing. With a look of doubt and suspicion on her face—Mom's no dummy!—she said nothing, which had pleased me. Mom had been through enough. After what had happened Wednesday evening—that bomb!—I just didn't want to involve Mom anymore, in any of this. I had made the decision not to inform her about my resolve to have it out the next day with Cindy. That damn low-life!

I would keep my silence about this showdown with Cindy. Mom usually left the house about eleven to go down and feed Dad and spend time with him. I would wait until she left, and then I would call Cindy and DEMAND to meet with her. Now! Today! This minute!

I felt like a run. So, that's what I did. I went for a long, slow run.

When I got back home from my run, Mom was up. She was in the kitchen, drinking her morning coffee. We had hot oatmeal and toast for breakfast.

The morning dragged on, or maybe it just seemed to because I was getting so anxious and nervous about my intended confrontation with Cindy. Anyway, I stayed in my bedroom most of the rest of that morning, mostly lying on my bed and trying to make some sense of all of this. What had Cindy been doing all of those Thursday evenings if she hadn't been attending an accounting class at Meramec? ... And had she been alone or with someone? ... Now, it was beginning to make a little more sense to me ... What if the guy—or guys!—she was seeing—giving that jerk, or jerks, the same good sex that she was giving me—got so enraged by this that he, or they, wanted me dead? … Could all of this have been nothing more than a jealous lover wanting revenge? First, killing Jeff, and then wanting me dead for having slept with Cindy? —And did she know about it and want it done, too?

At 10:30, I washed, shaved, and then returned to my bedroom and changed clothes, dressing in my jeans and a nice, cotton, long-sleeved, brown shirt. I had rolled up the sleeves of the shirt.

From the hallway, Mom said that she was leaving. She asked me if I was going anywhere and I told her that I didn't think so, that I was just going to stay around the house.

She left.

I waited about ten minutes after she had left, and then I left my room and headed downstairs.

As I descended the stairs, the front doorbell rang and was then immediately followed by knocking on the door, loudly and heavily.

Who the hell could this be?! I cursed silently.

I opened the door and cursed even more. It was Detective Carpenter! He was wearing a dark-blue suit and matching tie. I'll say this much for him, he's a snappy dresser—and he smelled good, too.

"What do you want?" I said flatly and bluntly, not in any mood for his crap.

"Where were you last night, Mayor, between seven and ten o'clock?" he asked matter-of-factly.

The bright sun was beating down on me, and I had to shade my eyes with my right hand.

"I'm not going to lie to you," I replied. "I was out, alone, driving around in my car. Why?"

With his arms and hands, he spread the sides of his suit coat back and then placed his hands on his slender, well-built hips, defiantly.

"Jerry Farmer was found dead in his apartment last night."

"What?!" I replied, totally taken by surprise—and shocked. My mind started racing. "You think that he was murdered?—and you think that I did it?!"

"At this point," Detective Carpenter began, "it looks like suicide—but I'm not ruling anything out. It was done with his own weapon—a bullet to his left temple from a .38 revolver. Plus, a suicide letter. In it, he stated that he no longer wanted to live with Jeff having been murdered, and with his killer still being free—and that would be you. He said so.”

I rubbed my forehead with my hand and then said, “How did you know that he had killed himself? I mean, how did you find out that he was dead?”

“An anonymous tip,” Carpenter replied. “A woman called it in. We tracked the number to a pay phone at a bar called ‘The Water Hole’ in the city, near Grand Street.”

Oh, my, God! I cried, silently. That was the name of that bar that Cindy had told me that Jeff and Jerry frequented often. What did all of this mean?! Now, I was totally confused. I didn’t know what to think—and then I suddenly thought of something else.

“Say, Detective Carpenter,” I began slowly. “May I ask you a question?”

“Go ahead,” he replied, staring at me intently and suspiciously.

“You said that Jerry’s gunshot wound was to the left temple— and not the right temple, right?”

“Yeah, that’s right,” he replied.

“Did you read that suicide letter?” I then asked.

“Yes, I did,” he said. “Look here, Mayor. What-what are you getting at?”

“Could you read the letter, Carpenter?” I persisted. “Was the letter readable—not chicken scratch?”

“Yeah, it was readable,” he stated, looking as if he was getting angry and exasperated with me. “What’s with all the questions, Mayor? I ask the questions. What gives?”

“Well, far be it from me to interfere with your investigation, Detective,” I stated, with a shake of my head, “but Jerry Farmer didn’t commit suicide—you have another murder on your hands.”

Staring at me, hard, after a few moments, he said, “What makes you say that?”

“The guy was a ‘Jesus Freak.’ He didn’t do anything with his left hand anymore: The left hand is the work of the devil.”

“And you know this about him—because?” he asked sarcastically.

"Because he told me," I replied. "He was sending you a message—a message that he was being forced to write that suicide letter, and that he was being forced to kill himself."

"Would you by chance happen to know who that 'someone' is?" he asked.

"No," I replied. "I don't."

For the longest time, Carpenter just kept staring at me, as if he were having trouble taking it all in, and what he should do about it all and me. Finally, he said, "I'll get back with you, Mayor—don't leave town." He turned around and walked away.

He had parked on the street behind my car. I waited until he drove away before I dashed out to my car. Before getting into my car, I removed my old flip-cell phone from my back pocket. I then got into my car, flipped open my phone, and with a shaking right forefinger, I dialed Cindy.

D-Day was here. The truth must, finally, be known.

Chapter Thirty-Three

Her cell phone must have indicated to her that it was me who was calling, because, first, I heard a lawnmower being shut off, and then I got a very angry and flat, "Hello?"

"Cindy!" I said quickly and emphatically, "Tom. I got to speak with you."

"Tom, I'm working," she replied flatly. "I can't talk right now."

"No, that's no good, Cindy," I stated adamantly. "Detective Carpenter was just here, and he—"

"Yes," she said, cutting me off angrily. "He was at my front door at seven o'clock this morning."

"Oh, so you know about Jerry?" I asked.

"Yes," she stated, angrily and flatly again.

"So, we have to talk, Cindy," I said emphatically.

"What about?!" she replied angrily.

"'What about'?!" I cried. "Cindy, we're both in trouble. I think Carpenter is getting ready to arrest either you or me—or both of us."

"Me?!" she cried. "Why would he arrest me?! I didn't do nothing."

"Well, you," I began, but then stopped. "Look," I said, beginning again. "Where are you? I got to speak with you—now!"

It was obvious to me that she hadn't wanted to tell me, but she did. I told her to stay there and that I would be there as soon as possible.

Cindy was in Fenton, which is about fifteen miles southwest from our house. I got on Highway 270 and traveled west. At Highway 44, I began travelling south. I exited at Bowles Avenue and drove to Williams and Larkins Road. I made a right onto it and began driving east. Yorkshire Estates subdivision was a mile down, on my right side. Boy, was it a beautiful subdivision, too—new and expensive-looking. I would say that it was probably about fifteen years old, and I'd also say that a house there was probably about two-hundred-thousand dollars. Two-story brick houses—red brick; beige-color brick; white brick—with multiple roofs to each house, and dormers, and such; all on pristine, well-maintained lawns of half-an-acre.

The street was a cul-de-sac, and Cindy had told me that she was cutting the lawn of the house that was three houses away from the end on the right side of the street.

As I approached the end of the cul-de-sac, I saw her white Ram pickup truck parked on the street in front of a house. I pulled up behind her trailer and parked.

Cindy was standing on the passenger's side of her vehicle. With her back to the door, she was leaning up against her truck, wiping her face with a white towel. She was wearing beige shorts, a short-sleeve denim shirt, and brown leather work boots. When she saw me pull up, she opened the door to her truck and tossed that white towel on the seat.

I got out of my car, and when I came abreast of her, she said real sarcastically, "Well, what's so damn important that you just had to talk with me—'now!?'"

Looking directly into her face, I said, "First, get rid of 'the attitude'. I don't need that. Second, where were you last night? —And don't tell me you were at Meramec! You're not even a student there. I checked."

She seemed stunned that I knew that. It hit her hard, like a punch to the face. She recovered quickly, though, and stated, again most sarcastically, "Well, ain't you such a 'famous detective.'"

"Again," I said, "lose 'the attitude'. So, where were you last night?"

Angrily, she said, "That's none of your fuckin' business!"

"Yes, it is 'my business' when I'm the prime suspect in not one murder," I stated angrily, holding up two fingers of my right hand, "but two murders … So, where were you last night?"

With her right arm stretched out, and pointing to my car, she said, "Why don't you get the hell out of here?!"

Wagging the index-finger of my right hand at her angrily, I said, "I'm not going anywhere until you tell me where you were last night!"

She got in my face, and baring her teeth in an angry grin, stated, "You want me to make you get the hell out of here?!"

"You got bad breath," I said flatly. "So, where were you last night?"

She stepped back, but was silent.

"Again, where were you last night, Cindy?" I repeated.

"I was at South County Mall, shopping! Okay?!"

"You're a liar, Cindy!" I shouted. "I don't believe you … So, where were you?! Where were you?! Where were you?! Tell me! Tell me! Tell—"

"I was at a hotel!" she screamed. "I was at a hotel!"

"With whom, Cindy?!" I said quickly. "Who were you with?!"

She was silent, but she seemed to be struggling with herself. I pressed on.

"Tell me, Cindy! Who? Who were you with?! Tell me! Tell me! Tell me! … Cindy! Tell me!"

"No one," she finally said, shaking her head. "No one. He never showed up."

"Who? Who never showed up?"

"Jerry," she said, simply. "Jerry."

"Do you mean to tell me that you've been sleeping this whole time with Jerry?!" I asked, shocked.

Quietly, and as if a calm of an overwhelming weight had been suddenly lifted from her shoulders, she said, "Yes. We have an eternal bond."

"What in the hell does that even mean?" I asked. "What does—" Then, I thought of something. "Is Faith Jerry's kid?"

She nodded yes.

"This just keeps getting better and better," I said mockingly. Then—THEN!—I thought of something else. "Did you call the police last night about Jerry from that bar—that Water Hole?"

She nodded her head again, yes.

"I didn't know what to do," she began. "Jerry always showed up. I kept calling him, but he never answered. I got worried. I drove to his apartment. I have a key." She was silent for a second, and then she said, placing her hands over her mouth, "I saw him. I saw him at the kitchen table. Dead. I ran. I passed the bar, and I thought that the police should know about him being dead. I called."

Looking straight at her, I said, "Lady, you're on your own. I'm done. I've had it with you."

I turned around and began walking away. No, I didn't get very far. I heard her crying, hard. I turned back around. Man, she was really bawling. She was holding herself, with her arms and hands wrapped tightly around her stomach.

Through her tears, she said, "I'm losing everything. Jeff's gone. Jerry's gone … I-I caught Faith cutting herself … My-my baby is cutting herself! … Why?! … Why is all this happening?! Why?! … Don't leave me, Tom! Love me. I need love."

Having said that, she ran to me, threw her arms around my neck and began kissing me on the mouth, hard.

I kissed her back—well, it felt good. She gave me tongue, too.

Finally, pushing her back at arm's-length, I said, "Do you want me to love you?"

She nodded her head yes.

"Then, you do exactly what I tell you to do. First, get on your cell phone and call the Mayo Clinic. I'll pay all of your bills. I'll pay everything. Just get on your phone and get that kid in that clinic before it's too late. Do it now, Cindy. This minute. Call."

She removed her cell phone from the back pocket of her shorts, turned around, and walked to the front of her truck. I guess she wanted some privacy. She was on the phone for about twenty minutes. After she had hung up, she walked back to me and said, "Well, it's done. We have to be there Monday at nine … I guess we'll leave Sunday."

"That's great, Cindy," I replied. "I'm proud of you." Thinking, I then said, "Say, Cindy. Did Carpenter ask you where you were last night?"

"Yes, he did."

"What did you tell him?"

"That I went shopping at the mall. Why?"

"What hotel did you go to last night?"

"The Hampton Inn on Lindbergh."

"How did you pay? Cash?"

"No," she replied, curious. "They don't take cash. I used my credit card. Why?"

"That perfect!" I exclaimed. "How did you check-in? What name did you use?"

With a shrug of her shoulders, she said, "Mine. I used my name."

"That's perfect!" I repeated, jumping up and down in place. "We have an alibi … Now, my phone is old, but I can take pictures and I can reset the date on it for any date I want. We're going back to that hotel right now. We're going to try and get the same room that you had last night, telling the person at the front desk what a great time we had in that room. Then, we're going to get naked, get in bed and take pictures. This way we have proof of where we were Thursday night, and if Carpenter should ask why we both lied, we just say that because of Jeff's death, we didn't want your kids to know that we were still seeing each other."

"Okay," she replied. "That sounds great."

"You drive, and I'll follow you in my car," I said. "Before we go to the hotel, I first want to stop at your bank. I want to transfer some money into your account."

Cindy placed her arms around my neck again. Looking at me so lovingly, she said, "Thank you so much for all of this, Tom. It really means a lot to me." She started to kiss me, but stopped suddenly. She placed her right hand over her mouth and said, "Do I really have bad breath?"

"No," I replied, smiling. "No."

We began kissing again.

Chapter Thirty-Four

Before we went to the hotel, we first stopped at Cindy's bank. There, I had fifteen thousand dollars transferred from my bank account into her checking account. After doing that, we went to the Hampton Inn. We were able to get the same room that Cindy had gotten Thursday evening. We did all of the things that I had said had to be done to give us an alibi—getting naked; getting in bed; taking pictures—and, boy, we had sex. It was GOOD!

I had gotten back home shortly before 5:00 PM, and the moment that I opened the front door, I could smell it. I knew what Mom and I were having for supper—bean soup. I could smell the earthy, pungent aroma of the big pot of it wafting from the kitchen. This was fine with me. I like bean soup. We have it on Fridays a lot. Although the Catholic religion years ago stated that it wasn't a sin to eat meat on Friday, Mom and Dad had gotten so used to not eating meat on Friday that they just kept observing and having 'Meatless Fridays.'

As I have said, that bean soup was delicious: I had two bowls of it, with three or four slices of bread—with lots of butter on them.

Feeling a bit stuffed, and as Mom was finishing the dishes in the kitchen, I slipped into the living-room, plopped down heavily onto the couch, and was about to turn on the TV, when Mom called out to me, "There's a letter there for you from Mr. Green. See it? It's right there on the end table, under the lamp."

I was sitting at the south end of the couch. The end table was right next to me. Seeing the letter on the end table, I replied to Mom, "Yes. I see it. Thanks."

As you know, Mr. Green is my CPA. That letter, I had assumed, was probably just a statement about one of my stocks or bonds. I didn't give it much thought—but, wow! That letter changed everything. Isn't life just like that? Everything can change, suddenly, in a moment. And it did.

Now, I want to apologize to you right now. I mean, you all have been kind enough to listen to my story for this long, and I'm going to reveal to you who is responsible for the killings and responsible for all that has happened—and it's not going to be very dramatic. Well, at least, not as dramatic as those two murders that I had solved for Claire. Now, the ending of that case had been dramatic; a "Thin Man" movie dramatic! But this is life, and not all things in life are dramatic. Please, though, stick with me. I promise you that I'll try to make the rest of my story as interesting as I can. I promise.

Anyway, I mindlessly ripped open the letter and began reading it. I didn't get far in reading, though, before my stomach tied up in knots; my body froze in shock; my mind raced for meaning and comprehension and less confusion—and then I just got boiling angry!

In the letter, Mr. Green stated that on Monday he had received the forms for my request of a 'change of beneficiary' of all my financial assets upon my death. This, he had stated, he was more than willing to do, but he wanted more confirmation from me, either in person, a letter, or a phone call. He questioned why I was changing my beneficiary from my mother to a person whom I had never spoken of before—a Mr. Singh Hu.

Son-of-a-bitch! In that one crazy moment of thought, I had been right all along. It had been Master Hu! That son-of-a-bitch. That fake! That charlatan! I couldn't BELIEVE it! I wanted blood.

Okay, okay. His motive for doing all of this, obviously, had been to get my money—which was dumb of him at best. Had he truly thought that he could get away with doing something like that?! Dumb. Okay, okay. I can forgive that. I can forgive him for killing Jeff and Jerry. I can even forgive him for trying to kill me, but—and I have said this before—DON'T MESS WITH MY MOTHER! That I would not forgive. Okay, he had been a government agent. Okay, he was a Kung-Fu Master. Okay, okay, okay. But I wanted blood. He would pay for what he had tried to do to Mom—or I would die trying!

I heard Mom walking across the kitchen. I quickly returned the letter to the envelope, folded it, and shoved into the pocket of my shirt. Mom came into the living-room. She scooted past me, in between the coffee table and the couch, and sat down.

"Well," she said. "Is there anything good on TV tonight?"

"That Halloween comedy is on tonight, Mom," I replied. "You know, that 'Ernest Scared Stupid.' It doesn't come on until eight, though. We could watch the news and 'Jeopardy' first."

"Okay," she replied.

This didn't last long, though. I couldn't take it. I just kept moving and turning in place as I sat—or tried to sit—on the couch. My skin was crawling, writhing, with volcanic anger. About five minutes into it, I exploded.

"Mom!" I cried. "I have to leave. There's something I have to do."

I started to rise from the couch, but Mom placed her right hand on my left arm.

She looked me in the face and said, "You have solved the case, haven't you, Tom?"

"Well," I replied, nodding my head, "I know who did it."

"Who?" she asked.

"I don't want to say just yet, Mom."

"But you want to confront him?"

"Yes."

"Oh, Tom," she said, shaking her head. "Why? Let the police handle this."

"I can't, Mom," I replied. "I can't. I have to look him in the eye and tell him that he's going to pay for what he did. I just have to do this, Mom."

After a moment of deep silence and deep thought, she said, "Be careful, Tom. Be real careful."

I leaned in and kissed her on the cheek, saying, "I will."

Once outside, when I had gotten about halfway down the sidewalk, I felt the urge to look behind me. I turned around and saw Mom standing at the living-room window; the same window in which we had strung those miniature Halloween lights of orange pumpkins. She waved at me and I waved back at her. There was a sense of finality to that wave of hers. It was as if she knew that she had to let go—like a mother bird, not wanting to, but knowing that this was long overdue—gently coax, push the tardy baby-bird from the nest. Fly away, little bird, and live your life, not mine.

Chapter Thirty-Five

I pulled my car into the parking lot that was behind the building of Master Hu's studio. It was a small parking lot—probably could hold no more than ten cars. I had hoped to find his blue VW parked there. No such luck. The only car parked there was an old, yellow convertible Ford Mustang. I knew that car belonged to Micky. Damn. I hated that prick.

I decided to go inside anyway. My goal now was to find Master Hu's home address and go there. I knew that he had an apartment that was near the studio, but I didn't know the address. He never locked the door to his office, and perhaps if I searched through the drawers of his desk, I could find something, like a bill, that had his address on it. I hoped so.

The glass front door to the studio was unlocked. Micky, like me, had a key. I entered the building.

I stood at the entrance. Master Hu's Office was just an arm's-length away from me, to my left. I looked at the clipboard on the door-frame to his office—at the sheet of paper on the clipboard of private lessons with Master Hu. It stated that Master Hu had a private lesson with Micky at 6:30 PM, Friday, which was seventeen minutes ago. No Master Hu was in sight.

Micky was on the wooden floor of the studio, dressed in his white Gi, with his green cloth belt wrapped around his waist. He was practicing his Tiger movements. His back was to me. Micky had once bragged that Master Hu had invited him to his apartment to discuss life and such.

I took several steps towards him.

"Hi, Micky," I said in a friendly manner.

He stopped, turned around, looked at me, nodded "Hi" back at me and then started practicing his movements again. I took a few more steps towards him.

"Is Master Hu around?" I asked.

Without stopping, he replied flatly, "You don't see him, do you?"

"Say, Micky," I then began. "Did Master Hu have class last night?"

"No," he replied. "He was a no-show."

"I need to get in touch with Master Hu, Micky," I said. "It's important. What's his home address?"

"I'm not your secretary," he started, with a smart-ass attitude. "Get a phonebook."

That was all I needed, man. I wasn't in any mood to take someone's crap.

I moved parallel with him.

"You're nothing but an arrogant, self-centered, rude punk, Micky," I yelled at him. "Master Hu has been more than kind and patient with you because I think he sees a lot of who he was in you and hoped that you'd change. You won't. You're a punk."

He stopped, turned to me, and gave me 'the middle finger' with his left hand.

I removed my tennis shoes and socks. I stepped upon the raised, wooden floor, and said, "Alright. It's about time someone taught you a lesson—and that's going to be me. We fight. If I win, you tell me Master Hu's home address; if you win, I'd write you a check for one thousand dollars. Are you 'man' enough to accept the challenge?"

"Let's do it," he replied eagerly.

I came abreast of him. We bowed. When we straightened up, we began circling around each other, feeling each other out. He crouched into a Tiger stance. I turned to my right side, and began making long, graceful, sweeping moves with my arms and hands. He brought his arms and hands out to his sides, exposing his chest. I took advantage of this and gave a side kick to his chest with my right leg and foot. It had been a trap. He blocked my kick with his left arm and punched me, hard, in the solar plexus with the open palm of his right hand. I went sailing back, with the wind knocked out of me. I didn't fall, thank God. I quickly recovered. He threw a front kick at me. I blocked it with my left arm and hand, and he brought up his other leg and kicked me in my left kidney. I bent over in pain. He grabbed my right arm in his hands and spun me across the room. My back hit a section of the mirrors of the north wall, shattering it. With the open palm of his left hand, he hit me in the nose.

Man, I told myself. *Stop fighting this guy. He's beating the crap out of you!*

He immediately kicked at me again. I spun to my left. The bottom of his foot hit that shattered mirror. Shards of it fell to the wooden floor.

I moved out to the center of the floor again, Micky on my heels. We squared off again.

Do nothing! I told myself. *Wait for him to make the move. Wait!* I did.

A few seconds later, Micky made a move. He acted like he was going to bring up his left leg and kick me. This time, I didn't fall for it. I knew that when I tried to block that kick, he would bring up the other leg and kick me. When I saw his left leg come up, I acted like I was going to block it. I didn't. Instead, I waited until he brought up his right leg. I went under the leg, first, with my arm and hand; then, with my body now under his body, I sprang up—throwing him on his back on the wooden floor.

He cried out in pain, "Oh, my back! My back!"

I straddled on top of him. Grabbing the one side of his Gi with my left hand, I began punching him in the face with my right hand. After about the fourth punch, I saw blood spewing from his nose. He must have felt it, because he cried, "Enough! You win! Enough!"

"Master Hu's address, Micky," I demanded. "Now!"

He told it to me, and I left.

It had felt great repeatedly punching that prick in the face. Yeah, I know that I was just taking all of my frustrations and anger out on Micky. While I had been punching him, I was seeing Master Hu's round, flat face. Well, he had tried to kill Mom, and I was so devastated. I mean, I had thought so much of the guy—his knowledge of life; his philosophy; his knowledge of Buddhism, and such. What a disappointment. What a fraud! Horrible. Horrible. Oh, well. I guess that's why you should never put someone on a pedestal—they will always let you down. Damn being human.

Anyway, I got back home a little after 7:30. Mom was in the living-room on the couch, waiting for me.

I sat down on the couch next to her. She was so overjoyed to see me, safe. I told her that it had been a complete waste of time, that I had not found him, which had not been a lie. I hadn't found him. After I had left the studio, I felt tired. I told myself that I would start again tomorrow, and that's what I told Mom—that I would look for him again tomorrow.

"For now, though," I said to Mom, "let's have some laughs. Let's watch that Halloween movie, that 'Ernest Scared Stupid.'"

We did. It did my heart much good to see Mom laughing and enjoying that movie. I had enjoyed watching it, too. But not as much as she had. I just kept wanting tomorrow to come. I just kept repeating that, silently: *Come on tomorrow. Come on tomorrow. Tomorrow. Tomorrow. Tomorrow.*

Chapter Thirty-Six

Tomorrow came. Today. Saturday, October 31st. Halloween. Halloween, a day when happy-go-lucky, innocent children dress up, wearing costumes and masks for play, for fun, for show, for candy. They shall pretend to be something they are not—a ghost; a werewolf; a vampire; a witch; Richard Nixon. All in the name of good, wholesome fun. No harm in any of that. Not like Master Hu at all. The costume and mask he wore was for deception, dishonesty, fraud and murder. I would demask him and reveal his true identity to the world—a phony, a fraud, a murderer. I would make him pay; hurt him; even kill him, if I could. Today was the day. Halloween.

Last night, I had told myself that I would give myself a treat; that I would not rise early, and I didn't. I didn't rise until 8:00 AM. I washed, shaved and got dressed: wearing my jeans, a light-brown shirt, and my tennis shoes.

When I entered the kitchen, I found Mom already there, dressed for the day—wearing her black stretch pants, a white blouse, and black leather comfortable shoes. She was sitting at the table, reading the newspaper and drinking a cup of coffee. A tall glass of orange juice had already been poured for me.

"Good morning, Tom," she said heartily as I entered.

"Morning, Mom," I replied, walking past her and to the counter to get a cup from above the counter and then pour myself a cup of coffee from the coffeepot.

"Are you still planning to do what you said last night that you were going to do today?" she asked.

"Yes," I said, pouring myself a cup of coffee.

"Well, then," she replied, with a heavy sigh. "You had better have a good breakfast."

Mom made us eggs, bacon and toast. It was hearty and delicious.

I left the house at 10:00 AM. Mom walked me to the front door. Just before I opened the door to leave, she said, "Be careful, Tom, and come back home—and remember, Tom. It's God's job to pass judgment on sinners; not yours."

"I will, Mom," I said. I kissed her on the cheek and left.

And so, the day began.

The weather wasn't too bad. It was a bit cloudy, but there was a cool, refreshing breeze to the fall air. I wondered if it would rain this evening. I hoped not. What with the kids Trick-or-Treating.

The address Micky had given me was just several blocks north of the studio, on Kingshighway.

It was an 'okay' neighborhood. An entire block of old, two-or-three-story, red brick buildings that were all apartments. The building of Master Hu's apartment was on the south corner of the block. The parking lot for it was to the back of the building, but I just parked on the street in front of the building. The building was divided into eight apartments, four on the first floor and four on the second floor. Master Hu's apartment was B2, second floor.

The wooden door to his apartment was painted a light beige. A plain-looking door.

Standing in front of it, I wasn't frightened at all. I took a deep breath, expelled it, and began pounding on the door with the palm of my right hand, which was clenched in a fist. I stopped and waited for an answer. When several minutes had passed, and no answer, I began pounding upon the door again. Still no answer.

The door had a deadbolt lock to it, which was about three inches above the doorknob.

I looked to my right, and then to my left, down the hallway, and not seeing anyone, I turned the right side of my body to the door and then gave it a side kick with my right leg. The inner doorframe flew off with a cracking sound and the door opened wide. Cautiously, I walked inside, shutting the door behind me.

It was a simple apartment, sparely furnished—to meet the needs of a man living a simple life. In the living-room, a couch, an end table next to the couch, with a phone on top of the end table: the phone had a built-in answering machine to it. In the kitchen, a small, wooden table with three matching chairs. In the bedroom, a single-size bed, with two pillows and a brown bedspread covering the bed. On top of the bed was a laptop. In the closet of the bedroom, I found few clothes. Yeah, the place was simple and spare. There wasn't a TV or a radio or pictures—or anything. About the only 'luxury' that I could see was that throughout the apartment, in large Terra-cotta pots, were mums: red ones; yellow ones; purple ones and on and on. My overwhelming impression of the place—it screamed it!—was of loneliness; a place devoid of human contact, and of love or being loved. I hated the place.

Before I left, I played the answering machine. There was only one message on it. It was of a man speaking in Chinese—so, I didn't get anything from listening to it. Towards the end of the message, the man began crying. What that was all about, I had no idea.

I sat in my car for a while, trying to remember some of the places that Master Hu had told us that he enjoyed visiting. One of them was Carondelet Park. I drove there.

I drove slowly through the park, searching for his blue VW car. He had said that he liked viewing the ducks at the two lakes in the park. I didn't find him.

Then, I remembered that he had told us that on a Saturday, he sometimes liked going to the Missouri Botanical Garden, to sit at the bank of the pond there and meditate, hearing the splashing of the multitude of goldfish in the pond. I drove there. The Missouri Botanical Garden is a HUGE place—and it cost me ten dollars to get in. I didn't find him. Then, I remembered the Buddhist temple he frequented. It was on Delmar. I drove there.

There, I spoke with one of the monks. He hadn't seen Master Hu in two weeks.

I was getting tired, frustrated and hungry. It was almost 4:30. Since I was so close to 'The Hill', a great place to get Italian food, I decided to stop at Zio's and have supper. I hadn't been there in years, and it sounded good to me to go there.

The food was great. I had a big salad, spaghetti-and-meatballs, and a glass of red wine—and their bread is to-die-for.

It was nearly six o'clock when I left Zio's. I decided to make one last run before going back home. I'd swing by the studio for a quick look.

It was dark by the time I arrived there. I pulled into the parking lot at the back of the building. There was but one lone car parked in the lot—a blue VW. I had found Master Hu.

Staring at the car, I shouted, "Got you!"

Chapter Thirty-Seven

Yes, I had found him.

As I walked upon the sidewalk from the parking lot to the front of the building, I felt a few drops of rain. *Oh, no*, I thought. *The kids—Trick-or-Treating!* There was a sudden, cold wind in the air. I heard the dry leaves in the trees rustling, shivering in the night.

The glass front door to the studio was locked, and the place was in total darkness inside. I had a key, though. I unlocked the door, opened it, and walked inside.

It felt 'spooky' in there, being dark and devoid of students and activity. To my right, against the south wall, was the light switch. I flipped it on. That was better. The fluorescent lights from the white, drop ceiling made the place less 'spooky.' I looked to the back of the building, to the door that led to the three small rooms back there. The door was open. It was dark back there.

Following the tiled path along the south wall, I walked to the door. I looked inside, to my left.

Through the string of beads that served as a door to Master Hu's sanctuary, I saw the spotted lights of many lit candles. I walked to the door.

Pushing the beads to the side with my left hand, I entered the room.

Towards the middle of the north wall, sitting on a mat on the floor in front of the human-size statue of the Buddha, both in the lotus position, was Master Hu. He was dressed in his black, martial arts, ceremonial garb, with a large, puffy, black bow to the back. His back was to me, and one of the two long, thin swords that hung on the wall behind the Buddha was now draped across Master Hu's lap. A white piece of paper was on the floor to his right side.

I walked up to him on his left side. His eyes were closed, and he seemed to be in deep meditation.

Referring to the sword, I said, mockingly, "I thought only the Japanese did the 'honorable' thing by committing suicide?—But don't let me stop you. Go ahead. Make the world a more truthful place."

He opened his eyes. Staring at the Buddha, he said, "You fight Micky last night. I see from front door."

"Yeah," I replied. "I kicked his ass."

"No," he said, holding up his right hand. "You follow. You learn. You used Micky's own energy to defeat himself. You know."

"Yeah, well, now," I replied flatly. "I've learnt a lot of things in the past few days—like you killed Jeff Farmer. Why?"

"He try to kill my student," Master Hu stated. "Could not find it within me to permit."

"No," I snapped angrily at him, "but you sure-in-the-hell tried to kill me—and my mother. All because you wanted my money!"

Still staring at the Buddha, he held up his right hand again, and said, "Not for me. For father. To build hospital in village. No matter now. Father dead. Die yesterday. Brother told me." Touching that piece of paper to his right with his right hand, he said, "I make confession. All here. I right wrong."

"I hardly think so!" I yelled. "You're pathetic. You really are."

Disgusted by it all, I turned around and started to leave.

Master Hu said, hurriedly and emphatically, "Mr. Mayor! Mr. Mayor!"

I stopped and turned back around.

"Don't stop learning," he said. "You excel—"

"Shut up!" I screamed viciously at him. "You don't give me advice. I have parents for that. I'm calling the police." I turned back around and stormed out of the room.

It felt so good to be back outside again. I eagerly drank in the cool night air. As I walked back to my car, I made a quick call to Detective Carpenter.

"Say, Carpenter," I said. "I got your killer—but you better hurry: He's committing suicide." I quickly gave him Master Hu's name and the address of the studio and hung up on him. I was tired and wanted to get home, but that didn't happen. I started to reach for the handle of my car, when three patrol vehicles pulled up and came to a screeching stop in front of me. They jumped out of the cars with guns drawn— the spotlights from all three cars were on me, blinding me—and one of the officers shouted, "Halt! Put your arms and hands behind your neck, interlacing your fingers!"

I did.

They approached me. One of them patted me down, while one of them said to me, "Are you Tom Mayor?"

"Yeah," I replied.

"Where's the person committing suicide?"

"In there," I said, pointing with my head in the direction of the studio. Two of them went running down the sidewalk towards the front of the building. The one who had done all of the talking stayed, with his gun still pointed at me.

"A Detective Carpenter instructed us to hold you," he said. "He'll be here shortly."

That 'shortly' turned in to being about thirty minutes later. Before he got there, a fire truck had come, an ambulance, paramedics, and a group of kids, dressed for the occasion, passed by, yelling, "Trick-or-Treat! Smell my feet! Trick- …"

Carpenter swiftly exited his car. As usual, he had his normal stick-up-his-ass, hard-nose, by-the-book attitude, and, as usual, he was dapperly dressed—wearing a black suit and green tie—and, as usual, he smelt good, too.

He spoke with the police officer for a moment, and then said, "Okay. You can holster your weapon, Officer." Looking at me now, Carpenter added, "But keep him here until I return." Carpenter turned and started walking down the sidewalk towards the front of the building.

About another thirty minutes passed before Carpenter returned—another thirty minutes! He spoke with the Officer first, saying, "You may leave now, Officer. Thank you for your assistance." The officer got back into his patrol car and left.

Facing me now, with the sides of his suit coat spread to the side, and his clenched fists on his hips, he said, arrogantly, "Okay, Mayor. You may go. You're cleared—this time. But watch your back. I don't like you, Mayor. I don't like your kind—rich, privileged. You people think that you're above the law; you're not. You'll get into trouble again, and I'll be there. I'm going to nail you, Mayor. So, watch your back."

"Well, thanks for the warning, Detective," I replied. "I'll be sure and watch my back—but you don't know me, Detective. You don't know a thing about me or about my life. I'll watch my back, and I'll keep my eye out for you. We'll see who wins. We'll see."

I got in my car and drove away, leaving Carpenter in my rearview mirror.

I headed home. Home.

Chapter Thirty-Eight

When I opened the front door, I found Mom sitting on the couch. The TV was playing. Seeing me, she sprang to her feet as quickly as her pudgy old body would allow. Dashing to me with open arms, she cried joyously, "Tom! Tom! I'm so glad to see you! You're safe. You're safe."

Hugging her, I replied, "Yes, Mom. I'm safe. It's all over. It's over." Gently pushing her back at arm's length, I said, "Say, is there any coffee? I could sure go for a cup of coffee."

We sat at the kitchen table, drinking coffee, and I told Mom all that had happened. Throughout the telling of it, she kept shaking her head, saying, "He must have been nuts."

We retired to bed at a quarter-to-ten. Mom looked incredibly tired: Well, the poor dear had probably worried about me all day.

As we were ascending the steps upstairs, Mom told me that she had had a great time dishing out candy to all of the little Trick-or-Treaters. She said it had been like being young again—like when Mary, Eve, James and I had been children. I was glad that she had had so much joy.

Before she entered her bedroom, Mom told me that she was going to take that test for possible Alzheimer's. I told her that I was glad, and not to worry about it; that no matter what, we would face it together—to the end.

In my bedroom, I immediately changed into my sweat-pants and T-shirt and got straight to bed. I couldn't sleep, though. I was too hyper. I just kept tossing and turning. So, I got up and began sitting at my desk, staring out the window at the night sky. I have been here ever since.

Well, that's my story.

Yeah, it's after 12:30. It's Sunday. A new day. A new beginning.

Mom was right about Cindy. She's not good for me. I need companionship; someone with the same likes and dislikes I have. Yeah, I'm going to dump her—but not before I know that Faith is okay. I'll keep in touch with her until then.

In several hours, the sun shall rise, showering us all with its warmth and its glory. Yes, a new day.

Soon it shall be Thanksgiving, and then Christmas—Mom and Dad's favorite time of the year.

I've been thinking a lot about Dad. I hate how I had abandoned him. I know, though, that if Dad had his mind that he would understand. Seeing him like he is—no mind, zombie-like—just kept reminding me of all of my 'dead-like' years of life. It was like I had to have a second adolescence. I had to separate myself from my old self and start anew; grow; cast off the fears of childhood; the fears of the outside world, the people in it and of myself—never to fear again ever being trapped in a box, like my dead brother James, forever.

No, Dad would understand all of that.

Yes, it is a new day.

I love you, Dad. See you at noon for lunch.

The End

The Author

After many years of being a "struggling" actor in LA, I turned to writing. I have had MS for several years now; I know physical and mental pain, so I need much laughter to endure it. Hopefully, my novels do just that—give you much laughter.

Books by the Author

Contents